COUNTERPARTS

by
Kurt B. Fischel
and
Audrey R. Langer

Acknowledgements to Svetlana Rovinskaya, David Rubin, and James R. Benson, for their invaluable assistance.

The characters in this novel, and their actions, are purely imaginary. Their names and experiences have no relation to those of actual people, living or dead, except by coincidence.

Library of Congress Cataloging-in-Publication Data

Fischel, Kurt B., 1917-
    Counterparts.

    I. Langer, Audrey R., 1929-   . II. Title.
PS3556.I757C6 1989   813'.54   89-3183
ISBN 0-929827-03-1

New Saga Publishers
P. O. Box No. 56415
Sherman Oaks, CA. 91413

ISBN 0-929827-03-1
First New Saga Printing, June, 1989

PRINTED IN THE UNITED STATES OF AMERICA

. . . Conceived together, separated by fate and happenstance, it was not until their encounter in the fury of a Soviet satellite storm that the first vague inklings awakened: they were <u>Counterparts</u>.

Other Books by the Authors
JIHAD ! - By Kurt B. Fischel & Audrey R. Langer

By Kurt B. Fischel
The Heat of the Rising Sun
The Visit
The Pursuit of Malevolence
They Came Bearing Gifts

By Audrey R. Langer
The Woman, Inge
Ashes Under Uricon

Part One

Chapter 1

(San Francisco)

"*O Borzhamoya*! God help me!" Tanya gasped, struggling to hold fast to the rail on the gangplank slanting from the deck of the "Kharkov" to the loading dock. Yuri had warned her about the steep slant, and the girl was grateful that dusk was about to settle over the city. Had it been earlier, the vessel would not have taken on as many tons of wheat, and the tides would not have receded so far out—which would have made the angle of the splintered gangboard even more precarious for a sway-backed, waddling young woman to negotiate.

Oooof, that sudden, breathtaking pain again, a serrated blade thrusting deep into the vaginal orifice. Moaning, Tanya clung to the rail, calling for Yuri Romayev who was still occupied with Captain Borodin. If Yuri were with her, she would not be so terrified. But the ship's political officer's greatest responsibility arose when they were in port, and certainly...

Another pain knifed through her, and she bent almost double, her palms so wet she almost lost her grip on the rail. In the cool breeze from the bay, her stockings and shoes felt moist, and above the sound of her own labored breathing, Tanya heard a faint splashing...as a puddle formed between her feet and streamed down the gangway.

"Yuri! Yuri" she whimpered, calling to the bridge in panic, but he had moved on with the other officers, out of sight. Warm amniotic fluid streamed down her legs as she stumbled awkwardly toward the wharf. *"Pazhah'lsta,* Yuri! Please, I need you!"

Police patrol cars were parked across the pier, and closer in were dark sedans with breeze-whipped radio antennae. Several tall Anglo-Saxon types in conservative business suits stood watching the loading of the Soviet vessel. From her training, Tanya knew they were American Secret Service. She trembled at the thought of being close to such danger...

Gripped by an agonizing contraction, she started desperately along the dock, shielding her eyes from the afternoon sun and scanning the top decks of the freighter for a glimpse of Yuri.

How could he desert her! But even she did not understand the significance of this emergency! She still had two months to go before the baby was due! And all had been going so well...

"Oi chort!" she gasped, clutching her abdomen as though to hold back the pain, barely able to catch her breath.

"Hey, Lady...! Lady, is something wrong?" a voice shouted, and Tanya stood transfixed, eyes streaming, as two San Francisco patrolmen closed in on her. The pain was too fierce, and one of the officers caught her as she swayed. Terrified, she pointed to her swollen abdomen and then up at the vessel's Soviet flag, but the patrolmen understood only that they had an emergency on their hands. She heard something shouted in incomprehensible English and realized that one of them had sped back to his patrol car and was pulling up at her side, the other officer trying to calm her.

"Just take it easy, Lady. We're gonna get you to a hospital."

"Nyet! Nyet!" she screamed as they maneuvered her gently into the back of the police car, but was shocked into sudden silence at the sight of great red splotches on the concrete and

the awareness that her legs were sticky and streaked crimson. The vehicle leaped forward, the driver shouting into his handset, the other officer supporting her against his chest.

She heard the rising wail of the siren, and then they were moving swiftly, swiftly...away from the waterfront and the "Kharkov" and the other freighters with their superstructures jutting skyward.

Her body convulsed in still another jolting spasm, and she cried, "Yurrrriiii...!"

It was the last utterance Tanya Ivanova ever made.

Chapter 2

(San Francisco)

The regular meeting of the section chiefs of the San Francisco Consulate of the USSR was in session, and the portrait of Premier Nikita S. Khruschev, his peasant features flesh pink against the somber background, looked sternly down at the conference table—his small porcine eyes disdainful of the stagnant atmosphere.

The Premier himself, having been denied the right to visit Disneyland, had created much international hoopla for himself, with a nasty swipe at the American executive staff for their inability to guarantee his personal safety while touring the vast amusement park. Once back in Moscow, he made it clear that he entertained only the dimmest hopes for the "Spirit of Camp David" talks with Dwight Eisenhower, and thus, the Cold War was relentlessly pursued.

The consular members tried to conceal their nagging boredom by focusing on what lay beyond the conference room window. Against the blue coastal sky, decorated by a few fluffy cirrus clouds, pigeons winged in ellipses from a roost atop a building in the city's business district. They looped silently, in the tight formation of some ancient aerial choreography, and their dipping, circling flight mesmerized several of the men at the table.

Chief Consul Sevastaniov, a gaunt man with the pale eyes of the idealist, listened with sour concentration to Muchagov's account of a recent row with American authorities.

"They rest their claim on the United States Constitution...," the brilliant but contentious advisor was stating, "...that children born in this country, regardless of parentage, are American citizens by birth and cannot be touched."

Opposite Muchagov sat the dapper Stepanov, chief of the cultural section. In his early fifties, he was renowned for having bedded every secretary hired at the Consulate, and the latest rumor concerned his involvement in a tempestuous affair with the wife of the Polish consul. Stepanov did not once look up from his incessant doodling as he spoke.

"The ship's captain is to blame for this sorry situation," he announced with contempt. "Why did he not put the woman ashore as soon as he learned of her condition? Since when does our Merchant Marine require the services of ship's cooks who are near full term in pregnancy...?"

"The birth was premature...," replied Padorin, the long-legged KGB station chief whose cover was running the communications section. "It was anticipated she'd return to Moscow well in time to give birth there. According to the staff at St. Luke's, she was only seven months along."

Igor Kondrashev, obese and almost bald, had become interested in the case when he learned that the girl, Tanya Ivanova, was from the Ukraine, and had prepared a detailed file of as many facts as were known. Rising, he took the file to Sevastaniov's chair and placed it, open, before the Chief Consul.

"You may find this of interest," he stated. "Here are photocopies of the employment file of Tanya Ivanova, born Lugansk, the Ukraine, in 1939. As you can see, she was just twenty. Very little formal education. Was apprenticed to her mother, a cook at the Hotel Dnieper in Kiev, when she was seventeen. Two years later she entered the maritime service as ship's cook, first on the old freighter, "Belogorsk," and then on the "Kharkov."

"A pretty girl," observed Sevastaniov, eyeing Tanya's photo. "Is the father's identity known?"

Kondrashev leaned over the Chief Consul's shoulder to turn a page in the file folder, displaying a glossy of Yuri Romayev and a glowing article of the man's Party record.

"The ship's political officer claims he's the father. States he intended to marry the Ivanova girl when they returned to Moscow."

"And where is Romayev now?" asked Sevastaniov.

"In Moscow, moving up in the Admiralty office."

The doodler, Stepanov, still busy with his pencil, erased a few lines as he spoke, brushing the rubber shavings from his pad.

"I understand that Romayev and Borodin almost came to blows when the girl was found missing and Borodin insisted on sailing on schedule. It was only after an interpreter from the San Francisco Police brought the report to the 'Kharkov' that they finally lifted anchor."

"How did the girl get to St. Luke's Hospital?" demanded the KGB man. "What was she doing off the ship?"

Kondrashev produced a page from the file folder.

"Here's the police report. Apparently, Ivanova was in premature labor when she left the Kharkov...seeking help, possibly. She almost collapsed on the dock, and two city patrolmen rushed her to St. Luke's, where she delivered within the hour."

An uneasy silence prevailed before the Chief Consul spoke.

"Well, Comrades...what are we to do about this unfortunate birth? How do we work it to our advantage?"

"Romayev has already been interviewed by Pravda and Izvestia. Paris Match is doing a feature article about this father being denied his natural custodial rights. It makes the Americans look like kidnappers. Excellent propaganda."

"Does anyone know how the mother died?" asked Padorin, his Ronson touching the end of his cigarette.

Kondrashev produced another page from the file and scanned it. "Post-partum hemorrhage and shock. She never regained consciousness. St. Luke's records the birth at somewhat after five, and Tanya Ivanova was pronounced dead at five thirty, all efforts to resuscitate her having failed. The police notified Captain Borodin from identification on her person when admitted."

"Poor girl," Sevastaniov observed sadly, glancing again at the photo. "Now, Comrades. Do we engage in a tug of war with the Americans over the nationality of this child?"

"Why not let it remain their responsibility?" Kondrashev proposed. "Let them take care of the adoption, the education...for about sixteen years...before we step back into the picture."

"To invite a Russian child back to his Motherland!" Padorin grinned, applauding the merits of the idea. "With offers of advanced schooling, career opportunities, fame, even reunion with their natural father and relatives, if possible. We could use such a child in the service of our country."

"Comrade Consul, it's a worthwhile suggestion," advised Muchagov with unusual fervor.

The Chief Consul glanced around the table with a weak smile. Elsewhere in the world, terrorists were at work. Intercontinental missiles were being placed each day as the Imperialists went on surrounding Mother Russia with their Trident submarines and cruise missiles. Why on earth, he wondered, was he wasting his time over a fatherless birth and a ship's cook who had died in delivery, when there were momentous world decisions to be made.

"Has it been established if this child is a boy or a girl?" he asked, not really caring one way or the other.

"Both," Kondrashev grinned, and the Consul's eyebrows flared.

"Both?" he repeated, and the others, astonished, sat forward.

"A boy *and* a girl," Kondrashev announced dramatically. "*Twins*."

Chapter 3

(Zermatt, Switzerland)

Filled with a noisy holiday crowd, the funicular wound its way through the Alpine winter wonderland to the Gronegrat Summit. The early winter sky was a darkish white, not a patch of blue on the horizon—a guarantee of even more snowfall to come.

From the car window, Harry took in the view of the majestic Matterhorn. In his sixteen years, he had done much traveling with his parents, but of all the resorts where Don and Sally Carroll vacationed, for Harry, Zermatt held special fascination, and he never quite got over the thrill of being there.

He had been surprised earlier that day to find that his new ski suit no longer fit comfortably. Three months past his sixteenth birthday, Harry Carroll was almost six feet two, his shoulders and chest developing the magnificence his athletic instructors had promised him as a reward for vigorous workouts. For some months, he had been trying to coax the start of a blond beard, and the only argument his father had ever had with him was about the length of his hair, which he consented, finally, to trim just below the ears. Thinking about buying a better-fitting skisuit, he decided it would be a pastel blue. With his wide-spaced, clear blue eyes and ruddy complexion, the girls looked at him more often and more boldly when he wore lighter shades. For Harry, that was becoming important.

He glanced at Yvonne, the girl his parents had invited on this trip as a favor to their Washington society friends, the de la Fontaines. Yvonne was dreamy-eyed with her private thoughts, gazing out the window at the mountain panorama. She, too, had told him he looked terrific in pastels, and Harry was confident she knew what she was talking about. Born into an aristocratic family of French descent, Yvonne, an only child, had traveled all her young life with the jet set, and had the best international connections.

Yvonne was beautiful and Harry enjoyed her company and the way she felt in his arms when they danced. She had been improving his technique in kissing the way she liked to be kissed. But both teenagers had plenty of growing up to do.

The funicular lurched to a stop, and the eager crowd spilled noisily out on the platform of the small terminal, anticipating the long downhill run. Paying little attention to the snow-covered peaks reaching to the sky like the spires of ancient cathedrals, the vacationers hurried onto their skis.

Sally Carroll tried to attract the attention of her son and husband, suggesting they meet at the luncheon stop. But Yvonne, red hair flying, was already into her first turn, with Harry in hot pursuit, and the Carrolls sighed, smiling, at each other. Then Don Carroll pushed off, Sally following closely in his tracks, taking the first steep hill in tight turns.

The snow surface was still crusty from the night's frost, and—skis flying—Harry skimmed easily over the groomed slope, rhythmically shifting his weight from one foot to the other, keeping his skis parallel and close together. This was his kind of life, his Seventh Heaven—downhill skiing on Alpine pistes glistening beneath cloudless skies, exhilarated by the speed, with the sudden, unexpected plunges challenging his skill and versatility.

He closed rapidly in on Yvonne, admiring the way she adroitly negotiated a steep "black" slope meant for only the very best skiers, keeping control of her body with sharp, forceful turns and her full weight thrown on the downhill ski.

Going deep into his knees, with his poles tight at his sides, Harry schussed past her, and from the corner of his eye saw her bite her lip in exasperation as he bested her.

"Show-off!" he heard her call, and knew she would head the tips of her skis straight downhill, determined to catch up. Harry knew Yvonne could schuss. Even if she didn't enjoy it the way he did, didn't glory in the headlong rush down the steepest slopes—he knew she'd try her darndest. With a graceful wave of his pole, he turned in front of a rock formation and coasted to a wider, more moderate slope where he decided he would wait for the girl. She'd catch up with him in a matter of seconds...

But when she failed to appear as expected, Harry herring-boned back up around the protruding rock to find that Yvonne had taken a spill. She had hit an icy mogul which threw her off balance, and now lay sprawled at the bottom of the steep slope, temporarily stunned. Her safety bindings had released the skis and her poles had slid downhill.

"Are you okay, Yvonne?" he shouted, and when she failed to respond at once, became alarmed. But as he made his way toward her, she nodded her head, which relieved him.

But another skier had stopped beside the prostrate girl, taking off his own skis to be of help. The rescuer was a youngish man, tall, attentive...and as Harry made his way uphill, the stranger assisted Yvonne to her feet, gallantly dusting the snow from her skisuit and collecting her poles.

In a tone clearly indicating possession of the girl, Harry called out to the stranger, "Thanks for your help!"

Yvonne stood composing herself as he reached her side, but he could see that the bad spill had knocked the wind out of her.

"She'll be fine in a moment," the stranger ventured. "Your sister is just out of breath."

And who in hell asked you, Harry thought, feeling jealous, curious about the man's appraising looks and the strong East European accent that clung to his speech.

"She's not my sister," he muttered darkly, studying the girl's flushed face. "You feeling better, Yvonne?"

"Aaaaaah, Yvonne is such a lovely name," the stranger warbled, extending his hand to both youngsters. "Excuse me. I am Igor Matlov."

Harry introduced himself, permitting the unfamiliar Mr.Matlov to pump his hand in greeting. At the stranger's suggestion, they stopped for hot chocolate at the way-station, selecting a table on the sun-soaked terrace, where Matlov placed orders for all three of them. Then he folded his arms and leaned across the table with a look of utter incredulity as he addressed Harry.

"You cannot believe how fantastic it is to run into you on this mountain!" he exclaimed, fishing his card from the breast pocket of his skisuit. "They told me in Geneva that you and your family were here on vacation, so I took the next train to Zermatt!"

"To find *me*?" Harry inquired, brows furrowed, wondering what the stranger wanted of him. Then, examining the man's card, he queried, "You're a consular officer at the Russian Embassy in Bern?"

"Why does that surprise you so?" chuckled Matlov.

"Well, you don't exactly look like a Communist," giggled Yvonne, coquettishly.

"And how does a Communist look?" Matlov smiled. "Shall I uncover my horns and tail?"

Harry shifted uneasily, eyeing Matlov with suspicion and wondering if their meeting on the mountain was really only the sheer coincidence the man claimed it to be.

The waiter brought three cups of steaming chocolate to their table, and Matlov played host, taking care of the bill immediately. As he nibbled at one of the slender cream-sandwich cookies jutting from the rich brown drink, he seemed to search for the proper words.

"I have something to propose to your parents, Harry," he said calmly. "But it concerns you."

"In what way?" Harry demanded, on his guard.

Matlov held his glance for a long moment.

"I think you have an idea how it concerns you," he said softly. "You see, my government occasionally demonstrates its particular interest in certain youths, all over the world, and invites these young men and women to acquaint themselves with the Soviet Union. You happen to be one of the chosen ones, Harry."

Harry's cheeks burned with embarrassment as his blood rose. *So this was it!* The old, haunting secret was coming to life. He'd hidden it in his heart for six years, from the day his parents had decided to tell him he was a special child...theirs because they had *chosen* him to be their son. *Chosen*, and legally adopted.

And now this stranger, this Matlov, from the Russian Embassy in Bern, was saying that the Soviet Union had chosen him.

"Whatever you have to say to me is of a private nature!" Harry warned the man, and Matlov was given to understand that Yvonne was not acquainted with the Carroll family secret.

"Of course," the Russian consul replied. "When would it be convenient to speak to your parents?"

"We'll all be at the 'Monte Cervino' tonight," Yvonne informed the man, and did not notice Harry's angry glare. "And if you do find us, you may ask me to dance...that is, if you know how."

"You'd better call first," Harry snapped, almost rudely. "My parents may have other plans for the evening."

"Of course," he was reassured, Matlov smiling politely like a man accustomed to respecting the privacy of others. Then the Soviet Embassy man flashed a brilliant smile at Yvonne, stating, "And yes, I do know how to dance, Mademoiselle, and I should be delighted if you would consent to dance with me..."

Harry set his cup down with an impatient thump and got up.

"We've got to be going," he announced, with a commanding look at Yvonne. "My folks will be looking for us, and besides, the slopes are calling. Thanks for the refreshments, Mr. Matlov."

"You were terribly rude!" Yvonne criticized him, following Harry back to the slopes. "Whatever proposition this man has to make to your father, you've done a great job of ruining it!"

Harry was bent over his bindings, his hair whipping across his face in the strong breeze.

"He was a waste of time!" he told her angrily. "And next time you take a spill, try not to collect any admirers...particularly not Russians!"

"Well, if it hadn't been for you, I wouldn't have taken that nose dive to begin with!" Yvonne scolded back.

Her words were lost on the wind. Harry was moving down the slope, zigzagging in precise, accurate movements, showing off his ability to wedel. Yvonne watched as she followed, smirking to conceal her admiration.

The persistent Matlov showed up at their table in a tuxedo doubtless fitted by one of Bern's best tailors, radiating such masculine charm that even the phlegmatic Don Carroll found himself on alert at Sally's reaction to the Russian's continental kiss on the back of her hand.

A disgruntled Harry was obliged to watch his favorite redhead swooning with delight whenever the Russian looked in her direction. Harry realized the girl was miles ahead of him in the uncertain arena of sex, and it was for him a continual struggle to keep building sufficient savoir-faire and sophistication to interest a fickle, vacillating charmer like Yvonne. And now this stranger had come along at the start of their vacation and seemed bent on ruining it.

"Our son tells us you're with the Russian Embassy in Bern," Harry heard his father remark uneasily, and caught a flicker of nervousness in Don Carroll's eyes. Obviously, he was uncomfortable in the Russian's company, but only someone who knew the older Mr.Carroll very well, and loved him very much, could possibly be aware of that. Harry beamed a message of strength and comfort to his father. Don't worry, Dad. I'm your son and I love you. This Russian bastard is not going to tempt me away from you and Mom. Not for any promise. Not for any all-expenses-paid vacation in Mother Russia. Not for a month or a week or a day. Not even for a *minute.*

"Oh, there's a song you kids like to dance to," a flustered Sally announced, with a special look that told Harry and Yvonne to leave the table for a little while.

Her small hand trailing behind her, fingers questing for his, Yvonne preceded Harry out onto the parquet. Harry began to lead her in the slow, sentimental rhumba, feeling the softness of the green Thai silk dress that Igor Matlov had been so quick to admire upon joining their table.

> *"Wo Deine Sonne scheint...*
> *Und wo Deine Sterne steh'n...*
> *Da hat man..."*

"What does Matlov want with you?" Yvonne asked abruptly as they danced. "What makes you so special to the Russian Government?"

It had been some time since he danced with her. Was she wearing a padded bra, or were her breasts fuller than he recalled? Perspiration beaded his upper lip, and he went into a fancy dance step, making her circle beneath the upraised arc of his arm, giving him a chance to break close contact with her until he composed himself. Then he held himself stiffly as they rhumba'd.

"Oh, I dunno. The past six months or so, they've been writing, asking that my folks let me visit their country. I don't really know what their reason is," he lied uncomfortably.

"Maybe you ought to go," Yvonne coaxed. "It could be interesting, and you could become a diplomat, like Matlov. In fact, he looks like an older version of you, don't you think?"

"Naaaaa..."

"He sure does! Oh, he's looking this way. Let's go back to the table, Harry. As soon as this dance ends."

Helping Yvonne back to her seat, Harry overheard Matlov invite his parents to a gala performance of the Bolshoi Ballet at Geneva's Victoria Hall the following month, if they were still in Switzerland.

"...and perhaps by then, the young Mr. Carroll will have had a chance to reconsider our invitation...and we shall make plans for his visit to the Soviet Union..."

Having concluded his remarks, speaking of Harry in the third person as though he were not even there, Matlov beamed up at him.

"I believe Mrs. Carroll and I should discuss this privately with our son, Mr. Matlov," Don Carroll replied, and Harry felt his whole heart go out to his father, observing the tremor in those ordinarily steady fingers as he asked Matlov where he could be reached.

"I'm staying at the Alpen Rose, a block or two from here," Matlov replied, his glance resting on Yvonne. There was an explicit invitation in his eyes, and she responded with the trace of a smile. Harry felt he had to get away from the table. If he had to sit there one more minute, he'd punch that Russkie S.O.B. right square in the nose

"I'll be in touch with you, then," he heard his father say, and seized that moment to wobble to his feet, complaining of too much sun and fresh air on the slopes and a violent headache, and asking to be excused.

Bastard Russkie...barging in like that! Harry's animosity had begun six months earlier, with the arrival of the first letter, which had been discarded as a piece of unsolicited advertising. But that letter was quickly followed by a series of telephone calls while Harry was at school and knew nothing about them. At last, there was a visit. A man and woman, looking like identical sacks of neglected potatoes in dour brown suits, had come to the Carroll home during the day, and remained long enough to see Harry when he arrived from school. Sally left it to her husband to tell the boy the purpose of that couple's visit, and although he took his time in mentioning the matter, he brought it up at the dinner table in a very matter-of-fact fashion, with much restraint, but the sensitive Harry was immediately aware of the tension in his parents' hearts.

"Naaaaaah, they can keep their invitation," he decided when his father explained the Soviet Government's eagerness to extend to him a six-month vacation upon his high school graduation which was coming up in June, 1976, offering him the opportunity to study at the Universities of Moscow and Leningrad.

"I'm not interested in anything that miserable country has to offer. I'm a hundred per cent American and I don't go for this 'Natural Ancestry' bit. They make it sound almost racial, and that's what Hitler was all about, right?"

His parents exchanged proud looks. They knew their son loved them, but the Russian intrusion into their lives had jarred and frightened them. Their attorney, knowing of their desire for a child, had arranged for Harry's adoption from an agency in San Francisco when he was only three months old. All they knew about the beautiful, healthy baby boy was that his mother had been ship's cook on a Russian freighter and had died in childbirth while the vessel was docked in San Francisco harbor.

He was ten when they told him of his adoption, and Harry accepted the news as the unraveling of one of the exciting mysteries of living. His one persistent fear was that some relatives of his real parents would one day come to take him away.

As Harry matured, he wanted to be like his father...strong, brave, respected by everyone...and could not wait for the day when he would be big and brave enough to defend his parents, his friends, and the country he loved. It became a lifelong ambition, developing more clearly every year of his life...

Excused from the dinner table, Harry returned to his room in an ugly mood, throwing himself upon the bed with arms flung over his eyes. Then he rummaged through his valise for John Le Carré's "A Perfect Spy,"which he had brought with him for evenings just like this, when his body was tired from skiing and his mind troubled by the encounter with the Russian.

Just thinking of the Russian made him search in his wallet for the advertisement he had carefully clipped from the international issue of the Herald Tribune, about a month earlier. It was a prominent ad in the newspaper's business section, and Harry was certain it was his destiny to have happened upon it. Alone in his hotel room, his heart drummed strangely as he re-read it.

CENTRAL INTELLIGENCE AGENCY
...where your career is America's strength. Not a job, but a unique professional career that provides an uncommon measure of personal challenge and satisfaction.

Harry never tired of reading the stirring ad. There was a paragraph on career growth and overall benefits which the sixteen-year-old found of little importance, but the blurb on qualifications fascinated him.

Strong personal skills, aptitude in foreign languages, previous residence abroad...

Just the thing for him, he knew. Still a long time off; he had first to graduate from high school! There would be four years at some university, and perhaps the CIA would require a graduate degree. But there would come a day, in five...perhaps seven years...when he'd knock at the Agency's door. Fluent in French and German, with years of travel in Europe, he could do one heck of a job for them. He could protect America's interests against the likes of Igor Matlov.

Dwelling briefly on Matlov, he reflected on what he knew of his natural ancestry. Yvonne had remarked that Matlov looked like an older version of him. Harry guessed Matlov's age at very late twenties. The man was tall, athletically built, had blond hair going dark and compelling eyes of no definite color. Yet Yvonne had seen similarities between them.

Well, maybe...

Carroll and Matlov, huh? A pair of Russian bastards.

He put the ad away and sprawled on the bed, thinking of taking a couple of aspirins for his headache. But that would be weakness. Instead, he shut his eyes and imagined himself as Agent Carroll, fighting the lonely battle of a courageous master of intrigue against the forces of evil. He visualized himself crawling along treacherous rooftops, or chasing his prey through subway stations in London, Paris, Berlin and New York. There were fair maidens to rescue from the musty dungeons of ancient cities in lands behind the Iron Curtain...

And one fair maiden in particular, with long red hair and ivory skin, lying on the floor of a bug-infested cell, hands tied behind her back, one strap of her bikini bra having torn from its clasp, the lace of the cup falling free of the pink aureole...

Keys jingled in the lock, announcing the return of his parents to the room adjoining his, and he sat up abruptly, hearing them say goodnight to Yvonne. How clever of them, he thought, to take for themselves the room between his and the de la Fontaine girl. Harry's cheeks burned at the thought that his mother suspected his erotic fantasies of women. What a relief, to have chambermaids take care of his bed linens when he traveled abroad, and a maid to see to the family laundry at home! For three years, his father had been attempting an all-important talk with him about the function of his body, and women's bodies, and the things he was to avoid. But those talks had always broken down into jesting and joking, concluding with Harry's relating some ribald stories he had picked up at school—stories that assured Don Carroll of his son's adequate education along those lines.

He gazed from his to Yvonne's window, wondering when she would turn her light off. She has more energy than I do, he mused. Maybe because she doesn't take school as seriously, or because she's about a month younger. He remembered their plans to ski from the summit of the Trockener Steg into Italy the next day, of having lunch there and returning to Zermatt by bus. He could already feel the excitement of the swift descent on the Italian side, could already savor the delight of spicy pasta...

Suddenly, Yvonne's window went dark, and there were light footsteps in the hall outside. Harry rushed to open his door just in time to catch sight of Yvonne entering the elevator. Dashing back to his window, he waited until he saw her emerge from the front portal below, cross the street and continue up the block. Somewhere a drunk was shouting obscenities, but Harry could hear only the rushing in his ears and the throbbing of his heart at Yvonne's audacious nocturnal escapade. His curiosity and sense of indignation propelled him into pursuit...down the emergency staircase to exit the hotel through the service area.

Surreptitiously, like an intelligence agent...

There were few people out and most of the houses were dark as Harry ran in the direction Yvonne had taken. Only the resort's hotels and restaurants were still open, their amber lights shining on snowy streets and alleys. At the first intersection, he saw no sign of the girl, but upon looking up, he discovered the blinking red neon sign of the narrow, three-story Alpen Rose, the hotel where Matlov had told Don Carroll he could be reached.

Dumbfounded, heartsick, and then—in turn—livid, Harry decided to go after Yvonne soon enough, he hoped, to wrest her from the lecherous arms of the Russian seducer. Was Yvonne that naive, after all? Didn't she know how dangerous it was for a girl to go to a man's hotel room at night...?

Shoulders hunched, his raincoat collar turned up, Harry stormed into the lobby of the Alpen Rose, through the red plush cocktail lounge toward the reservation desk. He would demand to be taken to the room of the Russian Consul Matlov. There he would pound at the door and shout Yvonne's name, insisting she come out. If she did not acquiesce instantly, he would shout that her parents had been notified and that agents from Interpol were on their way to take her into protective custody...!

"Oh, *mon Dieu*! Harry!" he heard a familiar gasp, and he turned to his left to find the iridescence of long red hair in the yellow-orange candlelight of the lounge and the shimmer of a green silk dress, as Yvonne sat discreetly at a table with a coffee cup half-way to her lips, staring at him in amazement.

Beside her, elegant in his impeccable tuxedo, sat Igor Matlov, equally astonished, a tiny cup of espresso in his fingers.

"Well, it's the young Mr. Carroll," he smiled congenially, but with a touch of malice. "So long as you're here, come join us. As you can see, this charming young lady has made me very much aware of her scruples and is neither in my room nor in my bed."

Humiliated, his face aflame, Harry seated himself at their table as Matlov signaled for another setting and coffee. Unable to meet Harry's eyes, Yvonne sat examining her fingernails, fixed spots of coral on her cheeks as though painted there, harlequin-style. When the coffee arrived, Igor raised his cup to Harry.

"*Nazd'rovia!*" he toasted the youth laconically, the broad smile patently false across the thin mouth, making Harry feel distinctly uncomfortable.

"I realize you're doing your job, Mr. Matlov," the boy said to the older man. "But you're intruding into my life and my parents' lives, and we don't appreciate it."

"I do see," Matlov replied, "and I sympathize. But just as your father carries out his duties, so do I and so do we all. It so happens that my government considers you one of ours. We've been following your growth and progress since your infancy..."

"Sir!" Harry exclaimed, his frenzied glance at Yvonne telling the Russian that the girl knew nothing of his tormenting secret.

"It's all right, Harry," Yvonne whispered gently. "Your mom told me two or three years ago that you were adopted as an infant..."

"And that your natural parents were Soviet citizens," Matlov finished for her, watching the electricity between the youngsters.

From his wallet, Matlov proceeded to remove a xerox copy which he flattened out and studied as though seeing it for the first time, casting sidelong glances at Harry.

"The resemblance to your mother is quite remarkable," he stated, handing the copy to Harry. "See for yourself. She was perhaps only a year or two older on this photo than you are now. This is Tanya Ivanova in her late teens, when she entered the

Soviet Maritime Kommissariat, a capable young woman from a simple peasant background in the Ukraine. Her mother was a professional cook. Apparently, her father died in the war."

A chill coursed through Harry at the sight of the pretty blonde looking seriously back at him from the photocopy. This, then, was his mother. Her name was Tanya. She had bled and died giving him life. He choked back a sob, aware that his eyes were stinging with tears, and that Yvonne was nodding solemnly, staring at the photo over his shoulder.

"And...and my father?" he managed.

"Unfortunately, that information is not available to me. I know only that there was no marriage record in Ivanova's file..."

Trying to cope with the torrent of emotions pouring through him, Harry handed the photocopy back to Matlov, whose hand closed over his, restraining him.

"Keep it," Matlov said with some feeling. "Keep it with your private papers. Someday, you'll have children of your own, and you might want to see how much they resemble their paternal grandmother."

Harry stared blankly at his coffee cup, his hands balled into fists, as Yvonne returned to her seat.

"These are ghosts from the past," he said through gritted teeth. "Why are you doing this to me? Why is your government creating such a disturbance in our lives?"

"Because you're old enough now to make decisions," Matlov explained. "Because you should know your true heritage..."

"*Heritage!*" Harry hissed. "Expect me to be proud that I'm some peasant girl's nameless bastard?"

"Harry!" Yvonne cried, aching for him.

"Don't impugn your mother's character that way!" Matlov commanded more sharply than he had intended, then softened. "Be grateful to fate for the life you've been given. And if your roots are so distasteful that you prefer to pretend they don't exist...well, that's all right, Harry. We'll not press you again."

Having made that statement, Matlov fished another card from his wallet and placed it on the table in front of Harry.

"Should you ever change your mind, call me. Your parents are leaving this matter entirely up to you. Now I must return to my Embassy tomorrow with the disappointing report that the young Mr. Carroll is reluctant to take advantage of the Soviet Government's generosity. I thank you for your time, and now I must bid you both goodnight."

Placing a pile of Swiss francs on the table, the diplomat pushed back his chair, and nodding to them with a forced smile, left the table like a man who has had his feelings injured.

"One thing more...before I forget," he added, returning with a thoughtful frown. "You've always believed you're an only child."

"Well, yes...of course!" Harry said with a quizzical look.

"Nobody ever told you about your sister?"

"My...my *sister*?" Harry struggled, staring wildly.

"Yes, Harry," Matlov replied, his expression dark and inscrutable. "The female child born within minutes of you. Your *twin*..."

Chapter 4

(New York City)

Jane had been tempted to get up twice during the all-night downpour to fling a metal ashtray into the yard to scare the screeching cats into silence. But the thought made her feel guilty. They were homeless and cold. And innocent. So was she. Except that in Connie Bishop's dismal flat there was no such thing as feeling cold, and in the few weeks Jane had been rooming there, she had complained incessantly about the stuffy heat.

"What were your parents...Eskimos?" Connie would laugh, and pretend to turn the knob of the radiator, but Jane knew it was pretense and kept still about it, feeling too much gratitude toward the older girl for having taken her in at sixteen the day Jane's mother died of metastatic breast cancer.

It had been Connie, too, who took care of details following Amy Sutton's death, and helped the highschool teenager clear her pathetic belongings out of the third floor walkup from which she was being evicted for non-payment of rent.

"I don't make that much waiting tables," Jane warned her when Connie insisted she move in with her. Jane was referring to her job at the Dolphin, a small coffee shop in the Eighties where she worked after school. "I can't pay you much until school's out."

Behind the wheel of her battered old Impala, Connie took in Jane's slender, willowy figure from bustline to ankles.

"We'll see about that once you're settled," she told Jane thoughtfully. "Do you dance?"

For a moment, Jane's face radiated a glowing memory.

"I used to take tap and acrobatics," she smiled. "But that was before my folks split up. The teachers said I was much too tall for ballet, but I was good. Then mom got sick and the money ran out and I quit taking lessons."

Connie gave her a comforting pat on the shoulder and proceeded south on Second Avenue.

Once settled, Jane was persuaded to demonstrate what she knew of tap and acrobatics, and Connie enthusiastically applauded the girl's natural rhythm, promising to teach her "more sophisticated stuff." Between Christmas and New Years, Jane learned a series of provocative bumps and grinds and developed an erotic dance routine of her own, and Connie was impressed.

Helmer, the stage manager at the Moulin D'Or, where Connie sang accompaniment for the strippers, looked at a snapshot of Jane Sutton and heard Connie praise her young protegée.

"I'll give her a week's trial if she's as good as you say she is," he agreed. "But on one condition. Bring me evidence that she was born in fifty-FOUR...NOT fifty-nine...and I'll give her a chance."

Thus, except for her school records and the memory of various acquaintances, Jane entered Show Biz as Jan Kuriliev, the Siberian Sailor, her specialty as a burlesque dancer launched early in 1976. Her act at the Moulin D'Or caught fire. She kept a promise to herself to achieve a highschool diploma by taking her equivalency examination, and by early spring was making enough of a living to repay Connie Bishop's monetary advances.

It was Connie's other advances that Jane couldn't handle.

Too deeply in Connie's debt to risk hurting her feelings by declaring her behavior inappropriate, she had tried to ascribe the girl's hugs and kisses to effervescent expressions of affection. But when Connie kissed her full on the mouth—tongue questing against Jane's tightly sealed lips—Jane drew away, hurt and bewildered, pleading in a shaky little voice, "Don't do that. I don't like to be kissed like that."

Connie looked flustered and said nothing, but Jane realized her friend was upset.

Yet it was through Connie that Jane learned her audience-drawing dance routines, how to undress in the most tantalizing ways, to expose portions of her body a little at a time, and how to keep her movements erotic and seductive. Jane was an apt pupil, eager for Connie's approval and for the boisterous applause she received from an appreciative audience.

And Connie devised the transsexual burlesque routine—Jane's transformation, through dance, from a reeling drunken sailor to a ravishing, long-legged blonde with small breasts and narrow hips—a dancer who could create the most arousing illusions with the use of her sailor cap.

"Study the way men walk," Connie instructed her. "When you come out on stage in your bell bottoms and sailor blouse, convince the crowd they're in for a comedy. Tuck your hair up tight under your cap and move like men move. You're narrow in the beam with and your height and flat boobs, you could pass for a young guy from a distance. Flirt with both men and women in the audience, so that they think you're gay...or at least bi...and when the mood music changes, you go into your strip."

"Think they'll like me?" Jane asked innocently.

"You'll bring the house down!"

She observed herself in the full-length closet mirror, listening to Connie's husky contralto handling the melody.

"Dahm...Dahm...Dadadahm...Darrrombombahn... bombom..."

"What is that piece?" Jane asked, thinking it was classical.

"Pete suggested a parody on the Russian Sailor's Dance. Why?"

Jane's heart hammered, and not from the exertion of the dance.

"Any particular reason for picking that piece?" she asked.

"No, except it's a hell of a lot more rhythmic than Anchors Aweigh! What makes you ask?"

But Jane had stopped practicing and was gazing out the window at the rain, remembering things her mother had told her before she left for the hospital that final time, things Jane could scarcely believe. Behind her, Connie was still humming the melodic selection and didn't hear the question Jane asked of the Universe.

"Could I really pass for Russian...?"

Generally, by Saturday night, Jane had warmed to her routine and executed it without a hitch. But the cats had kept her awake and there were purple patches beneath her eyes. Plus she was due for a period and her breasts were tender beneath the coarse tight sailor blouse. She always enjoyed seeing her transformation into a young seaman, as authentic-looking as if he'd just stepped off a gangway. Well scrubbed, ruddy complexion. Great blue eyes beneath long pale eyelashes. High cheekbones. The suggestion of a cleft in the chin. Nothing gave her a greater sense of fulfillment than to have a couple of pretty teenagers try to flirt with her on the streets or in the subway.

Big Joe, the counterman at the Times Square greasy spoon where she always stopped for a doughnut and coffee on her way to the nightclub, asked her the same question he'd asked for weeks.

"Still in port, huh?"

"Yep. For a while."

Big Joe leaned conspiratorially across the counter.

"Gettin' any lately?"

"Sure."

"Watch yourself, young feller. Plenty of clap around."

"You betcha."

The brief smutty dialogue reinforced her confidence in her disguise. If she could fool Big Joe, she could fool the audience.

Raindrops the size of half dollars were splashing off the sidewalk by the time Jane reached the backstage entrance, and she was soaked. One of the strippers, a chunky Austrian girl who did comedy burlesque, pressed through the door alongside of her in a hurry to get in out of the rain.

"Should've listened to my crazy mother!" she gasped. "She warned me to take an umbrella...!"

Jane winced at the girl's derogatory reference to her mother. At that moment, Jane would have agreed to any chore, any servitude, for the rest of her life, if necessary...if by so doing she could have her mother alive and well and close to her again. Loneliness had become the tragedy of her young life. She hated being alone, having nobody. Often, she wished she had the guts to end her life.

Through the dressing room wall, she heard the blare of the music, the shouting and laughter of the audience. The first show was always thinly attended, and the heavy rain would probably keep the numbers low that night...mostly young punks blowing welfare checks on pot, cheap booze and an occasional girlie show. Connie's contralto could be heard accompanying the club's café-au-lait kitten from Brazil, Juanita, in the opening lines of her number.

> *"Ah doan wanna set the whirl...on...figh—ugh...*
> *Ah jes' wanna start...a flame in yo' heart.*
> *In mah heart there is but one dee—zigh—ugh...*
> *An' that one is yoooo...Nobody but you..."*

The slow, docile fox-trot rhythm, with Juanita moving gracefully across the stage, making every suggestive move imaginable, evoked hoarse screams from the audience.

"Hey, take it off! Take it all off!"

The beat changed to a Latin tempo, Connie began a new song, as Juanita unbuttoned her blouse and peeled it back.

"When they begin...the bee—geeeen...
It brings back a night...of music so tender..."

Temperatures rose as Juanita stripped, the hollering intensi-fying as the little bronze bundle of curves got down to her pasties and G-string.

Jane never had to wait for Helmer's insulting signal to get her ass out on stage. She treated him for the oaf he was, and he begrudgingly refrained from imposing any authority on her. Somehow, he sensed in Jane the superior intellect.

The small band struck up the Russian Sailor's Dance, and Jane staggered onto the stage, an empty bottle of Stolichnaya vodka to her lips. Back and forth the tipsy seaman stumbled, swaying crazily, periodically tripping over both clumsy feet.

When Jane's mannish buffoonery had milked sufficient hilar-ity from the crowd, the music subtly changed its pitch and tempo, drifting into a hot jazz rhythm while maintaining the same melody. Imperceptibly, the uncertain stumblings of the sailor became a smooth, well-executed soft-shoe tap dance routine, the awkward limbs becoming well coordinated and nimble, evoking applause.

Jane had warmed to her act, the audience acclaim having stimulated her. With the lift of a finger, the sailor signaled the musicians, and the percussion increased in tempo and volume. What had remained unseen at the start of the dance now became apparent. The coarse, tight midshipman's blouse was separating down the front and the crowd was hushed. With a brief roll of drums, Jane's hand floated gracefully over her hip, and in an instant, one entire bell-bottom trouser leg was gone, exposing the long, exquisitely formed leg of a statuesque woman. Another roll of drums and the other leg appeared, Jane strutting across the stage, all that was left of her sailor trousers only the narrowest navy-blue bikini. Narrow-hipped or not, her modernistic dance movements left no doubt regarding the vul-var crevice, and the audience howled.

It had taken days of practice, but Jane divested herself of the open middy blouse in a blur of grace, her nipples stiffening at the change in temperature. Shimmying across the stage, she heard the roar of the crowd and looked beyond the footlights at the typical first-show audience. Dissipated senior citizens, the unkempt young, a balding but well-dressed tourist seated off to one side. There were always tourists in town seeking thrills, action...

Jane bestowed the coup de grâce, dragging her blue woolen hat from her head and shaking free her fine, shoulder-length white-blonde hair. The surprising vision pulled the crowd up, shouting, applauding, and Jane felt the familiar sense of triumph at having fooled them into believing she was a man.

Ducking into the wings, she threw the pea coat around her and took a quick, smiling curtain call. The lights went up and the curtain came down. She was free for another hour.

The backstage mess had a way of bringing her down from the heights of exhilaration to the depths of gloom, at the realization she was only a cheap young stripper in a sleazy club, trying to find a quiet spot for herself between shows, amid crumpled, lipstick-smeared wads of tissue, cigarette butts and ashes strewn everywhere across dressing tables, spillages of beverages and astringents. Her nostrils assaulted by the sour odor of sweat and cheap cologne, Jane considered braving the downpour for a walk around Times Square to clear her head, but decided on a racy paperback instead.

All at once, Helmer was at her side with a slip of paper in his hand. Generally, it meant an invitation from someone in the audience. Helmer had delivered a dozen or more to her in the weeks she had been entertaining at the Moulin D'Or. Always another guy out there, beyond the glow of the footlights, seeking a couple of hours on a waterbed in some cheap motel with porno films on TV...Jane had disregarded all of them. This would be no exception.

"Guy out there wants to meet you," Helmer announced.

"Uh huh."

"He's hangin' around for the next show."

"So?"

"I think y'oughta meet 'im."

"Why?"

"'Cause he's different."

"What's different about him?"

Helmer handed her the slip of paper and grinned.

"He's with the U. N."

Jane looked at the name written on the paper Helmer handed her. Karol Tobirian. Curious.

"Does he look weird?"

"Losin' his hair. Everything else looks okay."

Jane remembered the well-dressed balding man off to the side in the front row. She folded the paper thoughtfully.

United Nations, huh? What the hell.

"Okay."

Her first surprise was the stretch Cadillac with tinted windows and a uniformed chauffeur waiting in the lot at the rear exit. The United Nations license plates had caught her eye immediately. Her next surprise was Karol Tobirian's insistence she not be in sailor costume when he took her out.

"I'm sure you must have a dress and decent shoes," he said.

"I'll have to borrow some things. I dress up at home to save time...," she tried to explain, embarrassed.

"I'll wait."

She had dreamed of dining at the Waldorf-Astoria for years, but the idea of being there was suddenly threatening. What did this man want of her? Where would the evening lead?

He asked her to call him Tobi, presenting her with his formal card, indicating his attachment to the Soviet delegation at the UN, quartered in one of the international residences on First Avenue, directly across from the multi-flagged pavilion.

He complimented her for a convincing portrayal of a young male when she was obviously a very feminine young woman. Jane began to hold her breath in anticipation of the insinuations and invitations she felt sure would follow. But there were none. No request that she accompany him to his apartment. No pawing of her knees under the table. Receding hairline and all, Tobi was no run-of-the-mill-girlie-ogler. Tall, macho, with quick brown eyes and long delicate fingers—like those of a concert pianist—Tobi spoke perfect English in the slow, pseudo-mocking drawl of Eastern Europe.

Connie was awake at two in the morning, hopping to Jane's side as the tired girl crawled into her rollaway bed.

"Hey, I saw the limo. What was he like?"

"Nice. Took me to the Waldorf, can you imagine?"

"Fabulous! What'd he want you to do?"

Jane scowled at her roommate, punched her pillow and turned away. She hated when Connie insisted on inquiring about the most personal matters, as though she experienced a vicarious thrill by imagining Jane in a variety of encounters with men.

"He was just a nice man," was Jane's reply. "I'm sleepy."

Suddenly, Connie was on top of her, lips grazing the side of her face. Hunching herself up to shake Connie off, Jane felt the warmth of a hand cupping her breast. Revolted, she flailed out and sent Connie sliding to the floor.

"My God, Connie!" she gasped, trembling. "What the hell do you think you're doing?"

Out of breath, Connie was getting to her feet.

"Don't look at me so innocently with those baby blues!" she hissed. "You know goddamned well what I'm doing!"

Jane's mind was screaming half-formed truths she had tried to pretend did not exist.

"We're *girls*, for heaven's sake!"

"Exactly," Connie nodded, narrow-eyed.

"What's that supposed to mean, Connie?"

"You're putting me on, Jane. You've known about me ever since you moved in! Don't pretend you didn't!"

Jane's mouth was a small open oval of silent horror. For a long moment, the room was very still. Then Jane sprang up and dashed to her corner of the closet, rummaging through the hangers.

"What're you doing?" Connie demanded.

"Leaving!"

"It's the middle of the night!"

"That's okay. I'll find a place to stay the night."

Connie placed her hand on Jane's shoulder and it was flung away as Jane pulled on a pair of jeans and a long-sleeved sweater.

Why had the room become so hot and oppressive! Jane had been gradually adjusting to Connie's need for extra warmth, but all at once, the temperature in the room was more than she could bear. It was becoming hard to breathe, and her heart was lurching unevenly. Under stress, she had often felt this way. During ugly arguments between her parents before their divorce...just before important exams at school...when they diagnosed her mother's breast lump as malignant...the night her mother lapsed into a coma...And, now...

"Jane, don't do this. You look awfully pale," Connie said in a small, contrite tone, her belligerence gone.

"Well, thanks to your crazy ideas, I feel pretty shitty right now!" Jane managed to gasp.

"I'm sorry, Jane, honey. Please go back to bed. I won't bother you. I promise."

Jane, panting as though she'd run half a dozen miles without a stop, with her ears ringing and a cold sweat chilling her body, was in no mood to walk through treacherous streets to the Port of New York Authority Building where she could find a bench on which to doze off, or a green leather stool in Walgren's soda fountain. As lousy as she felt, the new day seemed a year away, and Connie's remorse sounded like a reprieve.

"I'll look for a place in the morning," she managed weakly. "And I'll settle up what I owe you."

Connie, defeated, returned to her bed with her head down, and Jane, fully clothed, fell into hers. The arrhythmia was evening out. Her breathing was slower, less forced. Her head seemed to be clearing. She looked sadly over at the girl who'd been there for her.

"I'm sorry, Connie," she whispered, with a helpless shrug.

"For what?" Connie whispered back. "For being normal?"

Karol Tobirian showed up at the Moulin D'Or for the last show on Sunday night and took her back to the Waldorf. They talked of her dreams of being a ballet dancer. Tobirian assured her that the Soviet Union would have found no difficulty with her height in preparing her for the ballet. They talked of Nuriev and Fonteyn, of Mia Plissitskaya and Maria Tallchief.

She told him she had moved into her own apartment off the Avenue of the Americas and he offered to help in any way he could.

She searched his eyes and found them warm, sincere.

"Why would you want to?"

"Because you're a lovely young girl."

She laughed as she described waging a losing battle with cockroaches and mice in her new one-room flat, and Karol Tobirian raised his glass to hers in the shadows of a small cocktail lounge on Fifty-Second Street. Then he handed her a small, stiff envelope, and in it was a Macy's gift certificate worth two hundred dollars.

"Say, look, Tobi, I can't take this..."

"...Why not...?"

"...You just can't give me money this way..."

"...It's for your new apartment. Buy anything you like..."

"Yes, but I..."

"...And I want you to spend next weekend with me."

Her mouth remained open. Somehow, she felt disappointed. It had been too good to be true. Tobirian had begun their acquaintance in a fatherly fashion, caring, protective, and she had begun to trust him, no longer afraid that she would be obliged to fight him off, or go through long, tiring arguments of resistance with the man. Why had he spoiled the idyll for her, so soon?

Despondent, she folded her arms and gazed downward.

"Sorry, Tobi. I can't afford to take any time off."

"I'll make it up to you. I've reserved a couple of rooms at a place I know you'll like. In the Adirondacks. Lake George."

Her pale eyelashes fluttered. He had said, "a couple of rooms."

"What are you looking for, Tobi?"

"Companionship," he told her simply. "That's all."

She was skeptical, her gaze probing for some time.

"Yeah," she smirked. "You'll cover my weekend income and take me on a dream vacation. And all you want from me is companionship."

Tobirian smiled and touched her hand across the table.

"I have a son five years older than you, Jane. Maybe you'll meet him some day…"

From the terrace overlooking Lake George she saw a slight haze hanging over the mountains. The long drive north through the Hudson River Valley and the elegance of the Regency Hotel made for a heady experience. Arriving in late afternoon, they had enjoyed a marvelous dinner and watched a blaze roaring in the fireplace. Tobirian had reserved adjoining rooms, each with its own bath, and the doors separating their rooms could be locked on both sides. Jane wondered if he would attempt to enter her room during the night, but exhausted from the long trip, he went straight to bed, and although she awoke several times and put her ear to the door, she could hear only the steady, soft sound of snoring.

Having breakfast with him in the morning, she found her initial suspicion waning. He listened patiently and attentively to her gossip with apparent respect for her opinions. Occasionally, he offered her a glimpse of his own considerable intellect. She was fascinated by the warm, lively eyes beneath bushy, dark brows, the elegant gestures of his fine hands. So much masculinity and strength, combined with so much culture, she thought, as she listened to him describe his youth in the Georgian Soviet Socialist Republic.

"Stalin came from my part of the USSR," he told her. "Do you recognize the name, Stalin?"

"Of course. He was the Soviet leader in the Second World War who later fell from grace," she answered, proud of her knowledge.

"You're remarkable, Jane," Tobirian commented. "Do you know how very few American sixteen-year-olds would be able to answer that question?"

Jane was about to respond with something coy, but stopped and caught her breath, staring at him in astonishment.

"Why...why did you say...*sixteen*-year-olds?" she gasped.

"That's how old you are. Am I not correct?"

She felt chilled. Something was wrong there. Very wrong.

"I'm twenty-one!" she emphasized. "I'm a stripper in a night club! I'm going on twenty-two...!"

Tobirian laughed, his eyes vanishing into narrow slits as his high cheekbones came up. He pressed her wrist in reassurance.

"Jane...Jane...," he panted as his laughter subsided. "It's all right, *Malyinki*. I know what it says on your employment papers. But I also know how old you really are. And your secret is safe with me. I'd never do anything to hurt you."

She sat stunned, goose flesh prickling along her arms.

"How...how do you know...? Who told you how old I am...?"

His soft, warm eyes smiled evenly into hers.

"But my dear little Jane, I know *everything* about you."

Her breath came in shuddering little spasms. For the first time since she had met Tobirian, she felt genuine fear.

"What's this all about?" she demanded, her throat dry.

Tobirian drew a deep breath and looked about as though searching for the best way to begin as Jane sat immobilized.

"What it's all about, little Jane, is that I propose to take you back with me to the Soviet Union, where you will become a student at the University of Moscow..."

"*You're crazy!*"

"...No, I am not crazy, and I wish you would hear me out before interrupting me again! I propose that you quit your job at the Moulin D'Or, take whatever clothes you absolutely must have for your trip, and accompany me to Moscow..."

Jane snapped her fingers in heated sarcasm.

"Right. Just like that. Tobi pays for my trip, my room and board, even for my tuition at the university..."

"No, Jane," he broke in gently. "Tobi doesn't pay for anything. The Soviet Government will see to that. My country offers free education to a number of promising foreigners..."

"Just how promising a foreigner do I have to be?"

Tobirian's eyes were dark and smoldering. He was not accustomed to sass from a youngster. It called for much restraint on his part, and somehow, he managed to convey to her the feeling that he was about to lose a very volatile temper. She sat subdued.

"I might add," he went on quietly, "...that my government takes care of its own. In your case, Jane, that's exactly what we would be doing. You're not a foreigner in our eyes, Jane..."

She sank back in her seat. *He knew.* Knew everything about her. How long he had followed her, she had no idea. But there was no sense trying to lie to the man when her life...to him...was obviously an open book.

"*Da, Malyinki,*" he whispered, and she felt strangely comforted by the sound of the musical Russian words. "We've kept track of you since your birth in San Francisco. That's where your mother died...your *natural* mother. Her name was Tanya Ivanova, and she was a beauty, just like you. We followed your adoptive parents, Craig and Amy Sutton, through your troubled childhood, through the divorce of your adoptive parents, through the privation you endured when Craig Sutton disregarded the court's order for child support, through your poor mother's final illness. We followed you right to this very table, where we now sit...you and I...to map out what you can do with your future."

Tears rolled down Jane's cheeks and Tobirian produced his handkerchief and brushed at them gently, like a devoted father.

She could not help weeping. This man was not a charlatan, not a liar. Everything about him had been legitimate. He had always kept his word with her. He represented one of the most powerful nations on the face of the earth. And he knew everything there was to know about her...

"Moscow University is a respected institution," he continued. "My country's capital is a fascinating city. I do think you would be very happy there."

The idea was so enthralling, so enticing. She, Jane Sutton, a burlesque performer with a highschool equivalency diploma, could go abroad, attend a university, and could become something in life! When would such an opportunity ever present itself again?

"What if I went to Moscow and didn't like it?" she probed, almost embarrassed to word the question. "Would I be trapped there...would your government hold me there against my will?"

"Arrangements will be made, quite properly, with your own State Department, Jane," Tobirian assured her. "They would be free to contact you at any time, to determine your state of mind. Of that, you can be sure."

Jane's mind was racing ahead. Was this a dream? Was it reality? Could she trust what he was saying? Any of it?

"When...when would this happen?" she managed to ask, clearing her throat. "When would we leave?"

"By the end of the month, Jane."

In only ten more days, then. Jane covered her face with both hands and sat there trying to quiet the hammering of her heart.

"Would you...would you be there with me, Tobi?"

"For a while, yes, Jane," he said with kindness. "Until you'd made good friends and contacts who would look after you."

In a little-girl manner, she spread her hands, shrugging.

"Tobi, this is so impossible!" she squealed, crying. "I don't speak a word of Russian!"

"You will learn, *Malyinki*. You will have teachers."

She wept unashamed, wiping her tears with her fingertips.

"When you call me '*Malyinki*'...what does that mean?" she sobbed.

Tobirian cupped her chin fondly, wagging his head.

"It simply means 'little one'...'*dear* little one.'"

"Oh, my God!" she wept excitedly. "Oh, dear God!"

"And perhaps one day you will have another surprise in Russia…"

"What?" she asked, flabbergasted. "What?"

Tobirian waited. The girl was too tense. A nerve throbbed in her throat as she stared at him with her great turquoise eyes.

"You may one day meet your brother, little Jane."

What kind of nonsense was this? Perhaps this was all a highly disorganized dream. Perhaps he'd slipped some drug in her coffee…

"M-my…my *what*?" she choked.

"Your brother, Jane. The child with whom you came into the world in San Francisco. Your *twin*…"

Part Two

Chapter 5

(Moscow)

A steady drizzle fell on the Kutuzovsky Prospekt, setting atremble all the pink petals of the windowsill's boxed geraniums. From their roots rose the rich, musty odor of soaked earth, drifting into the hotel room twenty-nine floors above the Moskva River, borne on the chill autumn breeze. It was the kind of cold breeze that filtered through flesh to settle in one's bones, the kind of breeze that whistled through the moth-caten trees of Central Park between Election Day and Thanksgiving. Jane took a deep breath , remembering, with nostalgia.

Strange, to be thinking of New York and Thanksgiving after so long. Strange, to be remembering the months of her mother's final illness, those terrible weeks of running back and forth to visit her at the hospital. Strange and sad, to recall her mother's death, and her job at the Moulin D'Or.

Where Tobi had found her...

*   *   *   *

Tobirian placed her with infinite care in the bosom of his family. Mirabianka, his wife, a dour but pleasant schoolteacher who spoke English as flawlessly as her husband, gave her their son's room upon her arrival.

"You've just missed Sergei," Mirabianka told her warmly. "He's an engineering student at Moscow State University and comes home only every other weekend. He, too, is doing well with English, so perhaps in two weeks, when he's here again, you'll be able to enjoy a simple conversation with him."

Jane glanced at the array of photographs on an oakwood drumtable in front of the living room window. Prominently displayed next to the traditional wedding picture of the Tobirian couple were older photos which appeared to be their parents, and one of a dark-haired youth with poetically brooding eyes and Tobi's classical features. She knew it had to be Sergei.

Each morning, Mirabianka—who very shortly became 'Mira' to Jane because it was the name by which Tobi addressed his wife—took Jane by bus to a special classroom in the school where she taught English and Social Studies. Jane found she was one of four students, all foreign, enrolled in a crash course in conversational Russian. The other three students were weeks into the course and making good progress, listening to tapes—all political in content—and learning the various Party slogans: "Long live the Soviet People, Builders of Communism!" and "Glory to Work!" and "The Party and the People are United!" As a youngster growing up in New York City, Jane had scarcely been aware of political advertising when an important election was coming up. But in Moscow, political advertising was ubiquitous. The very street names were impressive, indicating the country's obsession with politics and the spirit of the ideology that kept it alive. Karl Marx Prospekt, Lenin Prospekt, Revolution Square, Prospekt Mira—were some of the landmarks Jane noted as the constant politicization of public life. Glass-encased bulletin boards could be found on every sidewalk, posting Communist Party and Government newspapers for easy stand-up reading by pedestrians. Loudspeakers in the public parks blared martial music and continually broadcast the speeches of Party luminaries and special news reports.

Heroic statuary dominated the city. One of the first sights the Tobirians took Jane to see was the red marble tomb of Lenin in Red Square, the central shrine of Moscow. It amazed Jane to see the long lines of people from Moscow and everywhere else in the USSR and its satellites, visiting the place of honor. She spent a day with her hosts at the Exhibition of the Achievements of the People's Economy, covering five hundred acres and containing over one hundred pavilions displaying everything from farm equipment to Sputniks, and Jane gawked at the dynamic stainless steel figures of Communist construction—a young farm girl, a *kollektiv*, wielding a sickle in one hand, her other arm locked with that of a muscular young worker clenching a hammer in his fist.

"You'll get used to all this," Tobirian laughed when he saw the wonder in Jane's eyes. "After a while, you won't notice it."

Two of the students in Jane's class were teenagers from Zaire. A girl, Petra, about eighteen, and—obviously—her lover, Jomo, a year older. The other student was a tall young man from East Berlin. He had cold blue eyes and thick straight hair the color of sand, a perpetual pout to his mouth and a deep cleft in his chin. Jane found the African couple charming with their great dark eyes and gleaming smiles—particularly Petra, who wore her charcoal black hair in a fascinating array of colorful bead-strung braids.

The young German's name was Rudiger Furst, and when he made his introductory little bow to Jane, she fell hopelessly in love.

And even more deeply so, when she joined the other three to a tearoom on the Ulitsa Presnensky where they'd been told the best *vareniki* in Moscow were served. Tobi had been educating Jane in the value of the ruble and how to budget her weekly allowance. Checking her purse, she found she had enough with her for a brief excursion to the eatery. Besides, it gave her an opportunity to be with new friends.

Between the Africans' pidgin English and Rudiger Furst's schoolboy attempts, Jane understood much of what was said. She learned that, like herself, they were being sponsored by a government program of educating selected students from various countries—students considered to be prime candidates for eventual positions of trust in the government's service.

"Madame Prusovskaya say you from New Yorka!" Jomo exclaimed with glee, delighted when Jane understood his statement. "One day Petra and I come visit you in New Yorka. Then you and Rudi come visit us in our country, too!"

Jomo had linked the two Caucasian students—the two blonds, Jane and Rudiger—as a couple. That linkage was immediately noticed, and Jane was acutely aware of Rudiger's probing scrutiny, the ice-blue eyes beneath their hood of long brown lashes, the rosy flush across sharply-defined Nordic cheekbones. Either he would not, or *could* not, smile.

"So you are Jane," he stated. "Like Jane Mansfield?" and she nodded, her heart skipping at the drama of his strong accent. His glance traveled openly over her from head to toe.

"You are blonde like Mansfield," he conceded begrudgingly. "Otherwise, there is no resemblance."

Jane flushed at the tactlessness. She knew she was as flat-chested as a boy, especially in her heavy Russian outfits, with none of her long slender curves visible. Well, so Rudi was a T&A man, and Jane had long been aware that unless she were unclothed on stage, whipping an audience to fever pitch with an erotic dance, she didn't really cut it as a woman.

But Rudi was the first man ever to excite her fantasies, and when they studied together in Madame Prusovskaya's class, she often stole glances in his direction. Whenever she found him staring back, she became flustered and redirected her attention to her notebook.

The hardest thing for Jane to absorb was the Cyrillic alphabet, in which some characters looked exactly like English letters but were not, and while she caught on quickly to the spoken language, she feared it would be years before she'd read a first grade primer.

The role of women also bothered her. Jane would observe Tobi's sweeping, dramatic gestures as he extolled the virtues of his city and his people—while Mira, in nodding silence, agreed with every word her husband uttered. Even when he was wrong.

Returning from an evening's drive around Moscow, Tobi would park close to his residence on the Zhadanova Ulitsa— (never a problem finding street parking in Moscow!)—and with a signal to Mira, would lean over the hood of his Fiat and quickly remove both windshield wipers and the side view mirror, then all four hubcaps. These items would be hand-carried up to their third floor apartment and set down against the kitchen wall. When the auto was next to be used, they would be carried down and re-attached.

"Why on earth do you do that?" Jane inquired in all innocence.

"Because one has to wait long for spare parts," Tobi replied with a certain degree of discomfort, and Jane knew better than to have him explain his non sequitur. Thievery of auto parts and tools as well as of most manufactured products was carried out on a grand scale in the Soviet Union, and by the most respectable citizens. The news of this common criminality was kept under wraps.

Within two weeks, Jane had learned to do the family shopping at daybreak—queuing up before shops in the neighborhood, giving Mira a chance to enjoy an extra hour or so of rest. She had also started doing the household cleaning and laundry and learned from Mira certain arts of Russian cooking, for which she seemed to have a natural gift, and the Tobirians told her so.

The apartment on Zhadanova Street was a four-room affair, its square kitchen serving as a dining room, the windows of its modest living room looking directly into those of a building across the alleyway. There were two minuscule bedrooms with cracking walls and one bathroom in which the plumbing was noisy and unreliable, the showerhead managing to allow an uneven trickle of tepid water, while cockroaches crawled out of the woodwork and up the sides of the tub to flop in and swim grotesquely with the bather, their useless wings spread and antennae questing along the surface. After two such cockroach baths, Jane preferred the trickle of the showerhead instead.

But the Tobirians were proud of their apartment in one of Moscow's more modern buildings, for it boasted a private bathroom and an extra bedroom. The rent was higher than average, but Tobi was with the diplomatic corps and entitled to certain privileges.

The night before Sergei was expected for the weekend, Tobi borrowed an army cot from a fellow consul so that his son would be comfortable with living room sleeping arrangements, and he and Mira apologized for the extra crowding Jane would feel during Sergei's infrequent visits.

"Oh, I'm used to crowding!" Jane laughed. "Besides, you two are so good to me, I'll never be able to repay you for all this!"

"But hasn't Karol explained?" Mira asked, surprised. "We're being paid for your board and care by an agency of the government. Its funds come from a special program for foreign students."

Sergei was the thoughtful, taciturn type, with his father's features and his mother's pale complexion. His eyes followed Jane wherever she went, but he was apparently too unsure of himself to initiate conversation with the young American. He was, however, as fluent as Tobi in English, and after their first family dinner together—once Mira had shooed Jane out of the kitchen intimating she should get to know Sergei—he conversed with her about school.

"You speak English beautifully," she complimented him, and he turned bright red, the flicker of a shy smile lifting a corner of his mouth. "I know I'll never do as well in your language as you do in mine."

"Yes, you will. You'll see," he assured her. "You need practice. My parents should speak to you in Russian so that you are forced to train your ear and mind to understanding. Vocabulary and grammar will come in their own good time."

A sweet young man, Jane mused. Not dynamic, not the type to set her nerves on fire, but dear and charming nonetheless.

"When I come next time home," Sergei suggested, "...I'll have tickets to concert. Would you like to join me? There will be other students there. I will introduce you to those who speak good English."

"That would be very nice, Sergei," she agreed gratefully, and felt a rush of tenderness for the warm young man. He was someone she hoped she would hold as a treasured friend for years to come.

But her fantasies were filled with her fellow student, Rudiger Furst—with the sound of his voice and the thrill of his glances.

It was still dark when she awakened, and she had promised Mira to be one of the first on line at the greengrocers on the Ulitsa Solyanka, where they were to have a good supply of carrots, celery and green beans. The bedroom was freezing, the heat from the basement's steam boiler just beginning to clang through the tall, slender pipes that stood in stark ugliness in a corner of each room. Whisking off her flannel nightgown, she draped her terrycloth robe tightly about her, pulled a sweater, skirt and fresh underwear from a bureau drawer, and rushed the few steps to the bathroom.

It was always under the shower that she found time to think about what she was doing in Russia. True, in the United States, she had been without family and short on friends, depending on her looks and dubious dancing ability for a living. The future had been extremely bleak, almost hopeless. Had she not taken Karol Tobirian up on his offer, she would never have had the opportunity to study in Moscow, to travel abroad and enjoy this experience. She admitted that somewhere in the back of her mind was a small, subdued hunger to return to New York and escape from the grim, collectivist Moscow scene with its endless shortages and line-ups of citizens winding blocks long for commodities which Americans took for granted on a day-by-day basis. The Russian people were friendly, quick to offer advice and guidance, to be protective of the young, to demonstrate caring, parental helpfulness—and for Jane, that was important. Her life had been so lacking in that.

Using the last of the shampoo, she realized she would have to buy a new bottle at GUM Department Store, first chance she got. The water from the showerhead seemed to be cooler than usual and even the strength of its trickle was not up to par...barely a slow seepage, and she had a head of lather to rinse away. Furiously, she twisted the squeaky faucets to full volume, and the thin pipe coughed, gushing a torrent of rusty water into her face. Spitting, rubbing her eyes, she held her head under the nozzle until the shampoo was gone, bubbling in a snow-white froth at her feet.

Her eyes still stinging, she squeeze-dried her hair, dragged back the shower curtain and placed one leg out onto the tile floor. The moisture on her body chilled almost to ice in the draft that hit her, for the door had been flung open, and Sergei Tobirian, in a white undershirt and powder blue boxer shorts, was just entering, one hand to his crotch and a look of utter shock freezing on his face.

"Oh, my God!" Jane gasped, not knowing what to grab first, the edge of the shower curtain or the sleeve of her bathrobe dangling from the towel bar—accomplishing neither, and aware that despite his shock, Sergei's glance seemed fixed upon her full frontal nudity for several interminable seconds.

"*Oi chort! Prast'eeteh!*" the young man gasped, cheeks aflame, ducking out of the doorway and pulling the knob behind him.

Whimpering with seething embarrassment, Jane blotted herself dry with the rough towels and dressed in a wild blur of speed. Her hair streamed dark gold over the shoulders of her sweater, and sucking in her breath for a renewal of courage, she pulled open the bathroom door and ducked by the waiting Sergei without a glance or word. Once back in her room, she tried to calm herself, scooping her hair up under a white knitted cloche which Mira had given her for chilly mornings. Her feet and legs were still wet, but she pulled on a pair of woolen knee-high's and stepped into her anklet boots, shrugging into her winter coat and tossing a woolen scarf carelessly around her neck. The flush and gurgle of water in the bathroom, followed by racing footsteps beyond her bedroom door, told her Sergei had probably returned to his living room cot.

Swallowing hard, she started through her door and across the living room when Sergei, in a shirt and trousers and totally out of breath, stood before her.

"*Pazhahl'sta*, please, Miss Sutton. I am so sorry!" he gasped.

"It's okay, it's okay," she mumbled, trying to push past him.

"That was so clumsy of me..."

"It's okay. Forget it. Please."

"I am accustomed to...you know how it is..."

"Yes, of course. This is your house."

"I was in great hurry. I should have seen light on under door. I did not look. I am so sorry."

"Please, it's not that important! Just forget it!"

"I embarrassed you. I did not mean to. Please forgive..."

Her head was so hot she thought her hair would catch fire.

"All right, a'ready!" she exclaimed, lapsing into New Yorkese. "It was nobody's fault. Let's just forget it!"

She dashed toward the door and let herself out.

On stage at the Moulin D'Or, as a stripper, it had never occurred to her to be embarrassed by exposing herself to a full audience. But in the intimate confines of the small apartment, among strangers, she felt weak with shame that the Tobirian's young son had seen her in the altogether. With that wave of shame came the realization that Karol Tobirian, too, had studied her charms as a burlesque dancer.

"Oh, my God!" she exclaimed aloud, her breath forming a white cloud on the frosty dawn air, and several passers-by looked with curiosity at the pretty young girl walking hunched against the cold, talking to herself.

*   *   *   *

The salesgirl gave her dark, quizzical looks while wrapping the imported bottle of French shampoo and waiting for Jane to count the rubles in her hand. Jane knew her accent and her unfamiliarity with Russian currency marked her as a tourist, and the ordinary Russian shopkeepers and sales personnel had no great love for tourists, showing off their affluence and putting on airs.

Happy with her purchase, she started away from the toiletry department in GUM, hoping to make it back to the apartment before the downpour began in earnest.

Rain had been forecast for the entire weekend, and Mira had taken the single umbrella. But Jane needed that shampoo. The concert for which Sergei had obtained tickets was Sunday evening, and she felt fortunate at having made the purchase Saturday morning. At least she would look nice when introduced to Sergei's friends. Her Russian had been improving some, and both Mira and Karol had been praising her progress.

She still felt embarrassed in Sergei's presence, and he in hers. He had remained away the next weekend he was expected home, informing his mother of special exams coming up, for which he had to cram without any distractions. Smiling to herself in mischief, Jane wondered if she represented the specific distraction Sergei had in mind.

"Yahni!" a voice close behind her called.

Sensing that unfamiliar mispronunciation of name was meant for her, and recognizing the voice, Jane turned to find Rudiger Furst smiling at her in pleased surprise.

"Rudi! What are you doing here?"

"Shopping, of course. I see you bought French shampoo."

So! He had been observing her, the entire transaction!

"Yes, I'm tired of washing my hair with bar soap," she laughed.

Rudi spread his arms in an encompassing gesture.

"Welcome to Russia!" he chuckled, sharing a secret with her.

It was the first time they had ever exchanged more than a vague hello or goodbye. Somehow, the ice had been broken, and Jane felt strangely relieved.

"Where are you going now?" he asked, with the ponderous touch of the Teuton.

"Home, of course. They say it's going to rain hard."

"Yes, and the streets shall flood as they always do. I bought some soap and shaving cream. Hope it's not all turned to lather by the time I get to my place."

They walked out of the department store onto Vetoshny Street, then passed the small buildings and shops to the Ulitsa Kuibysheva.

"Do you live close by here?" Jane asked, wondering why her voice was quivering, and Rudi nodded, pointing up ahead.

"A block past Nogin Square. One room with a dirty window which I cannot force open. But it overlooks the Moskva River, and sometimes, late at night, I lie in bed and imagine what the breeze might feel like..."

Jane laughed liltingly, and Rudi brightened at her appreciation of his cynicism. He insisted on carrying her package, then lighted a cigarette and offered her one. She shook her head.

"That's right," he said. "I'd forgotten. Americans don't smoke. They have destroyed the tobacco industry. All American illness comes from tobacco, just like all Russian illness comes from alcohol, or hadn't you heard?"

She laughed again, glancing at him sideways as they strolled along the busy, crowded streets filled with shoppers. She could not help marveling at his exquisite profile. He reminded her of the very young Robert Wagner in the role of Prince Valiant.

He pointed out an octagon-shaped tower, commemorating the Battle of Plevna in the Russo-Turkish War, and the Polytechnic Museum. A low rumble droned through the gray-white skies, and the breeze from the river whipped up, aiming itself at the crowds like a blast of aerated ice. Jane felt Rudi's arm around her shoulders as they hugged the side of the building on their way to Nogin Square.

"And see that building over there?" Rudi asked, Jane recalling that Tobirian had pointed it out to her, but not remembering its significance. "That's the Central Committee of the Communist Party of the Soviet Union, out of which the funds come for our upkeep, yours and mine."

She looked askance at him. For the first time, it occurred to her that they were chosen guests of the Soviet Union, both of them.

A lightning bolt shaped like a pitchfork flashed over the building up ahead, and was followed by a clap of thunder so deafening that the sidewalk vibrated beneath their feet. People familiar with the signs broke into a run for shelter, and in an instant, the rain poured down and they were pelted by a combination of water and hail which soaked them through in very short order.

"Come on!" Rudi shouted above the splashing of the downpour and the sound of objects being flung about by the storm. "I live only a block from here..."

The room measured about eight by ten and yes, it did have one window covered with the dust of many years on the outside, but through which Jane could, indeed, see the grayness of the Moskva River. There was no clutter. Apparently an orderly and well-organized student, Rudi seemed to possess a thousand books on a number of shelves which he had evidently built himself along one wall. As Jane peeled off her soaked things, Rudi placed them on a wooden hanger and suspended the hook from the knob of an overhead cabinet. She noticed he had tossed his own jacket and scarf over the back of the single chair.

"It's not much of a place," he smiled. "But beggars can't be choosers. Excuse me while I fix us a drink."

He left for the community kitchen where part of a shelf in the collective refrigerator was allotted to him for his foodstuffs. Jane felt oddly relaxed just being in the room, waiting for his return, and wondering about her feelings, her expectations.

Returning, he held aloft two bottles and two glasses.

"I had a bottle of pshenichnaya, vodka made from wheat, and very good! And spring water. Sorry, no ice," he laughed, sitting down on the edge of the bed and pouring two glassfuls.

"Not too much for me!" she stopped him.

"Why not? It will warm you. You could have caught a chill in that sudden rain just now. This will help."

They touched glasses and smiled into each other's eyes.

The vodka was stronger than any she had ever tasted in New York. It burned its way down her throat and she made a face.

"It's strong!" she choked.

"That's the idea, isn't it? What good is weak liquor?"

They looked up as the rain slashed violently against the window, rattling the glass in its thin metal framing. Rudi poured himself another drink, and Jane watched him in fascination. In the eerie shadows there seemed to be an aura of white light around his head. Jane resisted the impulse to reach out and touch the thick, fair hair.

"Is it true, what I've learned of you, Yahni?" he asked, and there was a low huskiness in his soft whisper.

"What have you heard?"

"That you're an orphan of Russian parentage...?"

She sipped her drink, closing her eyes. He had been interested enough to find out about her background.

"Yes, it's true, Rudi."

"They chose me that way, too. Approached me while I was still in school back in Berlin. They had been doing things for me since I was sixteen. In seventy-two I was a medalist in the Olympics in track. They saw me as a sportsman, someone who could coach winning teams for them. But then they tested my brain and found I had one. So now, I'm being trained, just as you are..."

"For what, Rudi? What are they training us for?"

He studied her for a long, tense moment.

"You really don't know?"

"No. Tell me."

"If we come through our training well, and impress them with what we can do, we'll be foreign operatives in the KGB..."

"The KGB! But...but that's...," she sputtered helplessly.

"Part of their secret service. Exactly."

Amazed, she combed her fingers through her long hair, surprised to find the ends still sopping, feeling the faint splash against the side of her face. In a flash, Rudi was on his feet, scavenging in a cardboard box standing in a corner, returning with a folded Turkish towel...

"My God!" Jane exclaimed faintly. "I had no idea that..."

"Your hair is dripping," he interrupted, standing directly behind her chair and covering her hair with the towel, pressing the ends in its folds. "Let's dry you off..."

"Did you know this when they first invited you to Moscow, Rudi? Did you know what they had in mind?" she asked, the wild astonishment in her expression leaving no room for doubt that she had been innocent of any ulterior motive on Tobirian's part when he induced her to come to his country as a student.

"Not at first," Rudi replied, stroking the lengths of hair in the towel and blotting the rain from her temples. "I was a wild teenager out of a miserable orphanage, and the idea of being paid for sports was terrific! To run...and get paid for it? To play hockey...and get paid for it? To swim and ski and get paid for doing the things I enjoyed? What could be wrong with that?"

They were visualizing each other upside down. Jane felt herself breathing very deeply and swallowed several times to still the beat of her heart. Perhaps the blood left her cheeks...or some grimace, however unintentional but nevertheless irrepressible, darted across her face...but in a moment, Rudi was squatting in front of her, taking her hand in his and searching her face with concern.

"Did what I said upset you, Yahni? You look so pale..."

"No, I'm all right, really I am," she protested, enjoying the way he kept pressing the towel to her brow and the sides of her face and neck. "It's just that I had no idea..."

"They told me when I was here a few months. They'll probably get around to telling you fairly soon, I'd imagine..."

"Did you...did you agree to their plan?"

Rudi smiled his cynical smile and folded the towel across his knees, still squatting before her, holding her hand.

"How old are you, Yahni?"

"I'll be seventeen in September..."

"And you're a United States Citizen. You may be able to refuse them. I didn't have the luxury of such a choice."

There was a long silence. An arc of magnetism hung invisible in the air between them, but their innermost selves could ascertain the buzzing. Jane knew her lips were parted, as though she were sipping, imbibing his youthful male beauty, stirred by it to her very depths, hypnotized by it. She knew that the words tumbling forth from her mouth were constructed by one side of her brain, with logic and clarity, but that emotionally, she was drowning in a maelstrom of sympathy and longing.

"And have you come to terms with it, Rudi?" she asked.

There was a hesitant pause. He slipped his free hand about her waist and drew her up with him. She felt she was floating.

"Yes, I've come to terms with it. I'll do as they say."

"You won't resist them at all?" she breathed, eyes searching.

"What's the good of resisting what happens in our lives...?"

"But it should be of your choosing...of my choosing..."

He drew her close and she felt the clamor of his heart against her breast. His mouth was close to hers, his breath warm and sweet.

"Yahni, this moment is of my choosing. Is it yours?"

He had pressed the length of her body tight to his, the hard configuration of his desire starkly evident. She heard herself murmur, "Oh!" and crossed her slender arms behind his neck as his mouth found hers in a brief, brushing kiss, awaiting her response. As always, whenever stress overtook her, she became aware of irregularities in her heartbeat, a sense of breathlessness, the mildest wave of nausea and vertigo.

"Will you choose this moment, Yahni?" Rudi whispered.

His hand had worked up beneath her wool sweater to unclasp her bra. She felt the elasticized ends flap loose and the contoured fabric move awry across her breasts. A blast of wind and rain drummed noisily at the window. Lightning flickered three times in rapid succession through the shadowy room, and the outbreak of thunder was like the ripping of the gods against the veil of the planet. The room seemed to tremble. Somewhere, a book fell to the floor with a thud.

"I choose...," she sighed and closed her eyes in surrender.

The minutiae of erotic detail became blurred. Darkness, as of late dusk, had fallen over the city, and the storm streaked white slashes against the rattling windowpane. Rainwater seeped through the ancient crack in the framing, driven by the force of the north winds. Above the soft sound of Rudi's breath, Jane heard the tiny droplets of water plopping on a slow-forming puddle on the floor.

Even in the deep shadows, he was ruddy bronze and gold with the rippling muscles and sinews of the young athlete. The touch of his fingers exploring her delicate flesh was like electrical fire. Jane thought of the young god in her arms, the smooth, healthy firmness of his skin, the superb breadth of chest and back, the steel lock of his arms wound about her. He had spoken of winning an Olympic medal in 1972. That would have been in Munich, of course. Perhaps he had been eighteen at the time. She guessed his age at about twenty-two. An orphan, like herself, given the chance of a lifetime. What did it matter, in whose cause? The history of the world would not be written or changed one iota by the deeds of a Rudi or a Jane.

"Yahni, when I said you did not resemble Jane Mansfield, I said the truth," he whispered close to her ear, the tip of his tongue touching lightly over the sensitive structure. "You are even more beautiful. Really, you are."

She was too frightened to speak. It was forbidden, what she was permitting to happen...and with fear came a slight revulsion, not aimed at Rudi, but at herself, for having given in, for having undressed and followed willingly to his bed...in midday, with a young man who was also a stranger in this strange country. Rudi sensed the tension surging within her and raised up.

"*Was ist's, Kleines?*" she heard him murmur. "What's the matter?"

"I'm...I'm scared...," she quavered.

His fingers lightly brushed her disheveled hair away from her forehead and stroked tenderly against her cheek.

"Have you no experience?" he whispered.

"Not really..."

He did not move. All she could hear was his breathing. Then, "Would you...would you rather...not?" he asked.

There was such disappointment, such sadness in his voice that she clasped him close, loving the feel of him.

"Yahni, since first I saw you, I've wanted you..."

"Me, too..."

"Then don't be afraid. Just relax. You're so lovely..."

A tiny, wailing shriek rose all the way back in her throat.

"Ooooooh, Rudi..."

"Ssssh,*Kleines*. Don't be afraid. Easy...That's it..."

"Rudi...*Rudi!*"

"Don't cry, *Liebchen*. You're mine now...and I love you, little girl. I really love you..."

For the rest of her life, the sound of raindrops thumping at windowpanes, the coursing of stormwater creating a tympany of metallic gurgling through tinny gutters, the crackle of lightning and the droning roar of thunder would forever be associated with her initial experience with passion, the awakening of libido, and the rhythm of her body lifting and straining with his.

Had there been anyone else ever to say she was loved? Her mother had told her she loved her...a million times. But she scarcely remembered the face of her father. All she recalled of him were harsh scoldings and the gruff anger of his voice...the tension and contention that existed, unrelieved, between her parents. The feeling of guilt, that she had somehow come between them as an unwanted responsibility.

No, Jane could remember having been told by no person other than her mother that she was loved. That she was worthy of love.

Until Rudiger Furst, on a stormy afternoon in Moscow, in a tiny cell smelling of books and antiquity, took her with infinite tenderness and made her his own, telling her he loved her.

They were bathed in perspiration, their skin clammy to one another's touch, and Rudi excused himself briefly. When he returned to her side, he drew the billowy featherticking up to their chins and held her close.

"Are you all right?" he nuzzled her.

"Yes. I love you, Rudi..."

She could not remember ever feeling so safe, so protected, in all her young life. She wished the afternoon would last forever, never wanted to leave his side. The storm seemed to have spent most of its fury. Sporadic lightning flickered quietly now and then, the thunder had become subdued. The rain streamed, rather than struck, against the window. The din of flying metal objects in the streets below had ceased almost entirely.

"Forgive me for hurting you, Yahni..."

"The sheet is wet. I'm afraid I stained your bed..."

"Don't worry about it. There are laundries..."

She stroked his chest, awed by the firm rise of the pectorals, his skin now warm beneath the palm of her hand.

"What happens now, Rudi...?"

His mouth grazed against her forehead and he cupped her chin.

"We are lovers. What do you think will happen?"

"I don't know. Did you mean it when you said you loved me?"

"Yes. But don't expect me to tell you so every day."

"Then say it to me again...now," she pleaded.

He took a deep breath and rolled over her with care, toying with strands of her hair, gazing into her eyes.

"Whenever we make love, I will say it," he whispered.

She trembled and he held her close.

"I'll say it in my language, your language, and in our new language," he murmured into her hair, and she sensed the renewal of his desire as his hands glided over her body. She found herself fully ready for him, yearning, throbbing, hungry to be filled.

"Oh, I love you, Rudi...I love you...," she moaned.

He kissed her again and again, as his slow, careful penetration sent an electrical charge through her entire being, a charge zinging like the touch of a battery's low voltage against the palate of her mouth. She clasped her legs around him and rocked with him in steaming passion, ignoring the stinging abrasion of a new onslaught against freshly-wounded flesh, concentrating only on the excitement, the ecstasy leading to the warm bath of pleasure.

"Yahni, I love you...," Rudi gasped, keeping his promise. *"Ich liebe Dich...Ya lyublyutibyet, Duschitzka..."*

Sergei was proud to introduce Jane to four friends, students at Moscow State University enrolled in classes at both the old building on Prospekt Marxa and the new complex on Leninsky Boulevard. Boris and Natasha seemed to be progressing well in a romantic relationship. Vadim and Anna had recently announced their betrothal. All four were friendly to Jane, and spoke excellent English, albeit with strong "nya" and "lya" and "kh" sounds interspersed where they did not belong.

The concert was given at the Tschaikowsky Concert Hall on Gorky Street, opening with several sentimental songs by Mikhail Glinka, sung by a new young artist, Viktorija Sorgskaya, who followed with a long aria from Ruslan and Ludmila. Then the concert pianist, Alexander Miska, delivered an impassioned rendition of Rachmaninov's Concerto and Scriabin's Poem of Ecstasy, both of which brought tears to Jane's eyes.

The melodies flowed through her being like the warmth of Rudi's passion, and she could not wait for the next opportunity to be alone with him again.

After the concert, they went to a combination tearoom-dancehall, the Sofia, on Gorky Street, where an all-girl dance band played Russian and Polish polkas, gypsy music and popular American swing out of the 20's, 30's and 40's. Jane found the tea straight from the samovar much too strong and sweet, but Sergei introduced her to a special kind of *blini*, a cake-like affair filled with mushrooms and sour cream, which she found delightful. But she felt lost among the brilliant university students, particularly when they spoke of the literature of their country, the realistic works of Ketlinskaya and Ehrenburg.

"Have you read Solzhenitsyn?" Natasha asked with genuine curiosity, making no real attempt to discredit Jane intellectually.

"I'm afraid not," Jane replied, blushing, knowing she was out of place with this group of young men and women who were so superior to her academically. "I'm new to your language, you see."

"But surely you've read Pasternak's 'Dr. Zhivago'?" Vadim insisted on pressing. "You know that Pasternak was awarded the Nobel Prize for Literature in fifty-eight, don't you?"

The year before I was born, Jane mused. How much am I supposed to experience in less than seventeen years?

"I haven't read the book," she confessed. "But I did see the movie, with Omar Shariff as Zhivago and Julie Christy as Lara, and I cried and cried...It was so beautiful..."

"We must give Jane a chance to accustom herself to our language before we can expect her views on our literature!" Sergei laughed, coming to her rescue and pouring another cup of tea for her. "And besides, we're all at least five years older than Jane."

She gave him a grateful smile and sipped her tea, listening to the conversation, which concerned the didactic and moralizing tone of a whole genre of novels containing idealized, positive heroes and marked similarity of situation and plot.

It was all beyond her, and she gave up trying to understand them. Her mind wandered back to the previous afternoon in Rudi's arms, to the sensation of his flesh moving inside her body. Blood rushed to her cheeks at the memory, and she caught Sergei regarding her with more than casual interest.

"Will you dance with me?" he asked, and when she declined, he arose before her, extending his hands, saying, "This happens to be an American piece of music, I believe..."

Unwilling to embarrass him, Jane walked out onto the dance floor, aware that other Russian couples were doing a slow, tortuous version of The Twist to a melody that called for a fox trot. She recognized it as the background music from the motion picture, "The Sting."

Sergei led her easily in a comfortable fox-trot. He had put on his best suit for the occasion, and it smelled strongly of camphor. Yet even that sharp aroma was overladen by the musky fragrance of his aftershave, and Jane halted in her dance to stifle a few short sneezes.

"You're not catching cold, I hope?" Sergei inquired.

"No. At least, I hope not."

The rainstorm the previous afternoon? The drafty hallway in Rudi's apartment building? Hadn't she read of posthymeneal colds?

"You dance beautifully, Jane. I think my father mentioned you were a professional dancer in New York. Is that right?"

"I did some dancing...not a lot," she stammered.

Sergei seemed to gather confidence and drew her closer, his cheek damp against hers as he led her across the parquet.

I want to be with Rudi, she was thinking. Tomorrow is Monday, a school day. I'll see him. Perhaps we can be together...

The apartment was dark when Sergei brought her home. Karol and Mira had been asleep for hours. Sergei insisted on boiling some milk for the two of them before they went to bed. Jane could not stomach the odor of boiled milk, but did not wish to offend the young man who had tried so hard to make sure she enjoyed an entertaining evening. Actually, if she hadn't met Rudi, perhaps...

Sergei's dark eyes were intent upon her over the white rim of the milk glass. Jane sipped, resisting the impulse to pinch her nostrils together to avoid its stench. She smiled nervously and forced the boiled milk down, nauseated...

"You know, Jane, I must confess something," Sergei whispered.

"Yes?"

"I...well, I haven't been able to get you out of my mind since I saw you...that morning...Is it already a month since then?"

She gulped the milk, color rising in her cheeks, then took her glass to the sink to rinse it, making no reply.

"Are you still angry at me?" he asked, close behind her.

"I've never been angry at you, Sergei."

"Jane, you are the most beautiful girl I've ever seen..."

There was a look of hurt and exasperation on her face, and she made certain he could read it. Inclining her head in a gesture of departing, she whispered, "*Spasebo*, Sergei. Thank you, and goodnight," then slipped past him to her room.

*   *   *   *

"What do you mean, exercises?" Jane gasped in consternation at Rudi's announcement that he was being sent with a team of cross-country skiers to Tallin, the capital city of Estonia, across from Helsinki by the Gulf of Finland. It was late August, and the snows were expected within another month.

"It's a border control, I think," he explained. "They'll use those of us who are fluent in German. Some neo-Nazi groups in Estonia have been rearing their ugly heads, and the Russians want them infiltrated and put down before there's any insurrection."

"But why you, Rudi? Why *you*?" Jane wept. "You're still in training, learning the language, still being drilled. Why do they want to place you in jeopardy?"

He seized her with a light-hearted chuckle and drew her into his lap, stroking her hair and brushing her forehead with his lips.

"I must prove myself some time, must I not?" he stated, trying to lighten the mood for both of them. "I'm an expert skier, expert marksman, I speak fluent German and fair Russian...So...I'm useful now. More than ever before."

"But it's dangerous!" she cried, refusing to be comforted.

He gathered her up in his arms and carried her to bed, unbuttoning her cardigan and tickling her ribs to make her laugh.

"No, don't, Rudi. Please. I want to talk to you..."

"Later..."

She drew away from the hunger of his mouth.

"No, I want to talk now. Later you'll be too tired..."

"That's a promise...," he laughed, unfastening the belt of her jeans. There was no resisting him, no resisting the call of her own desire. She kept up a steady patter of complaint as they undressed. She wanted him to speak to Madame Prusovskaya, to intercede for him; he was not yet ready to go out on military excursions in the service of the government, the KGB.

"She has no authority, Yahni," he murmured, covering her face and throat with kisses, fondling her body until she thought she would positively wail with longing. "I won't be gone long. Maybe not more than a month. There's not really any danger..."

"You'll help put down an insurrection way up there in the Arctic Circle, and you say there's no danger?"

"It's more an observance than anything else, they say," Rudi told her, trying to hold her still, to begin making long, slow love to her.

"What would neo-Nazi insurrectionists be doing in Tallin?"

There was a noticeable chill in the room. The dust of age and a thousand rainstorms obscured almost all vision from the window. The glide of Rudi's thumb from the crest of her hip to her groin elicited her response and she sighed from her very depths as he took her.

"It's a city of old Germanic history, going back to the Hanseatic League and the Teutonic Knights. I'm not surprised there are anti-Communist sentiments alive there," Rudi panted, wondering how much, if anything, of what he stated, had been comprehended by the girl writhing and grinding beneath him. But one corner of her mind had indeed listened intently.

"I want you to be safe!" she cried. "I love you so, Rudi"

"Oh, you're such a nymph, Yahni," he laughed. "You just want me around because you can't do without me. I know...I know..."

She pressed her fingernails into his shoulderblades and clamped her leg muscles so tightly that he looked at her with astonishment.

"I want to hold you inside me forever," she gasped.

"Yahni...*Yahni...!*"

Afterwards, they lay wrapped in each other's arms, thinking of a cruel separation looming ahead of them. They talked quietly of Jane's progress, her high marks in Russian, in her political science classes, her studies in ideology, gymnastics, mathematics, chemistry, and weaponry...

"With everything you're learning, *Duschitzka*, I sometimes think I'm making love to the Soviet Union's most effective secret weapon," Rudi chuckled, nuzzling her, his hand stroking her bosom.

"Flattery will get you everywhere, *Duschka*," she giggled.

"Don't ever let them try to convince you to use your sex as a tool against the enemy," he warned lightly. "All of you, particularly here...and here...and especially here...belongs to me."

She loved when they played together, when he added humor and zest to their romantic interludes. But she worried about his leaving. There were things she had to tell him...

"I think, Yahni...," he conjectured, measuring the globe of her breast, "...you're wearing a bigger bra size since you know me. My little Yahni is growing into womanhood. When we first were here together, you had nothing in this department. And we saw each other so seldom, remember? Twice a month, if we were lucky. Either the Tobirians had plans for you, or you had a period...But the last month or so, what? Twice a week at least. Not a single interruption..."

Jane lay very still, observing him, one arm flung over her head, her lashes casting long shadows across her cheekbones. Something in her demeanor made him retrace his own words.

"Yahni...?"

"*Da, Duschka?*"

He grew serious, turning on his stomach and resting his weight on his folded forearms, studying her intently.

"If I remember correctly," he reflected, "I have made love to you twice and three times a week for at least the last six or seven weeks. No hindrances. No obstacles. Do you find something inconsistent with that measure of time and frequency?"

She said nothing. A corner of her small mouth twitched. In her eyes was a radiance he had never seen before. When her secret dawned on him, he drew a deep breath and caught her close.

"*Du lieber Gott, Yahni! Stimmt's?*"

She did not understand his native language, but there was an urgent plea for compassion in her eyes.

"Is it true? Are you pregnant?" he gasped.

"I think so, Rudi…"

He cradled her against him, stroking her, his eyes seeking something in his own private infinity.

"What do you want me to do, Rudi…," she asked sadly.

"I don't know, my darling. I don't know. We'll have to talk more seriously when I return…"

She buried her face in his shoulder and wept silently. It was not the answer she had hoped to hear.

"Yahni, listen to me," he whispered. "Do nothing until I return. This is our problem together, do you hear me? Do absolutely nothing until I return…"

*   *   *   *

October began with sleet and frost. Mira Tobirian was worried about Jane. The girl had not been looking well for a month, and had complained of loss of appetite and gastric upsets. Waiting for the bus to take them to school, Jane had made a choking, coughing sound and left Mira's side quite suddenly, walking behind a kiosk to vomit quietly into her handkerchief.

"Do you want to go home and rest?" Mira asked, concerned.

The girl shook her head. At home, her fears for Rudi would completely overwhelm her. The Tobirians knew nothing of her trysts with Rudi. Sergei still pursued her like a lovesick puppy, taking her resistance to his countless invitations to be inevitable, owing to her innocence and virtue. As the class opened, Jane's nausea abated, but the irregularity of her heartbeat seemed more pronounced, making her weak and dizzy.

The class had grown somewhat. In addition to the original four, three new students had joined the class. Nadia, a dark, olive-skinned girl from Armenia. A bespectacled youth, Zoltan, from Hungary, and Jean-Claude from France. All prime candidates for eventual service in the intelligence corps of the Soviet government.

Jane was still trying to clear her head, unbuttoning the collar of her blouse because the room was so warm and stuffy. She could feel perspiration running down the sides of her chest from her underarms and her heart was pounding furiously. Madame Prusovskaya was making an announcement, and something sad and woeful in her bland potato face made Jane look up, acutely alert.

"...every evidence, so far, that the American CIA instigators not only fomented the uprising, but armed the insurrectionists with sophisticated weapons! And we have now lost our young comrades, youths who could have done so much with their lives...Anton Krimsky, the assistant coach of the soccer team, and our very own Rudiger Furst, whom we all loved and..."

Jane's screaming drowned out the rest of her statement.

* * * *

Dr. Chornov gestured to Jane to be seated before his cluttered desk. Numb, she watched the man adjust his eyeglasses to peruse the chart in front of him. Attached to the inner sides of the folder were three strips of electrocardiograph tapes and two black and white sonograms clipped from the roll of echograph studies that had been completed the previous day. Stapled to the folder were X-rays of Jane's spinal column and rib cage, together with pages of laboratory reports and a review of the case history and symptoms. Jane stiffened in her seat as the physician removed his glasses and wearily rubbed his eyes.

"Miss Sutton, I'm afraid I don't have the best news for you. I've spent a lot of time going over your chart, and I've consulted with Dr. Radzinsky, head of obstetrics. We're both of the opinion that unless you terminate this pregnancy now, without further delay, you may not live to carry to term, or you may die in delivery. There is a serious cardiological problem here. Generally, it is not as serious as this. But in your case, it is, without a doubt, life threatening."

Jane's hands were balled into white-knuckled fists.

"What's wrong with me?" she asked in a tiny voice.

"It's a serious syndrome involving mitral valve prolapse, hiatus hernia with esophageal reflux and lateral scoliosis. Didn't anyone ever detect a heart murmur? Your pediatrician? School nurse?"

Jane nodded. She had often heard her mother mention her "murmur of the heart" but paid no heeu to it, believing it was nothing, not even worthy of mention.

"Yours is a true mitral stenosis. You cannot...you *must not*... continue with this pregnancy. It will cost you your life..."

Eyes devoid of emotion, the girl sat silently.

"In your history, you state you understand your mother died in childbirth. Did you ever find out the true cause of death?"

"No..."

"That could be significant. This syndrome tends to be genetic, passed from mother to child."

"I was adopted. I never knew my real mother."

"Yes, I read that. And what of your twin. You state you were one of a pair of premature twins, that you have a brother. How is his health?"

Jane stared down at her lap, biting her lips.

"His health? I don't even know his name!"

"Now, how is that?" the doctor wanted to know, curious.

"We were separated at birth...adopted by different couples."

Dr. Chornov mopped his brow and shook his head sadly.

"Too bad. It would have been interesting to know how he was faring. As you know, very often in the case of twins, one twin is the weaker, either physically or developmentally. In your case, I would venture a guess that you were the unlucky twin, and that your brother is hale and hearty."

Jane said nothing.

"Does that strike you as unfair, Miss Sutton?"

Jane sighed mournfully, replying, "All of life is unfair."

"But you can still have a full, productive life. Not every woman is born to be a mother. Some are destined for greater achievements. I know from the program in which you're enrolled that the government expects great things from you."

"That's good to know."

"If you'll sign the release papers, we'll schedule the abortion for Friday morning. You'll be hospitalized two days, so that we can monitor your heart condition..."

Jane was beyond feeling any emotion. Mechanically, she leaned forward, taking up a pen from its holder.

"Where do I sign...?"

*   *   *   *

Karol and Mira were at her bedside when she came to. A large, red clay pot of sunflowers stood on the windowsill, and Mira bent to kiss her forehead. Jane had been four months pregnant. It occurred to her that the sex of the fetus could be most accurately determined by that period in gestation. Did she want to know? Did she want to know if Rudiger Furst had given her a son or a daughter to bring into the world? Would she ever be able to live in peace with that knowledge.

Mira read the tormented, unspoken question in her eyes.

"It was a boy," she whispered quietly. "Better, perhaps, never to have come into this world than to die in its wretched wars."

Jane accepted the knowledge with stoic courage, then turned on her side and stared vacantly out at the late October rain.

"Does Sergei know?" she asked hoarsely.

"We felt it best you tell him yourself," Karol replied. "Our son has been in love with you since he met you. It's not our place to break this news to him."

"He knows you've had some elective surgery," Mira put in. "He asked to be allowed to take you home tomorrow. We said yes..."

*   *   *   *

It was the seventh of November, the commemoration of the Great October Revolution, celebrated by inspiring military parades and followed by mass pageants and sports displays. The whole city was decked out in brilliant bunting, gaily-colored streamers and flags. A brass band played patriotic marches as a long parade of men and armaments passed by the Soviet leaders who stood, in salute, atop the Lenin Mausoleum.

Jane, with Sergei at her side, stood listening to the pounding drums, the brassy march, watching the banners pass before her eyes—the thousands of uniformed men, the tanks, the artillery, the military might of the Soviet Union. She heard the cheering crowds, felt the surge of nationalism all about her.

Sergei pressed her hand comfortingly, and she stole a glance up at him, finding his grave, dark eyes watchful of her, sad and caring. He had taken her confession bravely, hiding his pain, and, it appeared, he was becoming reconciled to it. Jane had enjoyed the intimacy of another man, had conceived his child. Now the man was dead, and so was the child. Perhaps there would be a place for him in Jane's life.

The sounds, the music, the pageantry, all of it wove its way into the core of Jane's raw, vulnerable being. For this land, Rudi had died. For this mighty nation, the father of her never-to-be-born son had given his life. And who had caused his death, directly or indirectly? *Americans!* American secret agents, with their insidious underground networking, with their limitless money and support! They had murdered the young, innocent Rudiger Furst, an orphan summoned to serve the Soviets, like herself. He had gone out as an observer, and they had killed him, along with others, in that cold, remote Arctic city of ancient warriors.

I will avenge you, Rudi, my love, Jane said inside her soul. I will avenge your murder, my precious one, my eternal love...

*   *   *   *

Jane turned away from the twenty-ninth floor window of the Ukraine Hotel on the Kutuzovsky Prospekt, turned away from the gray line of the Moskva River. She took a final glance in the closet mirror, checking her appearance in the uniform of the Women's Brigade of the KGB. Two ribbons adorned the left breast of her navy blue jacket, one signifying her thirty months of service leading to her commission as an officer. The other signified her expertise as a marksman. She was proud of them both.

There were footsteps outside the door, and she leaped forward to admit the three people whom she had not seen in the fourteen months she had been away, traveling in the service of her adopted country.

"Tobi! Mira!" she cried, pulling them close and kissing them with ardent abandon. Tobi was beginning to show age, the hair at his temples whitening, lines showing in a slant from beneath his cheekbones to his jaw. Mira was as round and dour as ever, but her eyes sparkled at the sight of Jane in her handsome uniform.

Sergei, in his dark suit, a youthful professor of engineering at Moscow State, hung back until the reunion with his parents had died down somewhat. Then he stepped forward to receive Jane's kiss, full on his mouth, her arms holding his shoulders in a tight hug, with all the devotion of a younger sister who has been away.

"Are you ready for your big day?" Karol asked her, his all-knowing wise eyes soft and compassionate, and Jane swallowed hard.

"I hope you're ready, Lieutenant Sutton, because I happen to know for a fact that Admiral Yuri Andreievich Romayev is looking forward to this day as the most important event of his life!"

Jane smiled. Yes, she was ready to meet Admiral Romayev. She was ready to meet her father...

Chapter 6

(Silicon Valley)

A dark blue Nissan pick-up turned off the main highway in Santa Clara and pulled up to the high wire fence surrounding the Universal Electronics plant, stopping behind the one-story building. The soft crunch of its tires on the gray, moonlit gravel was the only sound heard above the rhythmic chant of the crickets.

A wiry figure with a bath mat tucked beneath one arm sprang from the truck on cat feet, removed a six-foot aluminum ladder from the flatbed, braced it against the fence and mounted to its top, quickly splicing the hot alarm wire to disarm the signal. With the protection of the bathmat over three strands of barbed wire, the trespasser bounded down on silent rubber soles and proceeded toward the pre-hung braided vine lassoed securely to the chimney, and scaled it, hand over hand. The lock of the utility tower's access door was easily forced. From there, it was only a matter of yards to the test area which housed the IBM XT computer with its newly-developed SRC chip.

The crime had none of the earmarks of a Mafia-type heist, nor did it contain sufficient evidence of international intrigue to warrant the company president's hysteria the following morning when he learned that the computer with its SRC prototype had been stolen.

Local law enforcement, unable to assess the value of the stolen equipment, were quick to describe the burglary as an inside job, a theft of expensive electronic machinery.

But in fact, the crime was the newest jolt in a series of tremors emanating from the hubs of high-tech industry to the very nerve center of the nation's capital, pushing the quivering indicator of the political Richter scale past a point which congressional leaders could not ignore.

Twenty million dollars worth of extraordinary computer chips were stolen annually from plants in the Santa Clara area, but the theft of the SRC chip represented the most damaging high-tech espionage at that moment, damaging enough to require the immediate attention of the President.

(Washington, D.C.)

"What do you know of this stolen super chip?"

Powell Wright, Director of Central Intelligence, knew enough. He had called for detailed reports the moment he was notified of the crime. The SRC was the biggest breakthrough in micro-electronics, its initials standing for Speech Recognition and Command. Not only did it recognize speech—it had a voice of its own.

Before Wright could answer that question, the President of the United States rose from his desk and gazed out of the window of the Oval Office, addressing his outrage to both men seated behind him, the DCI and Senator Carl Haskell of California.

"We can't let our high technology go on hemorrhaging like this, Gentlemen!" he warned, steaming. "We're not talking about a better kitchen appliance or a new concept in photocopying now! Sophisticated computer equipment is winding up in the wrong hands...and when it's the hands of competitors like the Japanese, that's one thing...but too damned much is falling into Russian hands!"

This was not news to Powell Wright. There had been many incidents of computers—used in military hardware, in simulators, robots, missile guidance systems—exported to friendly countries but diverted during transit to Communist-bloc ports and airfields. Wright also was aware of Customs' inability to fight highly-trained smuggling syndicates backed by the USSR.

The President wheeled around to face them, his color high.

"I want that voice-chip back, and I'm ready to make an all-out effort to get it back! Whatever it takes...a special team, a task force, with total jurisdiction, unlimited authority, unlimited funds! Hell, Carl, you can do some fancy persuading of the National Security Council when you set your mind to it!"

The Senator from California grinned, flushing as he nodded.

"And how about someone to head up the team?" the President demanded of Director Wright. "Have anyone in mind?"

The DCI envisioned the blond Robert Redford type whom he had observed with pride in the five years since his fledgling days at "The Farm" and how invaluable the man had proved himself to the Agency on at least twenty different assignments. Powell had bestowed a reward upon that man, making him the youngest Chief of Station in the CIA.

"Yes, Sir. I think I have the right man..."

Moving with heavy traffic through the woods of the George Washington Parkway, Powell Wright put in a call on the car phone to the Chief of Naval Operations, waiting to hear the familiar voice.

"Admiral, this is Powell Wright. I need to bring a man into Andrews from Islamabad...and I need him yesterday."

In the privacy of his office, he scanned the most recent dispatch his young COS had sent from Afghanistan, recognizing the sharp, incisive style, the quick grasp of situations overlooked by men who were twice the young Station Chief's age:

> This is not - repeat, not - Russia's
> Vietnam. Estimate less than twenty per
> cent of Soviet troops committed to
> combat. The war rages between Afghan
> insurgents and Afghans loyal to Moscow,
> with Sovietization in full swing and
> time, as always, on Russia's side. Their
> talk of pull-out has been propaganda to
> date; it may still be just that. I will
> be leading a covert action within days…
> certainly not an exercise in futility,
> but a much-needed morale booster for our
> clients.

Powell Wright closed the file and sat rubbing his eyes, then pressed the intercom button and spoke to his secretary.

"Margie, prepare a priority message to Islamabad…to Harry Carroll."

(Afghanistan)

Kipling had once insulted Afghanistan as being "a land without splendors" but did allow that "God took a giant step there," and left an imprint to last for all time. The majesty of Afghanistan seemed somehow linked to its timelessness.

In a mountain foxhole above the Salang Tunnel, Harry listened for the laboring of truck engines signalling the approach of the convoy, his right hand fingering the trigger of his automatic machine pistol, his left holding the switch for the explosives. It was an enigma, the USSR's war with Afghanistan. Parts of the country had remained almost untouched by time in the twenty-five centuries since the Persian, Darius, had marched through Jalalabad on his way to the Khyber Pass and the takeover of the Indus. Then came Hephaeston, Alexander's General, followed by whole legions of winners and losers, who raped the land and the women and introduced to the territory the policy of scorched earth.

Harry had been in the arena long enough to know that the Afghan plateau could be numbing cold in early morning, the whole country a meteorological puzzle, with bone-chilling winters and bone-softening summers. The arid, rock-strewn Hindu-Kush mountains, through which the supply tunnel ran, were actually foothills to the Himalayas.

To blow up the Salang Tunnel, thus cutting off the Soviet supply route into the country, required the best men, and Harry felt confident he had found two of them in Ranjit and Akbar Khan—earthy, proud men who lived hard, loved to laugh, despised foreign rule, and were not all that concerned with dying. Surrendering one's life fighting the Russian infidels would open the gates of Paradise. *"Insha'Allah...as God wills,"* was the essence of the Afghani *Lebensanschauung.* Existential nobility, the cut of man rising above daily triviality. Ranjit and Akbar Khan were both family men whose homeland was threatened. And homeland, to these men, meant more than soil, family and work. Their ancestors were buried there, and the history of their whole clan depended for sustenance on their continuing homage to it. Ranjit was known to spray bullets at the feet of any man who seemed inattentive to his commands. And Khan was a coarse, crusty man who addressed Harry as *Sahib,* and who claimed he knew the land as well as he knew the stretch marks on his wife's belly.

And Ranjit and Akbar Khan had Allah, which translated to something very few outsiders could comprehend—a deep abiding faith and trust in the merciful God of their fathers.

But they had too little with which to drive the enemy out. They needed Howitzers and bazookas, Stinger rockets and mortar-locating radars. Harry knew that ninety-five per cent of the shipments the USA landed at Karachi disappeared from Pakistani trucks on their way north, stolen mainly by the Baluchis, a people apart in that admixture of ancient tribes, who longed to break out from under Pakistani rule, and took whatever help the Russians gave them to do so.

But the mission had been planned for weeks, with Harry's sharply-honed perfectionism. Making the tortuous ascent in the battered jeep to their destination, sighting neither light nor human being on the way—not even a Russian soldier—reinforced Harry's feelings that the hills and gullies were pristine and inviolate, and that no matter what man did to them, they would, in the end, still represent God's footprint.

Using the cover of darkness, and from a vantage point of less than fifty feet, Harry and his confederates picked off the six Russian soldiers guarding the tunnel's entrance, after which Akbar, playing paymaster, bought more volunteers than were needed to place the explosives—the time fuses and the plastique—in mid-tunnel. The sight of colorful Afghani banknotes waving in scores of hands brought a grin to Harry's face as he watched through binoculars.

There had been a long, unexpected delay in the explosion within the tunnel, closing it off at the far end. Checking the illuminated dial of his watch, Harry feared something had gone wrong, and perspiration started on his brow, beneath the hood of his parka, and ran down his temples. Shafts of light were already visible from the lead vehicle of the convoy. In seven or eight minutes, the caravan of trucks would be nearing the entrance. If the explosion in the tunnel's center were delayed much longer, the convoy would be alerted by the blast and the whole operation, Harry realized, would become a bloody fiasco.

An entire row of trucks came around the bend, the dust of the lead vehicles dimming the lights on the ones that followed.

Still no explosion.

Akbar had sensed Harry's anxiety.

"I should have made sure, myself, that the charge was properly placed," Harry whispered with a mixture of regret and alarm.

Then the earth shook under their bellies, and a deep rumble followed, evoking a gasp from Akbar, "Praise be to Allah!"

And now, they watched Part Two of the operation, truck after truck being swallowed up by the mouth of the tunnel. It had taken almost twenty minutes for the entire convoy to negotiate the steep approach. As the last vehicle finally appeared, tail lights were already glowing red inside the tunnel as the convoy slowed.

"They've reached the point we blew up. They can't proceed," Akbar stated, speaking in Urdu, which Harry had learned with reasonable fluency.

"I'm blowing the entrance. You and Ranjit take care of the trucks remaining outside!" Harry shouted, pushing the switch.

The semi-darkness of the Afghan dawn was lit by a brilliant, incandescent strobe. The shock wave produced by one hundred forty pounds of tightly-packed gelignite sent a tremor through the entire mountain, as though it were a seismic fault instead of solid granite. There followed a momentary hiatus of silence and frozen movement. Then the face of the mountain crumbled onto itself, collapsing the strata above the tunnel entrance. One truck had partially entered and disappeared under tons of debris. The three trucks left outside the tunnel caught the withering automatic fire from both Akbar and Harry, the soldiers aboard instantly killed.

In the unnerving stillness that followed, the two men scrambled down to make sure there were no survivors, Harry concealing his emotion in the face of so much death, as they poked at the bodies and lifted the tarps of the trucks.

There were crates and cartons of foodstuff in the back of the trucks, and Harry knew the nearby villages could use it. He was already envisioning the celebration they would hold.

"I'd say we impeded the Soviet war effort, wouldn't you?" he asked lightheartedly of his Afghan friends, watching them nod in the flush of victory, huge equine teeth glinting in the moonlight as they laughed. "Maybe they'll wish they had withdrawn, as they've promised so often..."

He lay exhausted on the hard, narrow army cot in his bleak chamber, acknowledging his fatigue as a descent from the high—from the nervous cutting edge to which his exhilaration had driven him.

There was something magical about the swift, sure destruction of the Salang Tunnel, something that approached design perfection. Clinically, the tunnel sabotage was a "closed operation," an action seen through to a clean end, without casualties or complications, as the book put it. Knowing he had pulled if off successfully, making do with the barest minimum—rubber bands, Scotch tape, and the dedication of some excellent men— yet managing to cripple a significant military objective—made Harry's spirits buoyant.

To put one's all on the line in the ultimate struggle for an ideal was, in Harry's mind, sacred and beautiful, even transcendental. His was the same energy that fueled the crusades of extremists and idealists the world over, and, oddly enough, the same energy that fed the flames of terrorism.

One night in Zermatt, Switzerland, when he had been a teenager, he had made a deliberate choice. His mother had hoped he would go into medicine. His father had suggested architecture. His childhood sweetheart had expected him to use his law degree in corporate and constitutional legal battles in Washington, D.C., and eventually seek his success in politics. His failure to live up to her expectations had cost him their relationship. Yvonne had literally walked out on him to find her happiness with someone else.

Working for the Central Intelligence Agency, he was expected to use initiative and to perform the impossible, and to accomplish that, was given wide latitude and discretionary powers. When he had proved his merit beyond any shadow of doubt, he was promoted to Station Chief at the Embassy in Islamabad. It was the ultimate compliment Powell Wright could bestow, but it did cause some nail-biting among the troops, since Station Chiefs were not supposed to be on the scene, blowing up tunnels or otherwise endangering their valuable hides. There were those, among Powell Wright's aides, who saw Harry Carroll as a prima donna, a showoff who took unjustified risks. But others saw him as a levelheaded professional who always got the job done.

While his commendations referred to the service he rendered for his country, in his heart, Harry knew he had performed more risk-taking to himself than anything else. From earliest manhood, he had been a rigid pragmatist, his decision-making process little more than a *reductio absurdum* of accepted challenges.

He had disappointed his mother, who fretted ceaselessly for his safety. He had distressed his father, by refusing to surrender what Don Carroll called "a little boy's dreams of derring-do," and—most painfully, he had lost Yvonne de la Fontaine to a smug young Washington attorney with political aspirations.

Losing Yvonne had been his greatest sacrifice...

His pondering was interrupted by a small boy, screaming in Urdu, bursting into the chamber and pointing to a man approaching on foot. The man, dressed as an Afghan, was immediately recognized as a fellow American from the Embassy office. Harry sprang to his feet at once.

"Webster, my instructions were never to come here!"

"I know, Sir. I'm only following orders..."

"Whose?"

"Washington's, Sir. They want you there. There's a helicopter standing by and a plane waiting for you in Islamabad."

"Let's see the message," Harry ordered, and Webster withdrew from his Afghani outfit a folded sheet of yellow paper, on which Harry read the typewritten transcription:

```
HARRY CARROLL,
STATION 218, ISLAMABAD, PAKISTAN:


PROCEED WITHOUT DELAY VIA MILITARY
TRANSPORT FROM CARRIER ENTERPRISE MED
FLEET.  CLEARANCE AUTHORITY RED TO
ANDREWS AFB.  LEAVE TAYLOR IN CHARGE.
SECURE ALL PENDING CLASSIFIED MAT-
ERIAL.  BRING TOOTHBRUSH.


POWELL WRIGHT.
```

(Washington, D. C.)

"You look as if you've just gone ten hard rounds with a kangaroo!" he was greeted by Powell Wright on his arrival.

Harry had spent the day in a time warp, racing the sun, leaving Islamabad at five a. m., refueling in Ankara, proceeding to the Azores, and arriving at Andrews at five p.m. the same day. Wright had taken him home for dinner and a chance to unwind, briefing him about the men being summoned in for the micro-chip task force. Bob Carlson up from Rio. Bert Klemmer from West Berlin. And Natalie Soubrine, from Quebec...

Being in Washington always brought back memories that tore at him, would not let him sleep. Had he excused himself from his Director's hospitality and gone instead to a hotel, he would be at the bar, hanging one on. But he had always gotten along well with Powell Wright. Thus, standing at the window in Wright's residence, he gazed at the carefully-groomed lawn in the moonlight, the well-tended shrubbery and flower beds, a scene so strikingly in contrast with the turmoil he had just faced in the mountains of Afghanistan. He was, of course, glad to have been selected for an assignment of national priority, but could not help remembering the explosion of the Salang Tunnel and what it meant in the Afghan-Russo struggle. Still another thought niggled at the back of his mind. He had promised to meet Ranjit and Akbar Khan again in the old hut in Jalalabad in a week's time. Would Ken Taylor, his replacement, remember to meet them in his stead, and would Taylor win the confidence of both suspicious, hard-headed guerrillas?

Sleep out of the question, Harry paced up and down beside the bed. Spotting the Chesapeake and Potomac Telephone directory on the phone table, he thought fleetingly of calling Yvonne. It was only ten-fifteen. Surely, she would remember the man with whom she had studied and traveled and danced and skied. And with whom she had lived. He wondered what he would say. Would he be an embarrassment to Mrs. George

Chartrain, wife of a prominent Washington attorney? Oh, it was silly, imbecilic...

Annoyed with his thoughts, he tried to make himself comfortable in bed. What was he doing, pining after an old girlfriend? Ever since Yvonne, he'd lived by the "love 'em and leave 'em" rule, and it had proved a good principle. Conquests came easily, and he had learned how to terminate every liaison, no matter how enjoyable, the moment one word was uttered about commitment.

But there was an emptiness about all that, somehow. Living the uncommitted life kept him from giving of himself. And Harry needed to give of himself. It had something to do with his genes. For all his American ardor and upbringing and patriotism, there was something intrinsically Russian in his soul. Once in a while, it haunted him, the old Russian philosophy..."Why laugh, when you can cry!"...and he needed to share those feelings.

Surely, Natalie understood that. She was Russian. The DCI had reached her in Quebec...

*   *   *   *

Air Canada Flight 44 was held up an hour due to poor visibility and Natalie Soubrine took advantage of the delay to sip an extra cup of coffee and collect her thoughts. It was good to be returning to Washington. Something big, she'd been told. About time, too. She had begun to feel she wasn't earning her pay in Quebec. In her five years with the Agency, Natalie had often found herself playing the waiting game. Were it not for the intensive training periods every sixty days when she was not on assignment—training to maintain her skills in marksmanship, judo and athletics—Natalie knew she could never face the challenges of the job. At twenty-six, she felt past the first blush of youth, knowing that in less than a decade she would be standing on the threshold of middle age. Doubtless, there had been plenty of excitement and travel, plus at least a hundred heart-stopping moments when her very existence had been imperiled. But despite all that, whenever Natalie permitted herself to dwell on the meaning of her life, she felt cheated.

The idea of boarding the plane to Washington made her giddy with excitement. He would be there. A brand new Station Chief. Had he changed, she wondered. Would he still act uneasy and testy with her because of her obvious crush on him—a feeling he had never reciprocated? Couldn't he remember the ordeal of their first assignment together, as raw recruits, in the jungles of Luzon...?

She was not the last passenger to exit the huge transporter after it crawled to the gate and spilled arrivals into the colossal rotunda at Dulles International Airport. But to Harry, walking back and forth in the arrival hall, watching the B747 jetliner parked in the distance, it seemed that everyone else—all the students with their backpacks, all the wide-eyed servicemen, all the bewildered matrons traveling in pairs and trios, all the salesmen and government people with briefcases—had all left the transporter before her.

But she had only been submerged in that sea of humanity, approaching just as he started again toward the gift shop to kill time reading a magazine.

"Harry?" she called after him, addressing the wide shoulders, the white scarf resting at the nape of a sturdy neck, the dark blond edge of his hair. "Is that you?"

At the sound of her voice, he whirled around, the silkspun fringes of his scarf flying.

"Natalie! Where'd you sneak up from? I was wondering when the hell you'd be getting off!"

Laughing, she stepped forward to press her lips to his cheek in greeting, and he caught the fragrance of her Chanel, a fragrance he would always associate with Natalia Isaakovna Subrinina, when he recalled her full Russian name. He had not seen Natalie in over a year. She was as lovely as ever.

"You just didn't see me," she smiled brightly. "That's why, Harry, my friend, you'll never make a good spy!"

He stood in silent contemplation of the familiar face, rich in its beauty. Like Catherine Deneuve, whose perfume she wore, Natalie was one of the very few women who could gather her hair back tightly, allowing her face to stand or fall on its own, and Natalie's succeeded admirably. Were a portrait artist to select a perfectly sculpted face, with deep, shadowy hollows beneath high cheekbones—hollows yearned for by the highest-paid cover girls—a heart-shaped face with a complexion too fair for the sun and yet roseate from the health and vitality surging through her—that portrait artist would have chosen the face of Natalie Soubrine.

Harry took her arm in fraternal fashion to lead her through the rotunda toward the parking area.

"I'm glad Wright was able to reach you in time and that you're coming aboard," he said. "There's so much to go over..."

"My God, Harry! Can't we have a drink first?" she begged. "I haven't seen you in...what is it, fourteen months?"

"Jesus, Nat. Has it been that long?"

He had lost track since seeing her last. There had been a brief excursion in Zimbabwe, and from there, a few months shuttling back and forth between Marseilles and Istanbul. Then he'd moved on to Afghanistan...

Of course they'd have a drink. Seated opposite her in the airport bar, he thought back to their early experience together in the Philippines, when their plane had gone down in the jungle. It had been his third assignment with the Agency, her first. But Natalie had demonstrated class, guts, resourcefulness, and only a single fear, identical to his own. The fear of failure.

When their drinks arrived, she touched her glass to his and murmured, *"Nazd'rovia, Tovarich,"* her way of telling him she remembered his having once confided he was of Russian ancestry.

"You look good, Nat," he conceded. "Not a day older."

"Why, Harry! How gallant! The nicest thing you've ever said to me!" she exclaimed, and he held her lighter to her cigarette.

"Nobody's ever accused me of gallantry before," he chuckled, reflecting that what she'd said was probably true. Small talk and compliments were difficult for him. In his line of work, there was little time to be sociable. Finding the right words to tell a woman how he felt...that was an art form, and Harry had not been doing his homework.

"Well, now *I* have," she told him, letting the smoke curl out of her mouth. "*J'accuse.*"

"Don't tell me you're speaking French these days."

"I've been in Quebec, haven't I? How's my English?"

He thought before answering, sipping his drink.

"Competent. A little heavy. Maybe a little guttural. But...yes, competent."

She pouted, and he reconsidered.

"On second thought," he backtracked, "it's excellent. If I didn't know better, I'd say you were from Omaha."

The pout was replaced by a brooding smile. Mother Russia was never erased from Natalie's features.

"My fondest wish is to sound like a Texan," she told him. "I'd give five years off my life and four inches off my bust if I could."

"I wouldn't recognize you with five years off your life."

"You just lost the point I gave you for gallantry."

Smiling over the rim of his glass, he gave her an instruction. "Say all, Natalie. A-L-L."

"All."

"Good. Now say bidness. B-I-D-N-E-S-S."

"All bidness," she laughed.

"You've got it!" he joked with her. "Go to West Texas and tell folks you're in the all bidness, they'll take you for a hunnert-per-cent, cured-in-manure Texan. Now you've realized your fondest wish, and it didn't cost you a year...or an inch."

She flushed, because he gestured with his drink toward her bustline, and she thought how deliberately she had teased him. Harry signalled the waitress for another round and pulled his chair closer to hers. The focus of the conversation changed completely. Gone was the brief, carefree banter.

"Nat, we really can't talk here, but I'm so glad Powell Wright called you in. This job could well be the challenge of our lives. Bob Carlson and Bert Klemmer are coming with us."

"That's one helluva team," she noted, watching his eyes.

"I have no idea right now where it will take us. Certainly to Europe...maybe even as far as Russia..."

They exchanged a meaningful glance, then fell silent as the waitress set down another triple vodka and limewater for Natalie and a snifter of French brandy for Harry.

"Things could get sticky, Nat."

She touched his glass with hers again, whispering, "Here's to lots of successful stickiness."

He grinned. Her seductiveness was getting to him.

"Harry, remember Luzon? How you knew so much...when to drink the water, when to avoid it. The danger of the thornbush. How you stopped my feet from bleeding with strips of canvas. How you put my broken arm in a splint. You even hunted food for us. I didn't even know how to start a fire..."

"What are you saying, Natalie?"

Her reminiscence of five years back, of the first assignment they had shared, when he'd been a brash twenty-four with a law degree and two agency commissions under his belt, moved him strangely. She'd been a brand new foreign recruit then, just twenty-one and totally green.

"I'm saying, Harry, that if you were to ask me to join your team on Mars...I wouldn't hesitate."

Pale lights flickered in her gold-brown eyes.

Harry swallowed hard and held up his hand for the tab.

*   *   *   *

The DCI had called the meeting in an unprepossessing highrise on Fourteenth Street in downtown Washington. When he and Harry arrived, Craig Wesson was already setting up the film projector, and the screen was in place against the wall. Illustrations of the stolen computer and several pamphlets projecting the results to be expected from it when used in conjunction with the SRC chip were ready against the drawing board.

Still excited by the idea of having broken bread with the President of the United States an hour earlier, Harry felt powerful, responsible. More importantly, he sensed the exigency of his mission. Its weight was beginning to press in upon him, and he knew it would grow heavier by the hour.

Powell Wright had made him a Director. Pretty damn good for a guy not even thirty! Now he had to prove himself worthy of the promotion, had to prove that the DCI had used his unerring hunches in selecting the best man for the job.

"Am I too early?" Natalie's query sounded, and without looking up as Powell Wright greeted the girl warmly, he allowed himself only a glance at the high-heeled black pumps and slim ankles crossing the office's thick-napped carpeting, and then he was all business, an attitude from which his superiors and colleagues had learned he did not easily depart.

The soft sound of the elevator door opening down the corridor announced the arrival of Bob Carlson and Bert Klemmer. The reunion was brief and joyous, a flurry of handshakes and grins, and they were gestured to their seats.

Without further ceremony, the illustrations and pamphlets were distributed, and Powell Wright opened the meeting with the statement that the problem was of so serious a nature that the President had authorized a special task force to handle it.

"You represent the embryo of that task force," Wright told them. "In the wrong hands, this priceless electronic device is a threat to the survival of our nation. I've appointed Director Carroll as Lucky Pierre to put a group together to get it back. This is not a temporary assignment. Our President wants the unauthorized transfer of high technology out of the USA stopped...and stopped now!"

A detailed explanation followed, of the monstrous challenge lying before them. The chosen agents listened intently, their sense of responsibility building as Director Wright described the incident which had sent shock waves all the way to the White House.

"Installed, for example, in a fighter aircraft," Wright told them, "the SRC enables the pilot to obtain all pertinent information from his computer simply by listening to its voice. Conversely, he can fly the plane and operate his weapons systems by voice command, thus increasing his fighting capability a hundredfold. In short, the SRC represents a quantum advance in military technology, to say nothing of its use in space and in a thousand and one industrial applications."

There was a thoughtful silence among those present, then Harry spoke up wistfully.

"I would've loved to see that baby perform."

"That's why we're here this morning," the DCI replied, motioning to Craig Wesson to prepare the film. "This was done, using the SRC with exact-to-scale miniature models. Take a good look."

The film tape was threaded into a Kodak projector and the light was dimmed. The machine whirred and stock numbers appeared in swift sequence on the screen. Then suddenly, before their eyes, a Sherman tank, raising clouds of dust, was racing toward a number of simulated targets—a gun emplacement with two authentic-looking artillery men, a barn and three tanks marked with the Soviet star. Harry caught a searching glance from Natalie, then heard a deep voice, its owner unseen, on the sound track:

"Direction, three hundred fifty-five degrees, range four hundred yards. Two hundred rounds. Fire at will."

Immediately, the machine gun atop the tank blazed away, obliterating the dummy soldiers, transforming the 75mm anti-tank weapon into a twisted heap of smoking metal. The voice continued:

"Direction, forty-one degrees, range three hundred-sixty yards. Three rounds canon fire each. Commence firing."

The barrel of the canon rotated slightly and three shots followed. The first Soviet tank was enveloped in flames, the other two destroyed seconds later.

"The barn," the voice commanded. "Direction fifty-five degrees. Range six hundred yards. Three hundred machine gun rounds, six canon. Fire at will."

The first part of the film strip ended with the barn a raging inferno. Klemmer murmured. Carlson whistled. Harry and Natalie looked at each other with concern.

"Now watch this," Powell Wright instructed them.

The projector kept whirring, and on screen, an F-15 fighter came into view, as seen from a chase plane, its twin engine tail-pipes glowing. A voice, apparently from the chase craft, ordered:

"Seventy-five degree climb."

The F-15 lifted its nose and made a steep ascent.

"Correct to straight and level," instructed the voice.

The fighter abandoned its climb, resumed normal flight attitude.

"Arm left wing missile and fire."

Instantly, an Aim-9 Sidewinder missile detached itself, and with a slight puff of smoke accelerated and flew out of sight.

"Reduce engine speed to fifteen percent and trim for landing."

The F-15 went into a graceful glide, and after several turn-and-correction commands, landed easily on a runway, its touch-down as light as a feather. The aircraft was directed to a hanger and commanded to shut down both engines.

"This film could be deceptive," Harry complained. "We're looking at toy models here, miniatures..."

"Just keep watching!" his Director ordered gruffly.

The scene on screen had not changed. The aircraft was taxiing to a stop, and suddenly, several men in flight suits were rushing toward the fighter as it came to a stop. Harry leaned forward, narrow-eyed, holding his breath...

The air force personnel popped open the fighter's canopy. The seats were vacant. There was no pilot, no gunner.

"Hold on a minute!" Harry exclaimed. "This was the real thing!"

"That thing flew by itself!" Carlson gasped.

"Not quite," said Powell Wright, turning the lights back on. "It had our box with the SRC chip in its nose."

"...and the chase plane called out the maneuvers?"

"Precisely."

Harry's swift mind envisioned the new electronic phenomenon in the hands of some fanatical Ayatollah, a beast like Qaddafi, the old guard in the Kremlin...easily disabling the F-14 through F-18 fighters, as well as the B-1 and Stealth bombers. He pictured sabotage at sea, carrier-based planes bombing and strafing sister ships of the same convoy, destroyers colliding with battleships, American fighters turned kamekazi torpedoes destroying their own ships. Unstoppable carnage...

The vision grew too complicated, too ghastly. He could not remain cool and casual. There was suddenly too ominous a time-bomb ticking within him...

(Santa Clara)

In less than two hours, all four were on a special military flight out of Andrews, en route to Silicon Valley in California. It was agreed that learning as much as possible about the Speech Recognition and Command chip was essential. There would be time for regrouping later, for figuring out their separate assignments.

Harry came up the narrow center aisle of the twelve-seat cabin, exchanging a few words with Carlson and Klemmer, then proceeding to where Natalie was curled up against a window, immersed in a book on computer wizardry.

"You okay, Nat?"

"You betcha."

He nodded with a tight-lipped smile and walked off.

There was no question in Harry's mind that if he so desired, he could spend the night with Natalie. That invitation had been outstanding from her ever since their first association in the Agency. She had sent him many signals over the years, tiny nuances of encouragement only a fool would have failed to understand. But he had never taken her up on her invitations—admittedly, because of external prohibitions. Rigid department rules banned fraternization between operatives, a reasoning which was at once understandable and sound. Work in the Secret Service required instantaneous decisions and judgment calls—often in reaction to life-threatening situations. The tawdry history of espionage had proved over and over again that personal alliances between agents prevented clear, impartial thinking.

Besides, many female operatives were taught to use sex as one of their career weapons. Weaponry, quick-wittedness and physical brawn were tools of the trade for CIA men. Weaponry, quick-wittedness and seduction were the tools used by CIA women. How far the seduction had to go in any particular campaign depended, of course, on the individual operative. Whenever he thought of Natalie along those lines, Harry liked to pretend that she could tempt many men...but treat none of them.

Of course, his promotion to Station Chief did lift some of the force of that prohibition, and now that Harry was Director of a task force, he had still a wider prerogative. But in his mind, nothing had changed. He was still in the field, running things from the trenches, which seemed to waive his exclusionary status.

Proceeding up front, he glanced back at Natalie just before drawing the cabin door shut behind him. She was looking at him from beneath the hood of her long, dark lashes, just as she had looked at him before, and Harry swallowed hard, remembering the torrential downpours in the Luzon jungles, and the way she had felt, seeking shelter against his body.

The memory forced him to acknowledge still another force at work. Carrying out a mission with a woman, under a variety of circumstances—crawling along rooftops, sighting a target through Hasselblad scopes and firing a silent nine-millimeter self-exploding bullet over the heads of a crowd, sharing a bathroom, a toothbrush, and even a bed that could at any moment become a deathtrap—it all tended to reduce the normal expectations fostered by intimacy. Rather than annealing the bond, such closeness had the desexualizing effect of a cold shower. It was called the brother-sister syndrome and was commonly recognized in the business.

By the end of his first mission with Natalie Soubrine, despite the vision of sexuality that the girl brought with her, Harry was able to view her solely in terms of consistency, reliability, and professionalism...

*   *   *   *

The brown Santa Clara mountains presented a scenic backdrop to the sprawling complex of boxlike, ultra-modern one-story buildings surrounded by parking lots and neatly manicured lawns that comprised Silicon Valley. Having entered the peninsula between San Francisco and Palo Alto, they found the area resembling a vast chess board or a giant integrated circuit, with the air of a college campus. None of the usual signs of industry could be detected—no ugly factory walls, no belching smokestacks. But there was an intensity of competition observable among the members of the community, a purposeful activity often bordering on fanaticism.

The president of Universal Electronics was cooperative. In not quite ninety minutes, Harry and his team learned about the piracy and job-hopping that had come to be expected among the competing firms, and the existence of every kind of crime imaginable...

"Thefts to pay for drugs. Thefts to retrieve the gold from semiconductors. Thefts to save on development time. And, most serious of all, thefts to help the foreign competition catch up, help the bad guys build better weapons."

Harry and his team exchanged meaningful glances.

"Bad guys? The Soviet Union?"

"The Soviets, yes. But let's not forget others. The Poles, the Slavs, and particularly, the Chinese..."

Scales had been falling from Harry's eyes since his recall to Washington. From what he was learning, it was apparent that the whole world's greedy hands were reaching for the fruits of American ingenuity, and that it would be his job to preserve that fruit.

In new perspective, Afghanistan seemed like child's play to him, the Salang Tunnel only a curtain-raiser, a minor league event. Only a week earlier, he mused, life had been reduced to a few basics—food, water, a warm pair of gloves, and enough plastique and Afghani banknotes to blow a supply tunnel and impede the Soviet war effort. Prowling the wilds of Afghanistan, he had been out of touch with the dynamics of American industry. The achievements of the electronic whiz-kids of Silicon Valley were positively breathtaking, desired all over the world, and the more he and his team learned of what was going on in this swiftly-progressing world of mathematics and science, the more he realized how vulnerable the United States was becoming in its open well-springs of genius and technology.

Every detail of the robbery was explored. The building was examined, the security system, computer printouts of each employee's personal history.

Bob Carlson looked into what progress was being made by the local Sheriff's office. He did not believe that anything was ever swallowed up by the earth, and that once the Nissan pickup had driven off on the night of the theft that there were no further clues.

Bert Klemmer, inspired by his colleague's determination, set out to examine the vehicles of the employees in the parking lot.

Natalie Soubrine came up with the bright idea of contacting the local office of the Immigration and Naturalization Service, to scrutinize the background of several Asians whose pre-employment records appeared fuzzy to her.

All three were to join Harry and the company president later for dinner, at the "Lion and Compass"—a restaurant which was to the computer world what Sardi's was to the theatre district in New York City.

Harry looked around him at the parking lot when the valet drove off with the company president's snow-white Ferrari.

"I've never seen so many Rolls, Mercedes, and BMW's in one place at one time. What do the poor people around here drive? Cadillacs? Continentals?"

"We don't have any poor people, Mr. Carroll. Silicon Valley is America's latest gold rush area," the company president said.

At the bar, crowding rapidly for the dinner hour, the head executive of Universal Electronics discreetly pointed out to Harry some of America's youngest millionaires—those wizards who with ingenuity and entrepreneurship had helped create such giants as Apple, Amdahl, Signetisc, Avantek, Intersil, Siltek, and others.

Enthralled and elated, Harry was just beginning to sip his second brandy when he heard himself paged over the bar speaker. It was Bert Klemmer calling in, and Harry recognized the excitement in the man's low voice.

"Harry, old boy, I may have stumbled onto something. Found a truck in the lot that looks as if it might have transported a good-sized ladder. Belongs to a Chinese janitor in the plant. I'm going to check him out. Don't wait dinner for me or Natalie."

Harry took a deep breath. Perhaps this was the first break.

Part Three

Chapter 7

(Moscow)

Patrons glanced up from their dinner dishes in the popular twenty-first floor restaurant of the Rossia Hotel on Razin Ulitsa, near Krasnaya Square. Passing their tables was a handsome, distinguished-looking man in his middle fifties, elegant in his naval uniform with all its gold braid. Onlookers realized as the man passed that they had seen him before, that he was someone of importance, someone whose picture appeared every now and then in Izvestia and Pravda, and on televised reports of military and political situations. Those who were really in the know recognized their fellow diner as Admiral Yuri Romayev.

The woman following close behind was a tall, stunning blonde in the fashionable attire of an American tourist. There was nothing plain or dowdy about her. She emphasized her unusual height by wearing spike heels, and she could easily have been a magazine cover girl or alluring movie personality.

It was speculated that Admiral Romayev, who was long divorced and whose name seemed forever mentioned in whispers as being linked to one woman or another—now a famous tragedienne, now a ballerina with the Bolshoi, now a poetess said to be an intimate of Raisa Gorbachev—was apparently romancing a girl just about half his age. The maitre D' escorted them to a table next to a window which overlooked the Moskvoretskaya Embankment, offering a magnificent view of St. Basil's, that unique combination of nine commemorative churches, and of the Kremlin complex itself. There, a chair was drawn for the young woman to seat herself, and as she took her place at the table, she removed her black seal jacket with its silver fox collar and cuffs and showed herself off in a simple black wool dress against which a gold and amber lavalière was gracefully suspended.

The Admiral sat perusing the wine list, then pointed to his favorite Azerbaijani cognac, much to the delight of the maitre D' who hurried away to see to the swift dispatch of the high-ranking naval officer's order for drinks and dinner.

"How long do you think you'll be gone this time, Ilyana?" he asked the girl, reaching forward to light her cigarette, noting how her cornsilk page-boy bob cascaded from beneath the dramatic line of her black seal shako. It was always a source of sadness for Romayev to part from the girl. He realized she was a woman of importance with the KGB and that her assignments took her away from Moscow for months at a time, but the separations were always sorrowful. Admiral Yuri Romayev had come to fatherhood late in life, and had only begun to enjoy the delight of knowing his daughter when she was in her twenties, working in the service of the Soviet Government. She reminded him so poignantly of her mother...

"There's really no way to tell," she replied, and looked away from the dark gray line of the river below, her eyes misting for a moment, and she blinked several times to clear them. "But I will be in touch with you as often as possible."

Romayev nodded, proud of his offspring and of the contribution he had been able to make to his country. Over the edge of the fine linen menu, he watched her scan the table d'hotel, admiring her self-confidence, the way she carried herself, the charisma that clung to her, undiminished by the changing moments and situations.

Unlike his peers—and to their everlasting dismay and chagrin—Yuri Romayev was an avid traditionalist, a respected advisor to government leaders, but an advisor without iconoclastic compulsions. He seemed to have a better comprehension of the depth and breadth of Russian history than any of the lackeys surrounding the men of the Kremlin. Through the years of his maturity, Romayev had become a man of letters, but he was also a man of the People. The battles had been fought, the nation was united, the Revolution long a ringing success. For those reasons, Romayev no longer saw his duty as a rallying cry to the populace, yet he remained a man of history.

"A kopek for your thoughts," the blonde girl smiled at him, her pale fingers interlaced beneath her chin. Smoke from her idle cigarette spiraled upward from the ashtray, casting a faint mobile shadow across her face.

"Oh, I was thinking today, when I walked through the Administrative Building after the conference...," Romayev sighed, "...how many blatant contradictions of history can be seen from the East portal alone. You stand at the spiral balustrade and look out at the Spaasky Tower, and just beyond, to St. Basil's, both relics of our ancient glory. And there, immediately across Red Square, crowding out the old, sits the sprawling GUM department store and blue-tinted plate glass additions our modern architects have borrowed from the West. Modernizing the priceless forms of the Kremlin is nothing short of design butchery!"

The girl smiled secretly and lifted her cognac to him.

"Progress demands accommodation," she sloganized. "Communication today is paramount. At the risk of sounding like an unsympathetic foreigner, I remind you that until very recently, the Kremlin had a phone system only slightly better than Cairo's, the worst in the world!"

Romayev knew the girl was right. The Kremlin, originally erected in 1162 as a provisional fortress of wood against invaders, had been subjected every hundred years or so to design atrocities that were urgent and inescapable in the quest for better communications facilities. Frozen wood, and later, huge granite blocks for walls and battlements, provided little purchase for the needs of modern electronics. The Admiral was well aware of the fact that a delay of only a millisecond in communication could render the earth to ash. And a nuclear war, he realized, whether accidental or otherwise, would not produce select ash. Admiral Romayev was the Kremlin "dove" who—only the year before—had coined the unforgettable phrase, "One nation in ashes, the world in ashes," and was bitterly criticized by Kremlin hawks who believed that a nuclear war was winnable. However he tried to remind his opponents that Russia's "scorched-earth" policy of 1812 had robbed them of a hundred years of progress, his listeners were not men of history and simply argued more vociferously.

He sighed deeply. His daughter was leaving again, and he would miss her. The waiter was setting a basket of black bread and biscuits before them, along with small dishes of black Beluga caviar and sour cream, and as they partook of the tasty hors d'oeuvres, stood waiting patiently at tableside for their order.

"You're right, Ilyanitchka," he agreed with her, spreading his napkin across his lap. "I won't argue with you. Tell me, are your papers in order? Is everything ready for your trip?"

He knew full well how her identity would be transformed in an instant on the day of her departure. The name she had assumed with pride after meeting him for the first time at the age of twenty-two, — Ilyana Yurievna Romayeva — would be set aside.

The KGB officer who would fly, mainly by Aeroflot, from Moscow to Quebec, would enter New York State and proceed by Amtrack or by car rental, southward to Washington, D. C.,from thence to San Francisco, would carry the American passport of Jane Sutton.

"Have the *kulabiaka* and *blini*," he suggested. "They're delicious here, I promise you."

She gave him no argument. Already, he was experiencing the pangs of loneliness, anticipating the empty months that would pass before he would see her again, laugh with her again, attend the ballet with her again. Thinking of the ballet, he remembered that she had an appointment in the ballroom with someone else after dinner.

"Are you meeting your professor friend downstairs later?" he inquired, knowing that the basement restaurant boasted a good orchestra and popular dance music and an entertaining floor show.

"Yes, I promised Sergei I would meet him at nine."

The Admiral wondered about the mild-mannered engineering professor in whose company he had often seen his daughter. They seemed to be good friends rather than lovers, which gave Romayev pause to think. Did his daughter ever intend to marry and have children? In another year, she would be thirty. Such a beauty, so accomplished, and yet, no apparent romance in her life, except for a hint here and there of her seeing Sergei Tobirian, the son of a Kremlin international agent who was responsible for having found his daughter in the United States and induced her to return to her Motherland.

Karol Tobirian and his wife, Mirabianka, had retired and were living close to the Black Sea. Whenever Captain Ilyana Romayeva returned to the Soviet Union from some mission abroad, she rarely failed to visit with them, and the Admiral had to confess in his heart of hearts that he envied them the closeness she shared with them.

"Is there anything serious between you and Sergei Tobirian?" he dared to ask, pretending to be offhand about it, studying the menu.

"It depends what you mean by serious," she laughed lightly. "We have a serious friendship."

He looked directly at her, thinking how much like Tanya's her blue eyes glistened.

"He hasn't asked you to marry him, then?"

"He's asked many times."

"And your answer has been...?"

"I will never marry."

Yuri Romayev swallowed his disappointment along with a tablespoon of *akroshka* from the small bowl set before him. So she would never make him a grandfather, he lamented inwardly. It was something Romayev would have liked before the end of his life, to see a couple of grandchildren. But perhaps someday...who knew?

After all, he had never expected to be united with his daughter.

Miracles did happen once in a while.

Somewhere in the United States, he had a son, a son who looked like the male counterpart of Jane Sutton. Agents had watched the boy, all the way through his years of growing up, to the attainment of his law degree. And at that point, the agent assigned to keep track of the male Romayev twin had suffered a disabling heart attack, and the young man, Harry Carroll, had vanished from their surveillance.

Looking at his daughter, he wondered about his son. Was he all right? Was he practicing law? Why had nobody been able to pick up his trail again? It was the mystery, the not-knowing, that kept Admiral Romayev from ever discussing with Ilyana his curiosity about her twin.

Sergei had taken to wearing nickel-framed eyeglasses, which gave him a more mature, professorial air. The years had cost him little of his youthful features, however, and dimples still showed fleetingly at the sides of his mouth when he smiled. At thirty-four, he was an eligible bachelor, very popular on campus but committed to no particular husband-seeker, neither among his colleagues on the faculty nor among his serious young students.

"It's always difficult to say goodbye to a parent," he told her as they sipped their glasses of strong Armenian brandy. "One never knows when one will see them again. Do you feel that way, too, Jane?"

Her eyes had a far-away look. She was strangely sentimental.

"I feel terribly fortunate that I got to know my real father at all, and I'm grateful for the few years we've been able to see each other and spend time with one another. But I know what you mean."

Up front, across the dance floor, a popular vocalist in a slinky black velvet gown trimmed with frothy white lace and looking like a tamed gypsy, was entertaining the young crowd with an old favorite.

> "...yez l'nyi zna libi...
> Kak mnye doro'gi...
> Pad'moskov' nyi-eh...
> Vyech...er...ra..."

When the song ended, the vocalist stood bowing to the enthusiastic applause for a few moments, and then gestured to the orchestra leader to resume the dance music. It never ceased to amaze Jane how many modern American songs were hits among young people in the Soviet Union. She quickly recognized one of the songs that had made Billy Joel famous, "Just The Way You Are," and couples were stepping out onto the parquet and into each other's arms for the smooth foxtrot.

"Shall we?" whispered Sergei, and in another moment they were moving across the dance floor. She had always felt comfortable with him, had always found peace and strength in the circle of his arms. Although he had begun to pursue her with less fervor over the more recent years, having given up his quest as hopeless, nevertheless, he remained attentive and caring, remembering her birthday, days of special occasion, never failing to escort her to some function if she needed his company. Swaying quietly with him, trying to avoid the bumping of other couples, she nestled closer to him and sensed the quickening of his heartbeat. Without understanding why, her cool hand stroked the back of his neck, her fingers winding through the ends of his thick, dark hair. Perhaps it had been something her father said...

"When are you going to meet a lovely young girl and get married, Sergei Karolievich?" she asked him softly.

"A man should not marry except for love."

"And...don't you love anyone now?" she could not help teasing.

"Of course. And you have always known it."

They stopped dancing and stood still as couples moved around them. She saw the reflection of her own fair face and hair in his dark eyes. He was no longer smiling. The hand that had been holding hers was gripping hers.

"You still love me, Sergei?" she breathed.

"I've never stopped..."

His eyes were so serious. She felt herself tensing.

"*Pravda*, Sergei?"

"*Pravda*, Jane."

She hesitated for a moment. Then she pressed her cheek against his and whispered something in his ear. He followed her through the throng of dancers to their table and signalled the waiter.

He had not realized she was staying at that very hotel, the Rossia, and was surprised to see her press the ninth floor button on the elevator. When the doors slid open, they emerged into a plush-carpeted corridor and passed half a dozen niches brightened with well-attended plants on the way to her room.

She called down for a bottle of tminaya vodka, strong, with the flavor of caraway seeds, and it was clear to Sergei that this lady was very much in command, as befitted her rank and station in the Soviet Secret Service.

When the drinks arrived, she permitted Sergei to pay, but would have rushed to his rescue if he showed the slightest embarrassment.

They lifted glasses to each other, and she noted that his hand was tremoring slightly. He seemed unsure of himself, and anxious.

"I don't know how long I will be gone," she whispered. "For some reason I am sad tonight, and I would like company. Will you spend the night with me, Sergei Karolievich?"

There were no words to his reply. His glass in one hand, he took her in his arms and enfolded her tenderly. She could sense his excitement and drew comfort from the fact that she was wanted.

In the twelve years since the death of Rudiger Furst, Jane had devoted herself to her education and career, and with the exception of two or three meaningless encounters with male colleagues, had remained celibate and reclusive. At twenty-nine, at the height of her sexual prowess, Jane felt rather unsure, herself, as she undressed and stepped out of the bathroom in a soft woolen robe and found Sergei waiting for her with open arms.

But he was an adequate lover, a grateful lover, and the joy he expressed was a delight to her heart.

Afterwards, he lighted two cigarettes and placed one between her lips, confessing that he had liked that little touch of intimacy since seeing it in an old black and white film, "Now, Voyager," with Bette Davis and Paul Henreid. They snuggled close, Jane propping herself up on one arm and running her fingers occasionally through the dark, burly hair down the center of his chest.

"Marry me, Jane," he whispered. "I'll be good to you."

"You deserve better, Sergei."

"No one can ever be better for me than you."

"I'm committed to my career, Sergei. It takes top priority."

He drew her down on top of him, seizing the ends of her blonde hair between his teeth and locking her in his crossed arms.

"I'll make you pregnant, Captain Romayeva. Then you will have a different kind of priority," he laughed.

"I will never have a child," she stated.

"That's nonsense," he scoffed. "Any doctor who told you that should not be practicing medicine..."

"It's true, Sergei."

"*Nyet, nyet, nyet...,*" he insisted, playing with her. "Maybe it has already happened. And if not tonight, then surely another night..."

"Sergei...I had a tubal ligation twelve years ago..."

He had been chuckling, but fell still, his embrace slackening for a moment. He gathered her close and stroked the side of her face.

"Was it medically necessary, Jane?" he needed to know.

"Yes, Sergei. I'm not the woman you think I am," she breathed with some bitterness. "I only look like one. It's an illusion."

Sergei kissed the crown of her head and tucked it under his chin. Her revelation answered a number of questions which had for years remained mysteries in his mind.

"Is that why your career is paramount in your life?"

"Yes. Now you're beginning to understand. It's part of the secret of my success. I retain the illusion of being a female operative, but I am as deadly as any man, and often more so."

He digested that, knowing she was telling him the truth, knowing how bitter a pill it was to swallow, but also knowing he would never love any woman as he loved this versatile beauty.

"Your womanhood is no illusion to me, Jane," he murmured, kissing her. "When you return from this mission, I want you to marry me. It doesn't matter to me that you can't have children. I love you."

She covered him with her body, feeling the tension in him, the throbbing heat beneath her. Her mouth moved over his.

"Then make love to me, *Dorogoi*. I will be away a long time..."

(San Francisco)

The whole concept of being "away from home" depended on where Jane Sutton felt she was loved. The answer was clear enough. Her father, the Tobirian couple, and even Sergei—all in the Soviet Union.

Unwinding from a trip was always difficult. The shadows of an autumn afternoon made her San Francisco apartment seem sad and lonely. It was an ample apartment, one of the two bedrooms containing floor to ceiling bookshelves and a massive mahogany desk and comfortable leather chair for Sutton Enterprises' successful president, which was the designation on Jane's business card. An insightful distributor of technical articles. She advertised in the right magazines, made ever-increasing contacts, and in the several years she had maintained the small San Francisco headquarters, hundreds of scientific and theoretical papers had been catalogued and distributed to various technical periodicals, the constant flow of important material from her office to the Soviet Consulate not only admired but handsomely rewarded. The financial resources placed at her disposal by the system never ceased to amaze her.

KGB Captain Ilyana Romayeva, reverting in San Francisco to her identity as Jane Sutton, was one of the Soviet Secret Service's key technology operatives. Leonid Padorin, who had been the top KGB man at the Consulate when Jane was born, was the only consular official still at his post, and she conferred with him often. Now in his sixties, Padorin had long been a communications wizard, and under his guidance, her office, together with the equipment she required, had all been set up.

When visitors inquired about the small compact computer which rested on a wooden table beside her desk, she easily explained how it helped her review new titles, necessary information on authors, and other data important to a distributor of technical articles.

The computer was, in fact, hooked up to the central communications facility at the Soviet Embassy in Washington, enabling all Soviet agents to tap into that vital information bank. It possessed a built-in security system to prevent eavesdropping, and special secured lines. Access to coded transmissions were protected by the constant change of passkeys. Jane was thus enabled to examine documents stored in secret vaults in Washington, receive instructions, and transmit reports of her own, without the use of a single sheet of paper.

Maintaining the right image was essential, however. Padorin had made her acutely aware of that when she first took up residence in San Francisco.

"Avoid suspicion at all costs," he had told her with paternal warmth. "Keep in close touch with local friends and neighbors. If, among these, you must have a lover or two, then so be it. You're a beautiful woman, *Malyinki*."

He had used the term of endearment that Karol Tobirian had always addressed her with. Dear little one. She respected Padorin and followed his advice. Though her lifestyle was reclusive, her friends and suitors could not find fault with her warmth and congeniality when she chose to make them available.

Her refrigerator was empty, and there was nothing in the cupboards except some stale saltine crackers and half a jar of Yuban instant. After the long journey, she craved a good strong cup of American coffee. Humming to herself, she dialed the unlisted number of Chet Korngold, an attorney supporting two children, one from each of his marriages, a man who had made it known to her on their first dinner date that he would never re-marry. Chet Korngold's answering machine never failed to give her a laugh.

"Hi, there," his resonant voice sounded over the tape. "If you're a client or a woman or both, leave your name and number at the sound of the beep, and I'll get back to you in a matter of hours, if not minutes. If you're an ex-wife or one of my kids, I'll reach you in order of priority. But...*Sei gesund*, you-all."

Jane giggled, waiting for the high-pitched beep.

"It's Jane," she announced, in her huskiest, most enticing tone. "Got back in town today. Felt like a cuppa and thought of you. Call me when you have time."

Standing high on tip-toes, well over six feet, she rummaged in back of one of the overhead kitchen cupboards. Success. A bottle of Stolichnaya. Great! And shrunken ice cubes in the freezer tray.

Sipping her drink, she turned on the computer's power switch and tapped the code when the screen lighted. Nothing yet. Her hands went lightly over the keyboard, almost in a caress, the payoff for the intensive training at the prestigious International Relations Institute on Krymskaya Square.

Her proficiency had earned her a red I.D. card, unheard of for foreigners, KGB or not. The red card enabled her to shop in Moscow's very few luxury stores. Ordinary Russians carried blue cards. She remembered the one goal drummed into her head: Obtain technical know-how by fair means or foul. Years of development time and millions of rubles would be saved by wresting the latest in technological advances from the capitalists. Glasnost and Perestroika aside, Moscow was pleased with her success. Thus far, she was very special.

But there was also the risky side to the business. Agents kept disappearing. Some were never heard of again. Those were the clumsy ones, the men and women who became too smug, too cock-sure of themselves, making unforgivable errors which tended to compromise their nation. Moscow might overlook one error. The second was another story, however...

Like the man with whom she was to make contact the next day...

It took her a few seconds to realize that words, letters and numbers were forming on the screen, and her heart pounded as she entered the passkey, activating the descrambler. The alphabet soup of meaningless letters on screen dissolved in a blur.

```
PRIORITY MESSAGE.  EYES ONLY.  CIA TASK
FORCE  INVESTIGATING  DISAPPEARANCE  OF
SRC   CHIP.   CONTACT   PROFESSOR   AND
EXHAUST  LEADS.   COVER  TRACKS  AND  USE
NEUTRAL MEANS OF TRANSPORTATION. ADVISE
ETA HQ. MC.
```

She read the message twice, then shut down the computer, her hands sweaty with excitement. It was just about dawn, Moscow time. Someone at Moscow Center had timed her arrival perfectly. The language of the message suggested it would be simple for her to acquire the device. Jane understood that semi-conductors and micro-electronic inventions were red-hot items in Moscow. The message conveyed the fact that they were anticipating its prompt receipt.

Advise estimated time of arrival at Moscow Headquarters.

What a joke, if it weren't so threatening! And the CIA already going after it, to complicate matters. And Professor Smolerov, who had the contacts, but who was, she knew, expendable...

The phone rang, and in the panic of her thinking, she snatched it up with a sharp, "Yes?"

"Jane, Baby?"

Chet, of course. Not now. I need time to think...

"You there, Jane?" Chet Korngold pressed over the phone.

"You called back sooner than I expected," she forced herself to smile, calming her nerves.

"Where you're concerned, Baby, nothing's ever too soon," he intimated sensually. "Still feel like coffee? Or a couple of vodka Martinis with all the giant olives they can find at Emil's?"

The invitation sounded good. It would give her a little time to think. Besides, she needed to pick up a newspaper.

And she needed air...

"Sounds delightful," she murmured. "I can be ready in fifteen minutes..."

It was sunup when she started dressing. Sharp-looking black loafers over smooth black socks. A conservative gray three-piece business suit over a long-sleeved shirt with French cuffs adorned with genuine cat's-eye cufflinks. A striped, blue-gray tie. A military-type khaki raincoat with braided épaulets to enhance the width of the shoulders. A special snug blond wig designed to show carefully trimmed sideburns at the temples. A water-repellant rainhat with the brim curved rakishly down over one eye.

Voilà!, Captain Ilya Romayev, KGB.

Three local newspapers were discarded on the floor. She had learned nothing from them. Nor had Chet Korngold been of any help regarding the theft, pointing out that the scanty details which had been revealed in terse news broadcasts indicated that it had to be one of the "top secret" technological wonders the whole world was seeking.

Professor Smolerov had been startled by her phone call, some minutes after midnight.

Complaining of sheer exhaustion, she had cut short her evening with Chet Korngold and returned to her apartment to place that call. Her voice underwent a subtle transformation before she spoke. Her training in Moscow had included the masculinization of her voice. She had cleared her throat, tensing her vocal chords.

"Good evening, Professor. This is Goldleader One."

Chapter 8

(San Francisco)

Except for the soft purr of traffic from the street, Professor Smolerov heard only the eerie quiet of his high-rise apartment overlooking San Francisco Bay. The Harbor View Apartment which Moscow had rented for him as reward for his earlier triumphs boasted a long tree-lined driveway, awnings at street level with red and yellow stripes, an elegant lobby with mirrors reflecting the dazzle of crystal chandeliers, potted palms and uniformed doormen. A never-ending succession of Mercedes-Benzes, BMW's, Jaguars, Porsches and Citroens entered and left both ends of the parking area below.

Professor Smolerov turned up his stereo for Sibelius' Fifth and closed his eyes. He felt ready for the arrival of Goldleader One. His own .32 calibre Mauser was in its holster, and on the table was the weapon he knew Goldleader One preferred, a .38 S&W special with a four-inch barrel and a snappy grip. There was also a box of cartridges.

The call the previous night from his assignment leader had disquieted him, adding new wrinkles to his smooth face. At 53, Smolerov wore the look of a scientist and walked with the stride of a man who kept physically fit. The occasional flicker in his eyes betrayed a measure of ruthless ambition not generally found among men of academe.

He believed he had discharged his duties as well as any other operative. But what he had come to despise about his work was the sudden, unexpected, often clandestine meetings with mysterious contacts who would take him to task in the name of the organization, or even worse, of the Party or the Nation, and would then pile him high with extra work—as though supervising eight agents throughout the Silicon Valley and maintaining his own cover as lecturer at Berkeley no longer seemed to satisfy Moscow.

His dissertations on Slavic culture were famous throughout the university, and there were always long lists of students waiting for his classes. How easily he had established himself in the innocent, wide-eyed world of American education! A letter of recommendation from a well-intending dean on the Atlantic Seaboard, the transcript of several of his lectures delivered at the Sorbonne and at Dartmouth, and he was accepted on the spot. The ease with which his acceptance had been carried out convinced him he could probably import—without raising a single eyebrow—half his former colleagues from Moscow.

It had been over a year since he'd quit smoking, but finding a single crumbled cigarette in his jacket pocket made the craving return, and to calm his nerves, he placed it in his mouth and lit it. The thought of meeting Goldleader One in a matter of minutes made his stomach churn. That voice on the phone had been stern and imperious, insolent—with a certain youthful ring to it. His watch showed almost three. From the grapevine, he had learned that this individual was extremely punctual.

His security gate buzzed once. It was precisely three. Smolerov blew a low, begrudging whistle and pressed the speaker button.

"Theodor here."

"Buzz me in," said the insolent voice.

That voice had been rather accusatory the previous night, reminding him that he, Professor Smolerov, so close to Silicon Valley, had let the remarkable SRC chip slip through his fingers, an act viewed by Moscow Center as unpardonable negligence.

Scowling as he pressed the buzzer, Smolerov girded himself for a new tongue-lashing from a superior. But the enormity of the accusation had begun to weigh ponderously upon him. A technical breakthrough of immense proportions had taken place in his assignment area, and instead of pursuing it for his government, he had sat idly by while others—their identity and allegiances unknown—had rushed right in to grab it.

Footsteps outside his door. Then a light tap.

Smolerov stepped back, surprised, admitting a tall, slender blond man in khaki raingear who offered a hand in greeting. The Professor noted the lithe grace of the *danseur*, the searching eyes of the intellectual, and the peaches-and-cream complexion of Goldleader One, and wondered if this man ever had to shave.

"I am Captain Romayev," Jane announced in her strong, low voice, bouncing the Smith & Wesson in the palm of one hand and securing the cartridges inside an inner belt. "You are to lead me to the microchip and help me secure it for our Government."

The stranger's pale eyes pierced his with icy fire, and Smolerov felt paralyzed by their withering intensity. He asked himself how long he could withstand such intimidation.

He's making sure I know he's boss, he realized, no stranger to the system's peculiar way of dealing with losers. Any agents who had erred once too often or had outlived their usefulness would drown mysteriously in the Volga or be found hanging in the privacy of their apartments. Abroad, agents were found dead in bed, gas pouring from their ovens. Still others leaped from skyscrapers. They sometimes even left suicide notes.

"We must move quickly," Jane stated solemnly. "Your career is at stake, Professor Smolerov...as well as the health of your two daughters in Vitebsk."

Smolerov paled. He had to get his act together.

Li Yixin, headwaiter at the Jiangsu Restaurant in downtown San Francisco, eyed the two Caucasians as they entered, the older man sporting a full professorial beard and a wild mane of graying hair.

But Li Yixin knew this man had spent time in Beijing, and that except for the heavily-clinging Russian accent, his Mandarin Chinese was remarkably precise. Normally, Yixin ignored Caucasian tourists, leaving them to his underlings to pursue for their generous tips. But Professor Smolerov was on extremely good terms with the Jiangsu's proprietor, Eddie Hong. Yixin had long concluded that the two men shared a common interest either in a drug ring or a sizable stable of prostitutes. Why else would his Chinese boss spend hours with the Westerner in a remote corner of the restaurant, talking, laughing, and occasionally exchanging large sums of money.

He escorted Smolerov and his dinner guest—a slender man with piercing blue eyes and a soft, effeminate face—to a select table, according to them the deference reserved for friends of the proprietor, and speaking to them with that mixture of disdain and servitude at which the Chinese are masters.

Hearing Smolerov's fluent Chinese, Jane's respect for the man returned in some measure. From the fact sheets, he was slightly younger than Jane's father, and his record, which for the preceding several years had been anything but illustrious, was slipping badly. A widower with two grown daughters in Russia, he had been implicated—(according to his file)—with two female colleagues at the university, with several adoring students, with the woman from whom he had sublet the apartment, and with a member of the City Council who had a "thing" for dreamy-eyed Russian lecturers. Quite indiscreet. Now he'd be given a chance to erase the black marks against him by helping to recover the stolen superchip. If he failed…

Yixin posed courteously with his order pad. Smolerov smiled.

"I'll begin with bird's nest soup," he announced, winking at Jane to indicate his knowledge of Chinese delicacies. "That is,

Captain Romayev, a full-bodied chicken broth, brimming with minced chicken egg white...followed by a medley of perfectly cooked seafood, steamed to perfection in a clay pot, which people mistake for a casserole..."

Jane forced a grin to be sociable.

Was this the lifestyle of Professor Theodor Smolerov, long in the pay of the Soviet Secret Service? Were these excesses of gluttony and sex the sorry demonstrations of his dedication to a government that had placed its faith in him?

Then he deserves to die, Jane told herself. She would have no hesitation about pulling the trigger.

But Smolerov was continuing the litany of his order.

"...followed by deep-fried whole chicken emerging from the pot with a lacquer-like skin of crackling gold...fish enhanced by an aromatic mixture of soy, scallions, coriander, garlic, ginger, crab coral..."

"*That will do, Professor!*" Jane cut him off firmly.

Smolerov tried not to show his embarrassment. He pulled his chair closer to the table and told Yixin, "Please tell Mr. Wong I wish to speak to him."

A short, obese Oriental soon approached their table, casting an inquiring glance at Jane through tiny slit eyes. Smolerov explained that his guest was a colleague, that they could speak openly, and Jane listened to the clipped sentences as the men conversed in English regarding the stolen SRC chip.

"Why suspect Chinese?" Hong asked, sourly.

"Russia didn't take it."

"Maybe local thieves."

"True. But in whose interest?"

Hong lifted his chin toward Smolerov.

"Possibly," the Professor acknowledged. "But the boys from Beijing are everywhere these days."

"Yes, immediately followed by the so-called friends of the Imperialists. The Japanese," suggested Hong.

Smolerov shook his head impatiently.

"They don't have the balls," he whispered.

"No? Heard of Mitsubishi-IBM scandal?" Hong sneered.

"That's not even in this league!" the Russian pointed out.

Hong leaned across the table, his voice hoarse and low.

"What do you want, Professor?"

"The Chinese who stole the contraption," Jane put in.

Hong eyed the blond newcomer with suspicion.

"You're asking for the moon," he said after a reflective pause.

Smolerov looked to Jane to handle the fiduciary arrangements. Jane recalled the terse message on her computer that brooked no excuse and no delay. She considered the unlimited expense account which, with judgment and caution, could be tapped when necessary.

"Lead us to the thief who has the chip and you'll be five thousand dollars richer," she whispered.

"Not enough...," Hong shot back darkly, and then, as both Russians gloated over his stupid spontaneity like victors cornering and closing in on their prey, realized what he had admitted.

"You sonofabitch...," Smolerov smiled, his expression unchanged. "You've known all along."

"No! Not so! I can try to find out! It will take time!" Hong protested.

"It will take us forty-five minutes to consume the dinner your waiter is now bringing to our table, Mr. Hong," Jane menaced him quietly. "In forty-five minutes, you decide how to lead us to the chip, or this restaurant will not open for business tomorrow."

The ice-blue fire in her eyes underscored her pronouncement.

Hong struggled to his feet, almost tipping his chair over. With nervous uncertainty he moved toward his private office.

*   *   *   *

"I don't like leaving you here," Harry whispered to Natalie as they sat parked on Blossom Street amid the dirt, the stench, the squalid decay of the neighborhood. Small, drab, dimly-lit shops lined both sides of the street. Everywhere were Chinese, the old resigned and weighed down by life, the young quick and brave in their tight American blue jeans brandishing their portable stereos.

"I've been left in worse spots," she assured him.

"There's a pay phone in the corner diner. Call me the moment you've seen enough...or the second you need me. Okay?"

Their eyes met for a moment, digesting the *double entendre*, and Harry returned his attention to the street as dusk began to settle.

"You really think there's a chance this guy has the chip?"

Natalie's investigation into the personnel file of Sam Chu, a minimum-wage janitor at Universal Electronics, had made interesting reading. She went over the facts again with Harry.

"Worth investigating. The morning after the theft, Chu tells the personnel manager he just learned his brother is dying and needs emergency leave to return to Hong Kong."

"Coincidence," Harry observed.

"Except his security clearance lists one sister, no brother, in Hong Kong. Parents long dead."

"Well, you know how the Chinese are about family. Maybe it's a brother-in-law who's dying."

"You're trying to talk me out of watching this suspect."

"I just wish you were watching from a safer place, Nat."

The agent ignored his concern, staring through the windshield.

"There's more, Harry. Chu could've booked on CAAC, national airline of the People's Republic, which would get him there non-stop. Instead, he books on United, which takes him to Hong Kong via Honolulu and Tokyo..."

"Proves nothing," Harry scoffed.

"If he's our man, he knows the CIA and even the KGB will be examining every passenger and every bit of luggage en route to China. He doesn't pick up the last leg of his flight until Tokyo..."

"I see...," Harry said, chewing his lip.

"And for clinchers...," Natalie added with enthusiasm, "...our minimum-wage janitor pays cash for the tickets *and* for the girl he's taking with him. Linda Chan, about nineteen,

American-born, living with Chu about a year or so. Together they fly the friendly skies of United with a treasure in new Yankee technology riding in the luggage compartment."

Harry expelled his breath, acknowledging she was on to something.

"Nat, if you're right, this is probably the biggest acquisition to date for the minor-league technocrats in Beijing."

She put her lips to his cheek and left the car, but before she could close the door, Harry reached out for her wrist.

"Nat, promise you'll be careful."

"Stop worrying. See you later."

He watched her cross the street, remembering the brave little girl he had first met in a teeming monsoon deep in a Luzon jungle. Her first assignment. The Agency had sent her as replacement for Harry's sidekick, Jack Brady, who had come down with malaria. She'd arrived with provisions, first aid, and fresh underwear in her backpack.

Her signal had been the muted sound of the kiwi bird.

He had answered with the same soft cry.

Without batting an eyelash, she had dusted him free of the leeches clinging to the skin of his back...

He shivered as he drove away from Blossom Street, recalling the grim sight of leeches clinging to his shoulder, and the light touch of Natalie's calm, reassuring hand.

All he could see of her in his rear view mirror was the slim line of her figure in the darkened doorway, and the pale blur of her face.

*   *   *   *

Through Smolerov's powerful binoculars, Jane focused directly into the dingy apartment across the street. Neither agent had particularly entertained the prospect of taking up positions in the shambles of a condemned ruin, uninhabitable for a decade. The charred, vandalized structure seemed to be hanging together with spit and rubber bands, about to collapse at any moment to bury them both in foul, rat-infested debris.

But it was the closest point from which to observe the Chinese couple. Once Eddie Hong came through with the whereabouts of the superchip and identification of the thief, Jane developed a time frame and mapped out her directives, receiving more help from Smolerov than she had anticipated.

I was born in this city, Jane mused, looking through the field glasses. *Born here, with a twin brother.*

But that's where the link had ended, and Jane had learned to abandon the fact. Even her father, Admiral Romayev, while clasping her physically and emotionally to his heart, had been either unable or unwilling to disclose further information regarding the male infant with whom she'd come into the world.

A skinny Chinese girl paced through the dusky apartment, her form back-lit by the dying sunlight, two small pointed breasts jiggling against a flimsy yellow tank top as she moved. The ends of her short black hair kept catching at a corner of her mouth, and Jane wondered why the girl didn't just pin it back instead of constantly tossing it aside. But hair-tossing was sexy, wasn't it? She remembered that from her days as a stripper.

"She looks impatient for her lover-boy, no?" Smolerov intruded on Jane's thoughts, watching the girl through the window. "Why would she live with a man in his fifties?"

Jane maintained as much distance between herself and the Professor as possible. She didn't like the undeniable, rising lust in his eyes when he looked at her as Captain Ilya Romayev. Perhaps Smolerov had become jaded enough to swing both ways...

"Lucky old slant," he was muttering at that moment. "Imagine the fortunate Mr. Chu coming home to a hot little gash like that! Ever try yellowtail, Captain Romayev...?"

"Keep your voice down!" she snapped. "And look down there..."

A blue pick-up was stopping in front of the apartment building. A thin, middle-aged man in blue denims emerged. Dark butch haircut, homely Oriental. He locked his vehicle and disappeared into the tenement.

Jane magnified her view for greater detail as Linda Chan, breasts bouncing, streaked through the apartment to welcome Chu at the door, hanging on his neck, kissing the side of his face, as they moved toward their kitchen.

From the pocket of her raincoat, Jane drew a tiny two-way transmitter and pressed the button.

"Can you read me?" she asked in Russian.

"*Da*," a gruff voice responded.

She gave the command to proceed, then watched until a shiny red panel truck pulled up behind the blue Nissan and parked there. Two men wearing the uniform of the San Francisco Fire Department got out, one of them carrying a tool box, and entered the building.

"All right, you know what to do," she gasped to Smolerov, her heart hammering unevenly. "Once you see us leave the building, you may go. We'll expect you at the Consulate later tonight."

Without another word, she was gone, and from his watch at the second story window, Smolerov waited for the KGB officer to rush across the street and into the tenement. It was all rolling according to plan.

Linda Chan answered the front door, then returned to her lover in the kitchen. Smolerov knew she would now be informing Chu that the Fire Department had been alerted about a gas leak in the building and were checking every apartment.

Just as the Professor expected, Chu opened the kitchen window and leaned out to spot the red panel truck parked at the curb, bearing the designation "S.F.F.D." Satisfied that the inspection was legitimate, Chu closed the window against the evening chill.

With some smugness, Smolerov watched his agents, Brodsky and Kurzinov, in their Fire Department uniforms, begin their inspection of Chu's apartment. In another moment, Smolerov knew, Captain Romayev would enter—the blond KGB officer with the ice-blue eyes and the soft, effeminate features. It would all be done with calm and stealth. With smooth, lethal silence...

Cockroaches and silverfish scurried away from her feet as she mounted the creaking staircase to the second story. The antiquated corridor was pungent with the odor of cabbage. A naked light bulb suspended in a cylindrical socket from a rusted ceiling fixture cast bizarre shadows against the dirty, paint-peeled walls.

Just as Jane reached the open door of Chu's apartment, there was a sharp scream from Linda Chan. Brodsky and Kurzinov had discovered the computer on a bedroom bureau top. In a flash, Kurzinov's toolbox was opened, and both he and Brodsky were aiming automatic assault weapons at the hapless couple, forcing them into the living room.

"Surprised at you, Mr. Chu!" Brodsky mocked the Chinaman.

Entering with drawn revolver, Jane noticed young Linda Chan clinging to her lover, sobbing, "No! Please, no!"

"Leave the girl alone!" Jane commanded.

"Fu Manchu say, 'He who play with fire...get burned!'" Kurzinov sneered, firing. Chu, his chest blasted, sank to the floor, Linda falling with him, one protective arm riddled, holding him in a final clasp of tenderness.

"I said, leave the girl alone!" Jane cried, but not before Kurzinov fired again, the staccato racket of the weapon drowning out the deathscream of nineteen-year-old Linda, sprawled across the bleeding body of her lover.

Jane stared at the stream of blood streaking down the yellow tank top. The eyes of Sam and Linda were already glazing over in death, their mouths open, too, in howls of protest against the unanticipated finality of it all.

"Get the computer," Jane directed in a dull voice, suddenly unable to breathe, aware of too long a pause between heartbeats, of dizziness and imbalance. Kurzinov placed the weapons back in the toolbox and helped Jane strap the computer to Brodsky's sturdy back. Following them out, Jane stumbled and almost fell.

"Are you all right, Captain?" Brodsky asked, touching her arm.

She inhaled deeply and closed her eyes for a moment.

"I'm fine. Get a move on…"

Smolerov watched the two firemen emerge from the tenement across the street, one carrying a toolbox, the other with a
CTR strapped to his back, and make their way to the red truck,
followed by Captain Romayev who looked strangely pale and
unsteady. It elated him to know he had been instrumental in
the acquisition of this prize. It would win back some acclaim for
him. A promotion, perhaps, or a new assignment…

Down below, Kurzinov was at the wheel, the Captain alongside of him, and Brodsky squeezing in last, pulling the truck door
shut. Smolerov's instructions were to join them later at the
Consulate…

Who was that down below?

A dark-haired young woman had stepped out into the littered
street the moment the red panel truck pulled away, scribbling
the license number on a note pad and stuffing it into her
handbag. Then she looked up and down Blossom Street and
crossed to the tenement entrance to consult the names in the
bell panel.

"I'd better check this," Smolerov gasped as the woman
slipped into the lobby. He sprinted down the crumbling steps,
surprised to find that night had already fallen.

Moving stealthily along the shadowy corridor to the Chu
apartment, Natalie Soubrine checked to see if she were being
observed. As she entered, she braced herself at the sight of the
bodies lying in a bloody clasp of death on the living room floor.
A puddle of blood and tissue was still widening beneath them.

It had been overkill. Chu's chest was a gory hole and the track
of shells had all but severed Linda's head. Whatever the Chinese couple had possessed, their killers had made off with it.
Natalie had been curious about the two San Francisco firemen
and the peculiar red truck, but even more convinced her suspi-
cions were correct when they left the building with the rectangular gray case, a slim blond man in khaki apparently in charge
of the operation.

That man had looked strangely familiar. Natalie wondered where she had seen him before.

From snatches of an interchange among the trio, Natalie had picked up phrases in Russian...Natalie's mothertongue. Of course. KGB, snatching the prize from the Chinese. They would ditch the truck from which she'd recorded the license number...

From the bedroom doorway, she could see from the film of dust on the bureau top that a rectangular object had been removed. The identity of the thieves had changed...

"Put your hands up and don't move," an accented voice behind her commanded, and Natalie heard the apartment door kicked shut and a gravelly footstep on the splintered floor.

It was an older voice, a cultured baritone, not the soft tenor of the blond man in the raincoat, nor the harsh slur of the two disguised firemen. This had to be a rear guard of sorts, and from the tone of his command, Natalie knew his gun was trained directly at the back of her head. Her hair stood on end as she imagined the trajectory of a large calibre bullet aimed at her skull. Unless she gained a split second's advantage, she could be done for.

Her little ruse had worked before. She had to take the chance.

"You are making a grave mistake, Comrade!" she stated imperiously, in educated Russian.

Those few words jabbed at Smolerov's vulnerable insecurity. He dared not make another error and foil this mission...

But his uncertainty was all Natalie needed. In a blur of speed she wheeled down into a low squat, firing twice at Smolerov's legs.

His gun flew from his grip and his body folded grotesquely, as though it had been hinged. Screaming in Russian about his knees, he slid to the floor and fell silent. Natalie had shattered both kneecaps. Replacing her pistol beneath the ruching of her blouse, feeling its warmth against the surface of her breast, Natalie knelt beside him to go through his jacket. A small, leather-bound notebook had a calling card placed between its pages.

JULIO PORTO
— EXPORTS-IMPORTS —
LISBON, GENEVA

The phone beside the bed smelled of garlic. Natalie dialed, staring at the card as though it contained the key to the Rosetta stone. Bert Klemmer answered.

"The computer got away from me, but we've won a consolation prize," she told him. "Come to 47 Blossom Street...and hurry!"

The red panel truck wound north along the Embarcadero as the evening fog built, dense smokey drifts floating white before them. Jane was breathing more easily, her heartbeat more regular, pulses quieter. The throbbing in her temples had faded.

"There's the Buick I rented," she directed Kurzinov. "Pull in behind it."

Humming a gypsy melody, Kurzinov moved in tight at the curb behind the Buick with dealers' plates and cut the engine.

When they exited the truck, Jane preceded them to the door of her Buick, keys in hand, and turned to stare at Kurzinov.

"You will not be coming with us," she announced.

Kurzinov hesitated, then snickered in bewilderment.

"You want me to wait here in the truck...?"

"On Blossom Street," Jane cut him off, her eyes burning into his like dry ice, "...you were given an order, Comrade Kurzinov. You were told to leave the Chan girl alone..."

"She was a little slant bitch who'd have caused trouble..."

"*I* gave you that order, Comrade Kurzinov," Jane emphasized.

"Yes, Captain, but a girl like that..."

He did not see Jane's hand reach into her raincoat lining.

"You were trained to obey your superiors' orders," she stated.

"True, Captain, but I thought..."

"You weren't trained to think, you were trained to *obey*!"

There was a fiery blast as the .38 shell from Jane's revolver entered just below the Adam's apple and exited the Russian's medulla.

Kurzinov clutched at his throat with a few ghastly choking sounds and toppled forward. Jane stepped aside, making way for him to fall dead beside the car, then glanced at the ashen-faced Brodsky.

"Get in," she said quietly. "We're late."

Chapter 9

(San Francisco)

Padorin, relieving Agent Brodsky of the heavy gray case, and noting the man's pallor, welcomed Jane with a kiss. Brodsky had not yet recovered from the sight of his buddy pitching forward in death on the Embarcadero, nor was he now prepared to see Captain Romayev receive a kiss from the KGB Chief, and even less prepared to see Romayev peel one of his sideburns up from the temple, then yank the rubbery flap away from his head, revealing a cascade of cornsilk hair falling in dishevelment halfway to the shoulders.

"There, now, Comrade Brodsky," Jane smiled triumphantly to sooth the man's wide-eyed alarm and bewilderment. "I'm sure it doesn't bother you to take orders from a woman. And of course, this is a secret that will die with you, am I correct...?"

"But of course, Captain Romayev...Romayeva...," the man was quick to correct himself, acknowledging that yes, he would die with that secret.

Complaining that she did not take heat well and would tolerate no more than five to seven minutes of the new sauna in the Consulate basement, Jane followed Padorin to the dressing rooms, and with two Turkish towels draped strategically over her body, accompanied a totally nude KGB Chief into the sauna chamber.

"Here, thresh yourself," he said, handing her a bundle of leafy birch twigs. "It takes all the grime out of the system. You'll feel like a newborn afterwards. Of course, it's better if you're bare..."

The effect of the slow, fanning motion of the twigs was like a current of fire touching her skin, and in the dense white steam, the bureau chief was only a vague pink blob on the bench beside her.

"Ingenious, the way you're able to switch back and forth, Romayeva," Padorin wheezed, threshing away. "One minute a man, the next a woman. Do you realize that perhaps only half a dozen people at all our stations in the United States know you are really a woman? Your reputation as Goldleader One has been growing admirably."

"I'm happy to know that."

"You must know, of course, that Smolerov is under constant surveillance. Even during this transaction. We have reports now that he will not be joining us here tonight."

"Oh? What happened?"

"Evidently, the CIA got to him. He's hospitalized with both knees crippled, and very anxious at this point to exchange everything he knows for political asylum..."

Jane digested that news in silence. If Padorin were able to see her expression through the steam, he'd have found it inscrutable.

"Academics have always proven an untrustworthy bunch," Padorin continued. "Besides, he was a nasty pervert. It's no great loss to us, his capture. But of course, he will not survive his hospitalization, you understand..."

"I understand, Comrade," she whispered.

"Didn't he try to seduce you?" Padorin asked, leaning toward her with a grin that made her inch to one side along the wooden bench. "He's been known to seduce young men. Your masculinity would have been no deterrent to the old lecher. Can you just see his bewilderment if he started something with you, and found..."

"Comrade!" Jane interrupted, springing up. "I really can't tolerate this heat. And I must know about the courier we're using...this Portuguese...Julio Porto..."

"Yes, yes...," Padorin returned to his usual demeanor. "We make the delivery to him tomorrow afternoon. That old carpetbagger has handled a lot of hot stuff for us. He's been in the business a long time. You can trust him, Romayeva."

"Good. Now I must see to some communication matters. You'll excuse me, Comrade Padorin..."

On the top floor of the Consulate, Jane inserted her plastic card into a slot beside a steel door which led to the super-secret communications center. The door opened, and the clerk closest to the door removed a headset from his ears and gazed at Jane with the proper degree of appreciation for feminine pulchritude.

So the Professor had been crippled and captured. Jane requested reports on the Smolerov incident, knowing the routine all too well. Smolerov's own assistants would find their way to his hospital room, to make sure he never uttered another word to his captors.

But none of that mattered. The prized computer was now in her hands. Tomorrow afternoon, the appointed courier would begin its transport to Moscow. She would remain with it as long as possible.

Obedient to the authority in Jane's voice, the clerk with the headset moved down the line of files, checking the bins stacked in front of each communications specialist. The sensitive equipment in the center was hooked to powerful antennae atop the building to receive signals from towers, Soviet fishing trawlers cruising offshore and from satellites. Modern technology allowed eavesdropping on practically any conversation in America, any message electronically carried between individuals in industry or government. Full advantage of this opportunity was taken, assembling data ranging from trivia to top-secret communiques—and it amounted to staggering quantities.

The greatest problem presented by such an overload, Jane knew, was to sift for the comparatively few items presumed of value. Military moves, economic projections, political stratagems—were all there for the taking, and the bigwigs in the Kremlin convulsed with hilarity over the consistent demonstration of Yankee naiveté.

"They brag about their 'open society' but don't know the zippers of their flies are open," more than one Kremlin boss had been known to quip, while marveling at the windfall of technical and military information received each day. For years during her training, this acquisition of scientific and military input had been Jane's entire sociological orientation. Thus, the constant clatter of the communication machinery was music to her ears.

"I think this might be what you want, Comrade," the clerk said, returning with two sheets of paper. "Identical messages. One to the White House. The other to CIA Headquarters at Langley."

Jane read the message, written in the universally sparse language of intelligence personnel:

```
ITEM  IN  HANDS  OF  KGB  HAS  NOT  LEFT
COUNTRY. BEING HOTLY PURSUED. STRONGLY
SUSPECT PLAN TO EXPORT ASAP VIA NEUTRAL
COURIER. INVESTIGATING. CARROLL.
```

As Jane went through the formality of signing for the message, the technician was called away by another specialist as new copy came through the FAX terminal, and the sheet of paper was still warm when it was placed in Jane's hand.

"Thought you might be interested in this, too. Just came through the facsimile tube from downtown."

The thin paper was imprinted with copy from the front page of a San Francisco evening journal. Over black and white photographs of Sam Chu and Linda Chan, (replicas of their passport pictures) a bold headline read, "MYSTERY MURDER ON BLOSSOM STREET."

Jane studied the vital smiles of the murdered couple, recalling how they had looked in violent death. She signed for the FAX copy and went down to the lounge, where she ordered a Perrier and vodka and sat reflecting on the complications ahead.

So the CIA had already been closing in on the Chinese couple!

Damn right they were in hot pursuit! *Too* hot! Whoever had shot Smolerov could have been only seconds from touching Jane and her aides right there on Blossom Street!

Now the capture of Smolerov supplied the positive link to the USSR. Someone named Carroll was running the show. The newspaper article mentioned a dark-haired woman and a couple of men following the stretcher-borne Smolerov as paramedics moved him to the ambulance. Was Carroll a woman? A dark-haired woman? Jane sipped her drink and stared off into space. Were two top female secret service agents to be pitted against one another?

Normally, a CIA message to the White House would have been in code, Jane knew. This time it wasn't. They were probably frantic. Frustrated. Jane paid silent tribute to Moscow's insistence that the computer leave the United States in the hands of a neutral, out of the reach of the FBI, the CIA, the whole bunch of them. But they were a vigilant group of die-hards, and the stakes were high. Jane knew she had not lost them in pursuit.

"I'll have to watch out for this Carroll," she mused with a twinkle in her eyes. "If she's a woman, I'll give her a run for her money."

*   *   *   *

Bob Carlson, looking like a direct descendant of Eric the Red minus the beard, identified himself to the night manager of the

Mark Hopkins Hotel as a Federal Officer, and within minutes was in possession of a print-out of the guests, their residences, arrival dates and room numbers. Carlson's heart began racing when he spotted the computer listing of Julio Porto in Room 923.

"This is the man I must see," Carlson explained. "Very shortly, two men and a woman will arrive, asking for me. Please direct them to Señor Porto's suite."

He then pushed the button of his two-way radio to alert the team. Harry had chauffeured them to their assigned stations— Bert Klemmer to Ghirardelli Square, Natalie to the Sheraton, then had driven off to his own watch at the Hyatt Regency.

Reports had confirmed that one Julio Porto had arrived from Lisbon at JFK and continued on to San Francisco. The dossier on the man indicated that the Portuguese, on previous visits, had been a guest at those hotels for short periods.

"This is our neutral courier," Harry had told his team.

Ascending to the ninth floor, Carlson readied his weapon. He had always tried to be a very prudent man. Having dealt with international smugglers before, he knew them to be dangerous, to be handled with utmost caution.

The muffled sound of a woman's voice, a man's responding, took him by surprise as he tip-toed to the door of Suite 923 and leaned close to listen. He did not notice the two men drawing near until they were ready to pounce. There was only a brief scuffle, and by the way the two wrestler-types pinned him, their guns jammed into his ribs, Carlson knew they were professional guerrillas.

The room into which he was pushed was done in every shade of green with silver accents. Carlson held his breath, hoping his team had received his signal and that his three colleagues were on their way to undo the mess in which he had trapped himself.

A suave-looking Latin type, obviously Porto, and a tall, slim blonde woman jumped to their feet as the men forced Carlson forward, twisting his arms, one of the apes fumbling through his pockets, handing the contents to the woman.

She studied the gun, the two-way radio and the I.D. in Bob Carlson's wallet and her eyes burned briefly into his.

"Does the name Carroll ring a bell with you?" she asked.

Carlson's expression betrayed nothing.

"CIA, no question," she hissed to Porto and the guards. "He's bound to have alerted his team. Take him down the backstairs and out through the service entrance. We'll follow directly behind."

Porto understood the urgency of the situation. With his personal belongings thrown into a black canvas-type carry-on bag, he brought up the rear of the Russian contingent dragging a gagged and pistol-whipped Bob Carlson down the staircase. Nobody even thought to lock the door. Nothing had been left behind...

The disposition of Bob Carlson was left to Jane's henchmen. They were also instructed to move Porto to a more secure hiding place.

Jane parked her Buick across the street from the hotel's entrance, shifting over to the passenger seat, to appear she was waiting for the driver's return. She fixed her page-boy undercurl, examined her make-up in her compact mirror, then applied fresh lipstick. She wanted a glimpse of Carlson's cohorts. They were bound to show. Somehow, she felt compelled to see "the dark-haired young woman" sighted at the scene of Smolerov's shooting. In Jane's mind, the name, "Carroll," was linked with the identity of that woman. *Her opponent.*

Car after car and taxi after taxi arrived at the entrance to the Mark, Jane realizing it would be impossible to distinguish a casual traveler from an undercover agent for the CIA...

A Yellow cab pulled up, and even before it came to a complete stop, an attractive young woman with dark hair leaped nimbly from the passenger compartment, pressed some money into the driver's hand and rushed headlong into the lobby. Jane could not get a good look at her, but her heart vibrated strangely...

A big Oldsmobile pulled up, the driver abandoning it right in front of the main entrance, ignoring the uniformed doorman's surly protest, and charging into the lobby...!

Hah! *That's what I would do if I were in such a hurry,* Jane snickered to herself, catching a brief glimpse of the inconsiderate man as he vanished into the brightly-illuminated hotel. That's just what I...

Was her mind playing tricks with her...?

She imagined herself the driver of that big Oldsmobile, arriving late and breathless for a long-awaited reunion with some beloved, abandoning the car recklessly, its keys in the ignition, knowing that the hotel personnel would have to worry about it as she dashed toward her rendezvous...

Just as she, Jane...long before she became Captain Ilyana Romayeva, had rushed up a littered staircase to a single room off Nogin Square in Moscow...to be with a fair young god who fired the blood in her veins.

That's me, she gasped, inside her head.

I'm watching a videotape of myself, rushing into this hotel...

No hat. Soft blond hair, chiseled features, high cheekbones. The same type of raincoat, same agility, same grace of movement...

A sudden chill engulfed her, and she shuddered.

Some mystical perception sent a bell clanging and ringing through her mind, through her soul.

She knew that the man rushing into the hotel was her adversary.

She knew his name was Carroll...

And he was like her...*in every way...*

*   *   *   *

The rumble of a quarter-ton flatbed interrupted the quiet of the big city midnight. Instead of turning left toward the bridge, it crossed the boulevard and continued to the dirt road paralleling the Bay. The inky waters reflected the lights of the bridge like a trembling string of pearls, while on the other side of the body of water a big Nabisco sign blinked silent red and white messages to an unobservant world.

A few hundred feet down the dirt road, the truck stopped close to the water's edge. Two men in windbreakers, their faces shadowed by the visors of their caps, left the cab, and with great care, they lowered the tailgate. A dark bundle was unloaded and set down at the very rim of the concrete walkway encircling the Bay. Then, using several lengths of flexible wire, the men fastened two heavy cement blocks to the mysterious bundle, casting furtive glances all about to see if they were being watched. Lifting the heavy load, they swung it two or three times before heaving it into the water, where it submerged at once. There was a short gurgle, a few air bubbles rising to the murky surface, and then the waters flowed on impassively, carrying on their ripples a torn pack of cigarettes that somehow had escaped a watery grave.

Moments later, the truck was headed for the onramp. Just as it entered the intersection, it was flashed to a stop by a patrol car, and two police officers approached the cab with caution.

"S'matter, buddy," one cop called. "Don't your lights work?"

"Forgot to turn on. Sorry," came a heavily-accented reply.

"What were you doing down by the river?"

"Lost way through city. Missed ramp for bridge."

One of the cops leaned close, peering into the cab.

"What're you carrying in the truck?"

"Nothing, Officer," the Russian in the passenger seat replied. "Why you no look for yourself?"

The cop walked back, playing the beam of his flashlight over the bed of the truck. Then he returned, dousing the light.

"Get your asses outa here," he growled. "Next time remember to drive with your lights on!"

The truck drove off and the policemen returned to their car. A dispatch was coming in, radio chattering, alerting them to a mugging.

"Goddamn foreigners!" the irate officer muttered, starting up, hitting his lights and sirens. "Whatever kind of garbage the world vomits up these days winds up right here! 'Vy yooo no loook fooor yooo-say-elfff!' D'ja hear the Russkie bastard?"

The other cop nodded as the patrol car sped into action.

Down below, the wavelets of the Bay murmured of their secret.

*   *   *   *

Harry had begun questioning Powell Wright's judgment in selecting him to head up the task force assigned to recover the important superchip. His team was doing fine work and had come up with positive results from the start. Only his own efforts had been disastrous, and he felt he had disgraced himself as never before on any mission. He'd let his own people down with his inefficiency, his miscalculations.

Eyes burning from lack of sleep, scratching a two-day growth of golden beard, he stood gazing vacantly out at the Bay from the living room window of the Tudor residence nestling in contrast among the downtown highrises. Rumor had it that the Tudor home belonged to some hush-hush government agency, but the rumor could never be confirmed.

Behind him, slumped in fireside chairs and exhausted from the strain of the preceding seventy-two hours, Bert Klemmer and Natalie Soubrine exchanged understanding glances. Their frantic search for Julio Porto, the abducted equipment, and some trace of Bob Carlson had all been futile.

Suite 923 at the Mark Hopkins had offered mute evidence of a hasty departure — a tip-tilted lampshade, the shaft of a cigarette just begun and hastily snuffed out in an ashtray. Harry's practiced eyes found scuff marks on the green shag rug where someone's heels had ground into the fibers in a short, intense scuffle.

Even the San Francisco detective, an experienced sergeant on the force and a realist, advised Harry at the end of two and a half days of fruitless searching to call it off as hopeless.

Harry had sunk wearily onto the settee opposite the tip-tilted lampshade and the first-puff-only clinched cigarette and drew a deep, despairing breath, his morale at absolute nadir. A very faint fragrance, almost imperceptible, suddenly had filled his nostrils. He seemed to recognize it as the sweet, cloying perfume popular among Russian women. Sniffing again, he looked at Natalie.

"Do you smell that?" he asked. "What's that fragrance?"

"Somebody had some pretty sweet after-shave on," the detective grinned, inhaling deeply.

"It's 'Tatiana'...," Natalie decided. "Maybe they do make an after-shave, but I can't imagine Julio Porto using it."

It seemed senseless to spend any more time in the grim, vacant hotel room. Murmuring his thanks to the San Francisco police for their help, Harry drew himself up from the settee and was about to leave when he noticed something glinting on the headrest. With his thumb and index finger, he retrieved from the weave of the cushion a very fine, pale yellow human hair.

"You're not that desperate for clues!" the detective scoffed when Harry showed him the hair. "That's one of your own, m'boy! I don't need any fancy lab to run tests to tell me that!"

"I don't have hair this long," Harry disputed, estimating the length of the strand at close to six inches.

"Sure you do!" the policeman argued. "When a man starts losin' his hair, it starts on top, above the temples! Don't be so sensitive about it, Mr. Carroll. It happens to the best of us."

But Harry had placed the hair in his shirt pocket. Then, in conjunction with Natalie and Bert, continued to criss-cross the city, visiting the hang-outs of Eastern European suspects having ties with the Russians, monitoring all outgoing international flights, working with the local law enforcement officials to watch Soviet diplomats and agents around the clock. That surveillance likewise failed to turn up a single trace.

Harry felt Natalie's arms steal around him as he stood at the window. She pillowed her head against his back, her silence telling him she understood his anguish.

There had always been a commiseration between them, and her closeness always soothed him. He had been with Bob Carlson on a number of perilous missions. Carlson was one of the more seasoned veterans of the Agency, and the idea of his having been captured or killed burned through Harry's brain like a welder's torch.

"I'll never forgive myself if something's happened to Bob," he whispered, staring straight ahead.

"Bob wouldn't want you to feel that way," Natalie told him. "We're human."

"We're expected to be super-human..."

"And often we are..."

Shifting to face him, she found tears in his eyes.

"We've lost so much time, Nat. That chip could be in Moscow by now, and we've lost the race..."

"No, Harry. You'll turn it around. You'll see..."

"This time I'm stymied, Nat..."

"Maybe for the moment. But Harry Carroll gets what he wants out of life," she smiled encouragement to him.

Her gaze was mesmerizing. He felt he wanted to forget the mission and drown in those amber, gold-flecked depths. Through his cotton shirt, the warmth of her closeness was comforting and arousing. How many times had he desired Natalie Soubrine and held himself in check, living up to the code of the Agency? In an hour, they would be departing—Natalie and Bert for Geneva and he for Lisbon, in pursuit of Porto...

Her words had renewed his confidence, and with a smile he put her from him, hearing Bert Klemmer grunt to his feet behind them.

Harry's smile was still fixed on Natalie, and he cleared his throat of the accruing emotion.

"Remind me to tell you someday how great you are to have around," he beamed, then gestured to both of them, saying, "Now let's get ready to do some traveling..."

Part Four

Chapter 10

(Geneva, Switzerland)

Shortly after midnight, the concierge at the Hotel Richelieu in Geneva, Switzerland saw Room Number 67 light up. But he could make no contact with its occupant. Curious, the concierge noted that the room had been registered earlier that evening, just before he arrived on duty, to a Portuguese gentleman by the name of Julio Porto, showing a residence in Lisbon and listing Export/Import as his occupation.

Room 67 was a choice corner double with a balcony overlooking Lake Leman. Expensive. If he didn't follow up on the mysterious signal, the management could consider him derelict in his duty. He phoned the room, allowing a number of rings which went unanswered.

Concluding that the guest in Number 67 could be in difficulty of some kind—a case of dizziness, or perhaps even a *crise cardiaque*, the concierge dispatched his assistant, François, to check on it. The master key in hand, François knocked several times at the door of Room 67, then turned the key in the lock and the door fell open.

What François beheld would linger in his mind's eye for a long time to come.

Two men were on the floor, one with his throat cut in a thin, surgically clean incision. Blood soaked the body and the rug beneath it. The other man displayed no visible wounds. A dagger, its razor-sharp blade crusting with dried blood, hung loosely in his right hand.

François had been in the hotel when Porto checked in earlier that evening. He knew that Porto had gone to the dining room and had treated himself to a lavish meal and a bottle of 1984 Pinot Noir with the distinctive black and gold label of the Chevalier wines, one of Switzerland's best vineyards. He also knew that Porto retired shortly after 10:30 P.M.

With Swiss efficiency, the concierge, once notified of the findings in Room 67, placed three phone calls without further delay: the police, the Hôpital Cantonal, and the Journal Suisse. The grateful news desk would send him a discreet envelope within a few days, containing his reward—a number of crisp Franc notes.

The police notified the *Bureau des Détectives* that they had found one man with his throat slit, and another alive but unconscious due to unknown causes, possibly due to a blow to the head as a result of falling beside the deceased. However, neither a head wound nor a skin laceration could be found. The surviving man carried a Polish passport, possibly forged, which identified him as Leopold Wisniewski, a teacher, who had legally entered Switzerland two days before. No record of previous visits existed. Wisniewski's rented car contained his suitcase with several changes of clothing and a Japanese tape recorder. The interior of the car contained the lingering scent of perfume, indicating that a woman had been a recent passenger.

A probe of other hotel guests turned up no further information. However, the night concierge did recall the Pole, Wisniewski, crossing the lobby, accompanied by an attractive, dark-haired woman, and entering the elevator. He also recalled that three men who had been seated in the hotel lobby, reading the evening news, rose together and ambled nonchalantly to the stairway—which was generally used by guests who were ascending only to the mezzanine floor. From there, they could have taken the elevator to Julio Porto's floor, the concierge speculated.

A check of Porto's belongings, however, proved more interesting. One piece of luggage, the heaviest of the three items of luggage carried to his room, was missing. The hotel's bellboy clearly recalled that he had taken two suitcases and a heavy box from the trunk of Porto's car, a Mercedes with Portuguese license plates. That heavy box could not be located anywhere in the hotel.

Harry Carroll listened intently to Natalie's husky voice. He had lost Bob Carlson. He could not afford to lose Bert Klemmer.

"Where did they take him?" he gasped, his hands clammy.

"St. Antoine's."

"That's a dungeon! I'll catch a flight within the hour!"

"Hurry, we need you, Harry..."

He grunted a goodbye and hung up. Why would the KGB murder Porto, the man they had selected as their neutral carrier? Had the export-import agent from Lisbon decided to go into business for himself, offering the computer to any foreign power who made the highest bid?

Harry dialed Air Suisse and thought of Natalie.

She was in danger...and needed him.

Robert Lenoir, Chief of Detectives, hated foreigners. Seated at his giant desk, he contemplated the spire of St. Pierre and the narrow, cobblestone streets winding through Vielle Ville, the old town of Canton Genevoise, part of *La Conféderation Féderale Helvétique*. When he spoke of the foreign criminal element, the room temperature dropped, a result of his glacial attitude. He welcomed wealthy tourists to spend their money at St. Moritz or Zermatt. Or, if they came from the poverty of

Italy or Spain to wait tables, collect garbage, or do those other menial chores unworthy of the cultured Swiss...why, he would welcome those, too.

But when a foreigner abused the traditional hospitality of the tiny mountain country and broke its laws, then the full fury of Swiss law enforcement and jurisprudence was loosed on that perpetrator.

His sergeant had finished reporting on the initiation of the search for the woman and the three men. He also described what had been done to induce the Pole, Wisniewski, to talk. The suspect appeared to be in a daze or was pretending to be deaf and dumb.

"Make him talk!" Detective Lenoir barked. "Give him the works...lights, infusions, everything! Report as soon as he sings!"

Lenoir recalled with grim chagrin an Englishman's comment—some years earlier—that nothing perplexed him more than the hostility and rage demonstrated by the Swiss in handling foreign criminals. Lenoir regarded that comment as a compliment.

In Geneva, it was his responsibility to maintain law and order, and he enjoyed running a tight ship in the citadel of tranquility, the respected headquarters for hundreds of international organizations, including the Red Cross and the European branch of the United Nations.

Lenoir looked again at the gruesome photo of the murdered Portuguese, at the bloody gash across his throat. The most notorious throat-slitters in the world were the Turks, he knew, but the Bulgarians—with their deadly *Durzhavna Sigurnost*, their Secret Service, were a people of Turkish origin. The Soviet KGB relied heavily on them to carry out their dirty work—like the attempt on the life of the Pope.

Surely, Poles, too, were handy with the use of the blade. But the swift, straight slice across Porto's throat did not look like the work of a Pole. Unless the man in St. Antoine was *not* a Pole...

More than a decade earlier, the *Conseil de la Ville* had agreed to put the abandoned Prison St. Antoine to use for interrogation and detention of "heavies"—specifically foreign drug smugglers and political assassins. An interrogation room had been installed with the latest trappings, including a complex lighting system and tilting walls, painted bright red to destroy a prisoner's sense of orientation. And, of course, the new infusion techniques, which released serum into a prisoner's system at a prescribed rate.

Thus, in the complex network of international subterfuge and political intrigues, an American undercover agent carrying a false Polish passport was suspected of being a Bulgarian DS operative in the hire of the Soviet KGB.

The maximum-security cell contained a dirty mattress as its single amenity. An unshaved, disheveled Bert Klemmer considered how hospitable the Swiss were to the tourists, but how no courtesy whatever was extended to anyone suspected of a crime.

And he was accused of *murder*.

Porto, having returned to his room from dinner, had placed two phone calls, according to the hotel switchboard, shortly before eleven P.M. Klemmer and Natalie agreed to wait until midnight, at which time they assumed Porto would have retired. The plan was for Klemmer to break into Porto's room, effectively subdue him and make off with the computer by the rear door to meet up with Natalie, in the rented car parked with the motor running around the corner on the Rue Monthoux, ready for a quick get-away.

The best laid plans...

Bert's eyes watered as he gazed up at the high-wattage bulb suspended from the ceiling. His glance took in the stand-up toilet, the type he had last seen in the slums of Iraq, and realized the source of the stench permeating his cell.

He recalled having advanced cautiously toward the sleeping Porto's bed when a faint noise behind him made him spin around to face a moving wall of darkness, and two huge hands spanning his neck like a steel vise, choking off his breath. His attempts to break free futile, he felt the sharp sting of an injection. There was a rushing in his ears, a scrambling together of dim lights before his eyes, and he was out.

When the flash of cameras awakened him, he heard questions being fired at him in French, English, and some Slavic tongue that made him aware his Polish passport had been discovered. His silence infuriated his captors, and at last they dragged him into the cell in which he now found himself upon that foul-smelling mattress. The bars had clanged shut and they had left him to himself, warning him they would return.

He worried about Natalie. Had she, too, been taken by surprise? And was she now being grilled in another of these dreadful cells? Fortunately, she knew the language associated with her passport. To reduce the element of suspicion on this assignment, Harry had decided on Eastern Block identification, and Natalie had entered Switzerland as a Rumanian.

Natalie had been in tight spots before, he knew, and had never violated the basic rule of the Agency by confessing she was an agent of the CIA. On pain of death, no agent was to make such a revelation.

Pacing the cell, every joint in his body aching, Bert Klemmer felt he had screwed up, and those who flubbed an assignment—as he felt he had—were generally given the 'mushroom treatment' by the CIA bigwigs—covered with manure and kept in the dark indefinitely. An inglorious end to an otherwise distinguished career.

He had been proud to serve on the team of new Director Carroll, and the disappearance of his long-time friend and fellow compatriot, Bob Carlson, burdened his heart. Grimly assuming that Carlson had met an unkind fate, Bert had vowed to make himself even more invaluable to Harry Carroll. But it had not worked out that way. He wondered if Harry would arrive in Geneva to set him free. The Swiss, after all, were reasonable people. He consoled himself with the idea that eventually, they would concede that the man they had imprisoned was not the one who cut Julio Porto's throat. Then they would have to release him...

Along the shore of Lake Leman, where a few early-bird fishermen angled over the side of Pont Mont Blanc and stared expectantly into the rushing waters of the Rhône, traffic was gradually increasing. Sea gulls swooped and dipped, protesting the intrusion of the modern world into their domain.

The first street car came clanging out of a side street, soliciting early-morning passengers, and yesterday's litter was being swept up by orange-jacketed street cleaners.

Geneva was awakening to the new day.

An old, gray Citroën bakery truck wheezed to a stop at 'Moevenpick's' a popular restaurant at the corner of Rue du Rhône and Place Fusterie. The faded inscription on the side panels of the truck read, "Anton Weiss—*Boulangerie.*"

A wrinkled little man in a white uniform, moving with arthritic awkwardness, emerged from the cab to remove a number of trays filled with fresh-baked croissants and rolls.

Across the street, a dark-haired young woman sat watching behind the wheel of a tourist bus, attractive in her official brown uniform. She smiled at the only passenger she had in her vehicle.

"What I wouldn't give for one of those fresh croissants with lots of sweet butter!" she hummed.

"I know," her passenger grinned. "Five years off your life and four inches off your bust."

Natalie threw back her lovely head and laughed.

"You never forget a thing, do you, Harry?"

"That's why this assignment's been such a smashing success so far," he replied bitterly. "But no, my dear. You're right. I'll never forget your reckless commitment. The five years is one thing. But those four inches...well, that would never do."

Glad to hear him cheerful despite the sorry turn of events, Natalie gave him a reassuring grin and nodded toward the delivery man from the bakery truck.

"From here he goes to Vielle Ville, the Old Town. A stop at the little bistro just above the cathedral, and then we take over."

"You've studied his routine well," Harry complimented her.

"And remember, no English," she warned. "Any traces we leave are to be strictly Eastern Block, right?"

Harry nodded his agreement. It was amazing how easily Natalie had been able to acquire the bus. Half a dozen Hungarian tourist buses, none locked, their interiors reeking of body odor, had been parked at Rue Ami-Levrier.

"This one had been sitting with its windows open all night. It was the freshest of the lot, just begging to be driven off by a wild-eyed Russian like me," Natalie had chuckled.

Harry's answering grin was at once spontaneous and a display of bravado, and he knew his light attitude was not fooling Natalie.

He was *damned* worried about Bert Klemmer...

Connections from Lisbon had been terrible. He'd landed in Geneva at dawn, and upon his arrival at the terminal, found Natalie fast asleep along three plastic seats. He had ducked into the men's room to shave and brush his teeth before waking her.

Over a hasty breakfast, Natalie outlined the details of her daring plan. Watching the fire in her eyes, the dimples that appeared and disappeared beneath her cheekbones, the animation of her expression, Harry realized for the thousandth time how valuable she was. Together they tried to imagine every conceivable obstacle, and how to confront each in turn. *What if...?* Two urgent words in the vocabulary of game-players like themselves.

The arthritic little man emerged from 'Moevenpick's' and got back into his Citroën. As soon as he started, Natalie followed, keeping her distance...

(Moscow)

"Quick thinking on your daughter's part! She's to be highly commended!"

Seated before the desk of Admiral Romayev was KGB Chief Leonid Padorin. His long flight from San Francisco to Romayev's office in the Kremlin had wearied him, but the execution of Julio Porto at the command of Captain Ilyana

Romayeva had fired him with new strength, to marvel at the girl's quick, perceptive decisiveness and daring.

"You had no idea the courier was a traitor?" the Admiral inquired, squinting thoughtfully at his visitor.

"In this game, Yuri, everyone is suspect," Padorin sighed. "But Porto had been working with us over ten years. How could we know that some Arab bastard had made him a fabulous offer?"

Yuri Romayev held out his cigarette case to the Kommissar from San Francisco. Both men sat back smoking. The Admiral already knew the sketchy details.

Working with the Portuguese courier for the first time, his daughter had been keenly watchful. Nothing had escaped her attention. Not even the most minute hint of a business message—one recording among many left on Porto's private wire in Lisbon—in which the accent sounded Arabic and the wording cryptic enough to raise caution flags in Jane's mind.

During their flight from San Francisco to Lisbon, she had quite innocently asked Porto how it was to do business with the Middle East.

"I haven't done business with Arabs for years," Porto had replied with a wide smile. "And I don't intend to in the future."

By that evening in Lisbon—after having spent a number of hours on the phone—Jane knew that the computer and its superchip had been promised to one Ibn Rajmir, an agent procured jointly by Libya and Lebanon.

Porto's bank account had swelled with a deposit of a quarter million, funds wired in from Beirut the same morning he and Jane arrived in Lisbon.

Through the magic of international computer link-ups, the identity of the intermediary agent, as well as his antecedents, were discovered. It was not the first time that Ibn Rajmir had bribed a neutral international courier for the acquisition of top secret high-technology material.

The rest was easy. Picking up two aides upon arriving in Geneva, Jane, as Captain Romayev, joined in the stakeout in the lobby of the Hotel Richelieu. The moment Bert Klemmer made his move to follow Porto, Jane signalled her Bulgarian henchmen and accompanied them to the suite occupied by the Portuguese and the stolen computer.

Taken by surprise, Klemmer was easily choked into submission by the husky men of the *Durzhavna Sigurnost*, and pinned to the floor. Staring into Klemmer's bulging eyes as the injection was prepared for his radial artery, Jane could not help but wonder why the man lying at her feet bore no resemblance whatever to a Middle Easterner...

(Geneva, Switzerland)

Each time consciousness returned, Klemmer felt, in his disorientation, that he was just arriving at the fortress, St. Antoine, viewing the cathedral through the small, heavily-barred window in the rear of the police van. Reaching the crest of a hill, the vehicle stopped before an iron gate, the driver blowing his horn. A guard emerged from a side door, permitting the van through the gate into the prison courtyard, at which time Klemmer was brought to the guardhouse.

"L'Assassin polonaise!" he heard himself announced. It was not every day that a murder took place in Geneva. Certainly not one with international overtones, a Portuguese whose throat had been slit by a Pole...

The cell to which he was dragged was painted bright red, each wall tilted at another angle, the very floor sloping downhill. The topsy-turvy, unsettling dimensions of the room made him close his eyes, and when he was commanded to lie face down on a bare table, he clutched at its side when vertigo seized him and made him feel he was falling from its edges.

His arms and legs were tied spread-eagle, and a strap was fastened about his middle. Rough hands worked with his belt, his trousers drawn down to expose his white briefs.

"Whaaa...?" he started to shout, remembering just in time not to speak English, but in that instant, the cotton fabric of his underwear was pulled aside and a needle pierced his buttock, a burning sensation spreading swiftly through his entire body.

"Truth juice," flashed through his mind. Seldom had a CIA agent successfully withstood sodium pentothal or some other diabolic serum. Those few who were able had summoned remarkable reserves of willpower.

That was the beginning of the noises, the lights, the questions, monstrosities from another world, tormenting him, talking to him in strange tongues.

The beam of light was consuming the inside of his head, pulsating, like a strobe. Then sudden darkness. Only a few orange-colored rings remained, rotating beneath his eyelids, the afterglow of a thousand suns, moving like fading ripples on a pond. Then raindrops, gentle raindrops...dampness enveloping him. Falling rain, increasing to a stream. Then to a flood, water pouring from a thousand faucets, gushing, rising, lapping at his face, filling his ears, rushing into his nostrils...

"Help! Help, I'm drowning...!" he choked.

Faces of men bent over him. Serious, like the faces of surgeons during an operation. They whispered, wagged their heads, their dilated pupils mirroring his hapless state.

Then the piercing light came back on...the blinding, mind-exploding light.

The Citroën bakery truck wheezed through Vielle Ville and came to a stop at a weather-beaten stone fountain in the picturesque plaza of Place Bourg de Four. Surrounding it were small shops, restaurants, and a police station. The truck's squeaky brakes announced the arrival of fresh croissants, and a tray of baked goods was handed to one of the officers. Another tray was carried by the arthritic little driver into a hole-in-the-wall restaurant known as "Chez Jacques."

Natalie chose that moment to pull ahead of the bakery truck and head into Rue Etienne Dumont, a narrow one-way street leading to the next delivery stop. She waited in mid-block and after a moment, the Citroën appeared, the driver angrily blowing his horn at Natalie's obstructing bus. When the bus remained obstinately where it was, keeping him from his next stop, the little man swore audibly, limped painfully from his truck to the open window of the bus to inform the driver of the local traffic laws and just what he was about to do to enforce them.

He had barely begun his dispute with the amused lady bus driver when he was embraced from behind and lifted easily into the interior of the bus, placed on the floor with a gag in his mouth, and handcuffed into helplessness.

But not before Harry had pulled the white smock over his own clothes, drew the small man's visor over his eyes, and sprang behind the wheel of the Citroën. According to plan, he followed the Hungarian tour bus to the Promenade St. Antoine, where they parked beneath the resplendent chestnut trees opposite the Musée d'Art et Histoire—a stone's throw from the old prison.

It took only a moment for Natalie to abandon the tour bus and squeeze in among the pastry trays in the back of the Citroën. Then Harry proceeded toward St. Antoine Prison, stopping at the front gate to blow his horn.

With a wave of recognition, the guard disappeared to operate the electronic gate control, and Harry rolled through into the prison courtyard, where he slipped out to await the approach of one suspicious sentry on duty. One blow to the side of the head felled the guard, and Natalie, nimbly springing from the Citroën's rear, bent over the fallen guard with a hyperdermic needle. Harry heaved the guard's limp body into the back of the truck and grinned at Natalie. A good beginning...for a change.

Crouching low, they advanced toward the guardhouse, where two men were playing cards at a table, a third standing before a stove waiting for coffee to percolate.

With one well-aimed kick, Harry burst into the room, Natalie directly behind, and the guards stared into the barrels of high-calibre weapons.

Adding a Slavic accent to his French, Harry ordered the guards to raise their arms over their heads, turn around and bend over. There was no resistance. Natalie used three syringes, punching needles into three rumps, and in less than a minute, the guards had slumped immobilized to the floor.

Harry disengaged the communication equipment, pulling plugs and connectors throughout the room, then grabbed the heavy ring of cell keys from a wall hook. Weapons at the ready, he and Natalie moved swiftly along the corridor, Harry trying one key after another at the various doors.

On his fifth try, the door marked *"Chambre d'Interrogation"* fell open, and its interior stunned Harry's eyes. Irregular walls the color of fresh blood, a tilted floor, and—strapped to a table and delirious—Bert Klemmer.

The ordeal of his imprisonment showed plainly on Bert's tormented face, and as Harry and Natalie released their colleague they exchanged a look of concern. Then Harry slung the big man over one shoulder and followed Natalie back to the Citroën, from which they removed the still-unconscious prison guard, replacing him among the pastry trays with the dazed Bert Klemmer.

"Let's not shoot unless we have to," Harry said, taking the wheel and making a U-turn out of the courtyard, happily blowing his horn and waving with a smile to the bored gate-keeper. The gate opened without consequence, and they proceeded to the parking area where they had left the bakery driver on the floor of the tour bus.

"Good show. Eight minutes," Harry sighed with relief.

A stream of French obscenities assailed them both as Harry removed the gag from the bakery driver's mouth and unlocked the handcuffs. Then Harry pushed the little man back into his truck and kept him occupied with apologies while Natalie maneuvered Bert from truck to tour bus. To compensate for the rough handling the frail delivery man had suffered, Harry slipped a fifty franc note into his hand.

The tour bus was already moving when Natalie swung in beside him, pulling the door shut. In his rear view mirror, Harry spotted Bert Klemmer in a comfortable position stretched out along several of the fold-down seats. Natalie was consulting a map of Geneva, and he could only marvel at her ability to juggle several grave situations at once, keeping the same aplomb.

"Did Bert come to when you moved him?" he inquired with a nod back at the comatose Klemmer, knowing how vital the man's memory for details would be as soon as he had settled down from his ordeal.

"Just for a few seconds," she replied, directing Harry into the Avenue Louis-Casal leading to Cointrin, Geneva's airport. "And only to ask if we were able to get the computer back."

Harry grimaced. Yes, that was just like Bert, to think of the computer even through a serum-dazed brain. He swerved to the right, heading for the extreme end of the runways on the route marked "Direction Lausanne."

Just ahead was a green, unmarked CH 53 helicopter, its rotors moving at idling speed, its rear loading ramp down.

Half a mile to their rear were two police vehicles closing on them, sirens wailing and blue emergency lights flashing.

"We've got to cut corners...!" Harry announced, pulling Natalie into his lap as he swung off the road and headed straight for the chain link fence. With a resounding clangor and ripping of metal, they were through, eager hands from the helicopter crew helping them aboard, along with their unconscious friend.

As the green craft lifted off, raising a monstrous cloud of dust, Harry saluted down to the Swiss police who had converged in the area below and were stamping their feet in frustration.

"Sorry about that, *Messieurs*," he shouted, elated over the success of the rescue. Bert Klemmer moaned, about to be violently sick, and Natalie attended to him at once.

"Let him bring it up, all of it," Harry said with compassion. "I'm going to need his clear head for descriptions."

Natalie searched Harry's eyes for assurance.

"You did get word, then, didn't you...?"

He nodded, forcing a grim smile.

"Yup, m'Dear. They'll be moving it across Lake Constance..."

*　　*　　*　　*

Ludwig Waldvogel had never let Harry down. The East German Security Officer had proved invaluable time and again whenever Harry contacted him for help on an assignment. Ludwig's knowledge of political geography and the strategies of both European power concentrations—free world and Communist—was encyclopedic. Some years earlier, driving a jeep through the crowded streets of Teheran, Harry had seen the German surrounded by a mob of murderous Iranians, the dreaded Revolutionary Guards. Ludwig had already been stoned by a few of them, blood running freely from a gash over one eye, and his clothes were torn. One glance had convinced Harry that unless rescue were immediate, the German's life was not worth a tinker's damn.

Gunning the jeep's engine and speeding headlong into the wildly babbling mob, Harry drove up alongside the German and shouted to him to jump in. Reprieved from certain death, Ludwig jumped, and Harry made a fast get-away, shouting to the man to get down to avoid the barrage of rocks and stones hurtling through the air at their unprotected heads.

Once out of danger, Harry ascertained that Ludwig belonged to the secret service of the DDR, subservient to the Russian KGB. Ironic, he chuckled to himself. But you don't ask a man's political affiliation when you see his life threatened. He drove Ludwig to safety at the East German Embassy and from then on, Ludwig Waldvogel was in his debt.

It wasn't difficult to locate the German in Geneva. Harry telephoned him from Lisbon, reaching him at the GATT Trade Convention, and they arranged a meeting place.

At the busy main post office on Rue du Mont Blanc, without betraying so much as a blink of recognition, Harry and Ludwig stood side by side at a desk, pretending to fill out postal forms.

"I must stop something before it reaches your country," Harry whispered, his lips barely moving.

"Man or material?" Ludwig asked.

"Material."

There was no hesitation whatever.

"Bodensee," Ludwig told him. "Mannheim. Autobahn East."

Bodensee was Lake Constance, Mannheim a city on the Rhine, Harry knew. Probably a collection point. Autobahn East meant Berlin or East Germany.

"Mode of transportation?" Harry asked, realizing he was pressing his luck with the East German.

"Look for moving vans, like those used for household belongings," Ludwig whispered, and walked hastily away, Harry catching a glimpse of the slender East German disappearing in the crowd. It had been a brief, helpful encounter. Harry calculated he had given nothing and received much in exchange. He also knew he was fast using up his credits with the man.

But the trail was warming up.

Whoever killed Julio Porto and snatched the computer would move it across at Lake Constance.

*   *   *   *

Pale and drained, Bert Klemmer had been transported to an Alpine retreat where a medical team brought him back to reality.

He and the artist, Dominic Mattasini, were side by side at a drawing board presided over by Harry Carroll, Natalie Soubrine, and several other agents of the CIA stationed in Switzerland.

Dominic Mattasini, the best criminologist artist available to the Agency, had been pressing Klemmer for one detail after another regarding the three men who attacked him in Porto's hotel suite.

Bert had been reaching back into his memory for tiny details, describing the huge wrestler type who had immobilized him so that the other man's hyperdermic needle could be plunged into his wrist.

Mattasini's fingers had been flying over his drawings with swift, sure strokes, and as Harry and Natalie watched, two fleshy faces appeared beneath the criminologist's pencil. A moon face with flat, wide cheekbones and tiny simian eyes over a broad nose and heavy mouth. A square, lantern-jawed face with furrowed brow and heavy jowls. The two henchmen from the *Durzhavna Sigurnost* were on paper for the world to recognize.

"The third man, the one in command...," Klemmer said, straining his memory. "At the moment our eyes met, I knew I wouldn't be able to forget what he looked like..."

"Why?" Harry snapped. "What was unusual about him?"

Klemmer narrowed his eyes, thinking hard.

"He didn't look as though he belonged in command of that kind of operation. He didn't look evil enough, or rough enough..."

"Describe him, please," said Mattasini. "Was he tall, heavy?"

"Not as tall as the other two," Klemmer stated. "And quite slender. Altogether, a rather slim frame..."

"What about his face, about his expression," asked Mattasini.

"Handsome," recalled Klemmer. "Almost too handsome for a man. Prominent cheekbones, self-indulgent mouth, small nose...and the eyes...they were blue, very penetrating. Devoid of compassion...at least with respect to my situation."

"The shape of the head?" asked the artist, sketching away.

"I would say Nordic," said Klemmer, making an occasional suggestion to correct the artist's rendering. "Oval to long, with delicate ears. The temple hair was pale blond, and it looked like he never had to shave."

Mattasini's pencil worked in circles and strokes.

"How was he dressed?"

"A rain hat, brim pulled down over one eye. Military raincoat with braided épaulets..."

"What about ethnicity? When we first got started here, you mentioned you thought this leader was an American. What made you think he was American?"

Klemmer exchanged a doubtful look with Harry and Natalie.

"I don't know what made me say that," he admitted. "He could have been any nationality...of northern European extraction. But somehow, I got the impression he...well, maybe it was because his clothing looked American. The kind of raincoat you'd buy in Neiman-Marcus, perhaps. And his commands were...well, somewhat soft and relaxed...not gruff, like a European's."

"What about his disposition?" the artist wanted to know.

"Hateful," said Klemmer. "Toxic. Mean."

"Mean? Sadistic?" asked Mattasini.

"Cold and unfeeling. Like a dentist's drill," chuckled Klemmer.

Mattasini made a few more strokes, then tossed his pencil carelessly over his shoulder, spanking his drawing against the board and rising from his seat.

"There are too many conflicts in this drawing," he complained. "I'm receiving mixed messages. Masculine and feminine elements combined. Cold, unfeeling. Yet soft, relaxed. Casual American. Yet authoritative European. Something is very wrong here..."

"My God, I don't believe this!" Natalie gasped, gaping at the finished drawing Mattasini had placed on the drawing board.

The others crowded around, staring at the sketch.

"Why, this is ridiculous!" Harry gulped. "That's *me!* You drew a picture of *me!*"

"Bert, are you sure you're not still confused? Were you thinking of Director Carroll when you gave the artist this description?" Natalie pressed her colleague.

"No, I'm quite clear on it," Bert insisted. "Now I remember something else! I realized I'd never be able to forget that face because it reminded me so much of Director Carroll!"

Mattasini returned to the drawing and glanced repeatedly at Harry, then stood shaking his head.

"Incredible," he sighed. "If I didn't see this with my own eyes, I wouldn't believe it. It's your face, Director Carroll."

Harry, his heart pounding strangely, in awe at the idea of having a look-alike on the opposing team, studied the drawing.

"I sure hope I come across more macho than this," he said sheepishly, aware that everyone's eyes were fixed upon him...

Chapter 11

(Lake Constance)

The local commander of the German Border Police, the feared *Grenzpolizei* in Konstanz, showed Harry a map with many colored pins, designating manned positions, radar installations, and stretches of border continually patrolled by police accompanied by dogs.

"Soviet agents...," the commander explained in English heavily orchestrated by the musical coating of southern Germany, "generally exit Switzerland at this point."

His finger pointed halfway between Kreuzlingen and Romanshorn on the south shore of Lake Constance, then passed over the blue-colored lake to rest at a spot named Ueberlingen.

"They usually land here, then go north and disappear into the Eastern Zone."

"Why this particular route?" asked Harry.

"Because it's inconspicuous, Herr Carroll," the officer replied. "I'll have my colleague on the other side of the lake carry out tonight's mission. You'll be in good hands with Graf von Rathenburg."

Harry narrowed his eyes at Natalie and she shrugged. He was not entirely convinced by what the German officer had told him.

"One more question, please, Herr Kommandant. Why this complicated route, when they could leave Switzerland and head east via Austria?"

The German nodded, appreciating the question's logic.

"Because the Swiss can seal off their country tighter than a drum when they wish. Right now, they're on alert, looking for some KGB daredevils who murdered a Portuguese, broke into a prison to rescue the suspect they were holding, and in general have greatly upset their '*Mutterlaendli*'...their exemplary country...as they call it."

There the officer paused, contemplating with envy the good fortune of the Swiss.

"It's no easy matter to control all sixty kilometers of this lake," he explained. "The KGB...and all smugglers, for that matter, are aware of that. This stretch of the border is Switzerland's heel of Achilles, especially during our foggy season. We Germans have one hell of a time catching infiltrators who come across the lake. It's like your southern border with Mexico. Hard to put a lid on it."

By then, he had convinced Harry that this was a new game. All these European borders so close to one another—some friendly, some neutral, many openly hostile. Not at all like the endless steppes of Pakistan, Afghanistan and Iran...

Graf von Rathenburg, a solidly-built old patrician, settled back in his seat, happy to be entertaining guests, regaling them with the history of the Bodensee, where his family had made its home for over a thousand years.

Flushed with wine, Natalie asked how a man of his standing had wound up in the Border Police, and von Rathenburg replied forthrightly that his ancestors had been known to keep riff-raff out of that area, and that, "I'm doing essentially the same...being the local *Grenzpolizei Kommandant*."

"But how can a nobleman, a count, be a policeman...a civil servant?" Natalie pressed, and Harry noted the flush in her cheeks and how her eyes glistened from the effects of the heady wine.

"This 'Count' business is a leftover from olden times," he said agreeably, laughing. "After the First World War, all titles of nobility were abolished here in Germany. We became a Democracy. But, the people here are old-fashioned and still adhere to the old traditions. So they still refer to me as the Count. But my dear Fräulein Natalie, even a former count has to make a living..."

"And tonight's strategy?" Harry inquired, impatient.

Von Rathenburg became serious at once.

"We'll have patrols strung out from Ludwigshafen to the Austrian border. They'll have dogs and electronic listening devices. No one will land a boat here without being detected."

"And where will we be?" asked Harry.

"In a patrol boat, trying to intercept them," the Count explained. "If we fail, we can at least alert our people by two-way radio where to expect these rascals to land."

"Excuse me, Graf von Rathenburg," Harry interrupted, coldly serious, "...but these 'rascals' are heartless murderers working for one of the world's most evil regimes. They are never to be taken lightly."

Even Natalie found herself bewildered by Harry's sudden cold fury. The Count nodded philosophically, consulting his watch.

"True," he agreed. "It's almost time. We'll start now."

The "Enchantress," one of the border patrol boats, was tied up near the public landing in Ueberlingen. Bright boardwalk lights showed up the sleek, clean lines of her superstructure. Near her mast were several aerials, and a radar dish kept oscillating with alert energy. The crew, clad in the traditional blue of the German navy, were identified by the shoulder patch on their quilted combat jackets as *"Jungs der Grenzpolizei."*

Harry stood at the rail, his light raincoat marking him as an *"Ami"* to the few bystanders on the wharf and to the tourists in the area. Deep in thought, he listened to the purr of the craft's twin diesel engines as the "Enchantress" started across the lake. Natalie, in a short leather coat, stood back, reluctant to intrude on Harry's private musings.

"It's going to be a long night," Count von Rathenburg said as he joined them. "You two may as well go below to keep warm."

But Harry delayed leaving the rail, thinking back to his childhood when his parents vacationed with him on and around the Lake. He tried to catch a glimpse of the Nikolausmünster as the boat moved swiftly east, passing the cloisters of Birnau, the old Meersburg castle, its outline visible even in the darkness.

A chill wind kept gusting, whipping up the inky waves of the lake to iridescent white. Natalie shivered, hugging her arms to herself as she joined Harry at the rail where she found him preoccupied, frowning with inner turmoil.

"Troubles, Director Carroll?" she asked softly.

Coming out of his dark thoughts, he drew a deep breath, making no response, simply arching one eyebrow at her.

"The artist's drawing?" she inquired.

There was so little he could ever conceal from Natalie. Her quick perception was generally right on target in picking up on his feelings. Despite his distress, he offered a grin of appreciation.

"I suppose," he admitted. "One of Bert's most valuable assets has always been his total recall of details. I'd hate to think he was hallucinating, and I sure hope whatever those bastards poured through his system hasn't muddled his thinking and confused him."

"I don't think Bert's confused," Natalie reflected.

"You don't?"

She shook her head, gazing at the shafts of light on the water as the "Enchantress" moved toward its destination, halfway between Meersburg and Konstanz, to join its two sister craft at that point. "Until tonight, I'd forgotten…," she told him. "But the man Bert described to Mattasini…he was right there on Blossom Street the night they killed the Chinese couple."

"How do you know?" Harry rasped.

"I saw him," Natalie explained softly. "Everything Bert told Mattasini was correct. Right down to the style of the raincoat."

"And…he looks like me?"

"He could be your brother," she murmured, and their glances locked and held.

Suddenly, the lights blinked out and the crew appeared frozen in position, each man scanning the horizon for sign of a vessel in the darkness, the commander erect behind the radar screen, the faint light of the restless cathode ray tube tinting green patches across his features.

Moving in tight circles at minimum speed, the boat rolled and pitched, its engine noise confined to a low-key hum.

Harry felt the tension in the air, knew the crew of young Germans craved the victory of intercepting a strange boat coming from Switzerland, carrying Soviet spies. All at once he realized how vulnerable they were, all of them…

"Natalie, you go below to the cabin," he decided. "We could have fireworks up here, and it's getting colder by the minute. That's an order, Soubrine."

In the darkness, her unhappy pout was lost on him, but she obeyed, and Harry was relieved when the Count joined him at the rail, all fun-making and merriment put aside for the grim business at hand.

"Fog's building up strong all over the lake, Herr Carroll," the Count stated. "Fog is our worst enemy."

There was a murmur of discouragement from the crew as the eerie gray drifts enveloped the small craft, thickening quickly.

"Any chance this will lift again?" Harry asked the Count.

"Only a slim chance," came the reply. "Once the lake fogs over, it doesn't usually clear until late morning."

"Damn!" Harry swore. Then, "Any word from the other boats?"

"They're in the same pea soup."

A sailor called out from the radar screen, and Harry followed Count von Rathenburg to the monitor where a dot had been spotted, separating itself from the southern shore and advancing steadily toward their position. The companionway door opened and Natalie, who had heard the excitement, returned. Rathenburg, every inch the naval commander, was all business, issuing brusk instructions.

"Herr Carroll, I must insist you and the lady put on your life vests," he ordered. "In a fog like this we could easily wind up in the water, rammed by the bastards!"

"What about the other boats?" Harry asked, as he and Natalie complied with the Count's command.

"I told them to close in. One of us should catch them."

Tension and excitement replaced the initial discouragement, the crew staring out into the dark gray fluff, armed with rifles, ready to jump aboard the hunted craft as the dot on the screen approached the point of intercept.

"There!" a voice called. "Starboard!"

In a fleeting glint of moonlight, the outline of a fast-moving cabin cruiser was visible, snaking in and around the fog billows.

"Let's get her!" shouted the Count, ordering full speed, the sudden acceleration pitching Natalie against Harry's side. But in seconds, the fog formed a new white barrier and there was no trace of the cruiser.

"*Gottverdammt...!*" swore von Rathenburg. "We overshot. Kill the engines!"

At the radar screen again, he tried to identify the target among the other dots moving in the same vicinity, and shook his head in despair, Harry understanding that nothing could be done until the spy ship moved out to indicate its direction. Dark silence hung heavy and interminably over the small craft as they waited.

Then all at once, there was a muffled shout, and the target dot was seen pulling away from the other three, heading toward a point west of Ueberlingen.

Under the Count's command, the twin props of the "Enchantress" bit into the dark waters as pursuit of the cabin cruiser was resumed, the other two boats advancing to outmaneuver it.

The radar screen showed the target almost within reach, when suddenly, buffered by the fog, a crash burst across the lake, the sounds of grating and scraping and the shouts of men filling the night.

Immediately, two great fingers of radiance, the powerful searchlights of the "Enchantress," probed the fog to find the scene of the crash. The sharp bow of one craft in the German patrol flotilla had sliced deeply into the side of its sister ship, nearly cutting it in two. Men, hurled into the water by the impact, were struggling to make it back aboard.

His eyes filtering the darkness and the thick white film obscuring the details, Harry made out the indistinct beige blur of the cabin cruiser, its engines silent, bobbing just beyond the point of the collision between the patrol boats.

"Look there!" he cried. "It's the spy ship!"

The words had barely left his mouth when he noted what appeared to be a metal-threaded fishnet swinging wide over the cruiser's side, and heard a young sailor screaming for help across the lake. Von Rathenburg's boat moved swiftly to assist the stricken men. Shouting and bleeding, sailors were being pulled aboard, with lines thrown from one craft to the other.

Harry raced to the Count's side to implore his aid, but von Rathenburg waved him off, concerned only with the young lives at stake in the freezing waters, interested solely in their rescue.

"They're getting away, Harry," Natalie gasped in disbelief.

"I know," he said helplessly. "And if I can believe what I saw, they took one of our sailors with them."

The small dot on the screen reached the shore halfway between Ueberlingen and Sipplingen.

There it disappeared from sight.

*   *   *   *

Captain Romayev blew a long shaft of blue-white smoke toward the ceiling of the bungalow, staring with clenched fists

at the two Bulgarians and the battered German sailor unconscious on the floor.

"What did you get out of him?"

"Graf von Rathenburg was assisting two people in pursuit of
our cruiser. A man and a woman."

"Describe them."

"The woman...middle twenties, perhaps. Dark hair. Very
attractive. Possibly European-born. Speaks English with a
slight foreign accent."

"And the man?"

"Tall, well built. About thirty. Good-looking. Fair hair. Blue
eyes. Typical American."

"Did you learn their names?"

The men from the Bulgarian *Durzhavna Sigurnost* glanced at
one another, then down at the hapless shore patrolman.

"He didn't know their names, Captain."

The German sailor groaned. The youth and vulnerability of
his features could still be discerned beneath the massive welts
and ugly bruises. Captain Romayev stamped out a half-finished
cigarette and gestured to the captive.

"Take him back to the lake shore and leave him there. Alive.
Don't lay another finger on him. That's an order."

(Moscow)

Leonid Padorin's fingers quivered slightly as he lifted the
receiver for Ilyana Romayeva's call. *I'm either excited or I'm
growing old*, he laughed to himself. It was always exciting for
Padorin to communicate with the beautiful blonde KGB officer
whom he had known—literally—since her birth. On the other
hand, he had put in almost forty years with the intelligence
service of his country. It was time for him to relax and attend
to his garden—to spend his evenings listening to Tchaikowsky
and Gliere—to re-read the classics.

"Padorin listening," he said into the phone.

"You remember my telling you of my particular interest in a certain carol?" Jane's voice purred cryptically. "To orchestrate it properly, I must know all I can about this carol...conception, origin, history. Can I depend on you for these details?"

Padorin smiled.

"This carol...Is it often heard at the 'farm'?"

"In ever-changing variations."

"Give me forty-eight hours," said Padorin.

"Good. I'll be with Papa."

*   *   *   *

A tall man with thinning hair that had once been blond but with the years had turned a gunmetal gray sat fidgeting nervously as Admiral Romayev took a seat opposite him in the shadowy corner of a dimly-lighted tearoom. The stress of his furtive meeting with the high-ranking officer caused his left leg to tremor visibly, the result of a series of strokes following a major disabling coronary years before.

"May I speak freely, Admiral?" Igor Matlov inquired, brushing at the beads of perspiration starting on his upper lip.

"Of course, Igor."

The serving table jiggled from the uncontrolled thumping of the man's palsied knee, but the Admiral pretended not to notice.

"Comrade Padorin is looking for the file on Harry Carroll."

There was barely any visible reaction from Admiral Romayev. Just a whitening of the knuckles as his hands clasped the arms of his chair. A twitch in one corner of his mouth. A nerve throbbing in his jaw.

"How did this come about?" he asked thickly.

"Evidently, Captain Romayeva...your daughter...requested it."

Yuri Romayev's chest heaved sharply. Then he sank back, drained, in his chair, studying the other man's face.

"Let me hear the details, Igor."

Matlov groped for where to begin, wetting his lips. He reminded the Admiral of the time when Tobirian had induced

Ilyana to come to the Soviet Union, and when she started her training in Moscow. He also reminded the Admiral of his own failure to interest Harry Carroll, the Admiral's son, in the same opportunity.

"I remember, Igor," whispered the Admiral.

"You recall how...as you watched Ilyana's career taking shape successfully, and knew that Harry Carroll had entered law school in the States, that you told me it was no longer necessary to pursue your son?"

The Admiral remembered, his eyes misting for a moment.

"Yes, it was when you were recovering from your heart attack, Igor. I felt then it was one problem you could let go."

Matlov leaned forward, his hands limp between his knees.

"But I didn't really let it go, Yuri..."

The Admiral gripped the arms of his chair and leaned forward, his features blanched with anxiety.

"What are you saying?" he croaked.

"I'm sitting on a keg of dynamite, Yuri," Matlov panted. "And the fuse is ready to blow."

"Tell me!"

"Forgive me, Yuri, for being a sentimental Russian. I became fascinated with the boy and with his potential. When I recuperated from my heart attack, I renewed my observation of the young man. I did so, however, in secret. On my own."

Admiral Romayev's breath was coming in short spasms.

"And what did you learn? What has become of him?"

Igor Matlov straightened up in his chair and cleared his throat.

"Yuri, ironically, the KGB has an extensive file on Harry Carroll. They know quite a bit about him, what he's done..."

The Admiral was on his feet, demanding, "Why? Why would our Secret Service follow him? What does he mean to them, Igor?"

Matlov's eyes were round in supplication.

"Yuri...Harry Carroll is a Special Director of the Central Intelligence Agency...!"

"*What?*"

Matlov repeated his statement, and the Admiral sat stunned. "I don't believe this!" he gasped. "It's impossible!"

"It's true, Yuri."

The Admiral's eyes darted suspiciously about the tearoom. "Then I'm done for!" he choked. "And Ilyana...Ilyana...!"

Matlov hurried to soothe the older man's shock and fear. The Admiral was trembling, talking to himself in disbelief.

"Please, listen to me, Yuri!" Matlov begged, forcing Romayev to search his eyes for some ray of reason, or hope. "The file they have on Harry Carroll is the type of file they have on *every* enemy agent. They know what they need to know..."

"Then that's it!" rasped Romayev. "Then they know..."

"...No!" Matlov broke in. "They don't know the most important thing! Their file shows that Harry Carroll was born in San Francisco, in September, 1959, the son of Donald and Sally Carroll..."

Admiral Romayev sat aghast, incredulous, looking at the underling who had held his secret in the palm of his hand for so many years.

"They know what a threat this Carroll...now, *Director* Carroll...is to them. That he's the man who blew up the Salang Tunnel in Afghanistan a month or so ago!"

The Soviet Naval Diplomat, ranking high in the Politburo, showed an unconcealed pride in his expression.

"My son did that?" he gasped, with an undisguised grin.

"And much more, Yuri," Matlov conceded. "So much more. That's why I couldn't bring myself to tell you, until now."

Romayev sat nodding, staring off into space.

"I have never discussed this with Ilyana," he said.

"So much the better," said Matlov. "It could have hampered her own efforts, her own successes, if she ever knew..."

He paused, sweating, uncomfortable, reading the question in Romayev's burning gaze.

"...that her counterpart in the CIA...," Matlov continued, gasping and sweating, "...*is her own twin brother...*"

Chapter 12

(East Germany)

Natalie fumbled in the dark for the telephone. Its single buzz had been sufficient to wake her, and she listened intently to Harry's low, sensual whisper.

Three men answering to the description circulated had been observed in the office of a U-drive company on the outskirts of the lakeside village. Investigation revealed that a red and white van with bold lettering reading "Zimmermann Motoren Transport" had been leased, and inquiry made about the most direct route to Magdeburg.

A moving van. Its size was of no consequence. The computer was not of unwieldy dimensions. Exactly what Ludwig Waldvogel had predicted.

"Magdeburg," Natalie yawned. "That's in East Germany..."

"Precisely. And that's where they take off for Moscow."

"Then...?"

"Catch some shut-eye, Nat. I've put in a wake-up call for us. The U-drive personnel thought they'd take off at dawn, and I want to get the drop on them. See you at half past three."

Click.

She turned on her side, sleep out of the question. Harry's voice had awakened all her senses.

See you at half-past three...

Yes, Harry, I'll be there. But will you really see me?

What have you ever really seen of me?

What she loved most about Harry Carroll was the complexity of his make-up. She had loved him from that first moment he'd answered her signal with the muted call of the kiwi bird in a Luzon downpour. They'd known each other five years, had spent half a dozen missions together. Even when apart, working halfway around the world from him on different assignments, Natalie had managed to keep informed about Harry Carroll.

She knew she was a beautiful woman, and desirable. Too many close calls in the line of duty had attested to that. But was she special enough for a man like Harry Carroll? From what she'd heard of other agents, she calculated that Harry had sampled scores, if not hundreds, of women all over the world. He was a bachelor, still uncommitted. She wondered why. She had several times heard of a redhead named Yvonne de la Fontaine who had been his childhood sweetheart. That girl had dumped him for a Washington attorney soon after Harry had been recruited by Langley.

Was Director Carroll still nursing the scars of that old love? Would he ever settle down and be serious with another woman?

And...if ever he were ready...could she, Natalie, be that woman?

If only she had something different, something original, to offer. He had seen everything, every flesh tone, every shade of eye and hair, every body measurement, every delight imaginable that a woman could offer. She had more than once caught his erratic glance wandering over her body. A subdued lust. A certain degree of curiosity. But he looked at every woman that way, noticed what they wore, how they carried themselves, the way they moved.

Was all she had to offer Harry Carroll her unique courage? Her strength?

Naaaah. There were plenty of strong, brave women in the world. Of all shapes and sizes. Of all colors and backgrounds. Her mental spark, perhaps? The fine tuning of her brain? Plenty of beautiful brainy women, too. They were legion.

If only she were a virgin! Maybe innocence would be stimulating to a man like Director Carroll. From what she knew of the de la Fontaine girl, Harry had been a willing pupil, gaining experience in eroticism through Yvonne. So perhaps a pure, untouched innocent would offer to Harry Carroll the sense of heady power his ego demanded.

But even in that area, Natalie failed. She had traded her virginity for a dash to freedom across the Austrian border, almost a decade before...

When Isaak Subrinin heard the pronouncement of his sentence to fifteen years at hard labor in a corrective camp in Siberia for having violated several sections of the Criminal Code of the Russian Socialist Federated Soviet Republic, he smiled at his daughter, Natalia. Then, as he was led away, he spat in the direction of the prosecutor. Natalie had been sixteen then. She never saw her father again. She had heard the verdict. Her father had been found guilty of treason to the Soviet cause.

That was the moment when Natalia Isaakovna Subrinina resolved to leave the Soviet Union and everything it stood for.

As the daughter of an enemy of the people, emigration for her was impossible. The best advice she could get—mostly from Jews seeking an escape route—was to make it, somehow, to Bratislava in Czechoslovakia, and from there attempt the dangerous crossing into Austria on foot. Natalie had not yet, then, learned the meaning of fear.

It was mid-summer when she started on her trek, a rucksack on her back containing a few of her favorite books and a photo of her father. Local farmers informed her of Czech and Russian border guards in the area, suggesting she move in a westerly direction, preferably after sundown, as she neared the crossing.

Crouching stealthily through a mist, she moved over a well-trampled path to the parapet of an embankment, sensing she was reaching the Austrian border. It was when she straightened up to look about that she heard the footstep and felt her waist encircled by two strong arms. A Russian border guard switched on his flashlight to study her from head to foot.

"Not bad, not bad," he appraised her, tiny eyes glinting.

Terrified, but trying hard to conceal her fear, she lied, "My aunt in Vienna is sick, and I haven't been able to get a passport."

"*Da, da, Malyinki.* Yes, I know all about your sick aunt in Vienna," the Russian laughed in derision. "Listen to my proposition, you little beauty. You will be very nice to me, or you'll be given a free trip to the nearest jail."

The sixteen-year-old understood the insinuation.

"Why can't you just let me go?" she pleaded, bursting into tears. "I haven't done anything to hurt you."

In the darkness, she heard evil laughter, and felt his grip on her tighten.

"Listen, little one. Everything has its price. You lie down here with me for a while, or you go to jail. Very simple."

Tears streamed down her cheeks and she was trembling.

"And if I agree, how do I know you'll let me go?" she quavered.

Without another word, the guard tossed his cigarette into the brush, pulling her to the damp ground, ripping at her clothing.

"You don't know anything for sure," he wheezed. "It's the chance you take. Maybe I'll let you go and maybe not…"

He was a powerful man and his initial thrust was a double-edged sword piercing the core of her being. She screamed and writhed beneath him, and for just a moment, he held still.

"Oh, I see," he breathed. "Too bad. That's something my sisters are taught to save, to give only to the man they marry. And here you've gone and given it away for a thing called freedom. So sorry, *Malyinki*…"

Natalie bit her lip and clenched her fists to endure the agony of the renewed assault. It seemed an eternity before the guard's lust was satisfied, and he dropped back, gasping and soaked with sweat. Then he got to his feet, pulled up his trousers, and with a nervous glance in her direction, disappeared into the night.

Humiliated, her body sore and aching, Natalie climbed across the embankment on all fours and ran through the fields in terror of being captured by yet another border guard.

With the first rays of the sun came the view of a neat row of houses on the horizon, and as she drew closer, a sign written in German. She had reached Austria, and freedom.

The price had been high. Lying on her side on a comfortable featherbed in a small inn in Ueberlingen, waiting for the hours to pass, Natalie remembered the experience with revulsion.

No, she could not even offer Harry Carroll the mystique of innocence, unless it were the innocence of the heart and not the body.

But she loved him. Of that, she was certain.

Perhaps something in the dark mutuality of their backgrounds, something in their genes—a tribal trait going back to the dawn of humankind. But whatever it was, something undeniable in Natalie's soul reached out to the soul of Harry Carroll, and entwined itself with his forever.

At three-thirty sharp, she followed Harry to his rented Audi 500. It was cold and dark, the street lights of the village few and far between. Pale from lack of sleep, she stifled a yawn as he drove to the hotel where the van had been seen, being prepared for its journey to Magdeburg.

But the van was not there.

The night clerk at the hotel was in a vile temper at being disturbed in the middle of the night and spoke to them with disdain.

The three men using the moving van had left at midnight.

* * * *

Jane had placed her call to Padorin before leaving the south German village in the company of the two goons from the Bulgarian DS. The computer was secured in the back of the ample vehicle, and the three took turns driving and napping during the long journey on the autobahn.

Whenever she thought of the couple pursuing her all the way from San Francisco, she tingled with excitement. She knew only the name, "Carroll," and her two henchmen had precisely described the same man and woman she had seen rushing into the Mark Hopkins Hotel the night Bob Carlson was taken. Carlson had never spoken a word. He had taken the identity of his superiors and colleagues as well as the purpose of their mission to his watery grave.

But Jane remembered the pretty dark-haired woman—the one who had crippled Smolerov in the Chu apartment on Blossom Street.

Could they have misspelled the name in transmission? Carole?

A trace of a European accent, they'd said. Heading up an American secret service task force?

Just how closely matched was she, indeed, to this adversary?

And then, of course, that tall blond man with the high cheekbones. The man whose very appearance sent the blood pumping furiously through her veins.

About thirty, they had said.

Her own age.

Had Rudiger Furst lived to be thirty, he would have looked just like that...

* * * *

(Ueberlingen)

Powell Wright had been under constant fire from the Oval office over the disappearance of the SRC chip in San Francisco. In secret meetings with the President and the chiefs of the National Security Council, Wright was forced to make excuses for his task force's ongoing failures. The team had already lost one of its select stalwarts. Agent Robert Carlson had spent many dedicated years in the service of his country, and all indications pointed to his murder. The Soviets were not playing games. They knew the value of the microchip and were stopping at nothing to hold on to it. Whoever possessed that chip could—for a time at least—control the fate of the world. The Soviets were not about to permit the United States to hold that position for long.

Bert Klemmer, still weak and not yet ready for field work, met the DCI's Concorde landing at Charles de Gaulle Airport, and on board the private jet to Ueberlingen, brought Director Wright up to date on the status of the assignment.

"You're looking bright-eyed and bushy-tailed, Soubrine!" Wright beamed at Natalie as he entered Harry's hotel suite where the two agents, packed and ready to leave, awaited an important call from Munich.

Then, with a scowl at the ashen-faced Harry, snickered, "I wish I could say the same for you, m'boy!"

"I'm sorry, Chief," Harry confessed, contrite. "I feel like a first-class klutz. This Russian team has outmaneuvered me at every turn."

Wright nodded thoughtfully, enumerating, "You've lost Carlson. Klemmer's out of commission. And the computer's on its way to Moscow. Not a very pretty picture."

Harry felt Natalie's eyes on him. He had rarely, if ever, failed. This was the closest he had ever come to a tongue-lashing from one of his superiors.

"Do you want me off the case?" he asked, with such a mournful expression in his eyes that Natalie's whole heart went out to him.

Wright made a snorting sound to scoff at Harry's suggestion.

"God damn it, Carroll!" he fumed. "Am I hearing something like that from the man who blew up the Salang Tunnel? Knocked out the warning system in Tripoli? Brought Harrington and Carradine back from Zimbabwe? And saved the life of the Ambassador to Honduras, among many other things...?"

Staring at his shoes, Harry flushed. The fiery old Director had been his champion ever since his first days with the Agency, and he felt he'd rather die than ever let Powell Wright down.

"This mission has been a bummer from the word go," he admitted. "I wish with all my heart I had a more positive report to give you, something better than 'we're trying our best.'"

"That's good enough for me," Wright confirmed. "Now, level with me. Do you think you and Soubrine can proceed alone? Or do you want me to pull in additional help for your team?"

"We can handle it," Harry and Natalie said in unison, then laughed, and it broke the tension. Everyone needed that break.

It was when they were crossing the airstrip to a plane cleared for Magdeburg that Wright touched the most sensitive nerve of all.

"That Russian professor whose knees you blasted, Soubrine..., he didn't last long. And we didn't expect him to, especially once he requested political sanctuary..."

They reached the private jet, where Wright continued his explanation.

"...but before they got to him, Smolerov did manage to give us a lead on the guy heading the Soviet team. The guy everyone says is a deadringer for you, Harry..."

Alert at once to the enigma plaguing him, Harry asked, "What did you learn about him?"

Wright spread his hands contemplatively.

"Just about your age," he shrugged. "Good-looking sonofabitch from the pictures in our files. Name's Romayev. Captain in the KGB. Father's an Admiral with the Naval Kommissariat in the Kremlin. Naturally brilliant. Speaks English as though he were born and educated in the United States. That's about all we have."

Harry shook Wright's hand before boarding the aircraft.

"It'll be interesting to meet him," he quipped. "I just hope it will be soon."

Harry's contacts had reported sighting the red and white van in Munich, parked before dawn at a coffee shop on the Marienplatz.

When it took off, its direction was north on the autobahn. Harry estimated the van would be in Magdeburg, allowing for refueling and comfort stops, by early afternoon. At that point, he arranged for the private flight to Magdeburg, but still had time to see his chief during Wright's quick stop in Europe.

Once airborne, they checked their weapons, the validity of their transit visas, then sat back listening to the drone of the engines. The cabin seated twelve, but they were the only passengers, positioned directly behind the pilot. By the worried look in Harry's appraising eyes, Natalie knew she looked worn out.

"Sorry I got you up so early for nothing," he smiled at her. "Try to nap a bit before we touch down in Magdeburg."

"Oh, Harry, you know I can never sleep before an encounter like this," she reminded him.

Harry sighed and closed his eyes. He thought of what Wright had told him about his opposite number, the KGB Captain. Romeyev. About his age. Father an Admiral with the Department of Maritime Affairs in the Kremlin. It would be something to come face to face with that man...

"Somehow I feel good about this pursuit, Nat," he said, stretching his long legs. "I think it's about time for our luck to turn around."

"This Russian Captain sounds like quite a guy."

"Sooner or later he's got to let his guard down, make a mistake," Harry pointed out. "Then we've got him."

"And this assignment will end," Natalie said with sadness.

"And happily, I hope. Don't you?" he asked, forcing a smile.

Natalie shrugged, looking out at the fleecy clouds.

"Of course I hope it ends happily. It's just that...well, I will probably return to Quebec...And you...? God only knows where you'll be going next, Harry."

There was a huskiness in her voice he had never heard before. He took her chin in the cup of his hand, turning her face to his.

"There'll be other assignments, Nat...," he whispered.

"Yes. There are always other assignments."

Her tone was flat, caustic. Her gaze was through the window.

"Does this mean you'll miss me?" he tried to joke.

"Whenever I'm not with you I miss you," she said, her amber eyes meeting his squarely, and he waited a long time before replying.

"I can say exactly that, Natalie," he told her softly.

She lifted her chin free of his hand and stared at her lap.

"Not the same way, Harry," she murmured. "We both know we don't miss each other the same way."

Harry flexed his shoulders to ease the tension building in his neck. It was not the first time Natalie Soubrine had openly expressed her feelings. He had long been aware of her frank adoration, her affection, and that knowledge was at once a boost to his ego and a drain on his emotional energy. To stand back, distant and aloof, always pretending his mind was on a thousand other matters when she was near—often that was a difficult feat to accomplish. There were nights when he wished he could go to her room, slip into bed beside her and make love to her fiercely and passionately enough to make up for all the disappointments and emptiness they both had known.

But Harry knew himself, knew he could never do that to a girl like Natalie Soubrine. She was all heart, and therefore, very vulnerable. It could never be just a light, casual fling with Natalie. She would expect more...richly deserve more.

And that was more than Harry had within him to give...

"Someday, Nat...," he told her, staring at the back of the pilot's head through the window in the cabin door, "...Someday, I'll open my morning mail, and I'll find an invitation. A wedding invitation. I'll read it and say to myself, 'Hot damn, little Natalie finally got tired of playing international cops and robbers.' And you'll make such a beautiful bride..."

"You really think so?" she breathed, eyes closed. There was a wet spot glistening just below the long dark lashes resting on one cheekbone. It made him wince to see how his impersonal attitude wounded her, but he dared not let himself weaken.

"Yes, Nat. I really think so."

(Magdeburg)

Their transit visas were in order. Natalie traveled with a Roumanian passport as a computer analyst. Harry posed as an American journalist doing a series of articles on the variety of dialects and languages in the Soviet Union. The East German Airport Police would permit them easy entrance into the DDR. But their plan was for nothing so traditional.

As soon as the pilot notified them he was making his final approach to the airfield, to a comparatively short runway at its southwest end, Harry and Natalie sprang into action. From 1500 feet, through wisps of smokey gray clouds, Harry's eagle eyes caught sight of a dark, long-nosed transport plane bearing the five-pointed star of the Russian Air Force.

Harry noted the fiery light in the pilot's eyes as he gave him last-minute instructions. Fritz Kraemer, a 23-year-old flying ace recruited by Bert Klemmer during that agent's post in Berlin, had applied for consideration as a "regular" foreign operative of the CIA. Kraemer knew Harry Carroll's reputation, and knew that the Agency would give a good deal of weight to the success with which the Carroll-Soubrine team was dispatched.

Listening with one ear to the air traffic control tower, Kraemer nosed down for his landing—paying close attention to the strategy Harry was mapping out. It was going to be a rough touch-down, but he had done it before, and on more primitive surfaces than the narrow end of the airstrip.

Easing to a speed safe enough for both agents to exit the aircraft before it came to a complete stop was as worrisome as it was challenging, but since they seemed confident enough of their ability to carry it through, there was nothing for Fritz Kraemer to be concerned about.

Down...down...heavy puffs of gray scudding by. Mist in the air. Most likely a storm brewing. The tops of barren trees lifted their branches toward the aircraft's undercarriage. Kraemer heard a final whisper exchanged between Harry and Natalie as they stood tense behind him at the cabin door.

How pretty she was, Kraemer mused. What an elfin, tip-tilted nose, and that ready smile...and that body! Were there other women in the Agency as gorgeous as Soubrine?

Director Carroll had asked him if he'd done his compulsory military training. Certainly he had.

"Then you know how to use this," Harry had grinned at him, pressing a .32 Mauser into his hand.

Down below, and—as he leveled out for his landing—straight ahead, the Russian air transport stood waiting.

Steady...steady...Behind him a man and a woman were drawing deep breaths in preparation. There was a bumping jolt as his landing gear made contact with the far end of the runway, and he maneuvered quickly to correct a precarious wing slant. But the surface ahead was smooth and clear. Fritz Kraemer taxied into a slowing circle...

A heavy whoosh of air behind him made him turn just in time to see Natalie poised to follow Director Carroll out onto the tarmac. She reminded Kraemer of a cat as she sprang through— agile, devoid of fear. He wondered whether he could have that kind of nerve.

Du lieber Gott! his senses blared at him. What perfect timing! Ahead of him on the eastern apron of the airstrip was a tiny red and white van...

Harry somersaulted two or three times, breathing in accordance with his training, to keep his body buoyant. Then he lay prone, weapon in hand, watching, his heart in his mouth. In less than twenty seconds, a tightly-wound bundle with dark hair whipping about catapulted from the side of the slowing plane and rolled into a flattened position about forty yards away.

Good girl! Harry summoned enough breath to send her his kiwi bird signal. An indistinct white face turned in his direction and responded with the same call.

Scrambling to his right, crouching as low as his tall frame allowed, Harry reached a stretch of dark bushes in front of a chain link fence and motioned for Natalie to join him there. He calculated they were about two hundred feet from the Russian transport plane, and the red and white van was nearing quickly.

A soft crunching on the pebbly surface made him aware that Natalie had crept up close to his position. From the corner of his eye, he could see her profile—her body flat to the tarmac, her small hands clasped beneath her chin, the long barrel of her revolver pointed toward the approaching van.

The star symbol on the side of the dark transport plane gave Jane a measure of comfort. She was on her way home. So far, so good. It had been a rough go all the way from San Francisco, with the hot breath of the CIA scorching the back of her neck.

Too many close calls. Her opposite number seemed possessed of the uncanny ability to read her mind and know exactly what her next step would be. She hoped Leonid Padorin had carried out her instructions. She was eager to see the file on Agent Carroll.

"Get the crate unstrapped," she told the square-headed DS man. "There's rain in the air and we'd better be on our way. Follow me to the plane as soon as you park the van…and hurry."

With her masculine swagger, Jane crossed the few yards between the van and the plane, smiling up at the pilot who greeted her with a cordial salute.

Was it her imagination, or was there something moving out toward a clump of bushes in front of the chain link fence at the end of the runway.

I'm becoming paranoid in my old age, she smirked.

The pilot had begun warming the engines. He stood ready to assist her up into the cabin. Behind her was Square-head, awkwardly struggling with the crate containing the computer. Having driven the van to an inconspicuous position at the end of the strip, Moon-face was bringing up the rear, approaching with a dufflebag in each hand.

The first few drops of rain formed dark splotches on the gray roadbed, and a strong wind came up, forcing Jane to hold on to the brim of her rainhat as she started up into the transport.

"*Oi chort!*" she cursed. "Here's the storm now! We'd better..."

She never finished.

A shot rang out, and there was a high-pitched yelp from Moon-face. One of the dufflebags sailed through the air as he fell with an ugly thud to the ground.

The other Bulgarian dropped to one knee, bracing his weapon across the top of the computer crate. Jane cried out in surprise and there was a quick exchange of gunfire.

So she had been right! Nothing paranoid about her thinking! There *had* been something moving in front of those bushes!

From the cabin window, her revolver raised high beside her head, she caught sight of a dark figure, blurred now by the teaming rain, sprinting forward in a zig-zag maneuver, the storm whipping to one side several lengths of long dark hair.

Carole? Here?

The dark-haired female agent pursuing her since San Francisco?

Through the open cabin door, Jane screamed down at the Bulgarian, "Get her! Get her!"

The DS man was firing with both guns. A fork of lightning crackled through the heavens, followed by an ear-splitting clap of thunder. But above that din, Jane thought she heard the outcry of a woman...

The Bulgarian was crouched behind the crate, snapping fresh cartridges into his clips, taking advantage of the momentary cessation of the gunfire.

The computer...

Jane sprang out of the cabin, shouting to the pilot to help her get the crate on board.

Re-loaded, the Bulgarian agent was taking new aim across the top of the crate, trying to make out movement through the driving rain.

Bending low to see beneath the undercarriage of the plane, Jane spotted a sudden hurtling form—that of a person crawling rapidly, very close to the ground, and she fired her own weapon. Her gunfire was answered by a new fusillade and the whining ping of metal upon metal. Suddenly, there was a grunt of surprise from the DS agent, as a high-calibre shell tore through one of his eyebrows and exited with a gush of skull fragments and brain tissue from the back of his head. The man slumped backwards behind the computer, and Jane, screaming with shock and outrage, seized one side of the cumbersome crate and began drawing it toward the cabin door, waving her gun in front of her. Squatting in back of it, she fired at something dark slithering through the furious downpour toward the vulnerable plane.

She could have sworn she heard someone moan and gasp, and then, only silence.

"Hah!" she rejoiced, pulling with all her strength at the crate, shouting again for help from the pilot.

Another staccato burst of gunfire—this time aimed directly at the computer itself—each shell penetrating the crate and piercing the delicate, complicated mechanism within. Jane had leaped to the side for some semblance of safety as six bullet holes formed a good-sized circle in the crate's side, with one well-placed hole in dead center.

Swearing in both Russian and English, Jane pushed the bullet-riddled crate toward the outstretched hands of the pilot, who lifted it aboard the aircraft and waved to her in a frenzy to follow it in.

Her shoes squelching in the rain puddles splashing all around her, Jane shielded herself behind one of the plane's huge wheels, and with the utmost caution, lined up the indicator of her weapon with the head of the ever-nearing enemy.

I thought I'd killed you, she fumed within herself. *I could have sworn I heard a woman's scream...*

Suddenly, she was gazing at a head of hair as smooth and flaxen as her own. And beneath that pale fall of bangs, a pair of eyes as piercing and as crystal blue as the eyes she met daily in her bathroom mirror.

A mirror…What made her think of a mirror…?

Looking into the face of this enemy, even across a substantial distance, was like looking into a mirror! And this enemy was a man…a man with his own pistol pointed directly at her head…!

Harry stared for what seemed an eternity into the eyes of Captain Romayev. He could not budge. His fingers felt lifeless, paralyzed, unable to squeeze the trigger. He had emptied his previous clip of shells at the computer and had a full load of bullets ready to be expended in taking the life of the KGB officer in plain view before him.

Why couldn't he fire?

And why was Romayev…he could see for himself, now…his mirror image…why was Romayev not firing at *him*! Surely, there were enough unspent shells in that revolver trained directly at his skull to hit him no matter how speedily he moved!

But no shot was fired!

An inexplicable memory flashed through his mind. He was at a table in some Alpine inn, in Zermatt, and a man was unfolding before him a photograph of his mother. His natural mother. A blonde slip of a girl whose beautiful features had remained forevermore in some guarded corner of his mind. He saw the face of that old photograph superimposed over the face of the enemy only a dozen or so yards from where he lay. Romayev's face…it was the face of his mother. His Russian mother.

Her name was Tanya, he'd been told.

Motionless, Harry lay trembling on the wet macadam, his mouth and throat dry, his scalp tingling, his heart thudding against the ground, watching—helpless, as though he had died—the way Captain Romayev slid out from behind the airplane wheel, slim and graceful—no longer pointing the gun in his direction—sad, searching eyes locked with his in one long, magnetic exchange of glances.

Then Romayev sprang up into the cabin of the plane and disappeared from his sight. The noise of the engines mounted to a shrill scream, competing for acoustical decibels with the trammeling of the rain and the roar of the thunder.

Three seconds...then four...and the aircraft was moving down the runway, accelerating, picking up speed, half a dozen bullet holes gaping in its fuselage. Then it lifted off...

Only then did the strange, paralytic spell relax its hold on Harry. With a mournful lament, he dragged himself to the spot where Natalie Soubrine had fallen. There he gathered the unconscious girl in his arms, cradling her against him.

Over deafening blasts of static on Fritz Kraemer's wide area aircraft receiver, Bert Klemmer was informed of the more pressing details, and reported back to Harry what arrangements he had made for Natalie to be received at a West Berlin hospital where he had friends on the surgical staff.

Natalie was still unconscious, apparently in shock from loss of blood. It was only a short hop from Magdeburg to West Berlin, but time was definitely of the essence.

Kraemer handed the microphone to Harry who sat with Natalie in his lap, her head pillowed against his shoulder.

"She took one in the chest," Harry advised Klemmer in a dry, unemotional tone that sounded devoid of life. "Probably nicked the lung."

"Okay, Chief," Bert Klemmer replied. "I'm calling ahead to the Emergency Room. Fritz knows the hospital and where to put down. Be assured, they'll accommodate us for this emergency."

Kraemer had a map spread out across the dashboard and was indicating the hospital's location with his forefinger.

"Bert," Harry complained over the microphone, consulting the map, "that area looks pretty congested to me. Is there a landing strip nearby?"

He heard Klemmer chuckle lightly over the static.

"Leave it to Fritz, Chief," he was assured. "He can land that thing on the roof of an outhouse."

Chapter 13

(Moscow)

Slumped in her seat, Jane had for about half an hour been aware of irregular fibrillation, the dizzying weakness and vertigo accompanying it keeping her silent and motionless, trying to conceal her calamitous condition from the pilot, Sandor Topolov.

He had been glancing sideways at her repeatedly as they flew through the storm, the look in his eyes one of alarm. Jane knew she probably looked cyanotic, her lips tinged blue, her complexion ashen. Despite repeated deep, long breaths, she was unable to control the premature ventricular contractions her heart muscle kept throwing.

"Are you all right, Captain?" Topolov inquired anxiously.

"Da," she assured him. "Just pay attention to the flight."

What kind of prize was she bringing back to her government?

In its shell-blasted crate, she had no illusions that the computer was still intact. And it had been destroyed practically in her very hands. Her assignment had been to bring the revolutionary microchip to the Soviet Union—that complex chip which, when fitted correctly into the myriad complexities of a modern computer, could increase military might a hundredfold, a thousandfold, making its owner among the superpowers the absolute controller of the planet.

What she had retrieved from the Chinese to transport to Moscow was now a blasted casing and in all probability a ruined microchip.

Two excellent satellite agents were dead.

The prize had been destroyed.

And...the agent, Carroll.

Yes, a woman had indeed been there. Was that woman Carole?

Or was that the name of the man...the man she could not shoot?

Nor had *he* fired.

They had simply stared at each other, mesmerized by their likenesses, unable to fire the shot which would have been tantamount to suicide. The killing of the self.

Back there at the airfield, in those final moments, staring into the barrel of that man's weapon, she had felt certain of instant death being seconds away. They were adversaries; there was no reason for the enemy agent *not* to shoot to kill. All of their orientation had been to kill or be killed...

A duel to the death, of souls, hanging together through time and space. Had it been pre-destined that they not take one another's life...?

Lives could end in other ways. And very quickly.

THUMP-thump. Pause. Pause. Thump-THUMP...

The pilot looked back at her in concern.

She coughed several times. Then she smiled.

It would be all right.

Once again, she had foiled death.

The team of thoracic surgeons at the Berolina Hospital had encouraging news. Natalie had come through the surgery. She had received two blood transfusions and would remain in post-operative intensive care for about forty-eight hours. Upon arrival, her condition had been critical, prognosis guarded. She was, post-operatively, listed as stable and improving.

A .32 calibre shell had penetrated the right breast and torn through to the upper lobe of the lung. The shell had been removed, and there would be some scarring of the breast, but the lung had not been irreparably damaged.

"You may see her for only a few minutes," the head of the thoracic team told Harry. "She needs lots of rest."

In the shadowy intensive care unit, Natalie's face was as ghastly white as her pillow. When Harry entered, she was in the process of receiving a third unit of B-positive blood and an intravenous solution was being fed into the arteries of her other arm. She did not awaken during his visit.

"Hey, Nat," he whispered, lips brushing against her hair. "As soon as you get well, we'll laugh our heads off over this. You always wanted a couple of inches off your bust..."

But his words sounded tasteless in his own ears.

Had Natalie been awake to hear his quip, she would not have appreciated it.

Tears stung his eyes, and he kissed her forehead.

"Come through, Nat," he said softly. "Come back to us, Natalia Isaakovna..."

*   *   *   *

Igor Matlov was at a concert when the fatal heart attack took him, just as the strings came up for the second movement of Tchaikowsky's Fourth. It had started as incredible heartburn, followed by a terrible nausea, and he wondered what he had eaten to produce so much indigestion all at once. But like a weight in the center of his chest, the nausea became pain. And in minutes, the pain intensified, spreading over the left breast into the left shoulder and neck and down the left arm to the elbow...

And Igor Matlov collapsed, sweating profusely, in the dress circle of the concert hall.

"Please...," he gasped as ambulance interns rushed him to the hospital. "Please notify Admiral Yuri Romayev at the Kremlin..."

The Admiral received the call a few minutes past midnight, as he was preparing for bed. Matlov, a long-time member of the diplomatic corps, had expired within the hour after being admitted to the hospital. Coronary occlusion. Hospital attendants carried out the instructions written on Matalov's admittance papers.

"He had a family, did he not?" Romayev asked the aide who reported the news by phone.

"A wife and daughter. They are being notified as well."

"It's sad news," Romayev said. "But thank you."

He rinsed a glass in his small kitchenette and poured himself a cognac. Matlov had been living on borrowed time for years. Still, it was tragic that so young a man had to go. Romayev wondered why Matlov, in his dying moments, had felt compelled to have the hospital staff notify him, when there existed no relationship, no special bond, between Matlov and himself...

No special bond...?

But of course there was!

Matlov's file...the early file on Harry Carroll, the youngster who had refused the Soviet Union's offer to welcome him to his motherland with its bountiful privileges.

The youngster who had grown up...to become a Special Director of the Central Intelligence Agency of the United States!

Matlov, in his final moments of life, had remembered to alert the Admiral, in case anyone happened upon his secret file...

Romayev slugged down his drink and felt a tremor run through his body. He had to get hold of that file before anyone else did, for the sake of his position...for the sake of *Ilyana*...

Leonid Padorin, his frustration and anger rising, stared at the shattered remains of the computer. The bullet-riddled crate sat lopsided against the wall, mute testament to the destruction suffered by the complicated unit.

Useless. Totally useless. The entire mission had been a waste. How could she have brought back this evidence of America's determination not to permit the USSR to get hold of the wonder chip! It was an insult to the department! In its present condition, nothing whatever could be learned from its remains. The CIA agent who had fired at the computer casing knew exactly what he was doing. And now, other questions had to be addressed...

"Lieutenant Topolov," Padorin began, speaking to the man who sat anxiously before the birchwood desk. "Where were you when the attack began? What did you see?"

The pilot had been detained for questioning after submitting his written report. In civilian clothes, he cut a less dashing figure than as pilot of the transport plane. In his brief career, Topolov had never had occasion to be interrogated by the KGB, and it was a frightful ordeal for him. He wanted none of his words to be misconstrued.

"I was preparing for take-off, having made my assistance available to Captain Romayev and his party to bring the cargo on board..."

"Go on."

"It was raining very hard, and I truthfully don't remember hearing the first shot. But I heard the Captain shout, and looking out from the door of the plane, I saw that one of the men from the *Durzhavna Sigurnost*, the one who had just parked the van and was approaching the aircraft...he had just been hit, and I believe, instantly killed, Sir."

"And then what?" pressed Padorin.

"The other man, carrying the crate, set it down and kneeled behind it, firing across its top."

"Where was Captain Romayev at the time?"

Topolov ran a nervous hand through his dark, scruffy hair and tried to pin down details. Padorin watched him carefully.

"Well, it all happened so fast...I can't really be sure, Sir. But I think Captain Romayev was on board my plane, looking through the window in the direction from which the shots were coming. There was a lot of shooting..."

"What exactly did Captain Romayev do, Lieutenant?"

The young pilot frowned in deep concentration.

"If I recall correctly, the Captain jumped down, shouting something like, 'Get her! Get her!' and we heard a scream, like a woman's scream..."

"Is that when the other Bulgarian was killed?"

"I think so, Sir. Then Captain Romayev commanded me to help get the crate aboard, and was in the process of pulling it closer, when there was a lot of rapid firing, and the crate was hit...many, many times...just as you see..."

Padorin looked over at the incriminating holes in the wooden crate and nodded, his expression grim.

"Do you recall Captain Romayev firing back?"

"I'm sure he did, Sir."

"What makes you so sure, Lieutenant Topolov?"

"Because he was holding his gun, and there was a lot of shooting."

"And did you then lift the crate on board the aircraft?"

"Yes, Sir. I did."

"And the Captain followed you into the cabin and you took off?" Padorin asked slowly, emphasizing a point.

"No, not exactly, Sir..."

Padorin leaned back, drumming his fingers against his desk. There was something there he did not quite understand.

"Describe as clearly as you can what you saw."

Topolov swallowed hard. He did not want to cast aspersions on anyone, nor did he wish to be held personally culpable...

"It was strange, Sir. I can't be sure...but I don't recall hearing any more shooting, from either side. Captain Romayev was shielded behind one of the wheels, and then leaned out, aiming at the man lying on the ground about forty feet away..."

"And what happened?"

"Nothing, Sir."

"What do you mean by 'nothing,' Lieutenant?"

"Well, I expected the Captain to fire...," Topolov began, wetting his dry lips. "The man was an easy target, with his gun aimed directly at the Captain. They could easily have shot each other...But..."

"But?" Padorin prodded impatiently.

"Neither of them fired, Sir."

Padorin's expression remained cold, dispassionate, as he digested the young pilot's remarks.

"Why do you think that was? Were they out of bullets?"

"No, Sir. I remember the Captain emptying the gun later, during the flight. There were four shells removed..."

"Could the enemy have been out of bullets?"

"Possibly, Sir. I have no way of knowing."

Padorin nodded. The situation described was puzzling.

"Did Captain Romayev say anything to you during the flight back to Moscow? As to why no further shots were fired?"

"No, Sir. The Captain was evidently ill during the flight back. I was afraid he was about to have a heart attack, from the way he looked."

Once more, Padorin drummed nervous fingers on the birchwood.

"I have no further questions at this time, Lieutenant Topolov. You may go. And thank you, you've been most helpful."

Ilyana Romayeva glided through the restaurant in her Western-style new-look tailored gray suit with its padded shoulders and three-inch spike-heeled black pumps, knowing she would tower over the KGB Chief who had asked her to dinner.

Padorin had reserved a window table on the Rossia's twenty-first floor, and stood with a smile of greeting as his protegée approached. He had ordered a Schlivovitz over ice for himself, a French cognac for his lovely guest, and toasted her safe return.

"Sorry I let you down," she confessed with contrition.

"Perhaps not all is lost," he countered, encouragingly. "We've put a dozen of our best computer specialists on the unit. Maybe something can be salvaged."

"Oh, do you think so, Leonid?"

"I hope so. And I hope you're hungry."

She laughed, more relaxed. She had feared she'd be in for a hard time with KGB Chief Padorin, but so far, he seemed his usual ingratiating self, which diminished her concern.

"Leonid...," she whispered over a cigarette after they placed their order. "Were you able to uncover any information in your files about the 'carol' I mentioned?"

There was a perceptible hesitation before he answered.

"Why, yes, as a matter of fact," he stated. "The particular 'carol' you have in mind has been orchestrated widely in recent years. A newly-appointed Special Director on this microchip task force. Young, brilliant, lightning swift, and completely dedicated to his work. A worthy opponent, Ilyana."

"Then Carroll is a man, after all. I thought...a woman."

"There is a woman on the team. Natalie Soubrine. An experienced and accomplished operative. Russian-born, interestingly enough. From Kiev. Her father, accused of treason, died three years ago in a Siberian labor camp."

Remembering the eerie paralysis that had overcome her on the airstrip in Magdeburg as she studied the face of the enemy agent, Ilyana swallowed hard and blinked back the start of a tear.

"I think we shot Soubrine. Hopefully, she's dead," she said.

"I have no word on that yet. But tell me something, Ilyana."

She hesitated before raising her eyes to her superior's.

"I understand you had the opportunity to shoot...and kill...CIA Director Harry Carroll," Padorin continued. "Why didn't you?"

The crystal-blue of her eyes darkened with anxiety.

"I...I don't understand...," she stammered.

"A very simple question, Ilyana," Padorin stated softly, avoiding her eyes by consulting the wine list. "What was your difficulty in shooting Carroll?"

Jane's lips trembled and she ran her fingers through her hair.

"I suppose I...I think I was out of bullets..."

"Don't play games with me, Ilyana!"

She had never heard Padorin's tone so commanding, and it chilled through her. He was a commander in the Soviet Secret

Police. He flipped the wine list aside and his tone became softer, but just as relentless.

"The pilot reported you removed four shells from your revolver after you boarded the plane. He also told me you were feeling quite ill. Do you care to tell me about that?"

"There's nothing to tell, Leonid. I imagine it was just a bad case of nerves, and I was over-reacting..."

"You had just seen the CIA agent, Carroll, destroy the computer, something your country wanted very desperately to possess, and for which your life and several other lives had already been risked...and lost. Just at the moment when you could have brought the computer home to Moscow, you saw it destroyed. And according to the pilot, you aimed at the man...and never fired."

Padorin's eyes were cold as he searched her face. She felt icy perspiration across her brow and beneath the hair folded over the nape of her neck. She spread her hands helplessly.

"I don't *know* why!" she tried to explain, tormented by her own emotions. "It was very odd. The man's appearance stopped me cold. I felt I was looking at my reflection! I think I was actually spellbound for a few minutes...unable to think rationally...!"

Padorin pursed his lips, eyeing her suspiciously.

"I also understand that Carroll made no attempt to fire at you, either, Ilyana. Can you explain that?"

She tried to analyze the significance of his question, but could not do so on the spur of the moment.

"I can only assume he was out of ammunition."

The waiter brought drinks to their table and Padorin's warm smile returned as he lifted his glass to her.

"*Nazd'rovia, Ilyanitchka,*" his lips grinned beneath cold pale eyes. "We'll probably talk about this again, soon. For now, let's enjoy the evening."

All bureau drawers, every shelf in the closet, and all but one of the desk drawers in the Matlov apartment had been thoroughly searched. The center drawer was locked, and so far, the two men who had been conducting the swift search had found nothing. The sturdy mahogany desk was too fine a piece of furniture to smash.

"The widow may have the drawer key," one suggested, and they rushed into the adjoining room of the two-room apartment to speak to the widow, Evgenia Matlova.

"I never had my husband's desk keys," she told them.

"We must search the center drawer," one of the men insisted. "Where did your husband keep his keys…?"

"Perhaps in his briefcase…," the widow wept, and the searchers who had been dispatched to Matlov's apartment by Admiral Romayev returned to their examination of every zippered compartment of the dead man's briefcase. A small bulge in one of the inner compartments revealed the hiding place of the special keys. Several were tried, until at last, a small, thin key turned in the lock and the drawer was pulled open. Excited, they lifted one folder after another, scanning the labels, until one of them uttered a cry.

"Here it is!"

A manila folder, about an inch and a half thick, secured with criss-crossed rubber bands. Across the face of the folder was the handwritten name, "Carroll, H."

Sudden voices in the next room made them look up in alarm. The widow Matlova was speaking softly to two men who had just entered the apartment. Romayev's aides stood still, one of them holding the folder to his chest, gaping as two young men in the dark, dour attire of the KGB entered the room and took in the scene.

"The widow Matlova tells us you have been going through Consul Matlov's private files, Comrades," one KGB man stated.

"We're carrying out instructions, Sir…"

"May I see the file you have there?" asked the KGB officer in a pleasant enough voice, extending his hand.

With a nervous glance at his companion, the aide handed the file to the man from the KGB, who in turn glanced casually at the handwritten designation on its cover.

"Whose instructions were you carrying out, Comrade?"

The Admiral's aides, bug-eyed, looked at each other in fear. Then one of them cleared his throat and spoke up.

"We're with Admiral Yuri Romayev's office, Sir. He asked us to pick up this file..."

"Thank you," said the man from the KGB. "We'll take care of it for you. If Admiral Romayev has any question concerning it, he may call us at his convenience..."

The KGB man then held out his card to the frightened aide.

"The clerk handed it over without any resistance," was later reported to the man behind the birchwood desk. Afternoon shadows had darkened the wood-paneled office and the man at the desk flicked on the desk lamp, which added a yellow glow to the room.

KGB Chief Leonid Padorin looked long and hard at the old file, all four edges soft and fuzzy from years of handling. Written on the face of the folder in Cyrillic script was the name which had been keeping him awake nights for several years.

"They said they were acting on the orders of...?" he asked.

"Admiral Yuri Romayev, Sir," the officer replied.

Padorin nodded thoughtfully, then dismissed his men.

Quite calmly, he lit a cigarette and blew a smoke ring up toward the dusky ceiling. Then he drew the file onto his lap and slowly removed the rubber bands.

*　　*　　*　　*

Orderlies were mopping the tile corridors of the Berolina Clinic when Harry stepped out of the third floor elevator, seeking the room in which Natalie was recuperating.

The door was open, but noticing a screen around the girl's bed, Harry waited politely outside until he heard the scraping of metal on metal as the accordion-pleated screen was drawn back along its overhead framing. Finally, a nurse walked out, making notations on her chart, and gave Harry a quizzical look in passing.

Spying him, Natalie gave him a beckoning grin. He noted she was still receiving oxygen, two slender tubes inserted in her pert nose, tubes protruding from the oxygen tank upright on its support beside her bed. He observed she had received two floral gifts in addition to the long-stemmed roses he had sent.

"How's m'girl?" he beamed at her, bending to kiss her cheek.

"Getting better every minute."

He gestured with his chin toward the Bird of Paradise plant and to the exotic-looking glass terrarium with its pastel-colored pebbles and miniature cacti arrangements against soft, shifting sand.

"Powell Wright sent the Birds of Paradise," Natalie explained. "The terrarium is from Bert. Set it down on the tray here, Harry. I'll show you something…"

He reached over and set the pyramidal glass-enclosed plant on her serving tray. Natalie raised herself up and pushed a button fixed into the base of the terrarium.

The tinkling sound of a music box filled the room. Harry knew he recognized the melody but couldn't place it.

> *"What the world needs now…*
> *Is love…sweet love…*
> *That's the only thing…*
> *We need plenty of…"*

Natalie sang the lyrics, her voice alto and dry. He was impressed with Bert Klemmer's gift, commenting, "Nice of him."

"His card said he owed it to me," Natalie stated. "I could have done without that. I wish he could have sent it because he felt like it."

Her words were very clear, very poignant, and they hit Harry hard, as he realized how disappointed she could have been to read the card he had enclosed with his roses.

("A million thanks for being there when I need you most.")

Embarrassed, he asked, "Do you want me to tell Bert that?"

"No. Don't bother."

She moved her legs aside for him to sit on the edge of her bed. Against the white walls and linens, she looked exquisite with her dark hair and pale skin, her delicate features giving her the look of a high-school graduate.

"I was here a few minutes ago, but I guess you were indisposed," he told her. "The nurse had the screen around you."

"I was definitely indisposed. She was changing my dressing."

Harry glanced at the swath of bandages beneath the hospital gown, reaching the base of her throat, then took in the up-tilted orb of her breast. She caught his glance, and he flushed.

"Any more pain?" he inquired.

"Not really. They've been giving me something. Demerol, maybe. I'll return to Washington as an addict."

"Not you, Nat. Never you."

There was an uncomfortable silence.

"I never did find out what happened," she told him.

"Oh!" he responded. "Oh, well...I guess it went okay."

"Do you mind telling me? Just for my own curiosity?"

"Sure," Harry replied. "In the words of the Agency...it was a successful mission. There was no loss of life on our side, a substantial loss of life on the enemy's, and the objective was destroyed before it could prove harmful to the United States."

"Hey!" she laughed, jabbing at his arm. "That's marvelous! So you killed Romayev, did you?"

He was silent. Their eyes met.

"No, Nat. You and I...we got the two goons...but Romayev..."

"He got away?"

Another silence. She searched his troubled eyes.

"I let him get away, Nat."

"What do you mean?"

"I didn't kill him. I...I let him get away."

"For heaven's sake, why?"

Harry stared out of the hospital window at the distant steeple of a church, and the outline of a highrise against the clouds.

"Because I saw his face..."

"And?" she asked, breathless.

"And...it was my face."

He turned back to her and Natalie took hold of his hands.

"Harry...Who is this man...?"

Harry took one of her slim wrists in the circle of his fingers, stroking it tenderly.

"I don't know, Nat. I wish I knew..."

Chapter 14

(Odessa)

Industrial espionage had never made Jane particularly misty-eyed. Missions involving the theft of high-technology products had always seemed dull and businesslike to her, and had left her cold. She would have preferred observing a commando raid in some Third World Country or led a good squad infiltration into a hideout where some anti-Communist had taken refuge.

At its outset, the whisking-away of the microchip from the Chinese had seemed like a cut and dried operation, with nothing extraordinarily exciting about it. Certainly nothing to fire the imagination of a young, ambitious KGB officer. The only aspect of the mission that had appealed to her at all was its primary location—San Francisco.

So it felt good to get away. She hadn't seen the Tobirians in over a year, and knew that a few days in their cottage within walking distance of the Black Sea would do her good. She hadn't anticipated encountering the strange enemy agent—Harry Carroll.

Nor had she anticipated the effect he would have on her.

"Oh, it's been so long, so long!" Mirabianka wept, her arms wrapped tightly around Jane, swaying as she hugged the tall young woman. She had aged, Jane noticed, her body even chunkier, her plain features even coarser. But her smile and embrace were as warm as Jane remembered.

"And you're even more beautiful than ever!" announced Karol Tobirian, offering her welcoming hugs and kisses. "We hope you'll be staying with us at least a few months!"

"Oh, hardly!" Jane laughed, reveling in their affection, disclosing that she had just come off an exasperating assignment. "It'll be just a couple of days, I'm afraid. Three or four...and as soon as I receive a call from Moscow, I must rush back. But I simply had to see you, spend a pleasant visit with you..."

"We'll call Sergei and have him fly out," Mirabianka suggested excitedly. "He'd never forgive us if we didn't tell him you're here with us."

Jane remembered with some nostalgia the last time she had seen Sergei. Seeing him would be a most engaging diversion.

Over dinner, Tobirian mentioned that he, himself, had just come back from Moscow, having attended the funeral of an old colleague of his from the diplomatic corps.

"A fairly young man," he mourned philosophically. "Heart attack. Just like that. But being at the services gave me a chance to say hello to your father..."

"Oh, did my father attend the funeral, too...?"

"Yes, and Comrade Padorin...who broke his heart long enough to nod in my direction."

Jane felt a nervous buzzing in her chest and took a few forkfuls of Mira's culinary specialties.

"Well, Tobi...," she observed, "Leonid has never been the easiest person in the world to get along with..."

She was vaguely aware of a dark exchange of glances between the couple, and wondered what it signified.

She awoke at dawn, invigorated, anticipating the early walk she and Tobi had planned along the seaside promenade, Primorsky Boulevard, high above the water, from where they could view the picturesque panorama of Odessa Bay. They both dressed warm against the raw chill of sleet and frost in the air.

"Ay, Mira is so happy to be at her stove, preparing for a beloved guest!" Tobi said with glee. "Tonight she's serving borscht and pirozhki...just the way you loved them!"

Jane's spirits had lifted immeasurably as they trudged along, gloved hands deep in the pockets of their parkas. Up ahead were the Potemkin Steps, but they decided it was too chilly a morning to descend down to the bay, and turned at that point to traverse the promenade in the opposite direction. The more Tobi talked of the family dinner, and reminisced about Jane's early days with them, the quieter the girl became, and Tobi noticed.

"What's troubling you, *Malyinki*?" he inquired gently.

"Can you so easily tell I'm troubled?" she asked back.

"I know you, *Ilyanitchka*...what is it, fourteen years now? I know that look in your eyes when things are not right..."

Jane gathered her thoughts before speaking.

"Remember when you first spoke to me about my coming to the Soviet Union, Tobi? You told me something then that I've never been able to forget..."

"And...what was that, *Malyinki*?"

Jane took a deep breath and looked off toward the busy thoroughfare, the Deribosovskaya, which they were approaching.

"You told me that someday, I'd find I wasn't alone...That I would one day meet my twin brother...Were you joking then, Tobi?"

"Ilyana!" Tobi exclaimed in a soft, sad tone. "Why such interest, after so many years?"

"I'm past thirty now," she sighed. "If I have a brother...I would like to meet him..."

The aging consul gazed at her with deep compassion for a long time, then, morose and silent, walked toward the Soviet Army Square, Jane traipsing along at his side, searching his face.

"That's not possible, *Malyinki*."

"Why isn't it?"

"Because to the best of my knowledge, your brother never came to this country. I believe he refused."

Jane's legs felt weak. She could barely place one foot in front of the other.

"How can I find out for sure?" she pressed. "Where might I inquire about him, Tobi...?"

Tobirian stopped walking and placed his hands on her shoulders, his eyes very grave.

"Ilyana, listen to me. The only man from whom you could have inquired died last week. Consul Igor Matlov. It was at his funeral that I ran into your boss...and your father..."

(Washington, D. C.)

Washington, D. C. had never promised such comfort, rest and relaxation in all the years Harry had returned to it from different points around the globe. At the outset of the mission involving the microchip, he had dreaded having only abysmal failure to report to Powell Wright. Fortunately, such a report was no longer necessary.

He had never doubted the identity of his country's primary enemy, and knew well that in the area of industrial espionage, the Russian KGB was his chief antagonist. As always, in their inimical manner, they had left no stone unturned to accomplish their objective.

The battle for supremacy in the field of technology had seemed abstract and academic to Harry, offering no physical challenge and nothing so glamorous as running arms into a country like Afghanistan, or blowing up a supply tunnel.

But it had turned out to be a difficult, frustrating mission. Losing Bob Carlson was something he dared not dwell on for long. He had shared much with the red-headed Viking, and would miss him.

And what of his strange encounter in Magdeburg with the ruthless blond agent who resembled his mirror image...

What in hell WAS that! What did it portend?

The capture, torture and brainwashing of Bert Klemmer...the combat death of two Bulgarian agents...and the near fatal wound suffered by Natalie Soubrine...changed what had begun for Harry as an academic abstraction into a stark, awesome reality.

The Russian Premier sang siren songs of appeasement to the West, but his troops were very much at war with the USA on the technical front, more so there than in the political or economic arena. Not fought with charts and maps and pencils and word processors, it was a war fought with all the terrorist strategy at the disposal of the Soviets, with all their ruthlessness—including kidnapping, torture, and cold-blooded murder.

The mission had convinced Harry that Soviet agents had infiltrated the United States on a grander scale than he had ever been led to believe by CIA headquarters. Every move he had made, each of his actions in San Francisco, New York, Lisbon, Geneva and the Lake Constance area had been known in detail to the enemy.

His report to Powell Wright had been corroborated by trusted witnesses. Natalie Soubrine had described, right up to the moment she lost consciousness, the shoot-out at the Magdeburg airstrip. Bert Klemmer had included in his report the verbatim account by Flight Commander Friedrich Kraemer (of the Air Defense Force of the Federal Republic of Germany) describing what he had seen on the airstrip between the three Soviet agents who had the computer in tow, their Soviet pilot, and the two American CIA agents, Director Carroll and Agent Soubrine.

Harry found a genuine look of pride on the DCI's face when he arrived, for Wright had already digested the telex of Carroll's report and was content enough with that. He wanted the minute details for his own personal edification.

"Good thinking, Harry!" he exclaimed jovially. "To destroy the computer before Romayev flew it to KGB headquarters in Moscow. That was really spitting clean in their eyes!"

"There were four of them and two of us," Harry explained dryly, "And when Natalie fell, and the first Bulgarian, that reduced the odds to three to one. I had to decide at that moment whether I wanted to spill more blood or to reduce the technical risk to our side by destroying the thing they wanted most..."

Powell Wright's eyes were narrowed, and Harry felt obliged to look quickly away. It was rare his superior missed the tiniest inconsistency in anyone's report.

"Let's talk about it over dinner. My house," Wright said.

With Natalie flown to a private sanitarium in McLean, Virginia—a short drive from the nation's capitol—Harry breathed more easily. Not only was the staff there excellent, but the facility was safe. And Harry knew that Natalie required that kind of safety to recuperate from her close call. The flesh wound to the breast, the damage to two vertebrae—those would heal quickly enough. It was the torn upper lobe of Natalie's lung that worried Harry. Unless an agent were in tip-top physical condition and could depend on summoning maximum reserves of strength for exertion and endurance—that agent was of no use to himself or to the team with which he was associated. Harry had to wonder with deep regret if the Magdeburg fracas had cost Natalie her future as a field operative with the Agency.

"You be a good girl, now," he admonished her cheerfully, the moment she was comfortably installed in her sanitarium room. "Follow doctor's orders and get yourself all well and hearty again, because we need you."

Natalie shrugged self-consciously, flushing, looking around her room with its bright floral-print curtains and matching wallpaper.

Despite his customary reserve and impersonal manner, Wright had behaved in a warm, attentive manner, patting Natalie's shoulder and telling her to behave herself. Then he had drawn Klemmer with him, making excuses for them both, joking about having neglected his caffeine fix for the day.

Harry assumed Wright had pre-planned it that way, to give him a chance to spend a few private moments with Agent Soubrine, and from the look on Natalie's face, she suspected the same arrangement.

"According to what Bert learned from Fritz Kraemer, you shot a target on the wall of the crate and then hit it...bull's eye!" Natalie snickered. "That kind of shooting had to demolish whatever was in the crate."

"That remains to be seen," Harry sighed. "I hope I damaged it severely enough so that the boys from the Kremlin's think-tank can't figure out what made the SRC chip really tick."

He felt her gaze fixed on him and raised his eyebrows.

"Did Wright say anything to you about Romayev?" she asked.

"We're going to talk about it over dinner," he replied. "I'm sure he's upset, but pretending to be simply curious."

"And...and you, Harry?" she hesitated. "What are you feeling?"

He forced a smile, bending toward her for a kiss goodbye.

"At this moment...bewitched, bothered, and bewildered."

She slipped a cool hand around the back of his neck and drew him closer to her.

"I thought only women did that to you," she whispered coyly.

He kissed her with an impish grin.

"So did I, Nat," he murmured. "So did I."

Powell Wright poured two glasses of Zinfandel and the two men sat staring at the fire blazing in the hearth. From his significant relationship with the older man, Harry could tell how disturbed Wright was even before the questions began.

"Tell me what went through your mind when Soubrine was hit," he urged Harry gently, turning the wine glass in his hands.

Recalling the grim scene, Harry felt his scalp prickle and his mouth go dry. He remembered Natalie's outcry, recalled seeing her crumple. Just moments before, she had taken out the DS van-driver.

"I couldn't pick out Romayev through the storm," he told his superior. "I suspected he was inside the plane. I remember thinking Soubrine had been killed and burning up with fury...not really giving a damn at that moment about anything except blasting those sons of bitches to hell. And one second later, I blew the brains out of the other DS bastard firing at us across the top of the crate..."

Harry paused, swallowed some of the wine.

"Then someone leaped out of the plane and began tugging at the crate and shouting in Russian. I figured the pilot was in the cabin, probably armed to the teeth, and all I could think of was keeping them from getting away with the computer. I kept firing into the fuselage, re-loaded, and then emptied the entire clip at the side of the crate."

Wright swished the wine thoughtfully in his mouth.

"Was that when you took a look at Romayev?" he asked, and for just a moment, the look in Harry's eyes was one of surprise.

"That's when we looked at each other," he whispered. "And the world stopped."

There was a long silence. The fire crackled in the hearth.

"Neither of you fired," the DCI said softly. "Why, Harry?"

Through closed eyes, Harry saw again the sad, searching glance of his adversary. The impact of that glance was so powerful, his jaw ached with emotion.

"I don't know, Chief," he choked. "I'll never know."

(McLean, Virginia)

Northern Virginia didn't look its best on a wet, drab autumn morning, cheating the handsome estates on both sides of the highway of their usual elegance. It had stormed during the night, and the last golden leaves had left the trees.

Harry stopped for a light at the Old Dominion Drive intersection, feeling nostalgic about spending time with his folks again, glad that Don Carroll was taking life a bit easier and that Sally was still supportive of his idiosyncrasies. They had been good parents. The best. Harry never permitted a day to go by without thinking of them, never a week without a post card, never a month without a telephone call.

The road narrowed into a wooded area, with hills on one side and a gully on the other. A little further on, the terrain on the right leveled out, and a pretty two-story house came into view, surrounded by a large, tree-studded yard. It had been quite some time since Harry had been home in McLean. The small sanitarium where Natalie was convalescing was five minutes away by auto.

But for the moment, Harry was making another visit. Driving up into the circular roadbed, he pulled well over to the side to permit the passage of other vehicles. He hesitated before knocking at the front door. A curtain moved. A blurred face appeared at the window. There was a squeal of pleasure and a shout of joy as the door flew open.

"We hear through the local grapevine that our boy is special director on an assignment involving national security!" Don stated over lunch in subdued tones, as though to hush his words lest they be picked up by prying ears. Harry offered his father his very best "you're-on-the-right-track-but-don't-ask-me-about-it" grin, and the subject was abruptly and understandingly changed.

"I think someday Harry will tell us he's decided to throw his hat in the ring for some kind of a political post, so that we'll have the comfort of having him closer in our old age," Sally said with a mock pout, and Harry felt compassion for her, to be denied the warmth and closeness of the son she'd raised with such loving care. She deserved the tenderness and affection of a son, of a daughter-in-law, of grandchildren. Harry knew his mother was missing all that, trying to be stoic about reconciling with the fact that she probably wouldn't live long enough to experience any of those natural, wholesome joys.

They conversed lightly about Harry's travels, about Don's retirement and hobbies, about the economic situation and the state of the art in world diplomacy.

"Speaking of diplomacy," Don Carroll interrupted. "Did our letter ever catch up with you, informing you that Yvonne became a widow?"

Harry glanced up in time to catch the glance between his parents, and then Don Carroll was lighting the bowl of his pipe, puffing away, the aroma of rum and apple filling the room with the same warm spicy sweetness Harry remembered from childhood.

"Yvonne widowed?" he asked, surprised. "No, I hadn't heard."

"Oh, it's some time now," Sally said, gathering the lunch dishes. "What would you say, Don? Nine, ten months ago? Brain aneurism, we were told. Went to his office one morning and that was it. His secretary found him face down on his desk."

"How awful for Yvonne!" Harry gasped softly, his mind racing down a thousand half-forgotten streets and roadways, flashing on memories of a small, slim girl with a fine scattering of freckles across her delicate features and long, lustrous red hair...

"Well, they hadn't been making it, we hear," Don said in his confidential tone. "Quite possibly, if George Chartrain hadn't died, we'd have heard some scandal by now about a divorce, or an annulment, if that's what Roman Catholics are calling marital break-ups these days."

"What about children?" Harry inquired, pretended to sound disinterested. Inside his head, he was re-living the night when he informed Yvonne they would be leaving for Honduras, his first Agency assignment. He remembered how she had adamantly refused, even to consider the idea, and Harry had done what he later knew was a foolish thing—he had given the willful redhead a firm ultimatum: either she accompanied him to Honduras for the duration of his assignment, or he'd go alone. It was a night of choices for both of them. Harry chose his career. Yvonne chose her freedom from a relationship in which she would play second fiddle to Harry's work. She walked out that night, and Harry went to Honduras as a young, starry-eyed Secret Service agent.

And several months later, Yvonne was Mrs. George Chartrain.

"Oh, they didn't have any children," Sally was replying, and Harry wondered if the sense of elation tingling through him could be discerned by the smile of wonderment on his face.

His room looked exactly the same. Nothing had changed. The furniture, his bookshelves, his butterfly collection, his school athletic awards and pennants. It was all intact. He pictured his mother coming up there at least once a week to vacuum, to dust, to polish, to make sure the windows were sparkly clean. He thought of her picking up a photograph here, a book there, holding them, stroking them, living with her memories.

Have I let these wonderful people down, he asked himself.

For the sake of nostalgia, he withdrew a photograph album from one of the lower shelves and began going through it, page by page. He had mounted the photos himself, making sure each was identified as to date, location and circumstance.

Hah, he chuckled. Skiing in Squaw Valley. Swimming in the hotel pool in Guadalajara. A picture of himself receiving a trophy in forensics as a high school sophomore. He and Yvonne at the family piano. A whole page of photographs of a vacation in Zermatt. Yvonne in her ski suit, waving to him from the top of a slope. A group picture of Mr. and Mrs. Carroll with young Harry and the lovely teenaged Yvonne, in the company of a good-looking man with short, dark-blond hair, wearing a tuxedo, and identified as Igor Matlov. Harry looked long and hard at that photo. There was something compelling and stirring about it. The memory was a particularly powerful one.

Tucked into the album's centerfold was a large, flat envelope, yellowing with age. Harry's fingers trembled slightly as he removed it and opened the flap.

It was in there. The old photograph, fading now.

His heart jolting against his ribs, he withdrew the photo from the envelope and looked with burning eyes at the black-and-white picture of a young blonde girl of outstanding Old-World beauty.

"Ooooooh!" he heard himself gasp.

The gummed label which he had fixed to the bottom of the picture read, simply, "They said her name was Tanya. Tanya Ivanova."

The features were those which his mind had superimposed over the features of a man aiming a gun at him in Magdeburg.

The features of Captain Romayev...

The phone rang. Three times. Four. He was about to hang up, but paused when he heard the receiver lifted.

"Hellooooo?"

Voices hardly ever change. There was the same musical resonance, ever so slightly nasal. The same, almost totally-imperceptible trace of a foreign accent still clinging, still tell-tale.

"Yvonne, you sound as lovely as ever."

A long, hesitant pause.

"Who is this, please?"

The additional delay was tantalizing.

"I'm crushed, Yvonne," he whispered. "You've forgotten me."

A silence. Then a tentative venture, a wisp of breath.

"Harry...?"

And, with growing confidence at the sound of his laughter, an emboldened shriek.

"HARRY!?!"

(Odessa)

Jane nursed her cognac, holding small sips between her tongue and palate, allowing the fire to enter her tissues and warm through to her brain. She had borrowed a sweater from Mira and sank deeply against the comfortable cushions of the old sofa, sniffing deeply of the sweet, comforting aroma from the wood Tobi had piled on the fire. He had been playing a self-reversing tape of Khachaturian's "Spartacus," and Shostakovich's Fifth, and tempting Jane with new helpings of *blini* and *vareniki*.

Each of my senses is singing a rhapsody, Jane thought. This is my home. These are my people. Why have I ever doubted?

They had been talking light politics, avoiding all truly serious questions. Jane smiled, knowing that Tobi—old Bolshevik that he was—had served his country well all his life, had succeeded in evading the periodic purges, and was a master in party dogma and Leniniana. While most Soviet citizens were by and large quite non-political, Tobi remained the absolute political and sociological animal.

With impatient gestures, Tobi was in the process of stating, "And if ever you are in conversation with Americans in the future, *Malyinki*, you should simply tell them that if they take their nuclear missiles into space, so will we! Tell them we can make a better investment of all those billions...

He stopped, hearing a cry of joy from the kitchen, and then the laughter of a young man dearly loved. Jane got to her feet.

Mira entered the living room, beaming, leading by the hand a flushed and excited Sergei, his suit soaked dark with rain, and his eyes searching...until they locked with Jane's.

The lamp beside her bed cast a golden glow to the area around her, but it was barely enough light by which to read. Exasperated, she put aside the book of poems by Pushkin which Mira had recommended, and was just reaching for the lamp switch when she heard the knob jiggle and the door opened an inch, Sergei gazing in at her from the cold, wet service porch where his parents had arranged an army cot with piles of extra bedding for his brief sojourn with them in Odessa.

Earlier that evening, she had celebrated the rhapsodic rejoicing of all her senses. But she remembered now the one which she had omitted—the sense of her womanliness. And with Sergei in the doorway, even that would have its moment of fulfillment. Dimpling, she beckoned him in. He closed the door noiselessly and tiptoed to her side.

"Brrrrr!" he exclaimed, shivering and rubbing his arms. "I can't make myself warm on that service porch open to the elements! Even with all those bedclothes...!"

She patted the side of her bed suggestively and held out her arms. There was still a boyishness about Sergei that had always appealed to her. Beholding his tall, athletic build, the neat cut of his dark hair, the way his long lashes cast even longer shadows on his cheekbones—everything within her stirred with yearning. He seated himself and stroked her pale hair.

"So, Sergei Karolievitch!" she whispered with devilish mirth. "Tell me what brought you on such an impromptu visit to Odessa!"

He took her in his arms and she melted against him, needing his love, needing to fill his need as well as her own.

"Just the thought of a beautiful woman," he murmured, his mouth brushing over hers. "A wonderful, beautiful woman whom I have starved for all these many years..."

Through the wall behind her head came the sound of Tobi's nocturnal coughing, and Jane put her finger to her lips, her eyes flickering with merriment.

"You see?" she whispered. "It's useless. The walls have ears. Your parents will hear every sound we make."

"Are you sending me back to the service porch, *Duschitzka*?"

"No. Come get under the covers with me," she giggled without sound. "But we cannot make love..."

"Impossible!"

"Don't you respect your parents? Do you want to embarrass them so that they cannot look at us in the morning?"

Her hushed whisper was serious, but she was shaking with suppressed laughter, and Sergei worked quickly with the buttons of his shirt, the buckle of his belt, until his clothes were in a disorderly heap on the floor beside the bed and he was snuggling against her in his cotton underwear, one hand finding the hem of her flannel nightgown and raising it to her chin so that she lay exposed and vulnerable to his touch.

"How can one woman be so beautiful?" he was murmuring against her cheek, his breath quivering with passion as he caressed her. "Is it because you are American-born that you possess such a monopoly on beauty, Ilyana?"

"Sssshhh, Sergei...We must be very quiet..."

His kiss was indeed quieting, his mouth and tongue working in harmony with hers in a silence that coursed clashing and roaring through both of their heads, while his fingertips traced ever so gently through the flaxen *mons* to the moist vulvar crevice.

"Sergei..."

"I love you, Ilyana," he breathed. "*Borzhamoya*, how much I love you...!"

When at last they lay still, nestling in each other's arms, Sergei asked her again to marry him, and she shook her head.

"Let's be happy with what we have, *Duschka*," she whispered. "We don't even know from moment to moment how long we will live. How can people like us think of the responsibility of marriage?"

"What do you mean...people like us? I teach school..."

"But I am an agent of our government, Sergei..."

"So you will give it up, Ilyana. You will give it up and put away your guns and your service citations...And you will learn to put together meals like my mother does..."

He was kissing her again, his passion re-kindled.

"Sergei, you don't know what you're talking about..."

"...and you will keep house for both of us in Moscow and lie waiting in bed for me every night, just as you are now..."

She stifled her giggles in spite of herself, returning his wild, brushing kisses and arching herself at the urging of his hands. How enchanting his proposal sounded! How safe, and sane, and sublime...!

Through the wall behind her came the sound of the telephone ringing. It rang twice. She placed one hand in the center of Sergei's chest, her eyes wide open, warning him to be still.

Tobi's muffled voice was heard briefly, then a hushed exchange with Mira, and a rapping of knuckles against the wall...

"Ilyanitchka...," called Tobi softly. "A call for you..."

Jane pressed Sergei to one side and pulled herself up, her rumpled nightie falling down over her nakedness.

"What is it?" Sergei demanded nervously. "Who is calling you at this hour?"

As if in answer to his son's whispered question, Tobi repeated his call, "Ilyana...?" adding, "Come quickly. It's Moscow..."

Breathless, Jane smoothed back her hair and straightened her nightgown, racing on bare feet across the icy cold floor to Tobi's room, where the black receiver of the phone lay waiting.

"One moment, Tobi," she called softly. "I'm coming..."

Chapter 15

(Washington, D. C.)

"I can't believe you're here...just across the table!" Yvonne exclaimed, smiling at Harry in disbelief. "And you haven't even changed! You're as devilishly good-looking as you were six years ago!"

He reciprocated, telling her she was even more beautiful than he remembered. They held hands, and the mixture of her musky perfume and the heady wine made his head whirl. He wondered if she were experiencing the same excitement, and what it would be like to hold her in his arms again. But that was preposterous! After six years of separation, did he really expect he could breeze back into town and climb back into her bed...?

Seated opposite her in the Joshua Tree Restaurant, he had applauded her bravado in dealing with her young widowhood, but her response had made him wonder how much of her poise was bravado and how much of it was relief.

"I realize your husband's death was fairly recent," he observed gently, "...and probably you still have a way to go before returning to the social scene..."

"Now, Harry...," she grinned, one long graceful finger tracing a circle in the palm of his hand, "...you know me better than that."

It was all he could do to sit still, and his voice was husky.

"Is there anyone special in your life at this moment, Yvonne?"

She fluttered her lashes and smiled at him.

"Up to this moment, there hasn't been."

Her home was palatial. Yvonne had come from wealth and George Chartrain has provided most handsomely for her. Looking about at the tasteful appointments and the museum-quality art pieces in her living room, Harry realized Yvonne would never have to worry about supporting herself appropriately in Washington's high society.

"Chivas Regal, right?" she asked, pouring for him, and they touched glasses, Harry complimenting her on the beauty of her home.

"Well, George had the brains and the push...and my parents were there to head him in the right direction," she stated, then slipped her arm around him, her lips drawing closer to his. "All this could have just as well been ours, Harry...yours and mine..."

She tasted as sweet as ever, and when, without another word, she led him by the hand up the circular staircase, Harry found himself following, meek, unprotesting, unquestioning...

Certain of her charms and her artistry, Yvonne knew what she was worth and demanded nothing less. The demure and playful coquetry of her young womanhood had been replaced by the eager confidence of the aggressive female. Harry had been with aggressive women before, and had always given more than he received. But Yvonne had been his first love, the first fantasy of his boyhood, and somehow, he hungered for that illusion and did not want to spoil it.

He found himself going through motions, wondering what was wrong with him. There he was, holding in his arms a woman whose flesh he had invaded ten thousand times in as many dreams, inhaling her perfume, the pungent brine of her arousal, feeling the pressure of her legs, the edge of her fingernails in his shoulders, and...*God damn!*

Limp and exhausted, he swore beneath his breath as he rolled away to stare up at the sculpted ceiling, his chest heaving, his mind blank, and when Yvonne edged close with her head propped in the upraised palm of one hand, he apologized, furious with himself.

"Don't, Harry," she soothed him. "You're probably just very tired. Or maybe you were over-excited and I came on a little too strong. People do change in six years, Harry..."

She reached for a cigarette in her nighttable drawer and for a few minutes, smoked in silence. Lamely, he stroked her arm.

"I'm sure this is just temporary," she assured him. "We were marvelous lovers, you and I."

"I know, Yvonne. I remember."

She inhaled deeply and blew smoke into the shadows.

"I thought I'd never forgive you for choosing your career over me," she chuckled, reminiscing. "Then Fate paid me back for walking out on you. I married a total workaholic, a complete Class A personality. He literally worked himself to death..."

Harry searched in her eyes for the hope, the dreams, the longing he had always found lingering in those emerald depths.

"Well, he gave you the life you wanted, Yvonne..."

"Yes," she sighed, looking around the commodious room with its exquisite decor. "I'm happy with this life, Harry."

He sat up then and began pulling on his clothes.

"I wish you'd consider staying the night," she said softly, but he knew she would make no demand she already sensed was futile.

"No, Yvonne...I'd better be going..."

She regarded him as he buttoned his shirt, and he smiled weakly, feeling strange and embarrassed, out of place.

"Tell me something, Harry. Are you really happy with your life? Running from one end of the globe to the other, living in all those hideous places, always in danger, risking your life…"

"It's what I chose, Yvonne. We each chose our dreams."

Accustomed to displaying her body, she made no attempt to cover herself, and in the lamplight looked like a modern Titian.

"And…in these years we've been apart…," she pressed further, "…have you found no other woman to love…?"

As she voiced her question, his mind flashed back to a stormy monsoon night in Luzon, to the haunting call of the Kiwi bird, to a small, pale figure in regulation camouflage attire, with wide-spaced amber eyes and dark hair streaming…

"Maybe I haven't found the woman I could make happy," he said, and his reply seemed to give her comfort. She gave him a bright nod and drew the sheets up over her.

"Will I see you before you leave D. C.?" she whispered, watching him slip into his suit jacket and lean over her to place a kiss on her forehead.

"If I can get away," he managed. "I'll be in touch…"

"Harry…," she called as he started for the door, and he paused to glance back at her over his shoulder.

"Please take good care of yourself," she said. "Promise."

(Moscow)

A diplomatic rendezvous on a Sunday was rare. KGB Chief Leonid Padorin had been in on the arrangements from the start. Deputy Minister Antonin Simovich had told him to stick around, then had phoned Ambassador Roger Dunn, addressing him in English.

"I'll have my car call for you at your residence," Simovich told Ambassador Dunn. "I don't want the press around. If you get here in your ambassadorial limo, flags flying, every child in Moscow will know something is up. I've reserved a table for noon at the Ukraina. My chauffeur will call for you at eleven."

Two other foreign ministers were present when the American Ambassador was escorted into the private dining room by a Russian military officer. Two militia men stood guard at the door. There were introductions all around, initiated by the Deputy Foreign Minister, himself. The KGB Chief was identified only as Leonid Padorin.

Dunn nursed a Scotch and water. Simovich tossed down a vodka in one gulp and ordered another. Padorin sipped a cognac, observing, listening.

Then Simovich got down to the heart of the matter, admitting that the USSR had learned of the mysterious disappearance of one of the USA's latest electronic inventions from a factory in California, and sneering, "Some of your irresponsible newspapers have openly accused agents of the Soviet Union of stealing this device. They have told the wildest cops and robbers stories, implicating some of our people."

Padorin watched the Ambassador's craggy face for traces of a smile betraying pride, or victory. He secretly feared the USA's reaction if events proved that Moscow was behind the theft. While his country had openly and brazenly oppressed Hungary, Poland, Czechoslovakia, to say nothing of the Baltic and Balkan nations, and had defied world opinion by marching into Afghanistan, the USSR somehow felt obliged to dispel the impression that they subverted, spied and stole when it came to matters of technological supremacy.

Simovich spoke with gestures, a high-strung, emotional man with a face too gaunt for his obese, paunchy body.

"Now, Mr. Ambassador...," he went on, "...if we deny it officially, your government will take it as an admission of guilt. If, however, I personally assure you that we do not have your miracle device, maybe Washington will accept our word."

Dunn, his features expressionless, nodded.

"I appreciate your concern, Minister Simovich. I will be glad to relay your word," he said.

"You will personally inform your President of our innocence in this matter?" Simovich inquired.

"I'll carry your message to the President," Dunn assured him.

"Good! Then we can relax over lunch!"

Padorin remained silent, eyeing the Ambassador as the men consumed a substantial meal and made small talk. Now and then, Dunn looked, to Padorin, like a man disappointed with the reason for which he had been summoned to the meeting. The theft of a microchip seemed of little import to him. Padorin wondered if Dunn were astute enough to suspect Russia's reluctance to be caught with a hand in the cookie jar while the other hand was busily activating another dozen intercontinental missiles.

As soon as the Ambassador left, Simovich handed out some excellent Cuban cigars to the two ministers he had asked to remain together with Chief Padorin.

"My reason for calling this meeting with the Ambassador, Comrades," he began, gesturing with his cigar, "is because there are things done by some of our underlings which are extremely uncivilized...and downright stupid. We don't, for example, take the United States head-on over every little insignificant matter. We accommodate them in small things and stubbornly maintain our position when it matters. Am I correct?"

Padorin listened as one of the ministers spoke up.

"From my experience, you throw the Yankees a bone from time to time and they fall all over you for months. American Presidents are elected on a platform of unyielding militancy against the Soviet Union, only to soften and become more pliable after two or three years in the White House. Much bark, but little bite."

Simovich was tapping his ashes into the tray at his knees, and he did not look up as he spoke.

"Comrade Padorin," he began, the smile leaving his face, "would you agree that the most important word in the vocabulary of the KGB is INTELLIGENCE?"

Padorin felt the blood rise in his cheeks and chose to remain silent. If this encounter, which had not been entirely unexpected, were to be confined to verbal abuse, he could bear that. But there could be other consequences...and those he feared.

"From a report I've received...," Simovich went on, "...the KGB and its operatives have used anything *but* intelligence in the matter of this so-called 'super-chip.' The job was bungled. The unit was destroyed before it reached us, and...worse yet...the Americans know full well it is in our hands."

"That is true, Comrade Minister," Padorin replied respectfully. "There were a number of complications...mistakes..."

"And what is the mighty KGB going to do about it?" demanded Simovich, brow furrowed, eyes squinting evilly.

One of the other ministers spoke his thoughts aloud.

"In days gone by, those responsible for the fiasco were purged! We do not need operatives who prove counter-productive...or for that matter, Chiefs..."

A light snow was turning to brown slush on the sidewalks of Moscow. From his office window, Padorin watched the weary citizens trudging in their boots and galoshes, the spatter of mucky water inevitable on the backs of their legs.

The Foreign Ministry had suggested his initiating a purge of those responsible for the loss of the computer. Padorin would have been more impressed with himself had he been able, at that moment, to advance another recommendation, or even to refute the veiled order with a solid piece of logic. It was an unhappy state of affairs. Unhappiness in the Kremlin often affected one's health, at the minimum. Frequently, it affected one's longevity.

The KGB Chief let the curtain fall back into place and returned to his birchwood desk, in front of which Admiral Romayev was seated with a portion of Igor Matlov's file on his lap. The Admiral appeared to be drained, spent of hope and energy.

"Interesting?" asked Padorin sarcastically. "The son of an Admiral in the Maritime Kommissariat of the Soviet Union, with offices in the Kremlin, has a son who is a Special Director with the Central Intelligence Agency of the United States! I ask you, is that interesting?"

"Yes, Comrade...," Romayev struggled. "But it only appears that way. It's a matter of coincidence..."

"Don't play me for a fool!" barked Padorin, the veins prominent across his forehead. "You knew your son was with the CIA! And you knew there was a file in Consul Matlov's possession! Although I cannot for the life of me understand why you did not eliminate Matlov years ago, to safeguard your secret!"

The Admiral looked like a man already sentenced to death and anticipating the arrival of the firing squad. He took a deep breath and looked up at the ceiling, as though to the Almighty, for help in offering his explanation.

"Comrade Padorin, please listen to me. I knew of my son's existence, as Harry Carroll, only until he was in his late teens and determined to study law. I knew of his refusal to visit the Soviet Union. Igor Matlov would have continued pursuing him all through undergraduate school and into law school. We even talked about it, Igor and I. It was proposed that Harry Carroll could possibly be tempted to return to our country if we promised him an eventual position with the World Court, working toward world peace..."

"Ridiculous! That was *ridiculous*! shouted Padorin.

"...but none of that ever came to fruition. In the meantime, Consul Tobirian had persuaded my daughter, Ilyana, to come here, and I could watch her progress from close at hand. When Harry Carroll received his law degree, graduating with high honors, Consul Matlov suffered a disabling heart attack. At that time, funding was scarce...the program for bringing Russian-ancestry youths back into the fold was heavily cut back...and I decided not to pursue any further attempt to induce my son to come here. I thought that the case was closed..."

"You thought! *You thought*!" Padorin screamed. "And so the moment Matlov died, you sent your aides to pick up his file! Because you knew what was in there...and how it would incriminate you...to say nothing of your daughter!"

Romayev sprang to his feet, trembling.

"Ilyana knows nothing of this! *Nothing*!"

"You're a liar, and a bad one, Romayev!"

"I swear!" cried the broken naval officer. "Ilyana does not know that CIA Director Carroll is her brother...!"

Padorin's eyes bulged with anger as he pounded on his desk. "Doesn't she? *Doesn't she?*" he roared. "Then in Magdeburg, where he destroyed the computer, and she had the chance...*why didn't she kill him?*"

Romayev's eyes opened wide and he stared at the aging KGB chief. For a few moments, he digested what Padorin had just said, then reached out to the back of his chair to brace himself from falling.

"You are telling me...," he whispered hoarsely, "...that they *met*, Ilyana and her brother...?"

"You're a pathetic actor, Romayev!" Padorin hissed.

But his insult was tactical. Observing the ghastly look on the Admiral's face, Padorin was not at all sure that Romayev was merely acting out his stupefaction. He watched the Admiral sink, drained, with a long, breathy moan, into his chair.

"You want me to believe Ilyana has not told you?" he demanded.

"I haven't heard from her. She went on vacation..."

"Yes, to visit the Tobirians in Odessa. We know. I've been in touch with her..."

Romayev raised his eyes in supplication to the KGB chief.

"Ilyana knows nothing, Leonid," he choked. "Believe me..."

For just a moment, Padorin let down his guard and became a human being instead of a police state functionary.

"Yuri," he said, in a gentler tone. "Listen to me. Ilyana, as Captain Romayev...according to the pilot's report and her own admission...aimed her gun at Director Carroll's head. He was well within range. And she never fired..."

There was a low moan from Romayev. He sagged to one side.

"And...even worse, Yuri...your son, CIA Director Carroll...never fired at *her.*"

(McLean, Virginia)

The muted hospital TV seemed respectful of the incessant silence. The odor of lysol disinfectant rising from the floor of the corridor permeated the carpeted room. A narrow floor-to-ceiling window looked out on a concrete walkway with an attractive arrangement of shrubs and plants. From time to time a crow hopped down from one of the hospital eaves and found something to peck at among the bushes.

Nurses had admitted him, advising him Miss Soubrine was still in physical therapy and would be back in less than thirty minutes. Would he wait? Did he want a magazine?

Yes, thank you, to both questions.

Harry wondered why he felt guilty about having seen Yvonne. Clearly, the woman had invited him, no doubt about that. And, thinking back, he had to admit that he still found her desirable... Why, then, the feelings of guilt? Whom had he betrayed? And why, for the first time in his virile life, had he failed with Yvonne?

I'm losing my touch, he told himself with regret.

I don't have it any more, the cold dispassionate selfishness of the successful Secret Service operative.

I could have killed Romayev in Magdeburg. Why didn't I?

With patience, it might have been something memorable with Yvonne. Why wasn't it?

Yvonne had asked him if he had found no other woman to love. Something in the phraseology of that question had cut sharply through him at that moment. No other woman? Or...a woman other than herself? And he had instantly flashed on the young, trusting CIA fledgling, testing her wings on her first mission in a South Pacific monsoon, placing her safety in his hands.

He thought of that moment on the Magdeburg airstrip, when the Bulgarian's bullet had struck Natalie, and how she had collapsed face forward on the macadam, drawing her knees up as she lost consciousness. He remembered thinking she was dead, and how the very thought was agonizing. He had told Powell Wright that he 'didn't really give a damn about anything any more' when he thought he had lost Natalie...

I'm juggling too many emotions at once, he told himself.

There was a shuffling sound in the corridor and Harry looked up as Natalie, in a pink cotton wrap-around, entered the room with a nurse close at her elbow in the event she became weak and lost her balance. A look of utter delight crossed her lovely face when she found him sitting in front of the window.

"Harry! What are you doing here!" she cried happily.

He stood up to offer the nurse assistance in helping Natalie back to bed, but the nurse waved him off, and he re-seated himself. In a rather fortunate position for the accomplished *voyeur*, he discovered, watching from that angle as Natalie, her long legs anchored innocently apart and raised, allowed for the re-tucking of the blanket. For one heated moment, he caught the pale pink blur of an inner thigh, a vague tuft of dark hair...

"Well, don't you think I damn well ought to be here?" he laughed to conceal his prurient thoughts. "After all, we almost came to the end of the line together in East Germany, didn't we?"

Looking pleased, she shrugged against the pillows.

"Don't get me wrong, Director Carroll," she purred. "I'm very glad you're here."

"Have they said anything about when you'll be released?"

"They want some more X-rays before I go. And they say I'll have to take things easy for about a month and then come back for plastic surgery."

"Plastic surgery?" he asked, surprised.

Her hand fluttered to her breast.

"Yah. Seems I have a hole in my boob. They want to do a skin graft to patch it over."

Chuckling, Harry moved to the edge of her bed and she shifted aside to give him room to sit down. He glanced casually at the twin points poking against the cotton gown.

"I'd say any girl with a hole in her boob would have to be worth her weight in gold on the streets of Paris," he laughed.

"T'aint funny, Harry Carroll," she giggled despite herself. "Unless I have the plastic surgery, I'll never be able to wear a bathing suit without everyone staring at me..."

"They'd stare no matter what..."

"...or a low-cut evening gown when I'd attend any of those Washington galas you'll be taking me to."

His laughter faded away. He pictured himself arriving at a brightly-illuminated banquet hall in some fashionable Washington hotel—he, in a tux, and at his side—lambent shoulders bare over a black satin gown—a gorgeous and radiant Natalie...

He glanced again at the heaviest bulge of bandages, an inch or so above the nipple. The bullet had fragmented off the vertebrae and lodged in the upper lung. Scant inches to the center, to the left, it would have hit the heart.

"Listen, young lady," he said, clearing his throat. "You get well and come on out of this prison. I hear Powell Wright is planning some kind of special citation for you. You may wind up in Washington at a desk job yet, Soubrine..."

"Well, that wouldn't be much fun," she pouted.

"Why not?"

"Not if you're off on assignments everywhere else in the world," she said, leveling with him. "I want to be close to you."

Frank revelations of her feelings had always evoked jocular sarcasm from him, to place a definite barrier between them. But since the incident on the airstrip, Harry had not been feeling the same about many things. He slipped his arm around her shoulders, making sure it was her uninjured side that he drew close to him. They exchanged a grave, searching look, then he kissed her forehead and the tip of her nose, waiting for her giggle. She was silent.

"You're close to me, Nat," he whispered. "Very close."

Chapter 16

(Moscow)

"I want to go with you!" Sergei protested as Jane began sliding out of the car. "I don't want you up there alone!"

"You can't come with me, *Duschka*. This isn't an ordinary job. Your father has told you about Leonid Padorin."

"How soon will this meeting be over?" he demanded.

"I have no idea. I simply promise I will be at your apartment this evening, or I will telephone you."

"You promise, Ilyana?"

"I promise."

"Come here."

She leaned in and found his mouth, warm and sweet. There was stark concern in his eyes when they drew apart. She blew him another kiss and shut the car door behind her.

Her heart vibrated unevenly as she made her way to the gray brick office building with its narrow, dark windows.

What did Padorin want of her? So she had failed to kill the American CIA Director! So what of it! Yes, it was a judgment error, she acknowledged that without difficulty. But she had brought the unit back to Moscow. Damaged, yes, but in its crate. If the computer whiz kids in the Kremlin's science laboratories were worth their salt, they'd study the unit and its chip and put it back together again. She had risked her life! All *they* had to risk were a few hundred man hours of analysis!

The officer behind the reception desk in the vestibule announced her arrival, and Jane heard Padorin's voice on the intercom, stating, "Send her in."

He was seated at his birchwood desk when she entered and he did not rise and come forward to greet her as he generally did. She swallowed hard and looked at him through hooded eyes as he gestured her to a seat and lit a cigarette. There were stacks of files and reports on his desk. She wondered if they had to do with her situation, her predicament.

"Did you enjoy your stay in Odessa, Captain?"

Oh, so this was to be quite formal. He was not addressing her by her first name. She considered addressing him as Colonel.

"Yes, it was quite pleasant," she replied.

"The Tobirians are well, I take it?"

"Quite well. They send regards."

Padorin nodded grimly and looked out the window.

"You flew back with their son, Professor Sergei Tobirian, who teaches here in Moscow?"

"Yes. We're old friends."

"Just...old friends?" he probed.

"For now. Perhaps, someday, we will marry."

Padorin, rose, his hands clasped behind his back and walked in a slow circle completely around her chair to unnerve her.

"Captain Romayeva, while you were in Odessa, did you give any thought to the incident that occurred on the Magdeburg airstrip?"

"Yes, I did..."

"And what conclusions did you reach?"

Jane's teeth were on edge, and she wet her lips. She felt a pulse throbbing in her throat, perspiration trickling down the sides of her chest.

"I still don't understand exactly what happened there."

"You were hypnotized, perhaps?" he suggested.

"No, Colonel Padorin...nothing like that..."

Padorin did not wait for her to finish her statement. He rummaged through the files on his desk and seized one, thrusting it toward her.

"Do you know this man?"

On the top page of the inches-thick file he pushed into her hands was a grainy photograph of Harry Carroll. It jarred her to see that face, so much like her own, pale eyes staring at her.

"This is...," she began, pointing to the photo, "...this is CIA Director Harry Carroll. The man I saw at the airstrip."

"The man who destroyed the computer! Who killed two of our agents! The man you permitted to get away...unscathed!" he hissed.

Jane closed her eyes and remained silent. What did he want?

"Do you have any idea how important this man is to the Central Intelligence Agency of the United States? Do you know what he has cost the Soviet Union?"

Jane felt a familiar tightness start in her chest. She took a deep breath to calm down, her nerves twitching.

"I know nothing about him," she said. "Only his appearance..."

"Yes, his appearance! We'll get to that in a moment!"

He stood beside her chair, his strong breath powerful in her nostrils as he bent over the file in her lap, flipping the pages and pointing to the pictures.

"Here! Look, Captain! This was the Salang Tunnel in Afghanistan! The tunnel through which we supplied our troops. A passageway of tremendous importance to our war effort. Now...look here! This was taken the morning after Director Carroll and his mercenaries blasted the Salang Tunnel and massacred Soviet troops who were just entering! Do you see?

Do you see, Captain Romayeva? Look at the faces of the dead! Murdered by Harry Carroll!"

Jane was gasping. She didn't want to look at the gruesome photographs any longer. She wanted to get up and walk about. She needed *air!*

"Then obviously, I'm not the only one who failed to eliminate this Carroll!" she exclaimed, gathering new strength. "Why did none of these crack troops finish him off?"

Non-plussed for the moment, Padorin straightened up, then returned to his deliberate attack on her nerves.

"Only two days ago, we captured the new Station Chief, Taylor, at the CIA's Station in Islamabad. Taylor was not the same calibre of Harry Carroll. He was easy to break. Men like Carroll are often difficult to replace in sensitive positions."

Jane pushed herself up out of her seat.

"Please, I need air. May I use your bathroom?"

Padorin took in the frightened, white face, the gleam of perspiration on her forehead and the sides of her jaw. He placed his hand beneath her elbow and assisted her to the private door of his toilet, telling her not to be long.

Inside the yellow chamber, she relieved herself and rinsed her hands in the corroded sink. The medicine cabinet mirror above it was messy and badly in need of re-silvering, but she could see the terror etched in her features. I must calm down, she told herself. I must not let him do this to me. She brushed some rouge across her cheekbones and smoothed back her hair. Then she returned, refreshed, and sat down.

Padorin held out the file to her, thumping at it with the tips of his fingers. But he did not force it into her lap.

"Account after account, over the past five years," he told her. "Afghanistan was just the most recent. Carroll's name has become synonymous with the enemy's. In the Middle East. In Marseilles. In North Africa. In Zimbabwe. I could go on and on."

"Then why are you holding me totally and solely responsible for permitting the man to escape? Obviously, this Carroll leads a charmed life! Why are you holding me accountable for not having shot him? I've already admitted my negligence...owned up to my error! Now, seeing those pictures, hearing those accounts, I wish with all my heart that I *had* killed him!"

The ensuing silence thundered in her ears.

Padorin was looking at her with cold, cruel eyes.

"And *that* will be your redemption, Captain Romayeva," he gasped, and she did not comprehend what he had said.

"My...my redemption...?"

With a sigh, Padorin returned to his desk and stood looking hard at her, arms crossed in front of his chest.

"I may as well tell you...You know how the KGB handles those agents who fail in their assignments...who make costly mistakes."

A chill coursed through Jane. She looked down at her quivering hands and clenched her fists in her lap.

"The office of the Foreign Ministry has suggested you be purged," Padorin told her quietly, and Jane lurched forward, one hand fluttering to her throat, her eyes pleading.

"What of my record?" she wept. "Is no consideration given to my past accomplishments, the merits I've already earned? How can you crucify me this way for failing to kill a man whom nobody else has been able to eliminate...?"

Padorin stood deep in thought. She had made a case for her defense, he felt, but he could not acknowledge it. Her weeping softened something in the steel of his heart. He remembered the secret photographs taken of her in the American orphanage, when she was only an infant. He recalled a photo of her in a tutu, when she was five years old and enrolled in a dance class—Ballet for Beginners. The beautiful woman seated before him, face streaked with tears, eyes begging mercy—asked again and again why she had been singled out.

Suddenly, she found him standing before her. He took her face in his two hands, brushing at her tears, then held her forehead gently to his middle as he smoothed back her hair.

"In the eyes of the Soviet Union," he whispered, "you have more reason than anyone else to eliminate this man. And, yes, that will indeed be your redemption..."

He spoke softly as he stroked her, and she sensed that he had relaxed the formality between them, at least for the moment.

"...I will convince the Foreign Ministry that you are to be given another chance. You will seek out CIA Director Harry Carroll, and you will kill him. That will save your life, Ilyana."

Jane put her arms around the old man's waist and hugged him, thanking him for the favor bestowed upon her.

"I'll do it," she choked. "If that's the way I can rectify what went wrong in East Germany, then I have no choice..."

Her cheeks were awash with tears and she tugged at his hand, forcing him to look into her eyes.

"But tell me, Leonid," she wept. "We've known each other many years. Tell me, as a beloved uncle would tell a niece...why is this assignment being required of me exclusively?"

Padorin's eyes were grave. He cupped her chin in his hand and tried to smile, but faltered.

"You don't know?" he asked. "You really have no idea...?"

In the instant before he spoke again, Jane's mouth fell open as the realization which had been niggling at the back of her brain came ringing into full-blown reality, and she cried out.

"Ilyanitchka...Harry Carroll is your *twin*."

(Washington, D. C.)

The thoracic surgeons were satisfied with the CAT-scan and ultrasound studies. Natalie's lung was mending and they released her with instructions that she see them weekly for about a month while they discussed the plastic surgery required to repair the disfigured breast.

Powell Wright, himself, joined Harry at the sanitarium when she was released, joking with her about Harry's formal installation as Director, which would shortly be coming up, and inviting both of them to his home for dinner that evening.

"A bit of a celebration. After all, if what you did in Magdeburg could be publicized, you two would be national heroes."

Natalie had been given the choice of hotel accommodations arranged by the Agency, or a small efficiency apartment in Arlington, and she had opted for the latter. The DCI's dinner invitation overwhelmed the girl.

"It sounds wonderful," she beamed. "And boy, am I in the mood for a party. May I bring champagne, Sir?"

"Only if you feel so inclined," smiled Wright. "And you, m'boy?"

"Well, I'd kind of been hoping for a ticker tape parade," he grinned, "...but I'll settle for dinner at your house tonight, Chief, if I may contribute the caviar."

"Fine! Haven't had good caviar in ages! My wife'll give me the dickens, but please, my young friends...suit yourselves!"

The Wrights expected them for cocktails at seven. He would shop for the caviar and pick up Natalie, not necessarily in that order, about six. They would dine, talk about assignments— past, present and future—and then he would drive Natalie home. Early, because she needed her rest.

Close interplay with the girl was coming to an end. Soon he would be installed as the new Director, the cocooned boss of special operations. He would be expected to keep his distance from those who reported to him, including Natalie. The longer they had worked together, the stronger had grown his affinity with the young woman, the comradely understanding. Or had it become more...?

He dismissed those thoughts. Standing at the pinnacle of his career, he could not afford any enmeshment in a complicated love relationship. He did not want to own Natalie Soubrine, nor did he want her to put in a serious claim for his attention. However, he had caught himself, more often than he cared to admit, fantasizing about making fierce, passionate love to the girl. Thinking of the injury to her breast and the glimpse of a very private portion of her anatomy in the sanitarium certainly didn't help matters.

"I have to get her out of my system," he told himself as he parked in front of the store Natalie had chosen from the Yellow

Pages. "Design International" was described as being the source of everything in imports, from Russian caviar to Swiss chocolate.

"If you don't find it here, it won't be in Washington," Natalie said as they entered the large, elegant establishment on Connecticut Avenue. She would select her bottle of champagne and get a charge out of Harry's impeccable manner in ordering...

"I like my caviar firm and well defined," he told the Scandinavian sales clerk when he learned that the store stocked quite a variety. "It should have a smooth, creamy texture and a clean sea taste."

The middle-aged *Svenska Flicka*, her Nordic aloofness challenged by a customer who knew what he wanted, recommended a Sevruga Four Star.

"I hope it's fresh, not pasteurized," Harry nagged.

"Fresh, with firm grains and the taste of a sea breeze," she told him, adding, "The tin is one hundred twenty-eight dollars, if you're interested."

"I used to get twice as much for five bucks," Harry laughed.

"Not here in Washington," the Swedish sales clerk protested.

"In Iran," Harry whispered, cupping his hand to one side of his mouth as though imparting a secret of national proportions to her. "Before we allowed the bearded dervish to take over."

Regarding the Swedish woman's face, Natalie could only guess at what was going on behind those watery-blue eyes with the invisible lashes, but she could see what passed for Scandinavian fascination in that face.

"I'll put some dry ice in the insulated bag to keep it fresh," Harry was told with great courtesy as they prepared to leave.

Natalie was still giggling when they returned to the car with their acquisition of champagne and caviar, knowing that Powell Wright would be impressed with their offering no matter what his wife had to say.

"Some day, Harry Carroll," she announced blithely, "...you're going to impress a woman so much that she'll never let you out of her clutches."

Amused, and struggling to maintain the mock-distance between them, Harry went along with the prognostication, giving it a twist.

"That sounds interesting," he agreed. "But just tell me one thing, Soubrine. Which part of a woman's bed is the clutches?"

(Moscow)

Yuri Romayev stood at the window of his three-room apartment, looking down at the square. The light snow had turned to sleet and then softened to rain, and the streets displayed the shimmer of the few colorful neon lights boasted by several store fronts. He saw the taxi stop and the slim young woman emerge, take care of the fare, then start toward the entrance of his tenement. As she approached and became lost to his view beneath the overhanging ledges, he noticed a shiny black Zim automobile pull to a stop across the street and remain parked at the curb. From his window, Romayev could see two men clad in black raincoats seated up front.

So it begins, he thought. The final act. The circle closes.

The moment he opened the door and saw her face, he realized she had been told.

"Papa!" she choked, and he caught her in his embrace, rocking her like a child until they both regained composure. Then she sat quietly, staring into space, while he prepared a strong vodka over ice for each of them.

"Have you known all along?" she asked him gently.

"I knew he existed, but only as a boy, a student," her father said. "When you first came here, and Matlov fell ill the first time, I lost track of your brother. He seemed to vanish from the face of the earth."

"But surely, you could have found him again," she pressed.

"I might have," Romayev despaired, "...with my private funds. But I was so happy knowing you were here...that you were one of us, I didn't want to spoil anything. I just thought...someday, if my son surfaced...that would be all well and good. But I never dreamed he had been recruited into the CIA."

"Why not?" Jane rasped bitterly. "It runs in the family."

The Admiral sat in silence, hunched forward, his hands idle in his lap. He felt fear for his daughter, fear for himself. And the fear was agonizing.

"Now what, Ilyana?" he asked dully. "What happens now?"

"I have been offered an alternative to dying," she replied.

Of course. This was the way it was done. He knew that.

"And the alternative is?"

Jane got to her feet and went close to him, placing a cool hand on the back of his neck, massaging his back to comfort him in the pain gripping them both. It was some time before she spoke.

"My orders are...to kill Harry Carroll," she whispered.

Her father turned to her. Words would not come. Tears welled in his eyes and trickled down his roughened cheeks.

"I could not kill him in Magdeburg when I didn't know who he was," she whispered. "How can I kill him now...when I know that he and I were conceived together...?"

It was pouring when she arrived at Sergei's. Unable to find a taxi, she had walked a number of blocks and had taken public transportation to reach him.

"You're soaked through," he exclaimed. "Get out of those wet things and let's get you dry! It's freezing out!"

His single room was warm and cozy, but she shivered as she removed her clothes, peeling her underwear from her drenched body. Sergei came running in from the community bathroom with a large Turkish towel and wrapped her up in it, rubbing its deep nap all over her shivering form. He rummaged through her suitcase for a flannel nightgown and she donned it quickly.

"Hurry, get into bed!" he panted, drawing the blanket snug beneath her chin, then holding her close, giving her his warmth. He could tell she had been crying.

"Tell me what happened," he pleaded. "How can I help?"

"You can't help me, *Dorogoi*," she whimpered. "They're sending me away again, maybe for a longer time than before. And I will miss you, Sergei..."

She felt comforted by his strong arms, feeling the support, the protection, the love they offered. She knew she had made a mess of her life through a succession of improbable choices. And quite possibly, the strands of her life had been knotted into an inextricable tangle even before her birth. But perhaps Sergei Tobirian was the catalyst to unwind it all—to work out all those ugly snags and catches and make everything smooth and stable—for both of them.

"Can't you refuse, *Duschitzka*? Must you go?" he begged.

"I must go, my love."

He held her gently, their hearts beating in unison, and made no demand upon her for sexual intimacy. It was enough just to be close, to know the sweet reciprocity of the love that had developed between them over the years.

"Then, when you return, I'll speak to your superiors," Sergei announced in all seriousness, the utopian naivete of his Marxist upbringing making him believe he would be dealing with humane and reasonable men. "I'll tell them we're in love and wish to marry, and that they must release you. They will not refuse us that request, Ilyana."

Jane shut her eyes to discourage new tears and hugged him close, loving him for his idealism, his innocence.

She thought of the big black sedan that had followed her through the blustery streets, from her father's apartment to the place where she boarded the street car. Once inside the yellow-lit vehicle, she held on to a strap at the rear and peered through the rain-streaked glass as the sedan continued its pursuit close behind. She studied the men in the dark raincoats. One of them had been her aide on an assignment the year before. An ambitious, ruthless young man, she recalled—now stalking more selective game.

Tenderly, she stroked Sergei's hair and brushed her lips across his brow. She would not divest him of his innocence, his idealism...

"Yes, Sergei," she whispered through her heartbreak. "How could they refuse such a request...?"

Chapter 17

(Washington, D. C.)

The new agency's headquarters was located in a modern building on the corner of Fourteenth and "F" Streets, and for its cover, had been designated by the CIA as the "Capital City Engineering Company." In a flurry of activity, its communication equipment, including telex and computer terminals with hot lines linked to the rest of the intelligence community, was hurriedly installed.

Personnel ranging from clerk-typists to communication experts and computer analysts had transferred in from other agencies, and had gathered in a conference room to meet their new boss for the first time. The jobs sounded interesting, secure from physical risk, and were said to have presidential blessing— the new organization's main purpose to stop the theft of advanced technology—all of which meant good pay and a wide-open, optimistic future.

"I don't know if I'll be able to pull it off, Nat," Harry told the girl over coffee and apple pie in the building's cafeteria earlier that morning. She had insisted on paying for breakfast, to celebrate his formal appointment to the exalted position, equal to the head men at the FBI and the CIA. "I don't know if I can turn a bunch of raw recruits into an effective, smooth-running organization."

"If anyone can do it, you can," she whispered over the rim of her coffee cup, her eyes full of frank admiration.

Natalie was by no means yet ready to return to work, but there was no way she would be absent from Harry Carroll's first official act as Director of his own crew. Bert Klemmer was also on hand for the auspicious occasion.

Receiving the warm support of his dear friends, Harry straightened his tie, smoothed back his hair and walked directly to the podium, maintaining what he hoped looked like an air of control and authority. Tapping the microphone for silence, he called his people to attention and saluted them as a select group whose job would be to put an end to one of the most dramatic ills threatening the nation.

"...I'm talking about the theft of high technology, the only thing we have left to assure our military and economic survival."

His eyes moved from face to face as the new personnel listened attentively, and, satisfied they were a good group, he continued.

"The life blood of our technological fortune has been methodically syphoned from us in a period of a few short months:

"Item One. A court in Luebeck, Germany, convicted three men who were part of a far-reaching network of companies used for illegal shipments of American computers. The shipments wound up in Russia. The three men were about to send a two-million dollar Digital Equipment Corporation computer, via a Swedish freighter, to the USSR. The contraband was seized in Hamburg Harbor.

"Item Two. British officials seized a computer valued at three quarters of a million dollars on a dock in Poole, England, where it was about to be loaded on a vessel for export to Czechoslovakia. Two men, both directors of a British electronics company, were charged with attempting the illegal export of sensitive equipment to Eastern Europe.

"Item Three. A computer containing a brand new, highly-strategic Speech Recognition and Command chip was stolen by agents of the People's Republic of China..."

Harry mentioned brief details of the pursuit of the SRC chip, beaming directly at Bert and Natalie who stood together at the rear wall of the conference room. The new employees had learned of the ordeal both agents had survived, and—noting Harry's glance—turned their heads to applaud the two people whose contributions their new boss was acknowledging—and Harry applauded, too, his eyes meeting Natalie's across the room, his glance locking with hers.

"I could go on and on offering examples of what's happening to our technology," Harry went on when the hubbub quieted, "but I'm sure by now that's not necessary. I need dedicated, motivated men and women, people willing to work hard and risk much. We need teamwork, devotion to duty and respect for authority, and I demand discipline of those who work with me. If any of you wish to reconsider, you may return to your former positions, and for those who remain, I can promise only a long uphill battle, with many risks and frustrations..."

He mentioned small personal rewards and asked for questions. A spokeswoman for the group inquired if any employee would ever find himself at personal risk—the risk of attack in his own home.

"Yes, no doubt about it," Harry replied speaking over a flurry of exclamations sparking through the assemblage. "Technological theft, like terrorism, is a new kind of warfare. Keeping the fox from the coop is no easy job, and it does have its risks."

He resisted the temptation to turn the occasion into a lecture on the hazards of intelligence work, and when there were no further questions, decided he had shocked them sufficiently for one day.

Hell, he thought, give me a shoot-out in Magdeburg any day over this kind of pressure as he left the podium to return to his office, where he pressed a handkerchief to his forehead and waited for the group to file out of the conference room.

"Great talk, Chief," Bert Klemmer congratulated him.

"You were superb, as usual," murmured Natalie in her low, sultry voice. The touch of her cool hand in his sent an electric shock through his system. He wanted so much to kiss her.

*   *   *   *

(Moscow)

Deputy Foreign Minister Simovich lighted a Cuban cigar, which to Padorin meant he was deciding on a new approach. The KGB chief's palms were moist as he clutched at the arms of his chair in the spacious office. He understood quite well the pecking order of authority. He was part of it. At this moment, it was his turn to be under fire. Even Nikita Khruschev had experienced the ordeal of criticism and the horror it generally implied. That came with the job. Everyone in the Kremlin knew that.

"Think she'll do it?" Simovich asked, relaxed with his smoke.

"She has no choice, Comrade Minister."

"I disagree, Leonid. You forget that Ilyana Yurievna Romayeva was born in the United States. Her roots are American. The man is her twin brother..."

"...but she's never known him, Comrade..."

"...I say again, and don't interrupt me, Comrade Padorin, the man is her twin brother. She may feel a natural reluctance to carry out her orders."

"I've left her no choice. I've made it clear she has no alternative. That the Foreign Ministry has decided she is expendable."

Simovich gestured with his cigar, smiling with irony.

"What you seem to forget, my old friend, is that Captain Romayeva *does* have a choice. She'll be in her homeland. She can throw herself on the mercy of that government and plead for asylum. What will you think *then*, Leonid?"

"She won't do that, Comrade Minister. There is a young man here. A university professor. They are lovers..."

Simovich cut him off with a contemptuous snort and a disgusted wave of one hand, his voice taking on a thin, high pitch.

"Your bourgeois sentimentality amazes me, Padorin," he sang in exasperation. "Romayeva is a woman, with her life at stake. With a gun at her back, and with a choice of returning to her Soviet lover...or sanctuary in the land of her birth...which will she choose? Don't be an idiot, Comrade. A woman who looks like Captain Romayeva can find a hundred Americans eager to fiddle between her legs."

Padorin was drenched with perspiration, despising the coarse vulgarity of his superior. But he had to admit the man had a valid point. Casting about for something else with which to support his contention, he suggested, "Her father is here. You are forgetting Admiral Romayev, who has served us well."

Simovich again gestured with contempt.

"Yuri Romayev is an old dove, and has made mistakes. His daughter did without him the first sixteen years of her life. She can live quite contently without ever seeing him again."

Padorin tried to relax, inhaling deeply. What was his superior hinting at? What more was expected of him now?

"Our major objective at this moment is the elimination of CIA Director Carroll. That goal is two-fold. First, we rid ourselves of a nuisance who's been a thorn in our sides, and who, with his new position and power, promises to become an even greater one in the future. Second, we teach the CIA a lesson...that no individual in their organization becomes such a sacred cow that we fear to martyr him. Do you understand, Padorin?"

"I understand, Comrade Minister."

Simovich placed the shaft of his cigar on the lip of his ash tray, leaning forward and hugging his bulky arms.

"So *you* go, Padorin," he stated quietly. "You haven't been back to San Francisco in a while. The trip will do you good."

Padorin leaned forward, beginning to see the plan.

"You want me to follow Romayeva, then? You want me to observe what she does? And if she fails to carry out her orders..."

"Then she dies, Padorin."

The KGB Chief swallowed hard. *His* would be the smoking gun. Evidently, his 'bourgeois sentimentality' was being tested.

"I understand," he managed. "And if she seeks sanctuary..."

"Then she dies, Padorin."

Yuri Romayev had felt a premonition all day, ever since Ilyana had phoned her goodbye, that he would have a visitor that evening. I'm spending a lot of time at windows these days, he admitted to himself. In my office. In my apartment. Always watching. Living with fear. Sleeping with it.

I am not as brave as my children, he thought. They must have inherited courage from their mother...

A light tap at the door brought him out of a reverie of Tanya. On tip-toes he crossed the room and paused, holding his breath.

"Who's there?" he croaked.

"Leonid. Let me in."

The old KGB man sat glumly on the sofa while Romayev prepared drinks. For a long while, nothing was said.

"This is not an official visit, Yuri Andreevitch."

"So I would presume."

"Ilyana has told you her orders?"

Romayev nodded grimly, an untouched drink in his hands.

"Do you think she'll do it? Kill her brother?"

The Admiral shrugged, looking aside to hide his emotion.

"You've given her no alternative. It's his death or hers."

"These are your children, Yuri. What are your thoughts?"

Romayev faced him squarely without hesitation.

"You wouldn't wish to experience them, Leonid."

Padorin saluted the Admiral with his drink, then sipped.

"I could have arrested you, Yuri," he said, "...for the incident with the Matlov file. I didn't do so out of friendship."

"I realize."

"You've long been aware of my affection for your daughter. No, not as an old lecher with concupiscent longings...But as a man who never had a child of his own. Ilyana is like a niece..." Romayev nodded.

"Her brother means nothing to me. That man is a menace to our efforts and must be done away with. It is Ilyana who concerns me."

"What are you telling me, Leonid?" the Admiral asked after a probing silence.

"It will happen this way. She'll receive messages, that you have been taken into custody. As an officer in the KGB, she knows what that will mean. She'll be torn between her love for you and her chance for survival in the United States. At that moment, she will be most vulnerable. She may hesitate in taking the life of Harry Carroll. It is at that moment that I...or some other agent whose identity I do not know at this time...will be obliged to kill her."

Painfully, Yuri Romayev got to his feet and paced the room, his hands deep in his trouser pockets.

"I see," he breathed. "If she is concerned for my welfare, it could cost her life."

"Exactly."

There was a long silence. Padorin rose, finished his drink. The men shook hands, their countenances grave.

"We've been friends a long time, Leonid," said Romayev. "I don't remember your ever giving me bad advice."

"Thank you, Yuri Andreevitch."

They hugged tightly, briefly. Then Padorin was gone.

The Admiral continued to pace alone in his room. He searched from his window for some ominous parked car, for the sight of a raincoated man leaning against a streetlamp, reading a newspaper. He could see nothing, but that was deceptive. He knew he was being watched. Sooner or later, there would be footsteps on the staircase and a sharp rap at his door. He would be arrested. The charge did not matter. His imprisonment would be relayed to a woman who was being forced to prove her value to the Soviet Union by assassinating her brother.

An emotional pincer, a game the Soviet Secret Police enjoyed playing. A game at which they were rarely known to fail.

The Admiral picked up a gilt-framed photograph of Jane in her smart uniform, her citation ribbons proudly displayed. Her eyes smiled at him, telling him of her love.

He had lived his life. Nothing mattered to him but Ilyana.

His desk drawer made a grating sound as he opened it. The pistol felt heavy in his hand. Very calmly, he drew back the bolt, his eyes on Jane's photograph. The metal felt cold against his lips.

Admiral Yuri Romayev never heard the shot.

*   *   *   *

When the stewardess came up the aisle a second time, Jane requested a blanket. She rarely felt cold, and attributed her chill to nerves. The flight would be long and tedious. Moscow to Helsinki to Tokyo to San Francisco. Then a day or two getting her bearings before proceeding to Washington.

When this is over, she told herself, I'll undergo open heart surgery. The faulty mitral valve will be corrected...

Had there been such a technique available thirteen years earlier, perhaps she would have been a mother. She would have been raising a son. Rudi's son. How beautiful he would have been...!

Oh, what am I thinking of! It had never been meant to be!

"Yours is a classic mitral stenosis," the cardiovascular specialist had told her two days before she embarked on her trip. "It can probably be successfully repaired. But I urge you to see to your rest. Avoid stressful situations wherever possible, and as soon as you begin to feel the familiar symptoms—the fibrillation—you are to stop whatever is taxing you and lie down. Do you understand what I'm saying, Captain Romayeva? This kind of arrhythmia is quite deadly."

I'll consult with him again, she told herself. When I return to Moscow, I'll talk it over with Sergei. He wouldn't be happy with an invalid for a wife.

A wife... Had she ever seen herself in the role of wife? A homemaker, like Mirabianka? And she and Sergei would adopt a child, a little boy. The orphanages were full of abandoned waifs discovered by Russian troops in the mountain retreats of Afghanistan. They were beautiful dark-eyed, dark-haired children, a mixture of the scores of Indo-European and Eurasian bloodlines that crossed through that area over the centuries. Those war orphans were being brought back to principal Russian cities by caring Soviet troops.

And the world said the Russians were uncaring beasts...!

She had been adopted as an infant. It would be only right for her to return that favor to an unbiased Universe. Cuddling beneath the thin flannel blanket, Jane smiled, trying to fall asleep. All would be well. She had been trained to think only in positive terms, to dispel all clouds of doubt. Harry Carroll was simply an enemy marked for assassination. She had never known him. She would carry out her orders and return home. She had carried out such instructions before, had made the prescribed "kill" without batting an eyelash, and walked away from the scene. It would be that way again this time. It *had* to be. She could not think of Harry Carroll as her father's son, or of the fetus who had lain entwined with her in the womb...

No country is perfect, she thought.

Not the United States. Not the Soviet Union. She had suffered the effects of deprivation in the United States, and had been rescued from that life by the Soviets. She was grateful to the Russian government for the life they had made available to her. But she was not a fool.

Jane admitted that during her years in Moscow she had learned well and succeeded brilliantly. But her eyes had remained open. It was clear to her that the same people who eloquently preached the gospel of Marx, Engels and Lenin were somehow ready and willing to exchange their ordinary blue ID cards for the red cards of the élite. While they piously extolled égalitarianism, they strained at every opportunity to be included in the ranks of the privileged. Jane had observed them in their chauffeur-driven limousines, discreet curtains hiding their faces, or shopping in Moscow's hard-currency stores, or leaving the dust and summer heat of the Soviet capital to find comfort and refuge in their snug little *dacha* in the country. No, Jane was neither blind nor insensitive to the subtle disparities in Soviet society.

How many times had she seen prisoners being shipped to Bolshaya Lubyanka or even to Sukhanov, the most evil of Soviet prisons, from which many went to certain death or to the insane asylum—hideous punishment for a lucid, healthy dissenter. If the political system could not stand open discussion or criticism, she reasoned, wasn't that a terrible admission of weakness? True, *"Glasnost"* and *"Perestroika"*—the newest slogans for increased intellectual candor fascinating and titillating the West—appeared like rays of hope. But were they just part of a Moscow phenomenon, or would those ideas indeed take hold throughout the vastness of the country. And, most important of all, would they last?

"Yes, I'll have tea," she told the stewardess, still chilled despite the blanket. Hot tea would help. And then she'd sleep.

Self-questioning had opened her innermost soul to her own scrutiny. That was dangerous. At KGB headquarters in Moscow, thoughts such as hers would be brought to the surface by injection, until one stood before one's inquisitors, drained and naked, hearing their denunciation as traitors to the Soviet regime.

Her various assignments in the United States had buried those doubts and given her a greater sense of assurance. It had worked well and lasted for some time, until the incident with the computer in Magdeburg.

Up to that point, her reputation as a dependable officer who "got the job done" had been impeccable. Her position, her apartment with its equipment and furnishings, the near limitless funds made available to her upon request—that all spelled the fulfillment of her mission. The commitment she'd made to the "Motherland" was emotional and ideological. Although one might have concluded that she had been brainwashed by her educators in Moscow, and by "Agitprop," (the apparatus known for its insistence in pounding the party line into the brain of every Soviet citizen), Jane had always remained her own person, neither an enthusiastic follower of the Party line nor an outright dissenter, but an opportunistic entrepreneur, capable of putting on a variety of believable acts.

From her impoverished childhood in New York Jane knew first hand how quickly the poor in America could be reduced to their true status of have-not proletarians, and sneered at by the bourgeois middle class. She knew that Marx, Engels and Lenin would point smugly at the mottos of American capitalists— "may the best man win" or "the survival of the fittest"—as words with which to befuddle the issues, to hide the wanton exploitation of the masses. Often she questioned whether she could have lived happily in such a society, disregarding her doubts about its inherent wickedness. Wasn't she too much the "child of the new era, the daughter of the laboring people"?

The capitalistic press reported with great glee the return of so-called "defectors" to their Russian homeland, and American reporters always questioned why fugitives from the Soviet system would give up their "freedom" and the benefits of the "American Way" and, by their return, demonstrate their preference for life in a socialist society.

Jane, herself, had experienced culture shock upon returning to the United States after years of schooling and indoctrination in Russia. The West would never understand "*toska*", that longing, that depression of spirit experienced by those living away from Mother Russia. It was an anguished yearning, Jane knew, afflicting all Russians living abroad. Hadn't Svetlana Alliluyeva, the daughter of Josef Stalin, decided to return to Russia after seventeen years in the United States, talking of "*toska*" and condemning the West as a place where she never was really free?

Journalists, Soviet soldiers fresh from fighting, artistic and cultural celebrities, sailors, tourists, and even KGB agents like herself—had defected to the West over the years. A multitude of them. All criticizing the Soviet regime bitterly. Only to succumb, in the end, to a strange, mysterious homesickness.

Jane knew her superiors in Moscow were aware of her deep enmeshment in the Soviet system. If Stalin's daughter had been welcomed back, after all the derogatory statements she had made about her motherland, why—when once she had carried out this mission—would she, Jane, not be accepted back in glory, and permitted to resume her career again, if she so desired? After all, she thought, Moscow seemed to be going out of its way to demonstrate to the world how forgiving it could be, by according high visibility and remarkably respectful treatment to the returnees. Would her situation be dramatically different?

No, she assured herself. She had nothing to worry about. She would pick up a couple of confederates, plan her attack, and, very neatly, in her usual flawless manner, would dispatch CIA Director Carroll.

But what if she failed? She had failed at Magdeburg, had she not? And her opponent this time was her equal, in every way. Sharp, intuitive, brilliant, orderly. If for some reason she failed...

Yes, then she would plead for asylum.

Chapter 18

(Washington, D. C.)

On the morning of the White House banquet, although he had responded that he and his "guest" would attend with pleasure, Harry awoke with the realization that he had not yet arranged for anyone to accompany him to the affair.

Naturally, he could attend alone. Many CIA people, estranged from spouses or living the totally uncommitted life, attended Washington parties stag, confirming that relationships were difficult for them.

But would that be fair? He had been included on the President's guest list because he had headed the team to make sure the stolen computer chip did not reach Moscow intact. Harry had made sure of that. But in the attempt, one man had died, another had been brutalized, and a third member had almost lost her life.

"Nat, it's me," he said when she answered the phone, and he could tell he'd roused her from a deep sleep. "I figured I'd better call you early, just in case you agreed..."

"Agreed to what?" she yawned. "What's going on?"
Harry swallowed, selecting his words.
"A banquet...tonight...at the White House. I hoped perhaps you would like to go with me..."

"I hate you," she told him when he picked her up. "I can only believe I'm your utterly last choice for tonight."
Before him stood a vision. She had been to the hairdresser. Natalie Soubrine could never have styled her hair so glamorously, swept up with dark, feathery tendrils lightly curled along her forehead and gypsy-like at her temples. Her nails had been manicured. And how she had managed to find just the right ball gown—a gold affair that not only tied over one shoulder, high and broad enough to conceal the still-fresh scarring, but that also matched her amber eyes—that was amazing on an ordinary Saturday in Washington! But, Harry knew, when Natalie had to something, she went right out and did it.
He complimented her on her loveliness as they walked to his car, and she teased him by asking what he had done to merit a Presidential invitation to a White House banquet.
"I have no idea," he replied, chivalrously helping her into the passenger seat before settling behind the wheel. "He's invited various artists, I understand. Powell Wright says it's a kind of 'recognition' night."
"The President must have heard about the circular target you drew on that computer crate, and the bull's eye you shot in its center," Natalie laughed. "If that isn't artistry, nothing is."
Upon arrival, a Marine opened the door for them and Harry was again inspired by his old love, his penchant for architecture, at the sight of the famous building. Their identities were checked and they passed through the metal detector, continuing to where the guests were assembling in the East Room. Powell Wright greeted them cordially and presented them to the President, who beamed with a particular appreciation for beauty at the radiant Natalie, and when Harry noted the girl's glistening

eyes, he felt good—extremely good—about having asked her to accompany him.

Honored guests included well-known celebrities. Tricia Palmer, the popular singer, her café-au-lait looks contrasting with her white silk gown, showed off her gleaming smile as she greeted other guests. Wynn Fowler, the senior newscaster, more avuncular than ever, engaged in unsmiling conversation with a group of other men. And Efim Pankowitz, the violinist, looked as unkempt and distracted as a virtuoso was expected to look.

"Thanks for sticking close, Chief," Harry told Wright as they mingled through the gathering crowd. "Natalie and I don't know any of these people. We feel out of place."

"I don't mind the celebrities, Harry," Wright said, helping himself to another glass of wine on a tray as it passed. "What gets me is the unconscionable garbage these people discuss. Lately, I've seen so much unabashed obeisance to power that I feel we're trying to outdo Buckingham Palace. The people around the President arc making a Caesar out of him. It's disgusting!"

"Powell, *please!*" came the sudden frantic whisper from Wright's wife, who had just overheard his closing remarks as she joined them, and Harry exchanged an amused smile with Natalie.

Assisting Natalie into her seat, Harry surreptitiously glanced at the embossed card beside the place setting. The menu was a mile long.

Crab claws with dill-mustard sauce
French onion soup à la Maison Blanche
Smoked salmon
Roast beef and Yorkshire pudding
Creamed asparagus tips
Candied sweet potatoes
Baked Idaho potatoes
Baked celery with slivered almonds
Braintree squash rolls

Brandied nectarines
Ice cream
Linzer torte à la Olga
Fruits
California wines
Cognac
Mocha

Harry could not help remembering the starving children of
Third World countries where he had lived for short periods of
time. Out of the corner of his eye, he saw the look of awe on
Natalie's face as a long line of waiters, on signal from the
President, marched into the room carrying huge steaming serv-
ing dishes.

The Marine Band String Quartet played light dinner music
and good-natured laughter filled the room as the feasting began.

Harry slipped one arm around Natalie's chair and touched
her shoulder, whispering, "Are you okay, Nat?"

"I'm in another world. Are we really here?"

The cool satin of her skin made his hand tingle and he nodded.

He had barely tasted the French onion soup when a messenger came up discreetly behind Powell Wright's seat and whispered something. The DCI excused himself to the people
around him and followed the messenger into another room.

A phone call of some importance, Harry guessed.

What else would disturb a man at a Presidential banquet?

The thought had scarcely begun to form in his mind when the
messenger returned and politely handed him a note, written in
the DCI's bold script.

*Urgent you follow at once to my office. Make
your excuses and bring Soubrine with you.
Repeat, urgent. P.W.*

"We have to go, Nat," Harry told the surprised girl, folding
his napkin on the table and helping her up. Accustomed to

inconvenient interruptions, she made no protest. Together, they left the elegant dining room and began the long, brisk walk out of the White House.

A double whammy. That was how Wright referred to the twin dispatches. The Station in Islamabad had been hit, and hard. Two operatives killed outright, along with several Afghani aides. Harry's replacement, Taylor, overcome and taken prisoner, had not been seen or heard from since the attack.

Harry winced. Had they killed Taylor? Had they gotten any information from him? What of Ranjit and Akbar Khan, those two superb Afghan chieftains! Were they gone, too?

"But there's more," Wright continued, his face ashen. "Our man in Moscow waited until the rumor was confirmed. Admiral Yuri Romayev was found dead Wednesday evening. Suicide. Blew his brains out."

That name again. Ever since the mission began, it had been blinking on and off inside Harry's head. From previous data, he made the connection at once—the father of the KGB officer with whom he had shared an uncanny experience in Magdeburg. A suicide. So what? No rarity among people of the Kremlin...

He wondered how that piece of news would affect the CIA.

"Think, Harry," Wright said quietly, reading Harry's mind. "On that East German airstrip, you succeeded in destroying a valuable unit which this Admiral's son was ordered to bring back to Moscow. I believe you know how the Kremlin looks upon failure..."

"Yes. It's not acceptable," Harry said.

"Exactly. Possibly the young Romayev...the Admiral's son...has already faced the music of his peers and is either in prison or is dead. I'm not discounting the fact that the Admiral could have taken his life in a mood of despondency."

"Or...?" Harry pressed, marveling at Wright's consistent ability to put two and two together in fleeting seconds. An immense mind. That was why he was the DCI.

"Or...," Wright replied, "...the Kremlin is giving the young Romayev a chance to vindicate himself, by sending him on a suicide mission. My guess would be...to terminate the man who foiled him. Namely...*you*, Harry."

Harry remembered the pale, piercing eyes of his adversary that storming afternoon. Those eyes revealed a will and character equally as powerful as his own, capable of anything. He felt a chill run through him.

"You mean...they'd send Romayev here...to Washington...to try to take me out?" he asked.

"Why not? They sent him to San Francisco to pick up the computer, didn't they? I'll have an APB put out on him. But it's also entirely possible that the Kremlin has some other goons watching how efficiently this young KGB Captain blows you away...that they're standing by to pounce on you, themselves, just in case Romayev fails a second time. Maybe that's why the father, understanding that his son was in a no-win situation, ate his gun."

Harry glanced at Natalie's white face. How incongruous they looked, he in his tux and she in her gold silk ballroom gown, standing in a cluttered government office on a late autumn evening. "What do we do, Chief?" Harry asked, remaining calm.

"Double...maybe triple your personal protection. Don't let your guard down...not for an instant. Apparently that's the mistake this KGB Captain, Romayev, was guilty of in Magdeburg, and now they're making him pay for it. So take a lesson from that."

"When do you think this collision is to take place?" Harry asked, acknowledging what the DCI stated was most likely true.

"No idea," said Wright. "For all we know, you're being stalked right this moment...so watch yourself, Harry."

Bert Klemmer was quick to agree to the strategy. He would play Harry Carroll's double. He had done it before, effectively. In Natalie's efficiency apartment, both men examined themselves in her bathroom mirror. Harry was the taller by only half an inch, and both men were powerfully built. They were endowed with similar Viking-type features. All they needed was a blond wig, trimmed and styled like Harry's hair, to be worn over Bert's brown waves.

They had reached him at midnight, and by two a. m., he had arrived at Natalie's with a load of gear. Evidently, he was anxious to find himself in action again. The challenge of pretending to be Director Carroll, hunted by the KGB, was precisely the excitement Bert had been waiting for.

Nobody knew how the assault would come, or even *if* it would come. For the moment, they could act only on supposition. A high-ranking naval officer had committed suicide, after his son— assigned to capture a prized technological invention— had been defeated by the CIA. Why the suicide? Was it just coincidence, Harry wondered.

"When the KGB hones in on a tall blond man in the company of a dark-haired woman," Natalie pointed out, pouring coffee for her co-operatives, "...they'll make their move. And then Harry can appear from left field and get the drop on them. Right?"

"That's the simplified strategy," Harry grinned. "But what's this about a dark-haired woman? Don't tell me you're sticking around for another wild shoot-out, Soubrine! What about the boob that needs patching?"

Natalie giggled, noticing Bert's ready flush.

"The boob can wait," she said. "I want to see this assignment successfully wound up. What's the use of a beautiful body if the right man isn't around to appreciate it?"

Bert Klemmer shot a guarded look at Harry, who was pink from hairline to necktie. Harry sipped his coffee and said nothing.

(San Francisco)

The apartment was ice-cold, and Jane turned on the central heating. There was a puff of air, a low, musical bellow, and then the hum of warmth, accompanied by the disturbing odor of burning dust. Exhausted, Jane unpacked, wondering how easy it would be to pick up two men from the "team pool" associated with the Consulate. When Padorin had been there, he had always recommended reliable people, men working their way up—like the one who had trailed her in the big black Zim, in Moscow. She would have to be cautious in her selection.

Dialing the Consulate, she spoke to Kondrashev, whose father had been a consul there when Jane was born. Dmitri Kondrashev, the son, was about thirty-five, snotty, critical of everything and everybody. Jane disliked talking to him, but he was the one who would line up the kind of lieutenants she needed.

She wanted two men who were fast, athletic, eagle-eyed, known to respect authority, and expert marksmen. A rather large order.

Increased American suspicion and watchfulness of the consular offices throughout the United States had reduced the quantity of able men available to carry out new, dangerous assignments.

"I'll see what I can do," Kondrashev assured her. "Be here early tomorrow morning, Captain."

She finished unpacking and laid out her clothing for the following day, then ran the tape on her answering machine. The usual number of orders from bookstores, requesting specific copies of articles. Jane made notes on a scratch pad as she listened. Two messages from Chet Korngold, interspersed with bookstore orders, both of Chet's messages saying approximately the same thing:

"Janie-girl, where the hell are you? I'm getting worried! Or is this your way of kissing me off and telling me to go shinny up a tree? Wish you'd put my mind at ease that you're okay. Here's a hug and a feel and a long-tongued kiss from your legal eagle, Chet."

Jane smiled, letting the tape run out on what had accumulated in her absence. Then, all at once, a strange voice with an odd dialect. A man's voice, educated, with British inflections, but not quite. The underlying pronunciation of the words was different. The message stunned her.

"We are doing a report on naval officers charged with treason and imprisoned or sentenced to death. Anything you can recommend, from Captain Bligh of the Bounty to Admiral Canaris who was guilty of complicity in Operation Valkyrie in nineteen forty-four. This is Joe, and I will call again next week."

The closing beep was followed by three more bookstore orders, and the tape ended. Jane flipped back to re-play the strange message, her heart thudding with anxiety.

Naval officers. Guilty of treason. Imprisoned. Captain Bligh. Admiral Canaris...

There was no doubt about it. Her father had been taken into custody. Why? What did they want of him? And who was "Joe"?

Her breath coming in spasms, she dialed the Consulate again, announcing herself as Goldleader One, stating it was an emergency that she be put through at once to Kondrashev. The young Consul came on at his end with his peculiar nasal whine.

"I can't wait until morning," she panted, her pulses racing. "I'll be at your office within the hour, Comrade Consul."

Hurrying, she donned her masculine get-up, scrubbed her face of any hint of make-up, pulled on the rubber-scalped blond wig. Before leaving the apartment, she left a message on Chet Korngold's answering machine:

"This is special, from Jane. I've returned safely and am out on a shopping spree to replenish my cupboards. Will call you soon. May need some important legal advice."

(Washington, D. C.)

The waiting was tedious and unnerving, and Natalie's apartment had become an armed camp. Rather than risk exposure in the streets until more information came to hand, they had groceries sent up. Bert and Harry slept on two navy-blue futons which during the day were folded under Natalie's bed. In his

blond toupée, Bert Klemmer resembled an older version of
Harry, and from a distance, even Natalie had difficulty telling
them apart if they were dressed alike.

One snowy morning, the DCI caught them at breakfast and
ordered them to his office, pronto. They took Bert's car.

Powell Wright was visibly distressed, his complexion ghastly,
his voice hoarse and dry. Unusual for a man who had seen
everything.

"We've heard from the Investigation Division of the Immigration and Naturalization Service. Any citizen living on and
off in the Soviet Union and maintaining a residence here is
routinely entered in their files."

The three CIA agents hunched forward, waiting.

"The KGB officer in Magdeburg, Captain Romayev..."

"Yes...?" Harry pressed, his blood drumming.

"That person is also known as Captain Ilyana Romayeva,"
Wright said, his eyes fixed on Harry.

"What do you know?" Bert chuckled. "A female imperson-
ator in the KGB! What will they think of next!"

"Just the opposite," said Wright calmly. "*Admiral* Romayev
was very proud of his daughter! The blond at the airstrip that
day was no *man,* Harry!"

Harry was not even conscious of clenching and unclenching
his fists. All he could see were the eyes of his Chief, boring into
his, and hear the man's troubled, excited breathing.

"There's more," the DCI went on, trying to control his tone.
"This woman goes by another alias. Jane Sutton. Owner of a
clearing house for technical books. Resides in San Francisco."

Harry was aware of Natalie's amber eyes studying him. He
did not want to reveal the agonizing thoughts burrowing into his
brain. Everything in him resisted being informed of what was to
follow.

"Jane Sutton," he repeated the name dully. "Is this woman
here as a political refugee under the new 'open' programs?"

Wright came from behind his desk and perched on its edge,
directly in front of Harry's chair.

"No, Harry," he said. "She's American by birth. Born... thirty years ago...in San Francisco..."

A strangled sound escaped Harry's lips. He sprang up, wild-eyed, a tremor coursing through his sturdy frame. Hands shoved deep in his pockets, he swore under his breath and stalked off to stand silently before the office door, his back to the others. Natalie could feel the wracking pressure of the disclosure weighing on him. She could feel his pain...

"I'm sorry, Harry," Wright said gently. "You're here among friends. I can't begin to imagine what a personal blow this must be. But when you first came with the Agency, you informed us of your adoption as an infant...and your vague, unconfirmed understanding that you had a twin sister..."

Facing the door, working his shoulders to ease the tension, Harry chewed his lip and blinked back the tears.

"You don't have to say any more, Chief...," he choked. "There are things we just know, instinctively. Captain Romayev...or Romayeva...is my twin sister. And...Admiral Romayev...who blew his brains out over her...was my father..."

A gasp from Natalie, an unfinished exclamation from Bert.

"If you want my resignation as Director...," Harry continued, his voice gaining strength, "...I'll understand perfectly. And if you want me off this case...I'll step aside..."

Wright approached Harry and stood close behind him, somehow unable to reach out and touch the young Director who was fighting to regain his composure.

"Harry, you understand, this is something I'll have to discuss with the President and the National Security Council..."

"I understand, Sir."

"As far as I'm concerned, Harry, nothing has changed as of this moment. If, however, the circumstances are such that *you* feel you want to resign...then the Agency will understand that, too."

Harry blinked his eyes, facing the door, saying nothing.

(San Francisco)

Chet Korngold finished his second Stolichnaya over ice and drummed his fingertips thoughtfully on the coffee table. His expertise as an attorney was being tested, and he wanted to be sure of himself before giving Jane any half-assed answers on so ticklish a subject.

"Political sanctuary isn't always that easy," he told her. "Besides, you say your friend was born here. So he's an American citizen by birth. Was Soviet citizenship bestowed on this guy?"

"Yes, because he worked for the government," Jane replied.

"Then he had to renounce his American citizenship...," Korngold began, thinking of the assassin, Lee Harvey Oswald. Shaking his head, he went on, "I don't know, Jane. I'll have to do some checking, or talk to some attorneys who have handled matters like this or are more familiar with what the law says..."

"But you think there's a possibility?" Jane asked hopefully.

He could not assure her there was, and she was frightened. In another few minutes perhaps, or sooner, there would be a buzz at her security gate, and her two aides, Jancu and Mikulitsyn, would arrive to accompany her to the airport for her flight to Washington. There had been no further communique from the mysterious "Joe" and she was beside herself with worry about her father.

"Please look into it, Chet," she begged, and kissed him as the buzzer sounded. Chet took her bag down to the street where a dark Pontiac stood waiting. With a rushed "Gotta run. I'll be in touch," Jane entered the car beside the driver, someone in back placing her luggage on the floor of the car at his knees. With a wave of her hand from the open window, she was gone.

Her scalp prickled with an icy fear. What had she seen in the back seat of the sedan? Mikulitsyn was at the wheel. Jancu had just placed her valise at his feet.

There was a third man in the automobile. Next to Jancu...

Mikulitsyn's eyes were fixed on the road as he drove. Barely breathing, Jane slowly turned her head...

"Good evening, Ilyana..."

"*Padorin!*"

(Washington, D.C.)

Six days. Six lousy, stinking, empty, unproductive days, holed up in Natalie Soubrine's apartment, reading magazines, reflecting on the misery of his own private hell, waiting for word from the DCI that he was still Director of the new agency...that he was still *any* kind of employee of the Central Intelligence Agency! The CIA sometimes employed people of astonishing backgrounds, but Harry couldn't recall a single instance in the history of the Agency where an agent's father was an Admiral in the Kremlin's Maritime Kommissariat, and whose sister was a Captain in the KGB! Top security clearance was one of the first pre-requisites in the CIA. Top security clearance for Harry Carroll? What a joke!

"We're out of coffee," Natalie announced, examining the shelves of her cupboards. "I'm running out to get some."

"I'll go with you," Bert said, slipping into a heavy mackinaw and Natalie threw on her coat and wound a scarf around her neck. It had been snowing all day, temperatures well below freezing. Patches of sidewalk were like panes of slippery glass.

"Got everything with you?" Harry pressed, and they both touched the holsters at the sides of their chests.

"How about that little store around the corner?" Bert asked as they strode quickly toward his car. "They have a bakery..."

"Sounds good," she said and got in beside him. After a few unsuccessful attempts in the unusually bitter cold, the auto pulled away from the curb and turned left at the first intersection. Nobody noticed a sedan parked on the other side of the street, making a tight mid-block U-turn to follow them...

In front of "Sollie's Sundries," Bert told Natalie to make the purchase while he took a quick look under the hood to check the radiator, the hoses. With a gesture reminding him to keep his mackinaw unzipped, Natalie entered the grocery.

She had placed a large jar of Yuban on the counter and was going through the cooky rack, hearing the clerk ask, "Shall I ring this up, or will there be anything..."

A burst of machine gun fire clattered outside...one shocked, hysterical shriek! Three additional blasts persisted against the frozen silence.

"Oh, my God!" Natalie cried, her gun in hand as she raced to the door of the grocery just in time to see a dark Chrysler pull away in the gathering dusk. "Bert! Bert!"

The hood of his car propped open, Bert Klemmer lay sprawled in the snow against the front wheel, arms flung wide, head twisted in a peculiar position to one side.

"Bert...!" Natalie screamed, dashing to where he lay, staring at the bright red spray flecking the patches of snow all around him. Her heart pounding, she bent over her fallen colleague, as cars screeched to a halt and others honked their horns. The grocery clerk sped out, shouting for help, and several pedestrians formed a circle of horror at the grisly scene.

Bert Klemmer's classical profile looked untouched, lying with eyes wide open on a matting of blood and tissue spreading in an ever-widening pool beneath him.

The underside of his head had been shot away...

*　　*　　*　　*

Jane pressed hard against the sofa pillows in the hotel, unable to come to herself, unable to reconcile what she had caused with her innermost feelings of right and wrong, good and evil.

Her father, a *suicide*?

Padorin had informed her of her loss. Gently, with compassion. Strange, she had thought when she heard his words, for a top man in the infamous KGB to show such compassion about the death of an old comrade.

"What made him do it?" she kept weeping. "We were so happy..."

"He was despondent, Ilyana," Padorin had said. "He knew your orders, your assignment. How do you think he could feel, knowing his daughter had orders to take the life of his son, and that she could very well die, herself, in the attempt. It was something he did not want to face."

Jane paced up and down, wringing her hands.

"But why the message that he'd been taken prisoner, held for treason?" she cried. "All I could think of then was getting the job over and going home to help him, to stand by him and appeal for mercy in his behalf, regardless of the charges!"

"The purpose of that message was to force you to act, swiftly and decisively. And that message worked," Padorin said.

Exhausted, she sank down on the sofa, eyes closed, glad now, for the first time since aiming her assault weapon out of the car window, that at least the ugly deed had been done. Her brother was dead. She could go home. Her reputation would have been redeemed. She would receive another citation. And Sergei would be there...

But her father was dead! Because of her original failure...!

Taking her brother's life had not been as difficult as she had supposed. It had required much patience, much waiting in the cold. She had become numbed to the idea as her body had become numbed to the frost forming on the Chrysler's windows, day after day.

He had been a perfect target, lifting the radiator cap and bending forward to check fluid levels, not even looking up as the Chrysler came up the street. It was over in a moment. A rattling of shells from the weapon in Jancu's hands and a few short, spurting blasts from her own. The blond man had sprung several inches into the air with the force of the bullets, his body twirling sideways, limbs shaking grotesquely. Then he'd sprawled back in the snow clumped before the left front tire. Jane had seen the eruption of gore from the back of his head, the fragmentation of bone and tissue. She had turned away, drained and nauseated.

It was done. In the vernacular, a snap.

The telephone rang and Padorin lifted the receiver.

Jane saw him convulse, saw the blood drain from his face. He muttered something unintelligible and hung up.

"What is it, Leonid?" she demanded.

"Turn on the news, Ilyana," he choked. "You shot the wrong man...!"

The remains of Bert Klemmer were returned to Fort Worth, where his family lived, and his estranged wife, Nancy. A memorial service was held at "The Farm" in Langley to honor Bert's heroism. The risk of death was part of the job...

Powell Wright intensified his All Points Bulletin for the killers. His attempts to console Harry, however, were futile.

"Those shells were meant for me!" Harry sobbed, breaking down over the death of his friend. "He died my death!"

The DCI told Natalie to stay with him. She obeyed by begging Harry to stay with *her* in the Arlington hotel where the Agency had transferred her. Stunned and grief-stricken, the two sat slumped in abysmal despair. The silence was piercing, almost shrill, like one sustained treble chord on a pipe organ.

It was even worse this time. Bob Carlson had simply disappeared. But Bert was cut down, practically before Natalie's eyes, in a hit-and-run tactic that had to have taken days of the most efficient planning.

Natalie, too, felt guilty, for the few moments when she had let down her guard, and Bert had died in a hail of bullets. Had it been absolutely necessary to risk exposure for a purchase of coffee?

And yet, Romayeva had still failed. Sooner or later, her Kremlin bosses would learn of the mistake, and if she were already en route to Moscow, would deal with her upon her arrival. If she were still in the United States, they would insist she try again.

Natalie trembled at the thought.

"She's not invincible, Harry," she tried to console Harry. "She makes mistakes, just like all of us."

"There's too much blood on her hands, Nat."

"Maybe she's already left the country, and eventually we'll hear she was hung by her own cohorts in the KGB!"

Harry pulled himself up. He hadn't slept, and his eyes were red-rimmed and glistening, his beard growth heavy.

"I hope she hasn't gone back yet, Nat," he managed. "And that she turns up somewhere. Because, I swear, I'll get to her and kill her with my bare hands, if I can. She doesn't deserve to live! She's a cold-blooded, merciless killer...!"

"Harry..."

"It's come down to a test of will!" he steamed. "Either I die or she dies, or...maybe better...*both* of us! I've bathed in blood myself the last few years!"

"God in heaven, Harry, we all have! We're the same breed! None of us is less guilty than the next!"

"Natalie, this woman is my sister!" Harry cried. "Jane Sutton, Ilyana Romayeva...she's my flesh and blood! And despite that, believing that Bert was me, she slaughtered him...quickly, easily, KGB bushwack style! And is probably now congratulating herself on a job well done...her *butchery*, well done!"

"And you'd do the same!" Natalie shouted at him to bring him to reason. He appeared on the verge of hysteria, and she feared for him, feared for his future.

He stood still, staring at the floor, nodding to himself.

"Is it in our genes, Nat?" he whispered. "The joy of killing?"

"Please, Harry...," she wept.

He crossed to the bedroom of the suite and sank heavily down on the quilt, staring at the ceiling, his face revealing the torment raging within him. For Natalie, the moment was intolerable.

Was there a future ahead, for either of them? Was a dangerous KGB assassin out there somewhere, sworn to kill this man? Would Harry die in a spray of blood and horror, as she had seen others die?

Hesitantly, she seated herself beside him on the bed and put her arms around him, cradling his head on her shoulder, her lips against his brow and finding it cold and damp. She did not want anything to happen to this man who had saved her from a dozen deaths in Luzon, this man whose courage had been tested scores of times in the ugliest hell-holes on the planet, and who seemed to be going down in defeat because of a maddening blood-relationship with his sworn enemy.

His arms wound around her, drawing her down beside him.

"Harry...," she murmured breathlessly. "Harry, darling..."

Lost in a mixture of pain and desire, Harry drew her beneath him, covering her face with kisses, clasping her tightly as his mouth searched for hers, the stubble of his beard harsh against her tender face. She had never before experienced the hunger of his kisses, and the ferocity of his lust frightened her, made her realize that in a desperate longing for oblivion he was reaching out for her, for her warmth, her femininity, the way men the world over seek release and forgetfulness in the body of a woman. What she felt in the lock of his powerful arms, in the groping of his hands, was need, sheer need, and she responded to that need. She helped remove her clothing, felt the chill of the room against her unprotected flesh. But the warmth of his hands, his mouth, erased the sensation of that chill in one great flood of excitation.

Then suddenly, his vision cleared, his judgment returned, he was gazing down at her, his features a mask of pain.

"My God, Nat...," he gasped. "What are we doing?"

She trembled in his arms, holding him fast.

"We're putting aside the hurt, my darling...," she breathed. "Just for a little while. Oh, hold me, my love...Hold me..."

Could it really have happened? Could it be that out of the deep sorrow and despair that had engulfed them both had come an interval of supreme pleasure, a close knitting of selves as never before?

Her arms had formed two graceful arcs alongside her head, in a position of trust and innocence. Conscious of the still angry scar resembling a slanted cross in the upper portion of one breast, she attempted to cover it with her hand, but found her arms heavy with fatigue.

"No, don't, darling," Harry whispered. "There's nothing ugly about the wound. It's a badge. A badge of courage..."

She looked off, tears glistening in her eyes, and he drew her close, tenderly cupping the injured breast, placing a lingering kiss against the scar. She shut her eyes at the flood of renewed desire mounting within her as his fingers traced gently around the aureole, and his breath wafted feather-like across her flesh.

Is this real? she asked herself.   Am I here with him this way, tingling at his touch, knowing what it is to be a woman...*his* woman?

Hearing him murmur her name, she suppressed the desire to tell him of her love, of its depth, of its endurance, its strength. She feared such an outpouring would break the spell between them. That would wait, she knew, for some other time. Even if that other time would be their final farewell...she would simply have to wait.

"You've always been there for me...," he breathed. "You've always understood what I needed, and when. I've been so lucky to have you in my life..."

She read the uncertainty in his eyes, the torment.

"Harry, you sound as if everything is at an end for us now," she protested faintly.   "Is that what you're actually feeling?"

He smoothed back her tangled hair.

"What I'm feeling right now...," he murmured, "...is all the desire I've buried inside me since I first met you in the Philippines. Do you know how lovely you are?   How much I want you?"

Winding her arms around him, she drew him down so that they lay heart to heart, feeling the rhythm of the blood in their veins.

"Good Lord, Harry...," she gasped, "...I'm here! And I've wanted you just as long!   Don't you know that?"

For five years, she had lain awake nights, trying to imagine the rapture of intimacy with this man...and here he was, alive and real, reaching into the very core of her being, letting her clasp him, letting her hold that wonderment inside her...

A post-midnight downpour fell in Washington.   There was a perceptible chill in the hotel suite.   Rain and hail ticked and tapped at the windows, the vibration rattling in the modern metal frames.   From the street came the occasional sound of splashing when a heavy vehicle passed by.

Natalie stirred from a deep, troubled sleep, awakening Harry at once.   He drew the blankets up close over them and pressed her close. She felt she never wanted morning to come, never wanted to leave his warm nearness.

"What are you thinking?" he asked, his tone solicitous, and she knew she could never reveal her innermost secrets, her deepest longings to this man who had for so long held himself aloof from her, and for whom their union had been but an overt expression of emotional desperation.

"I'm thinking of your...of Romayeva," she replied. "She must have her own thoughts about all of this. Do you think she knows she is...your sister?"

Harry pressed his lips to her forehead.

"I'll confess something to you, Nat...," he said. "I think we both knew, beyond a shadow of any doubt, when we faced each other in Magdeburg. We knew, and yet we didn't know, because it was... well, so strange, so coincidental. And if the KGB's intelligence is as thorough as ours, she surely knew the truth before she killed Bert Klemmer..."

"It must be as agonizing for her as it is for you," Natalie stated, and when Harry began to dispute her contention, added, "You say you both felt the same on that airstrip, looking into each other's eyes. And neither of you fired a shot..."

"I know that, Natalie. We couldn't...in the first bewildering knowledge that something like that was possible. But don't you see, Nat? Knowing she exists...and that our father was a high-ranking naval officer in the Kremlin...has most likely ended my career. Do you realize that? I'm waiting for the moment when Wright tells me I'm not only off the case, but to hand in my badge."

"Yes, I'm aware that's possible," she admitted sadly.

"In fact, I've probably come to terms with that as a reality," he whispered. "Otherwise, I don't know how this...how I could have allowed this to happen between us tonight..."

His statement pierced through her like a sword.

"I thought it was a matter of need...," she pointed out.

"Yes, it was."

"And I was here to fulfill that need..."

He drew her close and kissed her, saying nothing.

"Shall I understand...from what you've just said...," she asked with great difficulty, "...that if you felt your position with the Agency was still secure...this would not have taken place tonight?"

He swallowed hard and waited a long time before replying.

"You know how I feel about the Agency code, the regulations..."

"Yes, I've known for years, Harry..."

"You know how I've always lived up to them..."

"...and they would have superseded your personal feelings tonight?" she interrupted, her voice cracking. "If Powell Wright had not placed your career in a precarious position because of your sister and father...you wouldn't have reached out to me?"

It was evident Harry was uncomfortable. He remained silent, and she drew away from him, trembling as she sat up.

"Tell me!" she demanded, and he touched her arm hesitantly.

"Natalie...please don't..."

"...I must know!" she interrupted.

There was a silence.

"The Agency is my life, Nat," he confessed at last. "I respect its rules. I...I'm sorry..."

Natalie sat very still for a long moment. Then she moved away, slipping into a pair of pajamas and curling up at the very edge of her bed, her back to him. She cringed when his warm hand touched lightly at her shoulder.

"Natalie, please don't be angry at me..."

"I'm not angry," she choked.

His warm breath grazed across her cheek, and then his lips. She felt him trying to draw her close again and everything inside her throbbed with longing.

"Nat, please come to me, darling...," he breathed sensually.

He was saying words she had waited years to hear.

But the magic had vanished and left only resentment behind.

"No, Harry...," she heard herself whimper. "Remember the rules..."

At dawn, the telephone rang. Wide awake, his heart heavy, Harry reached for it.

"Tried your hotel and got no answer," Powell Wright told him. "So I figured Soubrine would know where you were. I want you both in my office by seven. Something's breaking..."

"I must know, Chief...," Harry put in quickly. "Have you discussed my situation with the National Security Council...with the President...?"

"Let's talk about that when you get here."

Natalie gave him a questioning look as he hung up. He told her that Wright wanted them in his office at once. Expressionless, Natalie slipped out of bed and closed the door of her bathroom behind her. Harry heard the shower thundering on the floor tiles. He looked at the yellow line of light beneath the door.

The DCI had called him at Natalie's hotel at dawn. *"Figured Soubrine would know where you were..."*

There was something breaking...

Behind the bathroom door, a hurt and humiliated Natalie stood showering in a yellow light. Alone.

Harry Carroll hated himself.

Wright looked worn out and rattled, as though he had been at his desk the entire night.

He had discussed with the President and then with the big security chiefs of the NSC the peculiar family background of Task Force Director Harry Carroll.

"And...," Harry demanded, jaw set firmly, wetting his lips.

"There was some dissention," Wright admitted. "But when we put it to a vote, we overwhelmingly agreed that despite appearances, there were no ties between you and the Soviet Union."

His face illuminated, Harry was on his feet at once.

"You mean...?" he cried, breaking into a grin of relief.

"I mean we've got work to do!" Wright snapped, but with a responsive smile. "There's an I. Y. Romayev booked on

Aeroflot to Moscow, leaving Kennedy at noon today from the Pan-Am Terminal. There are a lot of Russians on that flight."

"I. Y. Romayev?" Harry mused, questioning the name.

Natalie studied the telex copy of the passenger list in Harry's hands, stating, "It could be her. She worked under the dual names of Ilya Romayev and Ilyana Romayeva. Both common names in Russia. But the father's name was Yuri, and out of traditional respect for the father, children take the father's name as their second names. When she was Captain Romayev, her name was Ilya Yurievitch. As a woman— Captain Romayeva—she was Ilyana Yurievna. Yes, I'd say this passenger is our KGB captain."

Wright's eyes were bright as he smiled at both of them.

"Washington National and Dulles are both pretty well socked in by this storm, and there's no forecast of its loosening up. But the skies over JFK are reported clear, and the Aeroflot plane leaves at noon. Feel like using your pilot's license, Harry?"

"If it gives me the chance to nail Romayev, I'll fly through a swarm of frogs and locusts!" Harry responded, determined.

"Please clear me, too," Natalie spoke up firmly. "Bert was within touching distance of me when this captain bushwacked him. If this passenger is our lady, I'd like a crack at her, too!"

"Chief, that wouldn't be wise," Harry protested. "I'm not that experienced a flyer, and Miss Soubrine was just wounded..."

Noting unusual hostility between them, the DCI put up a hand to stop their heated torrent of protestations.

"Soubrine's spoken for herself, Harry. And her background and knowledge of the language is invaluable in this case," he pointed out. "Now both of you get out to National as fast as you can. I'll alert Major Evans there to warm something up for you..."

Harry tried to speak up again, but the Director of Central Intelligence was already dialing a number, oblivious to him.

Natalie stood fidgeting with the straps of her purse.

"Nat, please, I'd feel a whole lot better if..."

"Do you think I give a damn about how you feel?" she fumed at him, then turned decisively away. "I'm going!"

Harry caught one of her hands and held it tight in his, forcing her to look up at him with pained, hooded eyes.

"I never realized you could be so hard-headed, Natalia Isaakovna," he whispered, in a suggestive tone meant for her alone.

"Why not?" she sizzled, staring straight at him. "We're Russkies, aren't we? It's in our genes..."

Part Five

Chapter 19

(JFK Airport, New York)

Wearing a helmet and flight suit, Natalie was helped into the sleek Northrup T-38, its two engines humming at idling speed. Harry, as pilot, turned on the headset and watched as the girl was strapped into her parachute.

He had wanted to go alone yet Powell Wright had permitted her to accompany him to Kennedy Airport, New York, even though he had not flown in months, and what lay ahead at JFK was an unspeakable danger...

Once the instruments were checked, Harry lowered the canopy and gave the thumbs-up sign. The blocks were removed and Harry increased engine speed to taxi to the runway. He was particularly fond of the T-38, and had criss-crossed the Middle East in its sister craft, the F-5 Freedom Fighter of the Imperial Iranian Air Force. Later, he had flown all over Pakistan in a T-38 wrangled from the U.S. Air Force.

The rain had faded to a drizzle when he shoved the throttle to full power for take-off, then pulled the nose up, almost vertically, rapidly climbing to twenty-five thousand feet, at which time he switched frequencies to check in with Evans at National.

"Any word from the FBI, Major?"

"They still feel she'll leave for Moscow today."

"Any change on that Aeroflot Flight three oh three?"

"Not so far, Director Carroll," Major Evans replied. "It'll board thirty minutes before departure."

Harry checked his watch, knowing he would be pushing things to the limit, even using afterburner. An idea occurred to him.

"Major, ask the FBI in New York to create a diversion. A fight, a fire alarm, anything to delay those passengers from boarding Flight 303. Understand?"

"Affirmative," came the brisk reply. "JFK traffic control says you're to come in directly, with no trouble reaching the Pan-Am terminal."

"Major Evans," Harry smiled into the mike. "When you're through with the Air Force, come see me. I need men like you."

The old confidence was noticeable in his voice. The DCI's assurance that he was still in solid had done wonders.

The T-38 was over Philadelphia when Evans signed off.

"Listen, Natalie," Harry stated, once more the Director, the authority figure, "The moment we reach that terminal, dump that monkey suit you're wearing and start spouting in your best Russian, put on any kind of act to get close to the gate. I'll work the waiting room and the check-in area. If this is Romayeva, she mustn't get away. And have your weapon ready. Got that?"

"Got it," she said softly, and they dared glance at each other.

Harry checked the fuel gauge. Just enough to reach the coast of New Jersey. He'd fly on re-heat almost into JFK.

Calling ahead to the control tower, he was reassured in the most musical Brooklynese that traffic was stopped until he made it in, and that the red carpet would be out at Pan-Am.

Over Ridgefield, New Jersey, Harry let down to ten thousand feet, clearly making out Manhattan and Long Island. The venerated figure of the Statue of Liberty, restored to her original beauty, stood in lonely splendor on Bedloes Island.

Natalie was wiggling out of her jump suit when Harry pulled the afterburner switch. An explosive noise was heard from the rear of the plane, and the aircraft jumped ahead as if kicked. "What was that?" Natalie shouted. "What did we hit?" "Took the TV antenna off the Empire State," he quipped. Then JFK tower came on, telling Harry he was on scope, that he was seen visually, and to come on in. All was clear.

Harry cut the afterburner and let the wheels down. The fuel gauge was close to the red line, meaning about fifteen minutes more of flying time. He carefully lined up the plane's nose with the runway, amazed at the sight of the busy airport so still, as though paralyzed. Not a vehicle moved. Planes sat waiting at the ends of runways, two and three in a line, their tail lights blinking.

Light as a feather, Harry touched down, repeating thanks to the tower, and the Pan-Am terminal loomed ahead, surrounded by blue and white 747's. Among them was one stranger—a four-engine Ilyushin 62, the Hammer and Sickle insignia on its tail.

Aeroflot Flight Number 303.

Harry braked sharply at the nearest gate and popped the canopy. He told Natalie to stay put until they brought a ladder. It was quite a jump.

They waited, and just before she stepped down, their eyes met.

"Nat...," he murmured, feeling helpless.

"It'll be okay. I know what to do," she assured him.

Then she was gone. He shut down the two J-85 engines.

"God help us," he prayed, stepping out onto the ladder.

A giant clock, ornate and imposing, looked down on the mix of people milling about at the international airport. Businessmen with their briefcases strode with the certitude of travelers who had endured the dreary routine a hundred times or more. Informal tourists congregated in loose clusters, using any excuse for the most boisterous hilarity. Armed security guards, pistols at their sides, moved warily about with alert eyes. Too many airports had become the target of fanatical Middle-Eastern terrorists, and the watchword was...*beware.*

Aeroflot, national carrier of the USSR, was checking in passengers for Flight 303, non-stop to Moscow. According to the latest weather reports, that city was buried in a foot of snow.

In her tailored gray suit, Jane sat reading the newest issue of Time, watchful of all who entered the enormous waiting hall. In her canvas carry-on bag was her plastic pistol, a sophisticated specialty weapon manufactured for the KGB by a Viennese gunsmith. A real dandy, measuring—even with its silencer--the width of a tabloid newspaper, and Jane had it wrapped in the New York Daily News. Its slim width reduced the telltale bulge of ordinary guns and enabled easy access to the trigger. It had passed through the metal detector, carrying six high-power shells, and had worked for her before.

She couldn't fail this time. If Harry Carroll showed up—as Padorin was positive he would—she would reach him as unobtrusively as possible, jostle against him, and send one or two bullets directly into his heart.

The moment he fell, she would lose herself in the crowd.

It would be the first time—post-natally—that she ever touched her brother...and the last.

Where was Padorin? They had separated upon arrival at Kennedy, but she knew he'd be circling around to alert her if he spotted the man she was to terminate.

No sign of him. Perhaps he'd gone to the men's room.

Jane stood up for a better view of faces in the crowd. An airport security guard came walking toward her—a black man with a benign smile and classical African features. Automatically, Jane smiled back, as one did with strangers, and the guard winked.

Great. That's what I need now, Jane thought bitterly. To have a black security guard think I'm flirting with him...

There was something familiar about the guard. Where on earth had she seen that particular face before...?

Oh, *there* was Padorin, engaged in conversation with another black security guard...a female...

What's wrong with my eyes, Jane wondered. Why did they look familiar? Had she seen such faces in National Geographic? They wore modified Afro hairstyles...the man's groomed close to the contour of his head...the woman's swept into an intricate basket weave of delicate braids.

Bewildered, Jane glanced at the oncoming guard, the black man with the winking eye...

Instantly, her trained mind focused on the replay of a message taped on her answering machine. Once again, she heard the almost-but-not-quite British inflections of an educated male voice seeking data on the imprisonment and execution of naval officers. The single message left on her tape by "Joe."

Her memory flashed back thirteen years to a schoolroom in Moscow. She saw the face of Rudiger Furst...

And Petra's...and Jomo's...

So that was Jomo on the tape, anglicized to "Joe."

The significance became clear. She knew why they were there.

"We just checked your boss through," the Pan-Am executive security officer told Natalie in a furtive whisper, having looked at her credentials. "Big blond guy in a flight suit. Said you'd be along right away. Are more of you still to arrive?"

"Not to my knowledge."

"You know, there are innocent passengers at that gate, and they're our first concern at this moment. If there's to be a commotion, we have to move them out of harm's way. I've called in extra security people. Is there some way you can arrest this person quickly and quietly and get the hell out of this airport?"

The airline man's face was lined with anxiety. True, every Aeroflot take-off and landing presented new problems. Security was the watchword that grew more demanding each day. The danger to innocent passengers increased with every flight.

"How I wish," Natalie sighed, envisioning a fast, bloodless capture of a disarmed and docile Captain Romayeva, taken back to Washington in handcuffs so that international negotiations at the highest levels of government could begin.

"I'll get a security guard to accompany you," the airline officer decided. "There's a pretty big crowd waiting to board, and we can delay the flight only so long before they start getting edgy."

He called to his people upstairs to send an escort, on the double. The wait seemed endless, and Natalie paced up and down outside the administrative office.

She would deal with her sadness later, after the urgency of this encounter. She didn't even want to reflect on the aftermath of her intimacy with Harry, an aftermath ruined by his avoidance and turning away...as though that ecstatic union never occurred. Or...even worse...acknowledged that, yes, it had occurred but was of no serious meaning, no consequence.

If at least he had only ridiculed her for attaching importance to what had taken place between them, she could try to hate him for that. But no. Harry would simply pretend that whatever they'd shared was an insignificant, casual fling—and that they were to go on as before, unlinked, disjointed. Were she to argue that point, Harry would give her his most benevolent smile and remind her that a few sexual intimacies didn't constitute a relationship, and that she'd be wise not to take "things like that" too seriously. He would insist it had been purely automatic happenstance—just as a man plumbing the depths of despair would reach for strong drink to ease the pressure of the moment—so had his body reached for hers. Because she had been there. Sorry if she understood it to be more meaningful than that...

Natalie took a deep breath. Perhaps this, then, would be her final job for the Agency. She couldn't see herself remaining on with a Harry who insisted on "living up to the code" and who would treat her in a coldly impersonal manner—or worse—in a fraternal manner. She would never be able to tolerate his denigration of the ecstasy they both felt to simply "one of those things."

But for now, the source of that ecstasy was moving about in the crowded room one flight above, seeking the sister he had never known…seeking to prevent that sister from taking his life, even if he had to take hers.

"Hello…," said a lightly accented, musical voice. "Mr. Dietz sent me to escort you upstairs. Anticipating trouble, are you?" Natalie took in the gleaming, wide smile of the dark-skinned security guard with her jet black hair done up in a braided basket-weave and began preceding the girl back toward the exit.

"Yes, there may well be some fun and game upstairs," she said.

"Okay by me," laughed Petra. "You just stay close to me."

There seemed to be no Americans in the crowd awaiting the take-off of Flight 303. Most were gray-haired, tired men, wearing suits that somehow did not fit properly. Many were United Nations staff members returning home. The USA was demanding a drastic reduction in the number of Russian personnel at the international organization in New York City.

The few women in the crowd—dowdy chain smokers—were most likely the wives of attachés and translators. They kept re-checking the contents of the giant paper bags they had with them, going over last-minute purchases. Harry had never seen a group of travelers so totally inundated with bags and packages. And, as they waited, they made frequent trips to a buffet table on one side of the room—a table stocked with trays of small rye-bread sandwiches, several bottles of vodka and orange juice, and a pile of small paper cups.

An announcement that the flight would be delayed had come through just before Harry's arrival in the waiting hall, and a number of travelers appeared angry and impatient. He wished he knew more than just a few phrases of Russian so that he could understand what the people were saying about the delay, and about the flight itself…

For the hunter, the anticipation of closing in on prey, the maneuvering for an advantageous position—those moments were the most exquisite, the most memorable. There was, associated with those moments, a spine-tingling excitement, a salivating of the palate for a deliciousness which could be equalled by only the most appetizing nourishment, by the most orgasmic rapture.

But this hunt was devoid of joy or pleasure. In this hunt, Harry knew only anxiety and torment. His twin was a murderess—the agent of a government which had been described as "an evil empire." She had arranged the cold-blooded homicide of his friend and compatriot, believing it was a CIA man named Carroll, the enemy of her country. But did she also know, at that moment, that she was taking the life of her brother? And, if she did know...did she even *care*?

Then why hadn't she fired at him in Magdeburg? What had made her hesitate, just as he had hesitated? Was it only the identicality of their appearances? Or was it something more...?

He wondered if he would find her there. With the flight delayed, the only place she could be at the moment was in the multi-gated waiting room. Harry wondered if his trip to Kennedy, in hopes of finding her there, wasn't totally asinine. The name on the passenger list, I. Y. Romayev, could belong to a dozen other people returning to the Soviet Union. But the DCI had felt it was worth checking out and had cautioned Harry to be extra careful.

"She's traveling under her own name, knowing the passenger lists are always checked, and knowing her name is a dead give-away. It's as though she has dropped her calling card...and expects you to call."

How would she dress? Was he to assume he was pursuing a woman? Or would he again—as he had in Magdeburg—confront a believable-looking man. This superb sister of his, with her multiple identities...

Repeatedly, he circled the crowded waiting room, making sure to look in the boutiques. He stopped in each of the men's rooms, pretending to wait for a stall, and studied the faces of the men as they came out.

The black guard with the polished accent, who had escorted him up from the executive office, was now trying to soothe a passenger who had become irate, evidently, due to the flight's delay. From where Harry stood, he could see that passenger, a man in his sixties, spewing his wrath at the security guard. It seemed to be a rather heavy confrontation. Why, he wondered, did both men turn in his direction, nodding and smiling his way before they moved apart...And why was the black security guard with the neat Afro and the wide, engaging grin returning to him through the crowd...?

At the same moment, Harry spotted Natalie entering from the corridor, a pretty black security woman at her side. Natalie's eyes met his fleetingly as she took in the milling crowd.

The same irate traveler up ahead seemed now to be addressing someone else...a gray-suited man with the brim of a fedora drawn down at an angle. A gray, wide-brimmed fedora...

Was it the shape of the back of that neck...or the way the gray tweed suit fit loosely across padded shoulders...?

Padorin's performance was stupendous. His outrage at the unexplained, tedious delay of Aeroflot Flight 303 made for great theatre! Between utterances, he skillfully hissed instructions—no more than two words at a time—advising Jane to inch her way toward a tall man in a flight suit, stationed against the wall.

"I've seen him," she replied in a low monotone. "It's impossible to do anything in this crowd. These are our own people here, Leonid. I don't want any of them hurt."

"Let me worry about that," Padorin sneered.

"When they start boarding, the crowd will thin out and it will be easier..."

"You're procrastinating, Ilyana! I must warn you again...Do not miss this opportunity!"

The spasmodic breathing had begun, along with the slight jolting in her chest. With fists clenched, she inhaled deeply.

"There are things we can and cannot do, Leonid," she said quietly. "We both have our orders. We both know what we are prepared to do."

Suddenly, Padorin's eyes opened very wide as he stared over her shoulder, but Jane knew better than to turn around.

"It's him, Ilyana," he rasped through lips that barely moved. "He's coming this way."

He started to drop to one knee, simultaneously reaching for the Beretta which Jomo and Petra had slipped to him upon his arrival in the waiting hall. Catching the glint of his weapon, Jane moved quickly to stop him.

"Don't!" she commanded him, and he glared up at her. "Now back up and stay clear of me! You haven't fired a gun in a long time, Leonid, and there are innocent people packed close in this room. Leave what must be done to younger people now. I'll take this..."

With one deft motion, she swept Padorin's pistol into her jacket pocket. A victim of his own emotions, the speechless man felt temporarily defeated by the young woman's brash behavior. She turned from him, resembling a sharp young computer executive carrying a rolled-up copy of a local tabloid.

From beneath the brim of her hat she looked at Harry Carroll. He was a short distance away...looking at her.

Natalie observed the milling, moving crowd. Petra hovered at her side as they stood in the corridor entrance. It would be difficult. If KGB Captain Romayeva was indeed the passenger whose name appeared on the flight list, what better place for Harry's twin to lose herself than in a crowded airport terminal, with the promise of immunity and sanctuary the moment she boarded the plane.

About twenty feet away stood a tall, slim man in a gray business suit, and something about him made Natalie hone in on the lower portion of his profile beneath the brim of his hat. She could not see his eyes, but could sense the direction of his glance, and followed it...

To *Harry's* eyes.

The total sequence, in all its grim detail—from one end of her peripheral vision to the other—became etched in her brain.

Both Jane and Harry stood frozen, seemingly unable to move.

Coming up behind Jane, a scowling, gray-haired man raised his arm like a maestro about to conduct a symphony orchestra. A signal of some kind? Jockeying for position at the other end of the hall, a sturdy, black security guard—even as Natalie watched—was just raising both extended arms, pointing his service revolver directly at Harry's back!

"Harry! Behind you!" Natalie screamed.

In a blur, Harry whirled, his weapon instantly in his hand, but across Natalie's field of vision fell the sight of *another* gun...a gun gripped in Petra's hand!

Trigger-swift reflexes reacting at top speed, Natalie brought her knee up hard beneath Petra's wrist, while the side of her hand came down in a fierce karate chop. Natalie heard the grunt, saw Petra's weapon wobble to the floor. In an instant, they were grappling furiously on the floor, and Natalie heard—above the hissing of her own breath—the sharp reports of gunfire and the screams of terror-stricken people! But it was all she could do to keep the hefty Petra from strong-arming her into submission as she strained with outstretched hand for the gun lying only a yard away...

For Jane, everything merged into a blast of activity, over-shadowed by a sense of impending doom. She had felt—rather than heard—Padorin come up behind her and heard the rasp of his command. Responding to that command across the hall, Jomo was doing a side-step, both arms extended, pointing a revolver at Harry's back.

So *this* was the reason for the KGB agents, Jomo and Petra, to pose as security guards in the terminal building! The turn-over in help occurred so regularly there that no executive could possibly be familiar with the faces of new personnel! Thus, not only was Padorin on hand to make certain she carried out her orders, but two other operatives were there to insure that she eliminated Carroll, or died in the fracas...if not by Padorin's gun, then most certainly by *theirs*!

With no hesitation, Jane raised the rolled-up newspaper to hip level, found the trigger and released the projectile.

It entered below Jomo's cheekbone and exited behind his ear, its impact hurling him backward. He landed heavily against the wall which he then decorated with a trailing swath of blood and tissue as he sank lifeless to the floor.

"Jomo! *Jomo!*" a woman's voice screamed, and Jane knew those agonized cries came from Petra somewhere in that crowd.

But before a further thought crystallized, she was seized in a powerful choke-hold by the surprisingly muscular arm of the desperate Padorin, who kneed the lethal rolled-up tabloid from her hand and snatched the Beretta from her suit pocket, jamming its nozzle into her ribs and dragging her backward in the direction of the boarding gate.

"You disappointed me, Ilyanitchka!" he hissed hysterically. "You and I are getting on that plane and returning to Moscow where you'll be executed and I'll be honored for bringing you in!"

Jane's choking response was barely intelligible.

"You're crazy, Leonid! Carroll will never let us get to the plane! He'll kill us both!"

But Padorin was barking gruff orders to the frightened Russian airline stewards who stood on the threshold of the L-shaped corridor leading to the cabin of the huge Ilyushin aircraft.

"Oh, I think not, my girl!" Padorin snickered, dragging her roughly with him. "Your brother won't harm a hair on your head!"

Waving his gun, Padorin shrieked for immediate obedience on the part of the airline personnel. Hearing the gunman identify himself as a Colonel in the KGB, several sprang to do whatever he demanded of them. They sped along the corridor to the cabin of the plane, preparing to take the Colonel and his prisoner on board...

Weapon raised, Harry pursued them, conscious of the terror in Jane's eyes—seeking no mercy but questioning the significance, the sanity, of it all. Once the gray-haired officer dragged Jane into that cabin, they would be protected by full diplomatic immunity, and he would be unable to touch them.

"That's Padorin!" Natalie's sudden whisper gushed in his ear as the girl darted close. "Communications Chief of the KGB!"

Harry continued inching forward toward the "L" of the corridor. Behind him, he knew, airport security police were arriving—to do what they could as the drama played out. They would be taking the semi-conscious Petra into custody and would see if anything could be done for Jomo. And, of course, herding the horrified onlookers to places of safety, bearing in mind that the most important individual was slipping away, using the body of a choking, fainting woman as his shield.

There was nothing any of them could do for Harry at that particular moment. To make any move could well prove fatal to the woman, to the CIA man inching after them, to both, or to all three...

"Let her go, Padorin!" shouted Harry, taking his cue from Natalie's rushed exclamation. "She's American by birth! This could become an ugly international incident, and you'll be responsible!"

"You're wrong, Mr. Carroll!" Padorin mocked him. "Captain Romayeva is boarding this plane. She has a date with a firing squad in Moscow!"

They were a few feet from the cabin door. Although he was behind her, Padorin was three inches shorter than Jane, and a portion of his face showed just above her shoulder as he kept dragging her backward.

It was one chance in a hundred, and if he miscalculated the tiniest fraction of an inch, Jane would die by his hand. If he permitted Padorin to board that plane with her, she would be executed in Moscow for treason. Harry had to take that chance.

Swiftly, as though he had stumbled, he feinted to the right, and the suddenness of his move caused Padorin to stir a few inches to the outer side to fire at him.

In that fateful instant...with Padorin's bullet zinging into a CTR screen atop one of the desks near the corridor...Harry fired. The shell whizzed past the angle of Jane's jaw and struck Padorin just below the eyebrow. He fell backwards without a sound, his eyes fixed and squinting...

Jane, her hands reaching for her bruised throat, stood aghast, looking down at the lifeless body of her superior. Then her legs buckled, and the floor came up very fast.

She could barely breathe. There were strangled sounds wheezing musically through her chest, and each inhalation was a supreme effort. The bright room kept fading to black and lighting up again. Her soaked clothes stuck to her flesh, and in her ears waves crashed and roared...

He was bending over her...*he, and the dark-haired woman.*

For a fleeting moment, Jane fancied she could see her head reflected in the pupils of his eyes. She was hatless; the blond male wig had moved lopsided, the rubber tight in its unnatural angle. The dark-haired woman knelt next to her, peeling back the wig to relieve the pressure on her head, and in the pupils of Harry's eyes, Jane could see her own pale blonde locks falling softly around her face, drenched with cold perspiration. The dark-haired woman was calling for help, but Jane could not make out the words.

"Has anyone called for an ambulance?" was Natalie's outcry. "Can we get some oxygen over here...quickly!"

She could not get enough air into her lungs, no matter how valiantly she struggled. Padorin did this, she thought. Choked me, did something to my windpipe...

My God, that deadly, irregular beat...! That lethal cardiac arrhythmia the specialists warned about! I must rest. I must lie down and rest. This has been too much stress...

But I *am* lying down! I'm not even moving! The valve isn't functioning as it should...not closing, not opening as it's supposed to! They call it...they call it the mitral valve...

Consciousness faded and returned, faded and returned.

So this is my brother...this splendid, beautiful man with a masculine cast to my very own features!

This is my twin. My enemy.

What did Padorin say before he was killed?

Your brother won't harm a hair on your head!

Well, Padorin was right! The old monstrosity was right!

THUMP-thump. Thump, pause. THUMP! THUMP! THUMP-thump, pause...

They can replace a mitral valve just as easily here as in Moscow. I will seek sanctuary...Yes, I will...I will send for Sergei...as soon as I'm well...

O, borzhamoya, Sergei, dorogoi...Ya sozha'layu...

My God, I'm sorry, my darling. I'm so sorry...

Everything went black. She was only vaguely conscious, vaguely aware that men in white jackets were bending over her, placing a mask over her nose and mouth, holding her wrists, checking the pulses there, then the temporal, the carotid...

THUMP! pause...pause...th-thump, th-thump...

Oh, the air feels good. Why can't I get it into my lungs?

Ah, there! How relaxing, to be able to breathe!

How do I speak to my brother? What do I call him?

His eyes are so concerned, so worried, so full of tears!

I must tell him...how proud I am of him! *My twin!*

She put forth one hand and touched his face weakly. He took her wrist and caressed it tenderly, gazing at her. Her strength ebbing, Jane raised her other hand and gestured—first to him, then to herself. He compressed his lips tightly, nodding.

She held up two fingers and smiled. Twins. He nodded.

How do I start speaking to him...? How do I tell my beloved twin all the things that are in my heart...?

With one straining effort, Jane pulled the oxygen mask away from her face and lay gasping up at him, smiling into his eyes.

"Our...our mother's name...was Tanya...!" she gasped.

And then it was very quiet, and very dark.

THUMP! pause... th-thump... pause... pause... pause... pause...

The young intern replaced the oxygen mask and took Jane's limp wrist in his hand, seeking the weakened irregular pulse. Then at her throat...at her breast...

The terrible question stood in Harry's streaming eyes.

"I'm sorry, Sir...," said the intern.

Chapter 20

(McLean, Virginia)

It was Petra who pleaded for sanctuary, stating she didn't wish to return to the Soviet Union, or to her own land, Zaire. Arrangements were made for the remains of her husband, Jomo, and of KGB Colonel Leonid Padorin, to be transported to Moscow,but CIA Director Carroll saw to the private burial of KGB Captain Ilyana Yurievna Romayeva in a memorial park on the outskirts of McLean.

Harry spent a number of hours interrogating Petra to learn as much as he could about Captain Romayeva. From Petra, and from the secret files the Agency had on Jane, Harry was able to put together some of the pieces—at least enough for a brief and honest funeral service. A Unitarian minister agreed to officiate, and for the sake of their son, Don and Sally Carroll agreed to attend.

The morning of the funeral, Powell Wright picked up Natalie. He and his wife had decided to attend to show Harry they were at his side in a very dark hour. As Harry had hoped, the minister managed, with truth and simplicity, to deliver a solemn and moving testimony of the measure of Jane's life.

"From the time she was conceived...," he stated with compassion, "...there hung over the life of this woman a double set of Fate lines. Born a twin, but separated from her brother and natural parents, her existence remained one of parallels and contradictions, almost as though she were continually justifying the absence of her twin...sometimes by *becoming her own twin*...in the parts she played, as both man and woman in her quasi-military career. Sometimes a daring and ruthless man, a brilliant and courageous soldier. Other times, a soft and loving woman...a friend, a daughter, and a lover. Yet from what we know of Jane...or Ilyana...all her efforts to develop a relationship with someone she loved ended tragically. It appears that once having lost her twin, she received the decree of some unkind destiny that she live alone...and die alone..."

Harry went by himself to the graveside. Natalie felt he should be alone with his deepest, most private thoughts as he bid farewell to his sister. She followed the Powell Wrights back to their car and waited until she saw him coming slowly down the hill.

He forced a smile when he noticed them waiting, coming up to speak to them through the open car window.

"I want to thank you for being here," he said. "It was very thoughtful of you, and I appreciate it."

The DCI suggested he take a few days off, remarking that Harry looked as if he hadn't slept in weeks. Harry, however, chose to continue working, reminding his chief, "It's better if I stay busy."

He looked over at Natalie in the back of Wright's Cadillac, but she avoided his glance.

"Well, suit yourself, m'boy," Wright agreed. "I'll be in touch with State regarding that African woman, and with the consulate in San Francisco. I'll touch base with you in a day or so."

"Thank you, Sir."

Natalie looked in the opposite direction as Wright drove off.

(Washington, D.C.)

It was ten of ten when he dialed her number. But the phone rang several times without answer, and at last he hung up, wondering where she could have gone. Perhaps she had taken Wright's advice and gone away by herself for a few days. God knows, Harry admitted to himself, she deserves the rest.

He couldn't help re-thinking the drama enacted at the airport.

To save him, his twin sister had killed Jomo. And across that same room, desperate to stop a would-be killer, Natalie had overcome Petra, a woman outweighing her by over fifty pounds.

He owed his twin his life, ironically enough.

And owed that same incredible debt to Natalie.

Where in hell had she gone?

Fixing himself a drink, he noted his fingers were quivering. Too much pressure had been building in the months and weeks just preceding...pressure of all kinds. Blowing the Salang Tunnel had been a breeze compared to the experiences which followed.

God damn, where was Natalie? He knew a number of agents who had been interested in dating her over the years...Those were the ones who didn't give a particular hang about restrictions in the Code...who described Natalie as an understanding little doll...

She had understood the strange mixture of his feelings about Jane—understood the gut-wrenching sorrow gripping him as he stood helpless, watching his sister die. He'd never had a chance to know Jane, to spend time with her, to joke and laugh with her about how truly alike they were...

Natalie had remained close at his side, holding tight to his hand in that moment of anguish when the paramedics covered Jane's face and carried her off on a stretcher. It was Natalie who spoke in Russian to the curious onlookers—ordering them to stand back—asking them not to press in upon a personal tragedy.

What would he have done without her...?

There were Christmas carols on the radio. Don and Sally Carroll would be trimming their tree, wrapping gifts. Had Jane ever known the beauty of Christmas...?

He remembered the trip back to Washington, after the shoot-out at the airport. He'd been entirely too distraught to fly, and Natalie had driven a Buick Century back to the Capital, permitting him to talk...to vent...

For the first time in his colorful and dramatic life, Harry had suffered a personal loss, with all its pain and pathos. He had known poignant and sensational moments in his career...

But losing Jane...losing his twin...that was something else...

"Did you see?" he'd asked Natalie as she drove, at last breaking a long, tormented silence. "Did you see her point to me...and then to herself, holding up two fingers?"

"Yes, I saw," Natalie whispered, aching for him.

"She knew...," he stated, holding back tears. "She knew we were sister and brother. It was a feeling that grew to confirmation...from the moment we faced each other in Magdeburg."

For a while he sat unspeaking, looking ahead to the wintery highway, churning with his own brooding thoughts.

"I couldn't tell this to anyone else in the world, Nat...," he whispered after a long silence. "But can you imagine that I felt *proud* of her? Oh, not proud of the country she represented, or of its ideology...but of *her*! Proud of what she was doing for what she believed in, proud of what she accomplished in her short life!"

Natalie nodded, blinking back her own tears as she drove.

"There was nothing superficial about either of our lives...," Harry went on. "And...I can't help feeling that *she* was just as proud of *me*! Honestly, Nat...does that sound crazy? Or do you understand anything I'm saying? Am I making any sense at all...?"

They slowed for the congestion of holiday traffic, and she noted how bright with tears his eyes were. Did she understand the helpless desolation engulfing him? Could she see how deeply he was in need of her compassion? Of course...but how much of it was she ready to release?

She put her hand gently over his on the car seat, pressing it.

"Only another Russian would understand," she said sadly.

Harry took a deep breath, gazing out at the white snow against a gray sky, nodding thoughtfully.

"Yes...," he breathed. "Someone whose name is Natalia Isaakovna *would* understand..."

She bit her lip, accelerating as the highway opened up.

"I'm grateful, Nat," she heard him say. "You must know that."

But she spurned his gratitude. It was his love she needed. Without that, nothing else mattered.

They would be in Washington in about half an hour. She would drop him at his hotel and proceed to her own, where, in her solitude, she could indulge her grief for the torment torturing Harry, for the pathetic life of his sister who had been so misguided by her fate. And for herself...in her bewildering loneliness .

..."I'll never get it out of my mind...," she heard him whisper. "Those last few words she managed to say to me. Were you close at that moment, Nat? Did you hear those final words? They keep ringing and echoing inside my head...'Our mother's name was Tanya'. She said that...just before she died...and it sealed all the bonds..."

There had been a chill, whipping wind when he exited the rented Buick in front of his hotel and watched her drive off. Alone in his room, his mind was filled with Natalie, remembering how she'd felt in his arms. He poured himself a stiff Scotch to help induce merciful sleep. He'd have a hangover in the morning, he knew...but what the hell...

She had been a vision, the evening of the White House banquet. My God, how long ago that seemed to him! Selecting, on extremely short notice, the kind of gown tailored to her special charms—the fabric and style that would best enhance those tempting curves—she had known how to do it. And he didn't think she needed any plastic surgery. In time, that cross-shaped scar would fade even whiter than her pale skin. A sobering reminder. "Hah, X marks the spot!" she'd say, "where a Soviet bullet almost took my life in an East German skirmish! And Harry, m'boy, you were there..."

Did he remember being there...?

That scar would always bring back memories...of so many things. He could develop a great fondness for that scar...

Oh, shit! Cut it out, he admonished himself.

He finished what was left of the Scotch and dragged himself to bed...to dream of a South Pacific monsoon...and the call of the kiwi bird...

Yvonne yawned hello after the phone had buzzed six times, wondering who'd have the colossal nerve to awaken her at half past seven on a winter morning.

"Oh!", she said when Harry apologized for the early call. And then, curious, "Oh...?"

"I figured, with your busy social calendar, unless I reached you early, I'd be out of luck," Harry told her.

Aroused and alert, she brightened, turning over in bed.

"Harry Carroll, I do declare!" she laughed. "What makes you call this December morning...?"

She paused to glance out the window, waxing sentimental.

"...with snow falling like Johnson's baby powder and the forecast of another few inches by evening?"

"Could we meet for breakfast?" he asked. "I need to talk to you, Yvonne..."

So, it was over—the dramatic assignment with its far-reaching effects—Natalie mused beneath the sting of a powerful shower. Wright's secretary had sent her a clipping from the New York Times, a brief account of the shooting at Kennedy Airport, wherein three Soviet agents had been killed and one taken into custody.

The story had been condensed into a tiny insert on the bottom of the front page, ending with "continued on page 17." No big deal. No photographs. Just a commonplace, daily occurrence.

Well, people in her line of work and Harry's didn't stay on the job for its glory. But Natalie often wished the public was better informed about the fine young lives sacrificed in the intelligence services. Only those closest to Harry would ever know the trauma he had endured, finding himself in an emotional duel to the death with the sister he had never known.

Maybe another man would simply have permitted Jane's body to be returned to Moscow, where she'd been schooled and trained. But that would have been an insensitive man, Natalie reflected. Harry was not insensitive. At least, not always...

Thinking of the look in his eyes when she dropped him in front of his hotel, she knew he would have more than welcomed her company in his room.

And probably, in his bed.

Only to tell her, afterwards, that it had been a mechanical happenstance, a man in despair and anguish, seeking relief in the soft warmth of a woman.

No. No more of that. This time, he'd stung her too deeply. In five years, while he had occasionally tantalized her with a kiss on the cheek, a fleeting embrace...at least she could not honestly say he had overstepped his bounds, or used and exploited her...

But this time...to experience the magic, to come so close to being a part of his very soul, to know beyond all doubt that he was exactly as convinced of their sexual compatibility as she was...and yet, to tell her, later, that the Agency was his life, and that she knew the Code as well as he did...

That was too painful. And he knew it.

Be happy with your new job, Harry, darling.

The new responsibility of running a whole crew of good people would gradually erase the emotional beating he had come through. So long as he had decided to remain married exclusively to his work, launching the new Directorship would be tantamount to enjoying a honeymoon.

Enjoy, my love, she thought.

Stepping out of the shower stall, she examined herself critically in the floor-to-ceiling mirror as she towel-dried her body. Breasts still full and firm, the wound fading to a pink-lavender. Tummy still flat, thighs smooth.

With a satisfied sigh, she rubbed the towel hard and fast over herself. That, she recalled, was supposed to be good for the skin, according to an old Russian saying.

Her body had served her as an exit ticket out of the miseries of the Soviet Union, and she had learned to use its promise, if no more than as a beacon, to facilitate her work as an undercover agent for the CIA. She had never given herself willingly to any man...not until that memorable night with Harry. Certainly she had dated many Agency men over the years...but had always used *her* allegiance to the Code as her way out of ticklish situations. Why condemn Harry for doing what she had done with others?

Did she want to try once more to win his love and loyalty? And what if she tried...and failed again? Wouldn't that be worse?

Dressing, she thought about him with deep longing, remembering the way his hands felt exploring the contours of her body, the tender but insistent way they excited her. It would be a long time before she would ever want a man to come close to her. So if she tried again...and failed...*so what*? It would be worse not to try at all...and never know...

Highly unlikely they would ever be sent on an assignment together in the future. Henceforth, he would be Director Carroll, and she would be relegated to the trenches with the other faceless agents. For the good of the country, that was probably wise. But it was not in accordance with her heart's desire...

Her father, the only other man she had ever truly loved—an ordinary man with a big heart and a tremendous sense of decency—had wound up in the icy steppes of Siberia because the Soviet regime measured its citizens by other standards. When her father had been taken from her, something inside her had died. When the CIA had recruited her in Vienna—seeking precisely her background and language skills—she had come to live in America, having found a home in the Agency, where she slowly healed...and looked for the opportunity to express her gratitude to a new country for opening its doors to her.

But at twenty-six, Natalie was ready to be a woman, with all the dreams, needs and desires of a woman. And perhaps it was Harry Carroll who had planted and nurtured that feeling.

The longer she thought about it, the more convinced she became that, yes...it was necessary that he know what she felt, and just as necessary that he consider it and come to a decision.

In the desk drawer she found some hotel stationery and sat down to write him a letter. She would put it on his brand new desk with a red and green Christmas ribbon decorating the envelope.

It would be totally honest, no camouflage, no manipulative phrases. Just all Natalie. Her holiday gift to him.

With her surprisingly feminine handwriting—the letters carefully formed and evenly spaced, she began writing:

Harry, my love,

I'm taking this means of communicating to save us both embarrassment. We've come through an awful ordeal together, and there are things that must be said. With all your intelligence and uncanny sixth sense, sniffing out the hidden and the obscure, you know I've been carrying a torch for you a long, long time. I do love you, Harry, and always will. But from my past experience with you, I must reserve the right to believe that my confession will fall on deaf ears. Thus, this letter.

You see, Harry...my sixth sense tells me we could live an idyllic life together. Not necessarily a tranquil life, but an interesting one, invigorating, filled with pleasant surprises. I envision the two of us, one evening in our living room, reading...the fire crackling and the stereo playing some piece by one of our favorite composers. And all at once, you look up from your newspaper and ask me if I remember the time we spent in Luzon, when I was so weak and sick in that putrid jungle that you had to press my fingers around the end of my tooth brush so I could brush my teeth. We've helped each other a lot, and saved each other's lives...more than once.

So I ask myself...why, Natalia Isaakovna, are you writing such a shameless letter to your Director? And my reply to that question is...because you mean so much to me, I must let you know, must make a statement of my love. Highly unconventional? For sure. But conventional I'm not. There are more than enough conventional girls out there already.

If I've come across as a gushing, love-smitten teenager, I'll hate myself forever. I am a mature woman with a fairly sound intellect and a very healthy body. If no spark can be kindled in your heart to investigate the measure of my love, then I will retreat, leave you alone, and send my best wishes for your happiness to accompany you throughout your life.

Always,
Your Natalia

With the letter folded into an envelope simply marked, "Harry," she donned her parka, stepped into her boots and left the hotel for Washington's winter wonderland of swiftly-falling, powdery snow—car headlights glowing yellow against incessant, swirling white mists. Holiday crowd clusters shivered at street corners, shoppers carrying colorful gift packages in a festive atmosphere which lifted her spirits.

Stopping once for an ornate Christmas ribbon and a couple of miniature pine cones to tape to the envelope, she went on directly to the offices of the Capital City Engineering Company on Fourteenth and "F" Streets, where two young budget analysts recognized her and were happy to place the Christmas letter on their boss's desk.

Light-hearted, she wished them holiday greetings and returned to her car. Chances were good he'd show up at the office the morning of Christmas Eve, to see to last-minute details before the long holiday weekend.

Oh, maybe it would be a great Christmas after all!

The thought itself made her happy, and she found herself craving a steaming hot chocolate and a rich, creamy éclair at a downtown coffee shop. Then she'd go back to the hotel, catch up on some correspondence, pay her year-end bills, take care of old things accumulating in her valises...

The snow was turning to rain, spattering her windshield, and she flicked on her wipers. On the streets, choked with vehicular and pedestrian traffic, umbrellas were appearing, people running from one shop overhang to the next to avoid the downpour.

"Oh, for heaven's sake! Look, it's raining!" cried a musical voice a few yards from where Natalie was inching forward on the car-clogged boulevard. Curious, Natalie studied the owner of that voice—a striking redhead in a black Persian lamb jacket, with a smart shako of the same fur rakishly set on her head.

"Harry, you didn't bring an umbrella, did you?"

A magically familiar rich tenor voice from the shadows of the jewelry store behind the redheaded woman laughed, "Don't blame *me*! At half past seven this morning, you're the one who said the snow was like Johnson's baby powder!"

Holding her breath, Natalie stepped lightly on the gas pedal as space opened up between her and the car ahead. Rolling forward, she glanced in her rear view mirror, trembling...

Director Harry Carroll, just emerging from the interior of the famous Washington jeweler, "Brilliants by Bernhardt," held the red-head's arm as they sped across the wide street to a parking lot, the woman's copper waves bright against the monotonous backdrop of white.

So that would have to be Yvonne, Natalie mused sadly as she returned to her hotel. A gorgeous redhead. She had heard about Harry's childhood sweetheart for years, about the society beauty who had dumped him for a Washington attorney who would *not* go roaming the world with the CIA in search of adventure.

The latest scuttlebutt was about Yvonne's loss of her husband to a brain aneurism, and the expectation that she would be returning to the social scene before very long...

So Harry had spent the night with her.

They'd gone to Bernhardt's to pick out an engagement ring.

Director Carroll had finally embarked on the committed life.

He was betrothed.

And why not? As a brand new Agency Special Director, wouldn't it be the most natural thing in the world for him to marry a wealthy socialite who could give him added prestige and enhance his career potential?

Yvonne de la Fontaine Chartrain had traveled all over the world, was well educated and brainy, to say nothing of charming and beautiful. A woman to fill the bill in every sense of the word!

Come on, now, Natalia! Blink back those tears and be happy for him! You told him in your letter you'd retreat, leave him alone, wish him happiness...

Now, keep your word!

You never had a chance with him anyway, and you know it.

The maid asked her to hold on. She'd see if Mr. Wright could come to the phone. They were having guests...a holiday gathering...

Then the DCI was on the wire, alarmed by her call.

"What's up, Soubrine? What's wrong?"

"N-nothing, Sir...I just..."

"Yes? Speak up! I can't hear you!"

Natalie heard music and the sounds of laughter and conversation. Warm, congenial sounds, starkly in contrast with the silence and gloom of her hotel room.

"I realize it's a holiday,Sir," she stammered. "But I was wondering if I could see you..."

"Yes, of course. I'll be in for a while tomorrow morning before we close for the Christmas weekend. How early do you..."

"Actually, Sir...," Natalie broke in, "I did want to see you tonight..."

Powell Wright heard something he did not trust in the girl's voice. He glanced at the dozen guests enjoying themselves over their cocktails and seafood hors d'oeuvres. Soubrine would never telephone, never make such a request unless it were vitally important to her.

"Then come on over, Natalie," he said. "You know how to get here..."

"Yes,Sir...and thank you, Sir..."

Harry sat at his desk with closed eyes, feelings he had never before experienced coursing through him. He leaned back in his chair, seeing imprinted against the underside of his eyelids the strong, handwritten sentence, "I love you, Harry, and I always will."

He took a deep breath, fingering the satin ribbon on the envelope, touching the tiny pine cones.

There was a buzz, and the switchboard operator in the all-but-empty office announced that the DCI was on the wire.

"Thought I'd catch you there this morning, Harry," Wright chuckled. "You workaholics are all alike. Can't stay away from the job."

"Yes, too bad we're so different," Harry laughed back. "Me, here at the office early this morning, and you, calling from the cozy warmth of your bed…"

"I don't want to talk over the phone, Harry. How soon can you finish up and get to my office?"

"Right away, Chief. What's up?"

"Let's talk when you get there…"

Wright's office was just as quiet and unstaffed as Harry's. With last minute shoppers out in full force, it was treacherous driving through town. In Harry's pocket was Natalie's letter…

The DCI looked uncomfortable, as though he'd had a sleepless night. Wearily, he gestured Harry to a seat in front of his desk.

"I thought it best I tell you in person. Soubrine's leaving us. She's resigned…"

Harry gripped the arms of his chair and propelled himself up. "*What!*"

"She phoned my home last night, asked to see me. I told her to come on over, spoke to her in my study. That's when she told me…

"But…you didn't *accept* her resignation, did you? You talked her out of it, right, Chief?" Harry asked, his eyes wide and frantic and his heart thudding.

Wright glanced at the ceiling, leaning back.

"Actually, no, Harry. I tried. But I couldn't."

Mystified, fuming, Harry paced in a short arc before Wright's desk, hands shoved deep in his pockets. He thought of her words…

"*I love you, Harry, and I always will.*"

"I don't believe this!" he gasped. "It…it's impossible!"

"She made last-minute reservations on a flight to Quebec for half past four this afternoon. Says she had some personal details to clear up there and will mail in her formal resignation letter from Canada..."

"Chief, I think I'd better..."

"Harry, has there been anything between you and Soubrine that I ought to know about?" Wright demanded fiercely, his face deeply lined with concern.

Color rose in Harry's cheeks and his jaw worked, but no words came. He stood tense and nodding before his superior.

"Yes," he admitted. "Yes, I guess you should know...that your new Special Director is a first-class horse's ass!"

The expletive broke the tension and Wright rose quickly.

"Then if I were you, you idiot...," he steamed at Harry, "...I'd get that horse's ass of yours to her place this minute!"

A light, hesitant step behind the hotel door. A faint clearing of the throat. Then a thick, weepy voice.

"Who's there?" to the unexpected rapping.

With effort, Harry forced his voice to deepen.

"It's Powell Wright, Soubrine," he replied. "Let me in."

"Oh!"

The latch clicked, the door opened, and her face was anguished at finding him there.

"Harry!"

She began closing the door in his face, but he strong-armed it ajar and pushed himself through, winded and gasping, gazing at her as though he had never seen her before.

"I don't understand you!" he wheezed. "Not at all!"

"Why not?" she sniffled. "You, with your summa cum laude, Phi Beta Kappa brain? There's *nothing* you don't understand!"

Her valise lay open on her bed, half-filled with clothing. A couple of clothes hangers were lying haphazardly on the small table top. Evidently, she was really leaving.

"Listen, Nat," he steamed. "The one thing I've never understood at all is the workings of a woman's mind! And yours has to be the most complicated of all!"

She walked past him to the closet, continuing to look through her outfits as she packed for her trip. It was obvious his sudden arrival had overwhelmed her and she was trying very hard to cope with it in a nonchalant manner.

"Evidently, Powell Wright told you I've resigned, and as you can see, I'm in the process of leaving Washington. So I'd really appreciate if you would just be on your way, seeing to your own life and letting me see to mine..."

Harry withdrew the envelope containing her letter and shook it in front of her face.

"How can you write me this letter and hand in your resignation on the same day!" he stormed. "How could anyone understand that!"

She flushed at the sight of the envelope, knowing he had most likely reveled egotistically in her declaration of undying love, and now, if given the opportunity, would taunt her without mercy.

Yet there was something sweet and vulnerable about the way he had chosen to fight her on the issue of her resignation. Of course, he'd be hard pressed to find another female operative as resourceful and skillful as she had been, and she didn't expect him to let her go without some kind of resistance.

She was folding a powder blue suit into her valise, aware that he was standing quite close to her as she worked, his breath warm on her cheeks as he gazed down at her. It was all she could do to restrain herself from a siege of uncontrollable sobbing.

"Everything I said in that letter is God's honest truth," she swore quietly. "I've never been ashamed of the way I feel about you. But Harry, it's a one-sided, unrequited feeling, and there's absolutely no way under the sun that I can go on working for you...or for the Agency, as a matter of fact...knowing you're married to someone else! In the words of the KGB, circumstances like that would make me...counter-productive..."

Even before she finished, he seized her shoulders so hard that she dropped the jacket she was folding. He forced her to face him squarely, searching her face in disbelief.

"What do you mean...'married to someone else'...," he cried. "Who said anything about my marrying anyone else?"

The heat of his hands radiated through her polyester blouse to the skin of her slim shoulders, and she feel her desire for him raging, her breathing thin and rapid.

"When a man gives a woman a ring, Harry Carroll...," she shouted back, with emphasis, "...it generally means there's to be a wedding in the near future. And you don't expect me to stick around playing international cops and robbers with glee and gusto while you and your fiancée are making wedding plans!"

"A *ring...*? *Wedding plans...*?" Harry protested, at a loss for comprehension. Then, because her face was close to his, her breathing labored, her lips parted to show the shimmer of her teeth, with the scent of her Chanel coming up strong between them, he caught her close and kissed her, wrapping her up in a tight embrace and imprisoning her in his arms. As his kiss lasted and deepened, Natalie's legs weakened and she staggered back to fall to the edge of her bed with his arms wound fiercely about her.

"What do you know about the ring, Nat...?" he breathed over her mouth, the movement of his lips across hers warm and moist. "No one knows about that ring except Yvonne Chartrain and me...and neither of us knew about it until yesterday afternoon!"

"I know that. That's what I mean...," Natalie choked, trying to find her breath, struggling to free herself from the circle of his powerful arms. "I saw you with her at Bernhardt's yesterday... holding hands and running out into the rain..."

Harry backed off then, holding her at arms' length and staring with wide-eyed wonder, then breaking into a slow grin.

"Oh, my God!" he gasped. "Is that what this is all about? You saw me with an old friend at the jewelers'...and you thought...you took it for granted...Oh, hell, Nat, is that the kind of louse you take me for? I'd sleep with you and then buy an engagement ring for another woman...?"

Stunned, she said nothing, sagging in his arms, trying to make sense out of what he had said, her eyes narrowed in suspicion.

Tenderly, Harry guided her back down atop the quilt, smoothing her hair, stroking the side of her cheek.

"Do you honestly believe that after all we've come through, that I could possibly love some other woman?" he asked softly.

"I'm hearing things!" she breathed. "God forgive me, but I'm hearing things that aren't real...!"

"For me, nothing's ever been more real...," he murmured.

She could not stifle the small moans of happiness that left her lips. Harry's fair hair fell across one eyebrow like a boy's, and she brushed it back gently, trembling at his closeness, the heat of his body through the wool suit.

"You're saying...you love me...?"

"I love you, Natalia Isaakovna. *Ya lyublyu'tibyet, Dorogaya.*"

For a little while, there was only the soft breathy sound of tender kisses in the afternoon silence. When at last Harry came up for air, he grinned and said, "But of course, if you still think you ought to quit...if the game's been getting too rough for you...I won't try to convince you otherwise."

She would be embarrassed having to admit to Powell Wright that she didn't really want to resign after all. He had been unhappy at the thought of her quitting. So unhappy, in fact, that he'd made haste to warn his fair-haired boy in good time to stop her.

"I'd like to stay so long as you're Director," she beamed at him. "You know better than anyone else how much I like my job."

"I know. But you see, I was going to offer you a better one."

"A better one...?"

"Well, this Directorship...it makes me just another Washington bureaucrat. Trapped here with the home, the car, the whole catastrophe..."

"And you want to make me part of that mess?" she giggled.

"Certainly. To cook my meals, wash and iron my shirts, my underwear...," he murmured, releasing her for the moment to search in his jacket pocket, producing an elegantly-wrapped little box. "And to bribe you into it, here's a little something..."

Together, they divested the jewel box of its outer wrapping, and Harry snapped it open, revealing a two-carat pearshape diamond solitaire set in yellow gold. With a self-conscious grin, he held it out for her slim finger, and had to force it over her knuckle.

"Firing ranges and karate practice gives you a good, strong hand. That ring won't fall off...not even in battle!" he joked.

Natalie examined her ring with wonderment and awe, weeping.

"It looks like a tear drop, Harry," she whispered. "Like an exquisite diamond tear drop!"

His lips grazed her forehead as he held her.

"Well, you know what we Russians always say...," he teased. *"Why laugh...when you can cry?"*

THE   END